ELISABETH SAMSON,

FORBIDDEN BRIDE

by
Carolyn Proctor

ELISABETH SAMSON,

FORBIDDEN BRIDE

by
Carolyn Proctor

Published by:

Joshua Tree Publishing
1901 N. Roselle Road
Suite 800
Schaumburg, IL 60195
www.JoshuaTreePublishing.com

All rights reserved. No part of this book may be reproduced or transmitted in any form or by any means, electronic or mechanical, including photocopying, recording or by any information storage and retrieval system without written permission from the author.

Copyright © 2004 Carolyn Proctor

ISBN: 0-9710954-2-6

Printed in the United States of America

In the 18th century Dutch plantation colony of Suriname, where wealth is measured by the number of slaves one owns, the educated Free Negress Elisabeth Samson, owner of several flourishing coffee plantations, desires the one thing her wealth cannot buy: a legal marriage with her consort, a white colonial officer.

But can she overcome the strict Dutch laws forbidding marriage between black and white against the powerful forces of the colonial Governor, the white planters who make up the Court of Justice, and the Society of Suriname, who covet her property, call her "whore" and accuse her of treason?

For the four people most instrumental in shaping my writing life: Virginia Dearborn, Paul Keye, Lobsang Samten, and Cork Proctor.

And for all my dear friends in Suriname.

PROLOGUE

The Suriname historical museum at Commeweijnestraat 18 has been closed and all but abandoned since the revolution and civil war of the 1980s. A stately remnant of Dutch Colonial architecture, the air of its interior was rank with the smell that only man-made items left untouched for years in a tropical climate can radiate.

Presently a small exhibition of artifacts is in place in the former military fortress of Fort Zeelandia, situated on a bank of the Suriname River where it could protect the Dutch colonial capital of Paramaribo. These relics allow a glimpse into the vibrant story of conflict, suffering, and triumph in this tiny South American country that is bordered by Guyana, French Guiana, Brazil, and a wild Atlantic coast.

The exhibition had been assembled by *vrouw* DeVries, a stout Dutch woman with springy curls and a determined air, who for the past twenty years has worked as director for the *Stichting Surinaams Museum*.

"I came from Holland just before the revolution broke out and couldn't get back right away, so I ended up staying," she says.

Standing in the old building on Commeweijnestraat amidst a jumble of boxes and furniture, I asked, "Do you know what all's here? Is there an inventory?"

"Nay, no inventory," said *vrouw* DeVries. "There may have been once, but if so it's long lost. It's something we need to do, but there's no one to do it, and no money to pay for extra personnel."

This was one of the reasons I'd volunteered to help. Already in Suriname on a two-year community development assignment, I'd become fascinated with the country's history.

Suriname is one of the three Guianas named after the Guiana Shield, a geological formation that makes up the northeast corner of the Amazon basin. Originally it was populated by peaceful Arawak and cannibalistic Carib Indians. Around 1615 both the Dutch and the English began establishing small settlements at the mouths of several of the rivers of the Guianas. In the terms of the treaty of Breda, at the end of the second Anglo-Dutch war in 1667, the victorious Dutch claimed the English territory of Suriname. As a bone to throw to the losers, the Dutch ceded their settlement of New Netherland—today's Manhattan Island—on the coast of North America. The loss of New Netherland was seen by the Dutch Republic as insignificant compared to the acquisition of an English territory that was on its way to becoming one of the most successful sugar plantation colonies of the West Indies.

"That trade's understandable," I said to *vrouw* DeVries when we discussed this. "After all, what can you grow in Manhattan?"

In the colony's early years under Dutch rule, it didn't do well financially. Bad management was cited, and in 1682 it was overtaken by a private organization, the Society of Suriname.

"The family van Aerssen of Sommelsdijck, the city of Amsterdam, and the West India Company were equal one-third partners in the Society," *vrouw* DeVries told me.

Cornelis van Aerssen, Lord of Sommelsdijk, left for Suriname in 1683 to become the newly Dutch colony's first Governor General. As such, he made great progress in establishing peace treaties with the native inhabitants, including the runaway plantation slaves who had already established their own villages along the Coppename River, deep in the jungle interior.

Three hundred years later, the colony of Dutch Guiana gained its freedom from the Netherlands and became officially the Republic of Suriname. Five years later, in 1980, the independent country was embroiled in a revolution and civil war. The conflict devastated its infrastructure and left the annual income of what population remained at barely twenty percent of what they had previously enjoyed under Dutch rule.

The task of inventorying and cataloging the remnants of the past contained in the Commewijnestraat building was overwhelming. Three days after I'd begun working there, *vrouw* DeVries was going over some ledgers in her cramped office as I unwrapped yet another unmarked box. Inside I discovered a cache of dusty books, bound together with what was once a strong hemp cord. I wiped them off and was surprised to discover a woman's journals, written in the 1700s.

"Do you know this name, Elisabeth Samson?" I asked *vrouw* DeVries as I stood in her doorway, one of the books in my hand.

She didn't look up right away from her work. "Aye, she was a free Negress during the Golden Age of Suriname."

"When it was a big sugar colony?"

"1740 to 1773, to be exact," she said. "But historians call the entire 18th century 'the Golden Century', because the planters were so wealthy."

"I've heard about their ostentatious living. That they demonstrated their wealth by the number of slaves they kept."

"They had the absolute best of everything money could buy," *vrouw* DeVries said, smiling. "Much different from Paramaribo today."

During this Golden age, the capitol, Paramaribo, was home to about 10,000 people, of whom seventy-five percent were African or Creole slaves. Less than 2,000 of the population were white, and a significant portion of them were Jewish. By the 1730s there were over 400 plantations with 20,000 slaves. At the end of the century that number had risen to 533 plantations with a population estimated at 53,000 people, not counting the native Amerindians and slave runaways. For every free person, there were nine slaves.

"The total survival and success of the colony depended on the slave trade," *vrouw* DeVries said. She rose from her desk and came around to peer at the book in my hand.

"Do you know anything about Elisabeth Samson?" I asked.

The little Dutch woman brushed a tumbled curl away from her face and took the book from my hand. With care, she began turning some of the fragile pages, studying intently. "Her handwriting is feminine but strong, clearly an educated woman. We do know something about the free Negress, Elisabeth Samson, but this is incredible. It looks like her journal. Where did you find it?"

I pointed to a ragged box torn open on the floor. "There are more in there."

Vrouw DeVries looked puzzled. "I never saw that box before. I'm not sure where it came from." Her Dutch accent thickened with excitement. "Is there anything else in there besides books?"

"Some old clothing and shoes, some fans, and what was probably once a wonderful velvet mask with a funny metal mouthpiece. A lot of it's been eaten by bugs." I shuddered. Suriname has its share of voracious tropical insects.

"How wonderful that we found this." *Vrouw* DeVries clutched the book to her bosom as if she were afraid I would take it back with me to America.

"Let's see how many there are," I suggested, returning to the box on the floor. When I sat down cross-legged, *vrouw* DeVries apparently felt it was safe to again open the volume she held.

"Many of the pages are torn, or eaten away. But the ink is remarkably clear. Most likely she used ink made from the cashew tree. The resinous sap was commonly used to make a very indelible ink."

We counted fourteen journals in all, and *vrouw* DeVries, who had been cautious about showing her feelings, was now ecstatic with the find. "I've never heard of journals by Elisabeth Samson. I don't think anybody I know has ever seen these. I have to call Andre at the University. This is unbelievable!"

"So who was she?"

"A remarkable woman, by all accounts. For the record, she was the first black woman in the colony to seek legal permission to marry a white man. That was forbidden, you know."

"You called her a free Negress. Was she born a slave then?" I asked.

"Nay, she was born free and became one of the wealthiest plantation owners in the colony. The only thing she couldn't

buy that other planters' wives had was a white husband."
Vrouw DeVries went on to explain that as a free Negress Elisabeth Samson could marry any mulatto, samboe, quadroon, maesti, or black man, so long as he was not a slave. White bachelors often took a Negro *huishoudster*, or housekeeper, and married white men often also had a *bijzit*, or concubine.

Later, after devouring the journals in one long sitting, I remembered *vrouw* DeVries's words. Elisabeth Samson had no idea at the time, I thought, that she would live on in Suriname's history because of the consternation and uproar her actions would cause on two continents.

PART ONE

MOFOKORANTI
(GOSSIP AND SLANDER)

1

<u>Paramaribo, January 1742</u>

I hadn't meant to tell Carl Otto what *vrouw* Mauricius and I had overheard through the open window at our new Governor's reception, but the words tumbled out of my mouth without thought, like bees escaping a smoking hive.

In the candlelight of our second-floor bedroom, where the night sounds of tropical frogs and insects were kept at bay, Carl Otto took me into his arms and tried his best, as always, to reassure me that the past is over. To avoid Carl Otto's embrace, Pansu, my darling little squirrel monkey, squeaked and scampered from my waist to the back of my shoulders.

Carl Otto's words after I blurted out "free whore" were little comfort. "They are only soldiers, Betje. Most of them are the dregs of the earth."

"But the woman—"

"The woman means nothing. Do you know her?"

"I didn't recognize her voice and in the darkness I didn't see her face."

"What can she know?"

"Everything," I wailed. "Everyone in this colony knows everything." This was not a little exaggeration. We are less than two thousand, not including slaves, indeed a close community. "I'm tired of being referred to as a whore; I want to be married," I whispered. "And I want children."

Against my neck I could feel Carl Otto's face relax into a smile. "I'm doing my best in the latter department," he said.

Then he pulled back and with one hand turned my face to his. "Betje, my sable darling. You know we can't marry."

"Everyone else can marry," I protested, refusing to acknowledge what I knew to be an unhappy truth. Carl Otto and I would marry this day if circumstances would so arrange themselves. Had flowed in my veins the slightest amount of white blood I could legally marry Carl Otto in the Dutch Reformed Church with the blessings of both God and our colonial government. But such is not the case; nay, since the period of our first Governor General of Suriname, Cornelis van Aerssen, Lord of Sommelsdijk, marriage between a Negro woman and a white man is not allowed.

It is a bitter irony the way our colonial governance regularly makes contradictory decisions. They disapprove of living in concubinage, yet object if a Negress wants to marry a white man. Nay, they even consider living with a man without marrying him to be whorish. Yet white men in this colony have taken Coloured women as concubines for eighty years, which situations are commonly referred to as "marriage, Suriname style." That is the strange state in which Carl Otto and I live.

"Do you think *vrouw* Mauricius noted the remark?" Carl Otto asked.

I buried my face in the warmth where his shoulder met his neck, and my reply was as a moan.

"Tell me exactly what happened, Betje," he said in a soothing tone.

The tart words flowed with a familiarity all the worse for their truth. I began to relate how the Governor's wife had remarked upon a painting in the Governor's palace depicting a plantation home situated atop a rolling green, and how it had been my pleasure to describe the place to her.

This painting happened to be next to a window that opened to an outside gallery. It being after sunset, the shutters of the tall windows in the grand reception hall had been opened to catch the slightest evening breeze, and bare-footed male servants walked about with tall fans of woven palm fronds with which they gently swept the air to keep the mosquitoes (this being the little wet season) away.

Outside the window some military officers and a few ladies, smoking their pipe-bowls, had been conversing.

"...an experimental execution to terrify their companions, and thus to make them return to their duty."

They were discussing the recent punishment of some recaptured runaways: one slave was hanged alive by the iron hook struck through his ribs, another tied and burnt to death by slow fire, and six women broken alive upon the rack. I was only half-listening, perusing the painting in a sense of well-being lulled by good food and wine, when I heard, "...the free Negress, Elisabeth Samson."

"The free whore, you mean." To my bitter realization, it was a woman who had voiced these words. The Governor's wife had dropped her eyes in embarrassment, for she had clearly heard. The lady had regarded me with a frankly curious look. Along with a sense of superiority, had I seen pity in her blue eyes?

The company laughed, and I directed *vrouw* Mauricius away from the painting and the window, wishing I had paid more attention, for when exactly had their conversation changed from the recaptured runaways to me? They could not know that we had overheard. I felt as if the entire room had suddenly become chilled, the candlelight grown cold and brittle.

Across the room Carl Otto chatted amicably with our new Governor. With my hand at *vrouw* Mauricius' elbow, nearly shoving her before me, I moved trance-like in their direction. The many greetings we received along the way suddenly sounded shallow and worthless. No matter how many slaves I own, nor how much property I buy, nor how well-cut is my habit, when I least expect them cruel words sprout like weeds in the garden of my soul.

And then Carl Otto, my husband—for that is how I think of him though he is white and we are not legally married—smiled at me, and the Governor himself with a slight bow welcomed my presence. His lady then complimented my satin stomacher, which bore many more studded jewels than her own. Normally this would have pleased me, but the words *free whore* still resounded in my ear.

Pleasantries had been exchanged, and Carl Otto, as a prominent Society lieutenant, had the honor to serve His Excellency his first glass of the rum here produced. Shortly thereafter I was relieved when Carl Otto begged leave to depart.

. . .

Not a planter's wife would have missed for the world the opportunity afforded this evening to meet and appraise His Excellency's lady, whose given name is also Elisabeth. But of course, she is white and I am black-skinned and therein lies all the difference that anyone would at first glance note. Her gown of claret-coloured velvet was exquisitely trimmed with a fine gold Belgian lace which, I expect, reflects the latest French fashion for our fair sex.

Oh, how the Governor's palace was set out for the evening! The black servants had spent the entire day just polishing the mirrors with their gilded frames. A thousand and one candle flames on double chandeliers contributed greatly to the warmth and glitter of the reception. Dinner was served on Japan china, and the facets of each crystal goblet were alive with dancing points of light. Seven kinds of meats, including venison, were served along with fowl and the sweet white *anumara* fish of the Suriname River. Pasties were plentiful on every table and there was a welcome quantity of Porter and Madeira, and our own fine *Sranan* rum, making me proud of the abundance our little colony presented.

In the right drawing room, light musical effects were accomplished by the players of the flutes, clavicin, cello and violins. A bright Vivaldi violin fantasy of cheery expression had the most merry effect on our company. Even the staunch faces of the white Dutchmen in the grand portraits adorning the walls seemed to smile down upon us.

All served as a perfect, dazzling stage for the plantation owners, powerful players in our Colony's various little political dramas. Mostly Hollanders, French Huguenots, Swiss or Germans, they respect my wealth, yet still call me "whore."

The Chartered Society of Suriname, that august group of Amsterdam merchants and politicians which has managed our businesses, and therefore our lives, for the past sixty years, has honored us with Johan Jacob Mauricius as our new Governor. Oh, we welcomed him in grand style. Of course, he will have to share his power with our own Court of Police, made up of white sugar planters who periodically rave and scrabble over what is best for us all.

Thanks to the many pipe-bowls which were being enjoyed at the Governor's reception, a gentle haze softened the glittering edges. I myself had enjoyed the fine Virginia tobacco—admittedly better than our own—that is exceedingly plentiful here. I would have found the evening perfect had not the charming discourse been interrupted by this most distressing incident in front of *vrouw* Mauricius.

. . .

The foot-boy entered our bedroom and I removed myself from Carl Otto's arms. Carl Otto sat down on the edge of the mahogany four-poster bed and leaned back on his elbows, one foot on the floor and one extended so that his jackboots could be removed.

"I like this new governor," he said.

I couldn't help but smile. "Of course you do. You're both German, both from the county Cleve." Pansu hopped from my shoulder onto the bed to examine Carl Otto's coat pockets, hoping to discover a treat of fruit or sugar candy. He chittered in protest when I picked him up to cuddle his soft grayish-gold fur against my cheek.

"No, it's more than that," Carl Otto insisted. He sat up and the foot-boy took his jackboots out of the room to be polished before they were put away. "I believe he has some good ideas on how to manage the Maroon situation."

That French word for runaway, *marronage*, has given everyday discourse a name for the offending slaves, Africans mostly from the coast of Guinea or Creoles born in the Colony who have for a hundred years plagued plantation production by regular desertion.

"The Maroons have always posed the biggest threat to the colony," I said, feeling an odd sense of relief that the subject had been changed from my unpleasant eavesdrop at the Governor's reception to something over which I felt I had power.

I crossed the room to place Pansu in his cage bed for the night. The mere mention of Maroons may cause most any planter to glance with unease over his shoulder. From established villages hidden well into the forest, they attack plantations seeking firearms, tools, and women.

"I'm glad you put that monkey away before he had a chance to tear at my wig again." Carl Otto removed his white wig of rolled curls, revealing hair the colour of the sand at Galibi, cut close to his head. "His Excellency has a master plan. He says there are only two ways to overcome the problem."

"Hopefully they are new ways. The present ones don't seem to be working all that well."

"His Excellency acknowledges that. He says we could destroy them in one fell swoop, but a campaign of such magnitude would be impossibly expensive. He wants to set them against each other by making peace with them, one group at a time. Do you think I should order a wig that's slightly shorter?"

"Well. That is a new idea."

"The wig or setting the Maroons against each other?"

I sat down on the bed next to him so that he could unlace the back of my stomacher. "I know Kwasiba should do it, but she's downstairs and I like it when you do it. Making peace with the Maroons, one group at a time...how do you expect the Court of Police will think about such a peace-making plan?"

"I think he'll have a hard time selling the idea. The planters will be afraid it'll encourage even more of their Africans to run away. There's too much contact as it is between Maroons and the family members they leave behind on their owner's plantation." He made an exasperated sound. "I fear I've made a knot of this lace."

"Take your time. The knot will work out if you relax a little."

I agree with Carl Otto's view of the Governor's forthcoming difficulty selling his idea to the plantation owners of the Court of Police. So far, at my coffee plantations on the Hoer-Helena Kreek, I have been extremely lucky not to have a problem with *marronage*. This may be because Toevlught and

Welgemoed are not on the Cottica River, closer to the coast, or up the Suriname River past Joden Savanne—the Jew's savanna—where many of the largest Maroon villages are hidden. Also perhaps because I make it a point of good business to keep my properties well-fed, their families together, and avoid ill-use of their bodies beyond what is normal in the course of their quotidian duties. Still, like any responsible planter, I'm aware of the threat posed by *marronage*.

"Mauricius seems aristocratic enough to garner some supporters among our *nouveau-riche* planters," Carl Otto said. "And he's made a good impression on the Jews, even though none of them will ever be appointed to high government or elected to the Court of Police."

The Jews, mostly Portuguese, keep themselves generally segregated from other people, except when it comes to parties and politics. The Jews have always enjoyed much freedom as well as the ear of His Excellency, the Governor. As evidenced by the number of them who had been in attendance this evening, I expect that will be no different with our new Governor Mauricius.

"Impressing the Jews is a significant beginning," I said. Jewish representatives by custom visit the Governor on the eve of an election to inquire as to which candidate His Excellency favors, and cast their votes accordingly.

The knot in my laces had been worked free, and I leaned forward to shrug out of the studded velvet garment that had flattened my breasts and narrowed my waist.

"Indeed, they know how to curry favor, and they know it's in their best interest to support the Governor." Carl Otto's hands were gentle as he kneaded the muscles of my bare back. His voice softened and he leaned forward to place a kiss on the skin below my neckline. "Ah, Betje, my sable beauty...you were so incredibly fortunate to be spared the lash. I was mad with despair when the sentence was handed down."

A second reminder this evening of unpleasant events that occurred six years past when I was just twenty-one. Having been born free and raised in a comfortable Waterkant mansion, I had been then quite naïve to the ways of the world.

. . .

Much later I lay awake in the big four-poster, listening to the night clatter of small creatures in the foliage outside the house. Beside me, Carl Otto's breath, coming as it was from his open mouth in soft inhales and exhales, was as reassuring as a heartbeat.

I thought again about the stinging words that had so ruined this beautiful evening, and how different everything would be if Carl Otto and I could marry, like my older sister, Maria, a Mulatto, married to the Dutch planter Frederik Coenraad Bosse.

Such fond memories I have of their wedding, the first Christian wedding I had ever attended. I was twelve and excited beyond words. The ceremony was to be held in the Dutch Reformed Church, the place of my Christian baptism two years earlier.

In the house on Waterkant, with its front porch view of the wide, brown Suriname River, the air was charged with the bustle of wedding preparations. When the dressmaker came upstairs to put the finishing touches on Maria's yellow wedding dress, my wide eyes watched every movement with a cat-like stare. I was sure that the way the lace of the sleeves fell from Maria's bare shoulders to meet the drapes of the ample satin skirt must resemble the most beautiful jungle waterfall I had ever imagined.

Twenty-seven-year-old Maria had been married before, at fourteen, to another white planter, the Swiss Pierre Mivela. That was the year before I was born. Ten years later he was murdered during a slave uprising on his plantation, Salzhalen. That is how Maria came to own both Salzhalen, a sugar plantation of more than 400 hectares on the Kabbeskreek, and the large three-story Waterkant house where I had lived as long as I could remember. Pierre Mivela had been kind enough to his wife's little Negro half-sister, and I had thought our world ended when Pierre was murdered by those marauding heathens.

The Dutch Reformed church was alight with heavy wax candles, even though it was the middle of the day. It was breathtaking to see Maria, on this day so well-adorned, stand to make her vows with her new white husband. It was truly a fantasy to inspire any impressionable young girl to dream, and

I was no exception. Every move Maria made was as my own would be, when my turn came. Her smile was that of a confident, willing bride, not a bride given in terms of family business, as is sometimes the case.

Maria was given away by our oldest brother, the free Mulatto Charloo, who had been manumitted along with Maria and our mother in 1713. As a Mulatto and no longer a slave, Maria was free to marry legally in the Christian Church. But I digress...I was saying that Maria's wedding to Frederick Coenraad Bosse most impressed me. My youthful imagination was alive with girlish love—rich dresses, magical candlelight, and the presence of all my family, including our mother, Mariana.

I saw her sitting in a front row with a dark-skinned man I didn't know. After the service, as everyone spilled from the church in excited groups, I ran to her. I wanted to throw my arms around her, but I was already twelve then, as I have mentioned, and knew proper restraint.

Yet this did not prevent me from asking, "*M'ma*, when will you come to see me?"

She stopped to stare at me, one hand raised to her bosom as if she had just run from the market and was out of breath. Her dark eyes regarded me with a strange distance.

"*Pikin* Elisabeth, *joe kon so bigi*," she said, speaking to me as she always did in Sranan Tongo. In truth, I hadn't seen my mother in nearly a year, but I didn't think I had grown that much. When I was younger she used to visit the house on Waterkant more often, and I had questioned her so many times that now she often ignored me. Anyway, I knew the answer.

Now here my mother stood, to me a perfect vision of a Catholic Negro Madonna. Her black hair formed a beauteous globe of gray streaked ringlets. The girl in me longed to touch her dress, embroidered with flowers and adorned here and there with a few gold spangles. As she regarded me she fingered a medallion on a gold chain around her neck. A shawl of fine Indian muslin draped her shoulders, and she carried in one delicate hand a beaver hat, the crown trimmed round with silver, a gift from her new son-in-law for the occasion.

"Will you dine with us today, *M'ma*?"

"Aye, Elisabeth. I will see you at *meneer* Bosse's. Run along now."

Only later, riding in the carriage from the church to the house, did I think that there was plenty of room and she could have ridden with us.

To console myself, I thought of the stories I'd been told of how my mother came to Suriname. When the planter Jon von Susteren moved from St. Christoffer in the Dutch West Indies to Suriname sometime around 1703, he brought his pretty young slave concubine, Nanoe, with him. She had already birthed a son and a daughter by him, Charloo and Maria. Her master had promised my mother that she and their two mulatto children would have their freedom upon his death. Indeed, he kept his promise and the instructions for their manumission were in his last will and testament. Luckily for my mother, the children were already baptized and von Susteren's widow, as his executor, had been duty-bound to carry out his provisions. After her manumission Nanoe changed her name to Mariana. New names for new lives, I suppose would be the reason for this action that seems to have become a tradition for so many slaves.

Mariana bore three more children before my free birth in 1715. Not a year later my father, the free Negro Sam, disappeared and was presumed to have been murdered in the jungle. Maria, at sixteen already two years married to Pierre Mivela, removed me from my whimpering mother's arms. Mariana, crazed by Sam's fate and consumed by *winti* spirits so that she knew not what was happening around her, relaxed her arms and thus gave me up. It was almost a year later when she arrived with her wits about her at Maria's house to inquire after me.

Though Maria had welcomed her visit she made it very clear to my mother that I would remain where I was, to be raised by Maria's hand and with the opportunity to be educated by Maria's husband. Maria had no children and had easily come to think of me as her own. Mariana had gone away without objection. I never hated her for that, indeed on the day of Maria's wedding to *meneer* Bosse it had been impossible to consider any unkind thoughts.

It was a perfect day with a blue sky stuffed with white clouds, the beginning of the dry season. As we rode through streets lined with fragrant orange and tamarind trees, the air itself was a veritable perfume and I was still in a dazzle from the thrill of the wedding.

When we rounded the corner at Waterkant, we were met with a sudden putrid wind blowing from the direction of the waterside fort, Zeelandia. At the base of one of the bastions of the fort were staked the remains of a black man who had been broken on the rack and disemboweled while he was still alive, then beheaded and quartered. In the heat of this beautiful afternoon, his rotting parts seemed to shimmer and dance in the distance as if they were still alive.

Charloo said, "The vultures are having their own feast," and removed his hat in respect for the 'kra, or soul, of the mutilated black man.

As we hurried into the house where all was light and merriment and sweets and wine, I gave a silent thanks to the grace of the Christian God that I had been born free and fortunately spared from the harsh realities of a life in slavery in the Colony.

I thought of my mother and realized she has never spoken of her life on St. Christoffer with the Dutchman von Susteren. I realized how very little I truly knew about the woman who gave me birth—what hardships, discouragements, joys or hopes she may have had before her manumission by the hand of von Susteren's widow. There is much I would like to ask her, but how to approach such sensitive, private subjects?

Acute was the disappointment I felt when my mother after all did not appear that day for the marriage dinner at the home of Maria and Frederick Coenraad Bosse.

2

Paramaribo, February 1742

Where to begin to record the sadness of these recent days?

The morning room was awash with a light that foretold a glorious day. Carl Otto and I were enjoying a breakfast of dishes of chocolate and passion fruit, here named *markoesa*.

"Much tastier than rusk biscuit," Carl Otto commented. He hates the rye bread cut through the middle and baked till it is hard as stone, the standard morning fare of soldiers and sailors.

"And no worms, pins, or broken bottles in it, either."

He laughed at my words. It was a black, but true joke.

From the back of the house came the familiar sounds of the comings and goings of the slaves from the separate *keuken* house where they prepared our meals. Their murmurings mingled with the morning calls of the *gritjibi* birds that populate the neighborhood.

When Dorotea appeared at the doorway, I was thinking of requesting a second dish of chocolate. With apprehension the servant regarded Pansu, sitting on the table holding the china bowl in both his tiny hands, the traces of chocolate he was licking indistinguishable against the dark of his muzzle. Because Pansu had bitten Dorotea when he first arrived in the house, she fears and carefully avoids him. Her eyes were wide but expressionless, one hand flat against the lap of her chintz skirt as in the other she held out something white.

"*Mas'ra*," she began, addressing Carl Otto. There was only the slightest hesitation before she continued. "Adoe come from *vrouw* Bosse's house with a letter."

The letter was only a simple folded paper. For messages sent within Paramaribo, there is no need to enclose them in an envelope. It is illegal for slaves to be taught to read and write, so the carrier of the letter would not be able to discern the words and spread *mofokoranti*—rumors—about the general neighborhood.

Carl Otto received the note and unfolded it. His brow furrowed and he heaved a great sigh as he followed with his finger the careful script penned by Anna Buys-Julien, Maria's neighbor and friend. When at last he looked up his face was pained.

"Frederik has died. Maria asks us to come."

The room dimmed to my sight and a bare whisper of air escaped my lips. Frederik Coenraad Bosse, just 52 years of age, had enjoyed, as far as we knew, perfect health. He had been an active member of the Court of Police. Under his tutelage I had learned to read and write, speak French, do numbers. He had even taught me to manage his account ledgers. Frederik had treated me as a daughter and had fair worshipped Maria. A myriad of warm and happy family scenes from their house on Waterkant flooded my senses, leaving me awash with sad melancholy.

"Maria must be devastated," were my first whispered words. Carl Otto shoved his chair back, making a harsh noise on the polished mahogany floor, and abruptly stood up. "He was such a good friend to you," I said. "We must go at once. *Kwasiba! My shawl!*"

. . .

It is only a five-minute walk from our house on Oranjestraat to the Bosse house on Waterkant. Like all the Dutch colonial houses on the street, Maria's is white-painted wood, and the foundation and stoop are of the red brick that comes as ballast in the ships from Holland. With shutters and trim of dark wine-red, the house is Maria's pride. Every morning the black servants sweep and wash the brick steps and stoop with soap and water; Maria makes sure it's kept spotless.

This morning, as we approached the front porch, the house slaves were already hanging the black cloth that proclaimed a home in mourning.

"Where is my sister?" I asked the little black boy who met us at the door.

"She rest, *mevrouw*, in bedroom. Doctor 'tend her."

I gathered my skirts, rushed up the stairs and entered the large room where just last night Maria had slept comfortably with her beloved husband. Now she half-reclined against a multitude of pillows set against the high, carved-cedar headboard that rose halfway to the ceiling. Her colour was pale, near to that of her sepia embroidered morning gown, and there were ugly dark shadows under her eyes, eyes that were still soft and beautiful despite the huge despair held therein.

"Dear sister, I'm so sorry." I sat down on the edge of her bed and took her hand in mine.

"She will eat *rien*—nothing, not even a broth." Anna said. Lines of worry creased the skin at the corners of her almond-shaped eyes. Anna Buys-Julien lives next door in the house on the corner and has been in mourning since just after Christmas for her own husband, Hendrik Buys, from whom she has inherited not only the house, but also the plantation Buys-en-Vlijt.

The white Dutch doctor looked helpless, and Maria murmured to me, "Send for *gra'man* Quassie."

I waved away the doctor, who seemed relieved to no longer be required, and sent a slave for an uplifting *sangaree*, the very acceptable combination of Madeira wine mixed with water and flavored with nutmeg and sugar. Between Anna and me we were able to coax Maria to sip this small refreshment, after which I sent another slave to summon from the plantation of his owner the Negro who enjoys the most celebrated reputation in the Colony as a natural medical practitioner, or *dresiman*.

. . .

Granman—or Great Man—Quassie belongs to a Jewish planter at Joden Savanne. On a recent visit to a Cassewinica plantation, Rosa Judea, Granman Quassie was taken in a raid by runaways. When later recaptured, he was interrogated by military officials and, undoubtedly influenced by what is said of him, promptly and fortuitously returned undamaged to his rightful owner.

It was a fortunate thing that news and the man both traveled quickly. Granman Quassie arrived at the house on Waterkant the following midday. Frederik's body was already wrapped and ready for burial, immediate attendance to physical remains being mandatory in our tropical climate.

Into the drawing room the *dresiman* was received with polite reserve. A kitchen slave served tea and sugar to us all with appropriate silence and then retired from the room. Maria, thin and wan, seated as straight on a cedar parlour chair as its woven *pitriet* back, greeted Granman Quassie in welcoming tones.

"I'm glad you had a safe journey on the river."

In an opposite chair, the Negro *dresiman* sat and sipped his tea, his squat legs and feet barely touching the floor. "Aye, I had a safe journey. The river spirits were generous today."

"My house is in mourning for the death of *meneer* Bosse, my husband," said Maria.

"I presume that is why this poor Negro is here," Granman Quassie said, adding two additional tablespoons of sugar to his teacup.

I thought that this must be a luxury to which he most likely is not accustomed, even though he often is allowed to leave his plantation to sell his talents elsewhere along the river or in the capitol. Thanks be to the generosity of the Jew, who knows a good investment when he sees it, Granman Quassie is able to collect money for his services, such fees of which he subsequently gives half back to his owner.

There followed some questioning of Maria, myself, and Anna with regard to poor Frederik's general health and behavior just prior to his untimely parting. Such inquiries were made with great respect by the *dresiman* and answered equally sincerely by Maria, all the while clutching her shawl about her shoulders, as if the big house itself was consumed with a death chill.

In the end Granman Quassie determined that a strong *obia*

would be needed to help Maria recover her strength and spirits. He would personally provide the ingredients for this talisman, but Maria would have to provide some of Frederik's hair as a necessary inclusion. Thus Maria led the squat Negro to the back of the house where Frederik's body lay in shroud. A servant brought scissors and the head was carefully unwrapped. Quassie mumbled a small incantation, held the scissors in his hand for a lengthy time, then handed them to Maria, for it was required, he said, for her to cut the hair herself.

The *dresiman* took the hair and quit the house on Waterkant for several hours. When he returned he had assembled everything in a small sewn packet tied with cotton string. This he gave to Maria with the caution, "Take this off only to bathe." He stressed the importance of this talisman to not only aid her recovery but also to maintain a calmness about the house should Frederik's *jorka*, or ghost spirit, come round to visit. "You must wear this under your camisole, next to your heart, for the entire twelve months' space of your mourning."

He also left Maria a few leaves of the plant everyone calls *kwasibitta*, for the great man Quassie himself had the good fortune to find out this valuable root in 1730. "Make a tea," he said, "and drink it every day until you feel the strength return to your stomach and your appetite restored."

Such is the reputation of this famous *dresiman* that I am confident Maria will be returned soon to good health. But oh, to lose a beloved white husband! For her spirit there may be no recovery from such a heartfelt loss.

After the departure of Granman Quassie, Anna sent for her baby daughter, Susanna, who was brought in by the child's Negro wet nurse. The presence of the Mesties Susanna indeed brought a smile to Maria's face. At forty-two years of age, it is Maria's greatest discouragement that she has not been able to bear children of her own. And with her husband now departed, I'm sure she will increasingly draw pleasure from the babes of her family and friends such as Anna.

It was with the greatest relief that I was able to depart my sister's house with this assurance that things would, eventually, restore themselves to normal and continuation.

As Carl Otto and I walked back to our house, my thoughts

fell to my own future. How I wish that Carl Otto and I would have a child to add to our family's wealth, a babe that could be outrageously spoiled by Maria in a loving manner similar to that which I enjoyed from her dear, departed husband, Frederik.

A child that will carry forward my wealth, and, being of mixed blood, will be free to marry as he or she should so choose.

3

Plantation Vlaardingen, March 1742

With the tides our tent-boat departed the waterside this morning at first light, so that in just past one hour's time our little party would arrive at our destination not yet tired from the rising heat of the day.

The little dry season with agreeable weather now being upon us, it was decided that a visit to Vlaardingen, our brother Quackoe's plantation near the mouth of the river Cottica, would be an amusing diversion. It would provide an opportunity for Maria to quit Paramaribo, and thus so reap the benefits to be had from taking the country air.

After the death of Frederik, I was eager for the presence of the quiet strength of Quackoe. I only hoped our brother Isaac (his name change from Jakje upon his manumission), with his fiery character, would not prove contrary and quarrelsome. Isaac and his children had departed for Vlaardingen the week past and would still be visiting there.

In addition to our persons, we carried provisions for Quackoe's table, for which reason an early departure was equally desirable. There were flour, imported tobacco, sugar and cinnamon, and some excellent salted mackerel imported from North America. Most well-received would be the parcel of medicines, which consisted of emetics, powders, and laxatives. Several securely tied bottles of claret trailed behind us a few fathoms below the water in order to render them cool and agreeable upon arrival.

Maria had included a present of pickled sausages and a half-dozen fowls from the detestable butcher Egbert Peltser. Though I still practice avoidance from making purchases from this disagreeable little man, I secretly agree with Maria that he is the best butcher in the Colony. I have not set foot in his establishment since his slanderous words that nearly cost me more dearly than I wish to remember. What he has forced me to live with, no free woman should have to endure.

Anna Buys-Julien accompanied us, as much to enjoy the outing herself as to be a comfort to Maria. Her little babe slept peacefully in the ample lap of her young Negro wet nurse.

The mourning habits of Maria and Anna notwithstanding, we were a colourful little group. Flags of yellow and purple and green fluttered from the gilt-edged roof that protected us from sun and rain. Matching cushions made our ride most comfortable. The oars, rowed by eight strong slaves of the most pleasing countenance, dipped rhythmically into the brown river waters in perfect time with the call and chorus of the men's singing. Their rowing being steady, the tent-boat, lightly built, moved along with astonishing swiftness.

As we approached the mouth of the river Cottica, a flock of scarlet ibis, commonly known as *korikori*, were startled as they fed for small fish and crustaceans in the mud banks between the mangroves.

"There must be over a hundred of them," mused Carl Otto. The morning sun was behind them, and as they rose noisily into the air the graceful flamingo-like birds were outlined in brilliant red against the blue sky.

We passed the time in light conversation, discussing all manner of things as they came to us. Carl Otto was fascinated with our new Governor Mauricius and called him "a most interesting man." Carl Otto is quite impressed, as are we all, with the fact that Mauricius, during a journey undertaken throughout Europe two years past, made the acquaintance of the controversial writer, Voltaire, at Château de Cirey in Lorraine.

"I hear he has made an arrangement with a merchant sea captain to obtain new books from Holland," Anna said. She reached over to take her little daughter from the arms of the wet nurse.

This was certainly bright news to the rest of us, as copies of such books in the Colony are few. "He enjoys reading, then." I helped her tuck stray corners of the cotton coverlet under the babe as Anna arranged her on her lap. Little Susanna, barely one year old, was now awake and squirming to reach Pansu, who sat in the frame of the tilt-window secured to my wrist by a gold chain so that there would be no chance he could fall overboard and drown.

"*Oui*. He also writes poetry and is well-known in the Dutch Republic for his essays. I want *ma fille* to enjoy the agreeable benefits of being able to read and write." As did many of our educated elites, Anna regularly employed the French language.

"It would secure her future in an agreeable marriage."

Carl Otto rubbed his chin in a thoughtful manner. "Indeed. I wonder what the aristocratic Mauricius will write about our little colony? I hear he has little sympathy for our *nouveau-riche* planters."

"*Quelle malheureusement*," said Anna. How unfortunate.

Fascinated by the shiny gold buttons on the sleeve of Carl Otto's jacket, Susanna leaned forward and clasped her baby fingers firmly about the button nearest her reach. Carl Otto smiled into the child's eyes so that her gaze would be distracted, then gently unwound her little fingers. He raised his arm to rest on the edge of the side of the tent-boat, his buttoned sleeve now out of her view and reach.

"His Excellency says we have, quote—no Dutch heart—unquote, so consequently we have no patriotic sentiments and don't consider the Netherlands to be our Fatherland."

"Well, it's not," I said, "Anna and I were born here, and you, my dear, were born in Germany." With my fan I tapped him on one knee to emphasize my point.

Carl Otto's smile was now returned to my direction. "It would be difficult to have an attachment to a country that is not now nor has ever been one's place of residence for oneself or one's children."

After seeing him engage little Susanna in such a patient manner, my heart fluttered at his direct reference to children. Though it has been two years and three months we are together, our union has not yet been so blessed. My heart ached with a longing I knew not how to curb.

There was a lull in our conversation as a raucous flock of green-rumped parrotlets passed overhead. I opened the woven basket that had been prepared for our refreshment and found baked buns, cold friend plantains, and sweet oranges. I handed a bun and a linen napkin to Carl Otto.

"I see no reason why *ma petite cherie* will ever need to see the Netherlands," said Anna, who broke off a small portion of plantain for Susanna. *"Voilà, chérie.* Everything she could possibly need is right here in Suriname."

Carl Otto said, "Did you know Mauricius accepted the offer to become Governor because he suffers from chest complaints and believed our climate would be salutary?"

"Really? And is it?"

"Apparently he now suffers less from that distress."

Maria laughed at this. "And *sans aid* from Granman Quassie?" She touched the place under her bodice where she faithfully wore the *dresiman's* talisman.

"Has he yet mentioned to the Court of Police his idea to make peace with the Maroons?" I asked.

"Nay, not yet." Carl Otto arranged the linen napkin on his lap and peered into the basket. "The oranges look delicious. I'm sure His Excellency will live up to his reputation as a successful diplomat and present it in a proper time."

"Soon, I hope," said Anna. No doubt she was thinking of the three slave women she lost to Maroons last month at Buys-en-Vlijt.

Susanna began to cry, and her mother held out a small bit of orange, placing it at the child's mouth to suck. Pansu watched Anna's movement in the hope that there would be an opportunity to snatch this tender tidbit from her fingers.

"I agree," said Carl Otto. "Before the day comes when we have a major rebellion. There will always be many more of them than us and, unfortunately, always a *vrouw* Stolker somewhere in the mix."

At the mention of this Dutchwoman's name, a cloud of distress cloaked me, as if a hundred *kori kori* suffocated me by beating their brilliant red wings against my skin.

Maria looked up, her expression as dark as her mourning

dress. "What outrage has *vrouw* Stolker committed now?"

With an uncommon degree of calm in his voice, Carl Otto proceeded to tell us a story of profound distress carried out by this white sugar cane grower's wife. "They were coming down the river to Paramaribo when *vrouw* Stolker felt herself disturbed by her slave girl's crying infant." He accentuated the telling with waves of his hands. "She ordered the mother to bring it to her, and when it was delivered into her own arms, she thrust it out the nearest tilt-window and held it underwater till it was drowned."

Maria's mouth made a little "oh." Anna clutched Susanna more closely to her bosom, and I felt my heart freeze.

"The crazed mother made to plunge overboard, but her attempt to end her miserable existence was futile. She was stopped by the rowers."

"And her punishment?" Anna asked, her voice so soft it nearly disappeared on the breeze of the river.

"Three hundred lashes." Carl Otto's right hand fisted. While to be a firm slave master is to demonstrate responsible citizenship, this was excessively bad usage on the part of the sugar planter's wife.

"*Vrouw* Stolker is not of very good character," I said, trembling with anger, "but that is outrageous behavior. A *babe*, no less!"

"*Quel dommage*." Anna shook her head in utter disbelief, and our company fell silent, for there was truly little else to say.

I stared across the vast expanse that is the mouth of the river Suriname where it meets the mouth of the river Cottica. Whereas merchant ships bearing our sugar, coffee, cocoa, and hardwood bound for the Netherlands would head straight out to sea, our little tent-boat veered right to head up the river Cottica.

Dolphins, I thought. There were dolphins here.

I had been an unwilling passenger on one of those ships—sentenced by a most miserable misfortune to an unknown destiny. I had stood at the rail with complete unhappiness at the receding vision of my beloved Suriname. The river, with its traffic of sugar barges, dugout canoes, military transports, tent-boats, and flat-bottomed *periaks* had held no interest for me then. I had been utterly languid and downcast, knowing not what the fates plotted to toss my way.

Before me I saw the bulbous face of the butcher Egbert Peltser. Such hate I had felt for him then! Now I felt a never-ending annoyance such as one would feel for a *sapakara* lizard impossible to keep from the hencoop.

What astonishment I had felt when first I saw the dolphins, breaking the surface of the water with their leaping play! I had heard of these river creatures and, as several of them followed the ship for a time, I became fascinated with their antics. What do they know of the cruelty with which one human can treat another? I wondered. Their faces seemed to smile, they never bumped one against the other, and they moved through the water with such ease as to slice through a lifetime without stress or care. When they no longer followed us, I had found myself left with an enlightened sense of uplifting and hope.

I strained my eyes across the horizon, hoping to see the dolphins again, and was sorely disappointed when none appeared to me this day.

On the river Cottica we began to pass a plantation here and there, beautiful estates with well-tended gardens, tidy out buildings, and fine plantation houses approached by sweeping lawns. Our rowers continued to sing and chorus, even as we passed a landing where a naked Negro was chained in a dog's collar and, no doubt on his master's orders, barked like a dog at us when we passed.

"Another poor soul destined to lose his wits to madness," Carl Otto said, gesturing with his palm held outward.

. . .

Our arrival at Vlaardingen was well-received. Having in advance heard the singing of our rowers, Quackoe and his little family awaited us on the landing. He had his arm about his favorite child, his grown daughter, La Vallaire, who waved a straw hat with a blue ribbon.

Beside her stood her Mulatto consort, Jean Planteau, and two-year-old Samboe—three quarter black—son. Standing to one side of them was my brother Isaac, with his four Negro children.

"Nanette regrets she could not come today," I said, explaining the absence of my Negro sister, two years older and most closest to me in age. "She suffers a slight soreness in her limbs."

As our little group crossed the lawn that separated the landing from the dwelling house, we heard the voices of the Negro rowers swell with exuberance. Covered in sweat, the men now refreshed themselves in the river without removing their only bit of clothing, a check cloth passed between their legs and secured to a cotton string about their loins.

Quackoe's home is an elegant white three-story affair in the Dutch colonial plantation style. The shingled roof is painted dark green, as are the framework and louvered shutters. The house is situated well back from the river, which could flood with the high tide during the wet season if not for the polder system of canals and floodgates. From this safe distance the family enjoys a magnificent view of the river Cottica. This area near the coast can be low and marshy, a situation that is welcomed by the sugar cane and allows our little Colony to produce some ten times what is produced in the West India islands. Indeed, Quackoe has done very well with his poldered land.

"You'll want to rest," said La Vallaire, waving her straw hat in the direction of the house. No matter what fashion dictates, she never dresses her springy hair, so that it seems to radiate from her head and shoulders in a wild, black explosion. Hats are more often found in her hand than on her head. "Come to the breakfast room."

"Send your slaves to collect the provisions we brought," I said.

"Oh, *tante* Elisabeth, can I hold your monkey?" squeeled Nanoe, my thirteen-year-old niece.

"Nay, me, me," pleaded her younger sister Liesbeth, breathless with excitement. Isaac's two youngest children were most unladylike in their competition to win my attention and gain the prize in the form of little Pansu. Startled by the girls' loud voices, the squirrel monkey squeaked and tightened his hold at my neck.

"He's very tired from the boat ride," I said. "But you can feed him at lunch."

What La Vallaire calls her "breakfast room" was the back corner of the house most affected by the sun in the first part of the day. La Vallaire has always been a bright girl quite enamoured of sunlight and laughter and games. Both the room and her dress were of a bright lemon colour, and the dark mahogany furniture seemed only to visit the room, not truly live there. Arrayed on the center of the long dining table was an expansive bouquet of orchids, *palulu*, wild greens, and the clustered balls made up of tiny cross-shaped flowers called *fayalobi*. Flowers and greenery are much favored by Quackoe's daughter, who also has a respectable knowledge of *busi-dresi*, the herbal concoctions from the forest that heal and cure all manner of human and animal ailments.

When we were all comfortably seated, La Vallaire shooed her two-year-old son away with a young servant girl to look after him. "I don't want your daughter near him," La Vallaire cautioned Anna. "Pieter has the ringworms and he scratches off the poultice if he isn't constantly watched."

"What are you using for the poultice?" Anna asked, with the exaggerated concern of a new mother.

"The usual—saltpeter, benjoin, flowers of brimstone, and white mercury in hog's lard."

Anna nodded, apparently satisfied that La Vallaire knew what she was doing.

"He'll be a very handsome young man if he doesn't stop scratching," said Jean Planteau, Pieter's father.

"That's because he's Samboe, of course," joked La Vallaire. Everyone knows that the combination of Negro and Mulatto, called Samboe, produces the handsomest of men and women. It is why Samboe slaves are particularly prized by planters for service in their households, and why Samboe girls find it easy to make profitable arrangements.

In fact at that moment a most attractive Samboe girl, naked to the waist in the common custom, brought us some refreshment. It was my favorite sweet drink, *mope*, from the hog plum. La Vallaire raised her glass to Carl Otto and said, "It is said that once you taste *mope*, you will never be able to leave Suriname."

Carl Otto, now nine years present in military service to the

Society, laughed, raised his glass to La Vallaire in a return toast, and settled his left hand on my knee.

I grew up drinking *mope*, I thought, and was nevertheless made quite able to leave Suriname. Thank you, Egbert Peltser and your libelous lady. I poured a small amount of the fruit juice into a porcelain tea cup and gave it to Pansu, who slurped the sweet liquid with unabashed enthusiasm.

Carl Otto turned to Quackoe. "What is the news at Vlaardingen?"

"There is never news at Vlaardingen." Quackoe took a swallow of his drink and smiled. "The best news is you are visiting today."

Of course, we all knew this was not exactly true. Janetje, Quackoe's Negro slave concubine and mother of his children, had disappeared last month under mysterious circumstances. It is most likely that she had been kidnapped by runaways, but on the other hand she may have gone off with them of her own accord. After all, she had had to remain a slave since, at the time my brother bought his children out of bondage—the most honorable thing a black man can do—he did not have guilders enough to buy also the freedom of their mother. None of the slaves will talk, and Quackoe is unwilling to flog and thus mar valuable merchandise over what he refers to as "the incident." What Carl Otto really was asking was whether there had been news of Janetje, and I'm sure Quackoe knew that but chose not to make any acknowledgement. La Vallaire directed a strange look to her father, but said nothing.

Quackoe, the third child of my mother and Sam, is a tall, quiet man. Quackoe is the only member of our family who can keep a secret; if he has made up his mind not to discuss something, that is the end of that. People who do not know how kind and gentle he is might call him brooding, and certainly a bad slave master.

He is quite a contrast from Mariana's fourth child, my Negro brother Isaac, whose father is unknown. Thirty-four-year-old Isaac is quick to laugh, loves to dance, and adores his four Negro children, whom he hugs and teases even though they are no longer small children. I fear Isaac has two sides, however, as evidenced by the change in his personality when he is too far into the most esteemed liquid product of our fruitful sugar colony.

"I was sorry to learn of Frederik's passing," Quackoe said to Maria. She lowered her eyes in response and stared down into the glass she held at her lap. My heart leaped to see her sadness.

"You are most kind, brother."

The truth is that Quackoe would not own the productive Vlaardingen and enjoy the life of a rich planter if it were not for Frederik Coenraad Bosse. Three years past, Vlaardingen belonged to a Hollander who had received it as a concession by our former Governor General Gerard van de Schepper. When the Hollander died, Vlaardingen was sold at a public hearing and that is where Frederik purchased it. When it came time to register the new ownership, it was registered as owned by Quackoe Samson. Everyone knew then that Frederik and Quackoe had conspired together to purchase the plantation for the manumitted Negro, but there was nothing the clerks or representatives of the Court of Police could do, or in fact cared to do, about it. No matter the extent of white disapproval, it is not against the law for free or manumitted persons to own property, just sometimes in reality difficult to accomplish. Quackoe had worked hard to merit the confidence evidenced in the transaction by his white brother-in-law.

Indeed, our Coloured family has been fortunate to reap the benefits of advantageous planning. At nineteen, I myself already owned the coffee plantation Welgemoed, which is doing quite well, along with two hundred slaves which are my own personal property, not the plantation's. A sense of well-being touched me when I thought of Welgemoed.

Across the lawn I saw the eight tent-boat rowers, black bodies glistening in the late morning sun, strolling towards the back of the plantation house to the *keuken* house. Their wet check cloths clung most revealingly to their privates. At the *keuken* house they would be served *pinda* soup in calabashes, which they would devour sitting on low stools in the cook yard.

"Today is the *anniversaire* of His Serene Highness the Prince of Orange," said Anna. This announcement brought smiles to our company, not because we were Orangists or cared that much for the Frisian stadholder William IV, that titular head of the Dutch Republic, but because the fact of his birthday made us feel festive, and gave reason to make celebration.

"Let us drink to the health of His Highness," said Isaac, slapping his hand hard on the table. La Vallaire sent for something more potent than *mope*, and also some slaves to fan us as the breeze had died down. Above the trees across the river a dark gray cloud was gathering, portent of a larger wind followed by rain.

We passed the hour drinking fine Jamaica rum mixed with *mope* and discussing the business of plantation management and the shipping of goods to Holland. All except Isaac, bored by this conversation, agreed that there is a potential fortune to be made from trading in textiles, silver, crystal, and liquor. With the guidance of my business representative, the commercial company Pieter Reydenius & Son of Amsterdam, I have begun of late to give serious consideration to such trade.

Ah, the fortunes of fate—what might have been my future in the Colony had I not been exiled? How could I have foreseen, gazing that day in abject melancholy at dolphins in the river, the fortuitous meeting with Pieter Reydenius that would make such a significant impact on my destiny and my fortune?

When we gathered in Quackoe's dining parlour for the midday meal, though the sky was darkening above us, we were inclined to casual conversation. All the children, even little Pieter with his ringworms, were in attendance, La Vallaire being careful to seat Pieter at the farthest end from Anna, who held Susanna on her lap.

"Sit next to me," I said to my youngest niece, Issac's daughter Liesbeth. Of Isaac's four children, only the Negro Liesbeth was born free. When she is older, she will be referred to legally as the Free Negress Liesbeth, as I am the Free Negress Elisabeth. Liesbeth is my favorite niece, perhaps because even though she is already eleven she retains that playful curiosity of children that I fear is an unfortunate loss as we grow older. Liesbeth exhibits a ready intelligence and is being taught to read and write, at which studies she has shown to be excellent. Her father, who can neither read nor write, I fear is already intimidated by her accomplishments.

Isaac said, "Next year, when Liesbeth is twelve, she wants to apprentice to a seamstress and lace-maker in *foto*, so that she may learn a trade." He spat the Sranan Tongo word for Paramaribo, derived from the slaves' reference to our formidable Fortress Zeelandia, where they are brought to be jailed and receive punishment. Clearly, Isaac is not happy with Liesbeth's ambitions.

"An admirable idea," said Maria.

"I want to be able to take care of myself," stated Liesbeth, with what I think is unusual confidence in one who has not yet the first blood experience of womanhood. Isaac scowled and downed a great portion of his drink in one swallow.

The kitchen servants arrived with the luncheon dishes—boiled cassava, two kinds of greens, little dishes of hot sauces, a tray of sliced venison, and a large pepperpot stew of various leftover meats and fish.

Anna and La Vallaire exchanged their favorite recipes for the pepperpot, and Liesbeth asked for two servings of the cassava, upon which she heaped sugar. Maria nibbled on a single slice of venison, though she complimented La Vallaire on its excellent taste. Nanoe and Liesbeth took turns feeding tidbits to Pansu. At last sated, the monkey turned his attention to the caged parrots at the far end of the room and the *pikolets*, the singing finches in their individual cages hanging from the top of the open window frames.

These pleasantries ended when Isaac began to question Quackoe about the next planter upriver, a particularly evil neighbor who is known to have slain one of Quackoe's slaves.

Quackoe, his face impassive, said, "A murder like that first needs be properly proven."

Isaac snorted and wiped his mouth with his sleeve. He was into his third tall glass of rum, I noted. "So he pays a fine of five hundred florins and needs pay no more to you for having killed your property."

"He may kill as many Negroes as he pleases," Carl Otto said, "As long as he pays the five hundred florins a head." Carl Otto is always quick to present the logic of a situation. His hazel eyes revealed no partiality regarding it.

"But he must compensate you, Quackoe, for the full value

of the slave." Isaac's voice rose in indignant anger.

"It first needs be proven," Quackoe repeated.

Little Susanna began to fuss, and Anna made a shushing sound to her baby. "*C'est dificile*," she said, "when evidence given by a slave is not admitted."

"My point exactly."

"So you are going to let the matter drop?" Isaac's tone evidenced disgust with his older brother's prudence.

Before Quackoe could respond, Maria said with an affectionate smile, "Brother, you are as forgiving of your neighbors as you are of your slaves."

"I prefer to let the matter rest," Quackoe said, with quiet firmness.

Outside, the anticipated storm cloud broke, and a loud clap of thunder accentuated Quackoe's pronouncement. Pansu scampered across the table and back into the security of my waiting arms.

As rain began to pound the house, Isaac said, his voice slurred, "In *foto* they say you are one of those owners who, for fear of disfiguring the hides of your handsomest slaves, forgive them with twenty lashes, when by their robberies they deserve the gallows."

Which comment earned him a stern look from Maria, who disapproved of such conversation at a meal where children were present. Quackoe helped himself to another slice of the venison and ignored the harsh words of his younger brother.

When all the meal had been consumed and the crystal and porcelain cleared from the table, the children went off to their pursuits, trailed by their elderly *creole mama*. The rest of us retired to the salon to smoke our long-stemmed clay pipes and relax before retiring upstairs for an afternoon nap.

Isaac slouched on the blue-figured velvet sofa, his mood as heavy as the rain which continued to fall in earnest outside. House servants hurried to close the louvered shutters against splashings from the downpour. The room, with its walls encased in made-to-measure, ornately sculpted paneling and rococo mirrors separating each window, took on an eerie light.

Carl Otto admired the work of the master joiners in constructing the paneling, and Anna complimented La Vallaire on the overall décor of the room. It was obvious that La Vallaire had with great care planned and orchestrated the furnishings of the room. She sucked the smoke through her pipe with pleasure as she received these compliments.

At length one by one we retired to our accommodations to take our rest. From an upstairs window I sang to the little monkey in my arms and watched the rain plummet down, the pleasant view of the river obscured by a watery wall. Long after Carl Otto slumbered in the bed, I remained watching the rain, thinking of all that had transpired at lunch, of Maria's quiet mourning, Liesbeth's bright future, and Isaac's callous words.

. . .

At dusk, the rainstorm having passed on, Carl Otto and I donned our clogs and took a walk along the raised bank of the river where young orange and *pampelmoes* trees had been established.

"Quackoe's done well with this plantation," Carl Otto said. "He tells me last year he transported five hundred and thirty-two barrels of molasses to Europe."

We came upon a sluice, that part of the polder system that controls the ground water level of the plantation and drainage of water. It is a well-built brick structure, recently made, and carrying a tile with the inscription of Vlaardingen's owner, Quackoe Samson. Upon seeing it, I felt a quickening of pride for my older brother's accomplishments. We crossed the little bridge and continued to stroll among the outer houses of the overseer and bookkeeper. To our right were the carpenter's lodge, storehouses, and stables. There were housed the horses and mules, as Quackoe does not rely on the uncertain levels of sluice water, though cheaper and faster, to turn the wheels to break up fresh-cut, jointed cane.

As the evening sun fell to ground, the slaves would be returning from the cane fields, where they are now finishing the spring planting of bananas, *tajer*, corn and wheat, these crops not exported but for consumption by the plantation's inhabitants themselves. Wisps of smoke from the cook fires outside the slave houses filled the air with a familiar pungency.

Oh, and it seemed that everywhere were the laughter and cries of children! Mostly Negro, but some Mulattoes, Samboes, and Karboegers—this last, the result of Negro and Amerindian intercourse. I never tire of observing the children as they go about their innocent games. I placed my hand on my own stomach, reminded that I myself may indeed carry a tiny Mulatto within my womb. This month I have hope, but in truth it is too soon to tell so I have said nothing to Carl Otto.

We employed a slave to walk a few meters before us and beat the ground with a palm frond to frighten away snakes. Such deadly, slithery denisons are hard to discern clearly at dusk, and I found myself clutching Carl Otto's arm. A full moon had already poked its head above the darkening line of dense treetops, and its pearlescent light caused the path ahead of us to appear as a white satin ribbon against dark velvet.

A troop of *kes'kesi*—capuchin monkeys—mischievous near the cane fields where they are known to commit havoc upon the leaves and stalks, now settled into their lofty sleeping places. Did my dear, little Pansu miss the squirrel monkey family left behind when he had been captured after his mother had been slain? Pansu seemed content to chitter from his place inside the little carrying bag I had made to secure him at my waist. The white fur circling his round, black eyes appeared stark in the rising moonlight, giving him the appearance of a creature comfortable with the night.

All this domestic harmony, plus the good humor of my handsome lieutenant, caused me to again dwell on thoughts of marriage. Carl Otto had been reminiscing about our happy reunion at Christmastime two years and three months past.

"In a vengeance, you wore your most fashionable gown for the party at the Governor's mansion."

Indeed, that season had ended a turbulent time. I had been feeling an emptiness from my mother's death the previous year, while I had still been in exile and therefore unable to be at her side during her final illness. My mother seemed to symbolize everything that I had lost during my lonesome years in the Netherlands, years that could never be recovered. The Christmas outing had been my first public appearance since my ordeal, and I had been determined to flaunt my victory, especially in the faces of Edgar and Sophie Peltser and the unscrupulous prosecutor, Jon van Meel. To my great disappointment, they were not in attendance, but this was forgotten by the attentions of the handsome white Society lieutenant.

The army of the Society of Suriname is comprised mainly of white adventurers and soldiers from all over Europe, young bachelor mercenaries. As such, they garner immediate perusal from the ladies of the Colony, be those ladies white, Negro, Mulatto, Mesties, Quadroon, Samboe, or Karboeger. Unfortunately, one cannot tell without references or further social intercourse which of the young men are indeed fugitives from justice hiding from the authorities of their home countries. In the end, why they are in military service turns out to be of little importance when they realize their horrible position and begin to die like flies because they cannot survive our climate and jungle. It is sad irony that more of them die of tropical illnesses and lack of strong constitution than warfaring confrontation with runaway slaves.

As a young woman of eighteen, I didn't give Carl Otto much thought when he first arrived in the Colony on December 11, 1733 as a cadet on the ship *Nieuw Clarenbeek*. Even though he was my same age, my first impression of Carl Otto was that he appeared too young to be in military service.

Carl Otto and I had been enjoying a budding friendship before it had been interrupted by the most horribly unforeseen of circumstances.

"You danced only with me," I said, remembering his attentions at the Governor's Christmas *fête*. This caused me to smile as we walked the graveled path atop the *dijk*.

"How happy I was to see you again, dear Betje. I had been in anguish that I had not declared myself sooner. Maybe there was something I could have done…" His voice trailed off in sweet sadness.

I leaned my head against his shoulder. "There was nothing you could have done, my love. Even had we been able to marry, I doubt events would have turned out differently."

"Ah, the law." Carl Otto waved the air with one hand as if with magic to make a foul odor disappear in the moonlight.

"I'm glad I didn't know that you cared for me," I said. "The pain of the separation would have been more than I could bear."

"Still," said Carl Otto, "it has come to the good in the end, my sable beauty. My commitment to you is no less than a church marriage."

Darkness had now descended well upon us, and we turned back towards the plantation house. The moon had heightened and its face glowed fair upon us. Fireflies reflected on the quiet waters of the Cottica River as Carl Otto stopped in the pathway to take me into his arms and bestow upon me a most passionate embrace.

...all come to the good in the end, he had said. But what good is there in being referred to as *whore* by the very persons who every day practice equally sinful living? Such is the incongruous life we live in our little Colony.

4

Paramaribo, July 1742

Three days past Isaac experienced a terrible accident which I feared to prophesy would result in his death.

Maria sent for Granman Quassie, but we were told the *dresiman* was far up the Suriname River at a plantation past Joden Savanne. I feared that even at high tide there was not enough time for him to make the journey.

Wednesday morning, Liesbeth had begun to read to me a book while I did some needlework, whence came the news that there were men at the door bearing the sorely damaged body of my brother.

It seems Isaac had been carousing with some men in a drinking establishment the previous evening. Sometime after midnight he became embroiled in an altercation that resulted in his body lying unconscious in a back road to the waterside tavern. He was only found at first light and near dead when brought to the house. His trousers and shirt were torn and bloody and his shoes had disappeared, no doubt stolen.

Having lain in the road for some hours wet and soaking, this being the heart of the wet season, he sank into a violent fever and was indeed in a most lamentable state. As I stood over the bed where I had him placed, he looked up at me in wild amazement, as if he did not know who I was. In spite of the fever in his body and the liquor in his blood, his black skin felt cold to my touch. I was aware that Liesbeth, speechless with fright, watched my face.

"Send for hot water to bathe him," I commanded her.

The white doctor, for a goodly sum of guilders, came to tend Isaac's many bruises and lacerations. Though he was twice drawn blood the first day, yet he remained weak and would not touch the hearty meat soup with barley that was brought.

"This is what comes of getting drunk on Jamaica rum!" said my sister, Nanette, when she appeared at the house.

"It's no help to judge now," I said, a stern edge to my voice. "Pray that none of his wounds become diseased."

I couldn't help thinking that if Isaac had taken a new concubine—the children's mother having already passed on—in addition to knitting and sewing for him she would have prevented him from keeping late hours.

The atmosphere now in our house on Oranjestraat was in an extreme state of agitation. However strongly I pressed the messengers to tell me who had performed this degradation upon my brother, no information was to be gained. Nothing would have given me greater pleasure than to find out the culprits and have meted out to them the harsh punishment they deserve.

Isaac's son, sixteen-year-old Jupiter, raged and made to strike the messengers, but Carl Otto stayed him. This was not the first time Isaac had partaken of a street brawl, but this time he was most seriously affected.

Liesbeth, pale and uncommonly quiet, would not leave her father's bedside. "Dear Papa," I heard her pray, "please don't leave us. I'll do everything you say if only you'll wake, and come back to us."

Her dark hand against the white bed sheet that covered her father's chest appeared cruelly stark and made me think of how easily life slips from one side to the other.

So distracted was I that when later I bathed myself I thought the blood I found to be Isaac's. My woman's blood has never come regularly with the moon and I realized that my time was upon me. Regrettably, after all I'm not with child. A heavy sadness fell over me so terrible that I thought at that moment I should myself succumb to deathly despair.

. . .

Dear laughing, pleasure-loving Isaac proved to be mortally wounded. He is with us no more. Liesbeth and her sisters, Nanoe and Cato, are distraught; Isaac's son Jupiter, in hot anger, vows revenge. But revenge against whom? For we have only been able to determine that two of Isaac's friends left him before the altercation and so claim no knowledge of what happened after midnight. The barkeep, as barkeeps do, knows nothing of what happened. Though Isaac is a free tax-paying citizen of the Colony, because he is black there will be no inquiry made by the Court of Justice.

"But we call the Governor 'friend,'" I persisted, "and you have friends among the Court of Justice and Court of Police!"

Tugging at his wig, Carl Otto appeared to weigh the matter with care before pronouncing that there is nothing further to be done.

By midday today Issac was committed to the ground and a memorial service held at the Dutch Reformed Church. All would have gone smoothly, as it should on such a sad occasion, were it not for a chance encounter with the Peltser family after the service.

How it came about was that as Maria, Quackoe, Nanette and I waited for the coach to be brought round, the butcher Egbert Peltser, his wife Sophie, and daughter Juliaana were also awaiting their own coach. As it happened both coaches arrived in the narrow road at the same time. Both drivers vied for the space next to a part of the road that was a bit higher and therefore dry, so that their masters could mount their carriages without soiling their shoes with the mud. This was even though we all wore clogs to protect our shoes, this being, as I mentioned, the wet season.

"Here!" commanded Peltser to his black driver, who forced himself so near to our coach that both horses, in the confusion of such close proximity, threw back their heads as if to bolt. There were loud neighing and awkward prancing of legs, so that mud was splattered on all persons standing near.

Maria, always most protective of the rest of us, spoke right up. "Watch your carriage," she said in an uncommonly loud voice, "There's no need to crowd."

"Ah, the Free Black woman Maria," muttered the butcher.

Peltser stepped forward, as if he would challenge my sister, and his wife sneered. "Go back to Salzhalen," she said. "And take your whore sister with you."

I gasped in frank distress at the directness of this confrontation. I knew I could expect looks and allusions from the Peltsers, especially the mean-spirited wife, but never before had she been so aggressive to me or my family. Even the daughter, fifteen-year-old Juliaana, a cream-skinned little thing with intense blue eyes, looked questioning.

"Get in your carriage and move on," Carl Otto said evenly. Where I held his arm, I could feel muscles tense in silent anger.

"There is mud on my dress," Julianna whined, leaning forward to pick at a place near her hem. Her tone was clearly indignant.

"You see what you've done?" shrieked *vrouw* Peltser. "It's an abomination that our lawmakers allow you and your kind to live freely in this Colony!"

My hand begged to slap her senseless, so incautious did I feel at such injustice. To his credit, the butcher propelled his wife in the direction of their carriage and Juliaana followed, gathering her mud-spotted skirts with care as if she were saving them to be studied later.

. . .

After the service for Isaac our family gathered at Maria's house. Tables were laden with food and there was plenty of rum and Madeira. Tobacco smoke permeated the main floor. Maria, adding to it with her own pipe, had slaves fanning the air so that it would not become stale, but remain sweet-smelling from the orange trees outside the windows of the dining parlour. Quackoe, after all had partaken of the refreshments, led us into the drawing room for the reading of Isaac's last testament.

It had begun again to rain. A house slave closed all the shutters, so the slightest sound in the rooms of the house seemed peculiarly hollow. With the light held at bay, we sat in a gloom that was acerbated by tobacco smoke and the heavy-heartedness of the day.

Isaac's testament was read by the civil servant, *meneer* Laban, an unpleasant little Dutchman of indeterminate age. His voice exhibited a grating quality not unlike the *tityari* birds that only cry at dawn in the jungle surrounding the plantations.

"Isaac Hannibal, a man who is not married, gives to his half-sister Maria Bosse 400 guilders and to his sisters, Nanette Samson and Elisabeth Samson, 300 guilders each."

This was good news to Maria, who had paid with 4,500 kilos of sugar to have Isaac buried in the church cemetery.

"To the clergy Hendrick van Perica is granted the sum of 200 guilders."

I made a little start at this pronouncement. Indeed we were all surprised that Isaac, who never made much of any kind of church-going, should leave the clergy such a handsome sum.

"The remaining estate shall be divided equally between Quackoe Samson, the brother of Isaac Hannibal, and Liesbeth Hannibal, the daughter of Isaac Hannibal."

So. Liesbeth's apprenticeship would be guaranteed. Isaac may have loved the drink that resulted in his downfall, but he had been and remained a good father to Liesbeth.

There were, however, scowls in the drawing room. Isaac's other three children, seventeen-year-old Cato, sixteen-year-old Jupiter, and thirteen-year-old Nanoe, had not been mentioned at all in his testament.

Cato, already a well-built young woman, pushed back her chair, which made a strident noise against the wood of the floor, stood up and departed the room in silent tears. Jupiter followed his older sister, as they were not often apart, and we saw no more of either of them for the rest of the day. Nanoe didn't understand what the reading of the testament meant for her, but she needn't worry as she, like Cato and Liesbeth, could remain under the care of the family until she married or took a consort or husband to care for her.

After the civil servant had enjoyed some drink and left the house, Nanette mused, "Do you think Isaac excluded them because they were born slaves?"

"They were manumitted with their mother," Quackoe said, as if that explained everything.

Carl Otto said, "That makes no sense." He is more

understanding of the intricacies of law than the rest of us, but perhaps not of human nature. I remembered all the quarrels between Isaac and his two strong-willed older children. "Granted, he didn't get on so well with Cato and Jupiter, but that does not explain Nanoe."

Nanette shrugged. "Everyone knows Liesbeth was his favorite." This could not be denied and I myself felt a tinge of guilt because of my own special love for the girl.

Carl Otto sucked air into his clay pipe and tapped the bowl with two fingers. "I fear for Cato and Jupiter. Those two are too troublesome for their own good."

<u>5</u>

<u>*Paramaribo, August 1742*</u>

Maria was happy to take in Nanoe and Liesbeth after the death of their father, and made the same offer to Cato. There was no reason to take in Jupiter, who was allowed to continue to live in the little two-room house my mother, now six years departed, had owned. Cato refused to come to the house on Waterkant to live, preferring to remain in the same house with her brother. Though this arrangement worried Maria, who desires to see Cato properly attached—preferably to a white man—it was a relief, I admit, to me, as I saw in the handsome, strong-willed girl a potential distraction for Carl Otto.

Thus Cato was not present this afternoon for tea and games at Maria's. I was happy to see that Liesbeth has come out of her withdrawal and is exhibiting again her quick, curious personality. Maria inquired after my suspected pregnancy. Liesbeth and Nanoe, just beginning their womanhood, were fascinated by such discussion.

"Won't you soon be too old?" Liesbeth asked.

"I'm only twenty-seven," I said, thinking the young have no concept of age. "I'm still hopeful."

Nanette laughed. "Kwasiba says there is a way to assure a pregnancy using the menstrual cloths."

Nanoe wrinkled her nose. "That's abhorrent."

"Kwasiba says it works," Nanette insisted. "The *wisiman* can do it."

"I'm not yet that desperate," I said. "Besides, some herbal

potions and African love charms can be dangerous."

We halted this conversation when Maria's servant girl brought a silver tray with a porcelain tea set decorated with the tiny blue English flowers called violets. Anything said in front of slaves may easily travel as *mofokoranti* all over the colony, if it is interesting enough. The last thing we need is for people to say the wealthy Negro Samson sisters are indulging in black magic.

When the girl departed the room Liesbeth, as if she had read my thoughts, said, "But the *wisiman* only does black magic."

"You're right. And his charms for tying the soul in fidelity are often so vengeful they can result in sterility, impotence or death," I explained to the girls. "That's why they're so dangerous."

Maria poured the tea and passed the China cups all around.

"Why don't you consult *Gra'man* Quassie?" asked Liesbeth.

"Because he's a *dresiman*, not a *wisiman*," scoffed Nanette. "He only heals and discerns who is lying and who is telling the truth. Besides, he's a man and men are not good with charms for the personal concerns of women."

"But that *wisiman* Kwasiba knows is a man. How come he can do it?" My niece was full of questions. I adore that about her, though I fear she has inherited her lively personality from her so recently departed father.

"He *can't* do it," Maria stated. As if to say that that was the end of that, she indicated that Liesbeth should pass the sugar, added a heaping spoonful to the hot liquid in her cup, and changed the subject. "When do you think you will go to Holland?"

Her question was directed to me, as I have been thinking of late that I must make the voyage to meet with my business advisor, Pieter Reydenius. The matters of importing and exporting have resulted in some questions that cannot be answered by letters that take months to travel back and forth across the seas. And truth to tell I should like to make visits to the great variety of shops at Amsterdam.

"I wait upon His Excellency," I said.

"Aye, I hear he has asked you to carry some documents for him," said Maria.

"Oh, little sister, I didn't hear that," exclaimed Nanette. "That's wonderful news."

"It's only a few things he's asked me to carry for him to Den Hague," I said. I'm still feeling honored to have been so selected. No doubt Governor Mauricius had heard about my past before he became our Governor General, but it's a credit to His Excellency that he has chosen to not let this affect his judgment of me. His trust in me proves how far I've come in pulling myself out of the blackness of scandal, but I did not say this out loud over tea. My brothers and sisters have made clear their belief that such darkness is best left in the past.

"I expect to go after Christmas, though I fear the voyage at that time of year will be rough," I said. Turning to Nanette I added, "I should like to take you with me."

"Oh, to the Netherlands?" Nanette's round face expanded to accommodate a wide grin. "I would love that!" In her enthusiasm she sloshed tea from her cup onto the saucer in her hand, and searched round for the white napkin that had slid off her lap and onto the floor.

"Why?" asked Maria, who is perfectly happy to stay at home at her Waterkant house or at Salzhalen, and often complains of the discomfort of tent boat travel.

"I want to go to Holland, too," announced Liesbeth. She bounded up from her rattan stool to stand over Maria's old English terrestrial globe. Almost upsetting its support of six balustered legs, she spun the globe half around, before fingering the spot on the varnished surface where lies the Netherlands.

"You're too young and it would be too much time away from your studies."

Liesbeth's sweet, heart-shaped face fell into an ugly pout. "Reading and writing aren't that important. *Tante* Nanette can't read or write." She pronounced the French word in the Sranan way, "tant-ah", though in addition to reading and writing, she is beginning to study the French language.

"Nor can I," said Maria.

This was news to Liesbeth. "Why didn't you learn? *Tante* Elisabeth learned."

"I never needed to."

Liesbeth appeared to consider this. She knows that reading and writing are important to me. Education combined with her beauty will provide Liesbeth with a significantly more promising future.

"Do you plan to take your monkey?" Nanette asked. It has occurred to me of late that Nanette does not like Pansu, though I cannot imagine why. The creature is such a sweet little thing—mischievous, aye, but adorable and so loving of my attentions.

"Perhaps not." I was in fact considering how such a voyage to a cold, harsh clime might adversely affect the constitution of my darling pet.

"Will you bring me books from Holland?" Liesbeth asked.

I brushed the back of my hand against her rosy young cheek. "Of course, my dear."

"What is it like in the Netherlands, *Tante* Elisabeth?"

"Cold. Much colder than first light in the little wet season. We will wear heavy clothes, and more, all the time."

"Won't it be hard to move around with so many clothes on?" Liesbeth asked.

We all laughed at this. "It's difficult to describe such cold when you've never experienced it."

"I don't care to ever experience it," Maria said. Finding the tea in her cup grown cool, she reached for the teapot.

This voyage will certainly be different from my first journey to Holland, I thought. It's interesting how immense a difference there exists between doing a thing you are forced against your will to do and doing the same thing because you choose freely to do so.

At that moment Maria was summoned from the room by her houseman. They spoke in hushed tones in the hallway. Maria was annoyed when she returned to our little group.

"One of the girls has been caught with the silver spoon that went missing two days ago," she said. "That girl had such promise, too. Now she'll be damaged goods."

"What punishment will you mete out to her?" asked Nanoe, though she really had little interest.

"I've sentenced the girl to a hundred lashes, after which three fingers will be cut off her right hand." Maria sighed. "Better than the whole hand, which would render her more useless and of less value. Of course she will no longer be a house slave. She'll be sent to the plantation to work with the field Negroes." This is the lowest possible position for any slave, and the most degrading demotion for a former house servant.

Our tea was refreshed and Nanette asked, "Is this porcelain tea set new, sister?"

"Aye, I purchased it from the ship that arrived last week. Didn't you get a message that the Jew had new merchandise?"

<u>6</u>

<u>Plantation Vlaardingen, January 1743</u>

Yesterday at midday we arrived at plantation Vlaardingen without incident in our overloaded little tent-boat. Carl Otto and I and Maria, Anna with her babe, and Isaac's girls. Maria still wears her mourning habit, though Anna Buys-Julien is out of mourning now and has commissioned an entire new wardrobe of stomachers, chemises, skirts, underdresses, hats, mantelets and shoe buckles. She is even having new umbrellas of some matching cottons made to shade her Mulatto skin from the intensity of the equatorial sun.

While Maria directed only one clothing box for herself to be loaded onto the tent-boat, Anna was accompanied by three. In addition to space for our usual gifts of provisions, liquor and tobacco, room had to be found to accommodate a large painting that Quackoe had purchased from one of the merchant sea captains and which has been stored for him in *foto* this past month. Rather than entrust it to slaves to transport on a flat-bottomed *periak*, he begged us to make space for it on our tentboat, which after much arranging and rearranging we were gladly able to accomplish.

Quackoe was awaiting the painting—for which he had paid 7,000 kilos of sugar—as eagerly it seemed as he awaited the birth of his second grandchild. Nineteen-year-old La Vallaire was due to be delivered next month, but as I shall note, this did not turn out to be the case.

The Mulatto Jean Planteau took La Vallaire as concubine

when she was sixteen, and I worried that she should suffer the difficulties of women who begin to bear children so soon. As it turned out, she did not have any trouble to deliver Pieter, but this time was not to be so easy.

La Vallaire had already taken to bed when we arrived, feeling weak and heavy in the humid air. Maria and Anna and I rushed to her side, trailed by Nanoe and Liesbeth.

"My dear, how do you feel?" Maria cooed.

La Vallaire lay amid an array of bedclothes, wearing a long dressing gown with scalloped details of lace at the sleeve and hem. She reclined at an odd angle, several pillows supporting the small of her back, and a light coverlet lay in a heap at her bare feet. Embroidered handkerchiefs, damp with sweat, lay in wads around her. For the sake of Nanoe and Liesbeth I'm sure, she appeared calm.

"Nothing has happened," she declared. "I'm simply resting." She had sent away the house slaves with their large, palm-woven fans, and fanned herself by hand with a smaller version.

"Is there anything you want? A *sangaree*, perhaps?"

"Please, that would be nice." La Vallaire seemed to brighten. "And tell that girl I want extra nutmeg."

Anna went to fetch the upstairs servant and give her the order. Maria brought brocaded footstools from a corner and placed them around the bed so we could sit for a visit. I have always preferred the footstools to chairs, which seem uncommonly high. Maria set her own by the window so she could enjoy a pipe bowl and blow the smoke out the window and away from her pregnant niece.

Sipping her *sangaree* La Vallaire did look to be quite at peace, though her ebony hair was wild like tangled jungle vines round her bare shoulder where the dressing gown had slipped.

"Does Jean know you are ill?" asked Maria. Her voice was stern with concern.

"I'm not ill." La Vallaire exhibited a slight smile that gave the appearance of using all her energy. "I just get tired. I'm resting, that's all. There's no need to send for Jean. He'll be here on Friday, in any case."

I respect the Mulatto Jean Planteau as he has provided well

enough for my niece, but he remains married to a Mesties woman with whom he already had children when he discovered La Vallaire. Maria cautioned La Vallaire about bestowing her favors upon Jean Planteau, but the girl, in the heat of first love, would hear none of it. La Vallaire is happy with Jean, a minor civil servant who only visits week-ends at Vlaardingen. This is why La Vallaire rarely goes to *foto*, but remains content to live an idle life at the plantation.

. . .

When I entered the dining parlour for lunch, Carl Otto and Quackoe, already seated at the table, were discussing Cato and Jupiter.

"It's thievery, well and sure," said Carl Otto.

Quackoe nodded and heaved a great sigh. "I find it difficult to believe. You know how *mofokoranti* spread, but I've heard it from three sources."

"That doesn't make it true," I said, arranging my skirts to sit in the chair Carl Otto held out for me. "Whatever it is. I should know." I set Pansu down on the vacant chair next to me. "So what is this *mofokoranti*?"

From behind me, Carl Otto took my hand as I sat. He did not let it go, but held it as he sat back down. "It's not good news, I fear."

I looked from his solemn face to Quackoe. Maria and Anna and the girls came into the room and now Carl Otto rose to see them to their chairs. La Vallaire had elected to remain in her bed, and I worried that she had declined nourishment. Servants were already bringing in platters of succulent dishes of piranha from the river, and chicken accompanied by yams and a spicy plantain broth.

In quiet earnestness Quackoe said, "It appears that Cato and Jupiter are helping Maroons."

We were all indeed alarmed at this news.

"*Cato?*" I asked. "What is that girl thinking?" I knew she was trouble.

"Helping them, how?" Maria demanded.

"That's not sure." Quackoe paused, as if to be sure he had

the right facts. "Some say they are helping slaves escape the plantations, which is thievery, but I'm sure that rumor must be extreme. But one of them was seen about the waterside, trading something to make a purse."

"A trade?" I asked, perplexed. "What's wrong with a trade? Was it Jupiter, then? What sort of trade?"

"That's not sure, either. But it was Jupiter. He appeared to be selling something for ready money, and the man he was engaged with was recognized as a person who is known to visit the Saramaka Maroon villages."

The villages he spoke of were in an area where the parallel Saramacca and Suriname Rivers run closely together. The Maroons of the area call themselves Saramaka as they have established hidden villages on the upper Saramacca River.

Carl Otto passed a platter of piranha fish in an excellent sauce to Maria and said with his usual injection of reason, "That in itself isn't illegal. Without men like that Governor Mauricius will never be able to contact and propose peace to the Maroons."

"Still," breathed Anna. "They could find themselves *se compromettant*, compromised—even be killed." She voiced my very fear, and the sound frightened me even more.

"Has Mauricius told the Court of Police about his peace-making ideas yet?" I asked Carl Otto.

"Not officially, but he's mentioned it to several persons of authority and influence. I do believe he's campaigning, if you will, the idea."

"And the response?" I longed to hear something positive.

Carl Otto placed a bit of fish in his mouth, chewed a moment, and said, "Not good. Nay, one could even say the idea is not being well received at all."

I felt as if the very floor beneath me swayed. "It does go against everything the Society has established as government in the Colony." My voice came out in a whisper. "And it's no good if Cato and Jupiter are involved in helping runaways."

Liesbeth spoke up. "They have to do something. Don't you want to find Janetje?"

Quackoe paled. It had been over a year now, and no one had heard one word since of his concubine. From one of several cut crystal bowls laden with fruit on the table, Quackoe selected a ripe mango. No one spoke as Quackoe began with a little silver knife to peel it.

"You are right, Liesbeth," he said at last. "I fear the entire colony will suffer the most terrible and bloody misfortune if the Maroon question is not settled—*soon*."

. . .

I knew not the hour of darkness when I was awakened by Maria, who summoned me in haste to La Vallaire's bedroom.

"Quiet! Don't wake Anna or the girls."

"What is it?" My voice was high pitched with alarm.

"La Vallaire has begun her labor."

"But it's too soon!" I exclaimed.

Indeed, La Vallaire had passed her water and was breathing with effort when we entered the room.

"The midwife—" she gasped.

Maria grasped her hand; La Vallaire's knuckles were white with strength. "Who is the midwife?" Maria demanded.

Sweat beaded on La Vallaire's forehead. "The slave woman, Afinesa—the house—behind the *keuken* house." Her breath came in measured tones.

To me, Maria ordered, "Fetch her."

I ran down the back stairs and out the door to the cabins behind the house with the cook chimneys, where all was dark and silent. I ran to the first house and flung open the unsecured door. Fearful faces greeted me.

"Afinesa," I panted, "the midwife—your mistress—it's early—need to hurry—" The words came out of my throat in incoherent shots. A middle-aged woman came forward nodding her unclothed head, unperplexed by the sight of a black woman in a fine European nightdress invading her door at a dark hour.

"I take you there," she said.

She led me from her house to another and knocked on that door. A muffled voice called out, "*Soema de?* Who's there?"

"*Misi* need the midwife," my guide answered.

The door opened and a corpulent old Negress with linen-white hair stood there, grasping a check cloth about her ample body.

"Hurry," I commanded.

"I come." Her soft voice had the calm induced by the delivery of hundreds of babes. She seemed to me interminably slow as she followed me back into the main dwelling house and up the stairs to the bedroom. Maria had lit several candles and two oil lamps, and the room was infused with a warm, honey glow.

La Vallaire received the midwife with great relief, as a child welcomes the return of its mother from a long day at the market. Now Maria and I became the slaves, fetching cloths and arranging for hot water at the direction of Afinesa, who was the very picture of calm and composure.

She made La Vallaire open her loose robe, a tea gown fastened with ribboned cord, so she could lay her hands on the huge, round belly. As she moved her roughened, wrinkled black hands around the expanse, she cooed to the child within in her own African language, which none of us could understand. When the midwife had something to say to any of us she expressed her instructions in Sranan Tongo.

She urged the expectant mother out of the bed and made her stand. La Vallaire doubled over with a contraction and the midwife directed Maria and I to support her. La Vallaire draped an arm about the shoulder of each of us. Afinesa gathered La Vallaire's frilled teagown into the fold of flesh where her breasts began to roll over her big belly and there retied the ribboned cord. La Vallaire's naked abdomen and buckling legs were now quite exposed.

In this manner Afinesa coaxed our threesome about the room, causing La Vallaire to walk with great awkwardness between the contractions. This activity continued for some time. La Vallaire said little, but now and then a moan passed out along with her breath. She was given *smeri-wiri*, the birthing drink of stewed herbs. She sweated greatly, and wet cottons were brought with which to wipe and refresh her face.

Afinesa, in spite of her bulk, moved with ease and confidence about the room, little affected by the heat and humidity. She continued her calming African singing and only paused when she needed to direct our little group in one way or another.

I know that there is pain to be paid for the pleasure in the making of children, yet I greatly envied La Vallaire. I have taken the pleasure too many times not to be granted my own pain and the greater pleasure that follows as a mother takes her newborn babe to the nipple. Oh, to be sure I long so for a child of my own—gladly in these hours would I have traded places with La Vallaire as she suffered!

When the birth moment came the midwife guided La Vallaire away from the Turkish carpet by the bed to a place on the wooden floor where cotton sheets had been laid, knelt down between La Vallaire's bare legs and caught the babe in her fat, widened fingers as it entered this mortal world.

Then the most wonderful thing happened: Afinesa handed the blooded infant to me to hold so she could cut and secure the ends of the birth cord, saying all the while in her songful African language what must be a prayer of thanks. I was dizzy with elation. The sound of this tiny boy howling forth his first cries were to me utterly melodious.

And then my sweet moment of oneness with this new child ended as I had to pass it back to the midwife. While Afinesa occupied herself with the business of wiping down the newborn, Maria loosened La Vallaire's nightdress and we helped the new mother back into the bed.

It was first light by the time La Vallaire had been delivered of the boy. It appeared so frail I feared for its life, but it took lustily to the breast, and Afinesa assured us with a hearty grin that this was a good sign.

During the hours this occupied, Maria and I had been more nervous than either the midwife or the mother-to-be, since neither of us has had the fine fortune to undergo the blessed trial.

. . .

Over breakfast of chocolate, baked buns and the sweet pink citrus of the *pampelmoes*, Nanoe and Liesbeth questioned us with girlish eagerness.

"We want to see it," they chorused.

"Of course you do. But they're sleeping just now. Be patient. Your cousin and the babe aren't going anywhere," I assured them.

"Will she put the blue spot on its forehead?" Nanoe asked.

I laughed. "Where on earth did you hear that?"

"To keep away the *ogri* eye," Liesbeth said. Placing on the forehead of a newborn a smudge of blue powder is a tradition among the native Arawak and Carib Indians who inhabited this land long before Captain Willoughby traded it to the Dutch. A babe may wear such a mark until it begins to walk.

"Nay, Liesbeth. She won't do that."

"Does she have a name for it?" Nanoe asked.

"La Vallaire has given the boy a fine Holland name," I said. "Jan Simon Petrus Planteau."

7

Paramaribo, May 1743

"Governor Mauricius was just saying that he's advised the plantation owners they can nominate four persons for the vacated posts," Carl Otto said to me as I returned from a nearby buffet table. "His Excellency will then select two to replace van Sandick and de L'Isle,"

The Governor, standing next to him, nodded his agreement. A square-jawed man wearing an expensive wig of rows of pale gray ringlets which graced his shoulder, even in polite conversation engages one in a fearsome stare that would intimidate the most shy of persons. This greatly belies his poetic nature.

For the occasion of the departure of our two favored neighbors van Sandick and de L'Isle, garlands of fresh orange boughs were draped over paintings, mirrors, and windows of His Excellency's mansion, making for a gracious, perfumed air. The mansion is a most impressive two-story structure with wide exterior galleries on all sides, a magnificent residence of which all Surinamers are very proud. Not only are the floors made of mahogany, but also the shutters that secure every window. Curved balustrades of this beautiful wood grace the wide cedar stairway from the main hall to the second floor, and cut crystal chandeliers adorn every room. Indeed, all of the furnishings are exceedingly rich, provided from a fund gathered by the planters, as the Governor himself only makes 10,000 guilders per annum. Surely there is no other Colony with a residence so refined for its august leader.

His Excellency Johan Jacob and Elisabeth Mauricius are the most gracious of hosts. The farewell dinner two weeks past was a tribute to the planters Jan van Sandick and Daniel de L'Isle, two gentlemen of the Honorable Court of Police who, having secured their fortunes in sugar and now yearn for their mother country, are quitting our little Colony for Amsterdam and do not plan to return.

A reception line of citizens and civil servants gathered on the expansive lawn that fronts the Governor's mansion, through which line were escorted the two planters. This took some time as everyone seemed to have some words of honor for them, for they were admired and will be missed, and there was much shaking of hands. There were some who put an arm about the men and heartily slapped them on their back shoulders—a curious European custom.

The banquet which had been prepared for the gathering was served in the main dining parlour of the mansion by Negroes in elaborate blue livery decorated with gold and silver buttons and braid. Those wearing silver served the food, and those wearing gold distributed the drink. Hundreds of newly arrived spermaceti candles gave off a sweet perfume in addition to the warmth of their light. The meal was extensive, to be sure. The cook slaves had been working throughout the previous night, and some ninety dishes were served in all, from fish to fowl to fruits, of which Suriname has in abundance. These dainties and delicacies were served on gleaming silver platters, in porcelain and beautiful Japan china bowls, and we drank from the most expensive crystal goblets of intricate cut.

The two departing planters moved among the throng of well-wishers as if this were just another party to which they had been casually invited. It is true that we are all accustomed to such rich entertainments, but *vrouw* Mauricius must be recognized for her organization of such magnificence of drinking, dining, and music as we enjoyed this evening. This fine lady, habituated to such entertainments as the result of her husband's European travels, had everything under perfect control for the occasion.

Regarding Carl Otto and her husband in serious

conversation, she said, "You can speak of all the politics you want tomorrow."

Elisabeth Mauricius is a soft-spoken woman whose skin rivals porcelain. With no effort she gives the appearance of clearing from all unpleasantness a space around her husband in which he can perform his social duties without undue distraction. To change the subject she announced, "I've been thinking I should like to organize a literary social group."

"Such learned societies are the rage now." Governor Mauricius smiled with indulgence at his wife. "Everyone seems to be curious about everything. Why, just before we left Amsterdam we saw some experimental demonstrations by the most interesting man. He brought with him to our house all manner of magic lanterns and illumination cases. In our living room he actually dissected a butterfly!"

"It was so stimulating!" *Vrouw* Mauricius waved her silk fan at her bosom. "He belonged to a group of regents and merchants and scientists and philosophers that met every week to discuss the most intellectual subjects."

"We may have trouble finding scientists and philosophers in the Colony," Carl Otto said.

"But we certainly have merchants and people who would *like* to be regents," I offered.

They smiled at this and *vrouw* Mauricius hailed a servant passing by with a silver tray of Madeira in stemmed glasses.

"I mean to say that many gentlemen from the upper and middle classes participate—ministers, physicians, higher public servants—and educated ladies, too, of course." She tipped her glass in my direction.

"I don't think they'll be including *Gra'man* Quassie," whispered Carl Otto. In my attempt to stifle a laugh I came close to spilling the wine from my mouth.

The Governor wiped a bit of grease from his fingers and said, "They don't really *do* anything. They're most interested in simply watching experiments. Perhaps ours might be of a general orientation. A focus here on natural history—zoology, botany—would be the sensible thing. I should think a collection of specimens would be quite easy to put up."

"Or you could instruct them in the acquisition of poetic

skills," *vrouw* Mauricius. Turning to the rest of us she added, "My husband is quite a poet, you know. He's even had some works published."

I was astonished to see our Governor General blush, and I don't think it was from the Madeira he'd consumed.

"Sometimes they offer prizes for the best poems or essays on certain subjects," his wife continued.

Mauricius recovered his composure and said, "Certainly the flowering of arts and sciences in the Colony would be desirable and pleasant. This Colony could greatly benefit, it seems to me, from a concentration on poetry and eloquence."

"I think he means," said Carl Otto, "that we should indulge ourselves in more learned pursuits instead of the common entertainment of spreading *mofokoranti*."

I made a mock toast to him with my wineglass. "I can see that we will spread our rumors in rhymed verses instead of Sranan Tongo," I said. A ludicrous thought struck me then that I might describe the shameful ordeal of my past in rhyming phrases, providing the darkest of nursery entertainments.

"Will our new nominations for the Honorable Court of Police need to write poetic essays to enhance their chances of selection?" Carl Otto inquired with one raised eyebrow. His voice carried twin tones of curiousity and amusement.

His Excellency's square face bore a thoughtful expression. "It certainly would not be required, but such poetic skills would naturally lead to the enhancement of a man's intellectual discourse."

"I should like a reading society," I said. "If we could enjoy more access to books, Your Excellency."

Governor Mauricius nodded agreement and tugged at one of the gray curls that fell about his shoulder. "Reason and experience make it undeniable that the practice of useful arts and fine sciences will improve the daily society, and such progress can be expected from joint efforts. I support my wife in the idea of instructive gatherings—bringing learned neighbors together in friendship and common interest to raise the level of our society."

"Perhaps there might even be published a periodical in the model of the *Hollandsche Spectator*," *vrouw* Mauricius suggested.

I have only seen one volume of this influential Dutch review founded by the Dutch journalist Justus van Effen; which periodical he copied from the very successful English *Spectator*, and which I found to be a most enlightening as well as entertaining journalism.

Carl Otto stared into his wineglass, which he twirled in his fingers so that the dark liquid swirled dangerously close to the upper rim. "Are we not merely cultivating Dutch taste and literature?" he asked.

"Nay," said *vrouw* Mauricius. "We cultivate our own taste and literature."

"At least it would provide us with more reading material," I reminded him. The direction he made with his question could only prove of controversy, and we need no more of that.

Others joined us and His Excellency had need of socializing in another direction, and *vrouw* Mauricius also left our company with a promise to lend to me some of her books.

. . .

We thoroughly enjoyed ourselves at the Governor's mansion and went home to our house on Oranjestraat just as the eastern sky turned rose with dawn. Our carriage wheels rolling on the ground pink sea shells of the street made a fresh crunching sound, and the *gritjibi* birds were just breaking into morning song. The day promised to be sparkling and quite possibly free of rain.

"Do you have planters in mind you prefer for the nomination to the vacated posts?" I asked.

Carl Otto laughed. "Ah, one is as bad as the next. Perhaps it's the curse of governing that one can never find a candidate completely innocent and pure of heart."

My consort has the ability to see the simple truths of things and his words brought a smile to my face. "I take it that means, no, you do not have any preference. Well, nor do I," I admitted.

"I do hope His Excellency is successful in his campaign to make peace with the Maroons," Carl Otto said.

"My dear, it is the dark side of the business of slavery. I don't know that a successful peace can be had."

As we entered the house, Kwasiba appeared, chewing on a sprig of new growth from an orange tree. Her black face, fair to look upon, showed anxious disturbance. Since she has been mine for two years past, I have come to know her well and I am not disappointed to be able to count on her quick service. She was there now to take my mantelet, help me undress, fold and put away my stomacher, skirt and underdress.

"*Misi* 'Lisabeth," she said in a conspiratorial whisper, "*Fufuruman* come to house of *misi* Bosse."

This startled right out of me my weariness after a night of dining and dancing. "A thief? What you say, girl?"

"Adoe jus' come from visit to cousin there. *Misi* Bosse come home early from party at Governor's, she find many things stolen from her house." Kwasiba bobbed her madras-wrapped head with a righteousness that only information heard first-hand can bestow.

"What sort of things?" Carl Otto asked.

"Much silver plate, linen dinner cloths, gold watch, many ells of velvet ribbons gone missing."

"My sister keeps most of that in locked cupboards."

"Aye, *misi*. Locks broke. Wall of one cupboard chopped in."

"Who was there? Was anyone hurt? Did anyone see the thief?"

"Nay, *misi*. Only house slaves. They no see *fufuruman*, but he there."

. . .

Our households have been in a state of great disturbance since the evening of the Governor's party. Maria is in a condition of extreme agitation over her missing household goods, and has not been able to find the culprit among her house servants, as would be the first assumption.

"Who else could commit such an outrage?" She demanded. Without hesitation, each of the house slaves present that evening has received one hundred lashes of the whip and banishment to Salzhalen, where they are now of the much lower position of field slaves. Maria has ordered from the joiner and furniture maker larger, thicker cabinets to be made and new locks of a different design to be forged. She is busy training a new household, and suffers from the frustrations of same.

Carl Otto has been in a foul mood as the result of *mofokoranti* he heard following the same evening. Summoned one day to a military meeting of some sort at Fort Zeelandia, he arrived early and while still in the hallway overheard a casual conversation between two officers. In the discourse my name was mentioned in a most derogatory manner. He will not disclose the details. Though an uncomfortable unease has overtaken me because of this I have not pressed him. There is more urgent business to which I'm obligated to attend.

For our departure to Amsterdam, Nanette and I have been absorbed with packing clothes and sundries, and selecting which two slaves shall accompany us. As Nanette does not concern herself with such things, I had to set the time for her to make the necessary visit to the notary to record a last will and testament; one does not responsibly set out on such a voyage without one's affairs in perfect order. Nanette made her sisters, Maria and I, and our brother, Quackoe, her heirs.

We had plenty of time this morning as the ship *De Beekvliet* awaited at the waterside for the tides to be auspicious for the departure. In addition to passengers, the ship will return to Amsterdam weighted with the products of our Colony. Nearly forty vessels sail every year from our busy capital port of Paramaribo, each laden with coffee, sugar, cotton, and timbers of our beautiful hard woods and cedar.

As I peered over the railing, a molasses barge, newly arrived from some upriver plantation, sat nestled at anchor aside. From it the Negroes delivered up on board the large hogsheads of molasses. Their bodies were marbled with sweat as they moved with care to avoid the two long oars with which they propelled the barge.

We had the good fortune of a sunny morning with fat, cotton clouds populating the sky.

"Pretty sky. Bad omen," Kwasiba said, though she has never sailed herself, and has spent little time at the waterside. Still, her words and demeanor were disquieting and I was annoyed that she might fall into a spirit of dire warning. For a moment I considered that it had been a mistake to choose to bring her with me to Holland, but in truth I have become dependent upon her services and am comfortable with her presence. Attired in her best madras petticoat and head wrap, she fingered the buttons of her short jacket as she regarded everything around her.

There were many more people about the waterside than usual this morning, as it was also the departure of the planters van Sandick and de L'Isle, our neighbors so elaborately feted by His Excellency. Van Sandick's wife is accompanied by four slaves. De L'Isle's wife will follow him later, but he has brought his two stout sons, who were not aware that they attracted Kwasiba's gaze.

Not the least amount of attention was paid to the four recaptured runaways at the foot of the fortress wall strung upon the gibbet by the iron hook through their ribs. Not yet but soon dead, their pus-filled wounds already ran with maggots, expelling the most foul odor upon the breeze. Ladies will be thankful, I believe, if Governor Mauricius is successful in abolishing the law of 1721 making mandatory the death penalty for the act of *marronage*; his recommendation is that rebellious slaves should, "be condemned for life to one or another public work, but not before they have their tongues cut out and are castrated."

When on board the ship *De Beekvliet* I recognized the planter Daniel du Peijrou, I moved in avoidance to the far railing, for this is the neighbor who murdered one of Quackoe's slaves, for which act Quackoe has never been compensated and quarrel is still pending. Standing with du Peijrou was the planter Jean Couderq and next to him the man whose loathsome face will haunt me till I die.

"Come with me," I said, grabbing Nanette by the arm.

"Where are we going?"

"To our cabin. I can no longer abide the smell nor the sights."

"But we have yet to sail," my sister protested. "Everyone is waving to us."

"Let them wave." I caught myself, realizing my tone with Nanette was unduly harsh. I forced a smile. "You then stay and wave for both of us." I turned in controlled agitation and left her standing bewildered at the ship's rail. Tears welled in my throat, and this surprised me, for I thought I was past the harshest of feeling for what happened to me those years past.

Seeing the abhorrent face of the investigator Jon van Meel brought everything back in a heated rush.

. . .

Already at the age of 21 I had been doing well for myself, as I may have already mentioned. My brother-in-law, Frederik, who taught me to read and write and keep accounts for his liquor importing business paid me well for the work. I had been able to purchase slaves of my own and even some land for a small coffee plantation, so I was considered a woman of property. I enjoyed the dresses and hats of fashion, imported from England and France via the Netherlands.

It was with the greatest devastation that I became the instrument of unjust accusation and scandal. It happened that in July, 1736, Egbert and Sophie Peltser had a situation that required the law. Sophie Peltser herself, for I suspect her husband had not the stout heart, went to then Governor General Johan Raye, with a personal request. The Peltsers had a home on Gravenstraat rented to one H. Bellart, whose payment of the rent monies was several months neglected. They wanted the man justly removed from their property. Governor Raye agreed to see to the matter.

The next day *vrouw* Peltser was enraged to see *meneer* Bellart still residing on her property with no visable intention to remove himself. In her anger, she rushed to Governor Raye's office to demand he take more immediate action. I can surely imagine His Excellency's annoyance at her audacious act.

"Does she not think His Excellency has else to do?" Frederik wondered when he heard the story.

Sophie Peltser, an impatient woman to begin with, was in such a state of agitation that as she descended the red brick stairs of the building she knocked her fan against the painted iron railing and was heard to make unsavory remarks against His Excellency's person. When Frederik related this to Maria and me I laughed out loud at the image of the social climbing Dutchwoman, her face splotched with indignation, breaking a good fan and behaving altogether most unseemly for a white lady.

The next day Frederik entertained us with, "The renter Bellart has been removed from their house, but His Excellency has heard about *vrouw* Peltser's remarks."

The corners of Maria's mouth slackened. "What was his response?"

"He summoned the butcher and his lady to his presence and had, I can tell you, some severe words of admonishment for them, after which he bade them directly to take leave."

We were enjoying a *sangaree* in the serene comfort of our own drawing room at the time and had no reason to make much of these events. "And that was that?" I asked.

Frederik shook his head. "Nay, afterwards *meneer* Peltser, outside in the very street, declared that the governor is too arrogant, and that de Cheusses would have been a better governor."

The man to whom Peltser referred was Governor General of our colony for a very short period two years past.

"Jacob Alexander Henri de Cheusses introduces a property tax system and encourages the cultivation of herbs and Peltser thinks that makes him a better governor?" This was indeed an amusing viewpoint. "Who heard this?"

"A solder and an assistant to His Excellency," said my brother-in-law.

I shook my head in disbelief at such extreme behavior.

All would have been forgotten, I suppose, had not the whims of fate the following day put me in a place to hear the treasonous words for myself. I had occasion to visit the butcher shop and to my face, *vrouw* Peltser, relating the story with zealous detail, called His Excellency *schuim*. Such a word is only used to describe the basest mongrel of a sea dog, and I was shocked speechless.

"My own husband is above that man in honor and station," she stated. My confusion at these words must have shown, for she continued, "You know that Governor Raye was ordered to turn in his sword when he was in the military! He is not fit to govern our Colony."

At home I repeated this to Maria and Frederik. Maria sighed and continued her needlework, but my brother-in-law was thoughtful. "You must tell this to Governor Raye," he said.

"Oh, I couldn't possibly repeat such slanderous remarks." The very thought of saying out loud to the highest authority in the Colony such insulting words made my throat tighten.

"It's the truth, Elisabeth," Frederik said, "and he has the right to know what is being said against him."

"Couldn't *you* tell him?" I asked, reluctant to go any further with it. Without being able to say why, I felt that the words of a white man would make a greater impression than those of a black girl. At this same moment a cold stirring of air passed over my shoulders, so that I shivered without knowing why.

"No, I didn't hear the words." Frederik's stern countenance fell full upon me. "You did. You are the witness, and you know that by law these words are treasonous."

In the end he persuaded me to visit the Governor and tell the story as I experienced it.

At the Governor's mansion I was received with welcome and offered a refreshment. I was made to wait for a few minutes in the entry salon, but that is not unusual nor was I in any way concerned.

Governor Raye greeted me wearing an attractive green waistcoat with darker breeches and fine leather boots, as if he had been planning a horseback ride. Whatever his plans, he sat down beside me and directed one of his servants to fetch him a rum punch. We chatted together for a few minutes before he pressed me to the point. With the greatest reluctance I related the events in the butcher's shop, and *vrouw* Peltser's exact words, for they were sorely etched in my memory.

Governor Raye became upset. His pale eyes hardened, appearing as glass locked in a tense white frame. Several times he interrupted to ask me, "*Vrouw* Samson, is this really true?" and each time I answered, "Aye, Your Excellency."

Suffering I believe from some ancient military injury, he rose awkwardly from the sofa, nearly spilling his rum punch, and paced the floor in heavy steps that punctuated his anger.

"*Vrouw* Peltser has insulted the highest authority," he declared, his voice dark with tension. "*Vrouw* Samson, you are sure this is true?"

"Aye, Your Excellency."

In his fury, Governor Raye issued forth soldiers to apprehend and arrest Egbert and Sophie Peltser. The Peltsers were subsequently taken to Fort Zeelandia for interrogation by Governor Raye's military captain and the prosecutor Jon van Meel.

An overwhelming feeling of premonition grasped me as I stood alone on the porch of the Governor's mansion after being dismissed from His Excellency's presence. It was as if the curling tentacles of the most aggressive jungle vine were growing around me, about to ensnare me in an unforeseen nightmare.

In their own obsequious fear the butcher and his wife denied everything, and thus began my dark ordeal.

8

Amsterdam, December 1743

Nanette is smitten with tulips. Of course there were almost none remaining in bloom when our ship *De Beekvliet* docked in Amsterdam this September past. The weather was fine yet the trees lining the canals were already acquiring a bright, golden tone that heralded winter in the Netherlands. Everywhere we went Nanette pointed out every drawing and painting of the coloured flower, as well as the tulip motif in carvings and stone. At first I deigned to humor my sister, but now have tired of so many visits to the tulip merchant in preparation for a selection to carry back to Suriname.

"Nanoe and Liesbeth will love them," Nanette declared with enthusiasm. "I want a complete medley of colours—reds, yellows, the striped ones, that beautiful lavender!"

"You will need a special case constructed to carry the bulbs back in safety," I said.

"Ah, little sister, you are always the practical one." Nanette's dark eyes fairly sparkled with her passion for the waxy tulip blooms.

I smiled, remembering my own first sight of tulips. It was in the same month that I arrived in Amsterdam to begin exile from my beloved Suriname. At that time for me the tulips represented all that was strange and startling in Amsterdam, a colossal metropolis of streets, canals, and grand edifices completely foreign to me. I, who had arrived frightened and, I was sure, without friend in the world. Though there were still sunny days in that September, already the air was considerably colder than tropical Suriname, a foreboding sign of the darker, frigid winter to come.

My feelings for Amsterdam now are more agreeable, and I asked my sister, "Do you know what the French philosopher Montesquieu said to his traveling companion Lord Waldegrave?"

Nanette shook her head.

"He said, 'I would prefer Amsterdam to Venice because in Amsterdam, you have the water without being deprived of the land.'"

My sister found this comment to be quite agreeable. It was my pleasure to introduce her to this crescent-shaped city with its ring of canals fanning out from the center and ending in squares that formerly supported the city gates.

Amsterdam seems larger than I remember. Everywhere are narrow, bustling streets, gabled houses, towers and churches, old wooden footbridges, sluices, and arched stone bridges, and the place is alive with the music of carillons and barrel organs.

I am told there are now 300 bridges in all about the town, and one near our lodging even made entrance to low dungeons where prisoners suffer the additional torture of continually wet feet. Some of these wide, arched bridges are constructed of elegant sandstone block masonry with striking balance beams and porticoes, but the limited headway causes a captain the necessity to lower his mast to pass thereunder. On a calm day, the arches are reflected most charmingly in the canal waters.

This ring of canals is the most stylish residential area. Noble four-story houses with stoops and side steps face the canals, their brick facades clad in sandstone and decorated cornices. These are the homes of prominent citizens and wealthy merchants, the latter arranging their cellars and top floors so as to serve as storage space for commodities which they move about the town by boat. These houses, narrow at the road and lengthy towards the back, feature tall fronts customarily crowned by ornamental gables to hide from view their saddle roofs. These gables are most impressive, enlivened as they are by grand crolls sculptured in the forms of classical divinities, eagles, horses, lions, dolphins, and sea gods. On a recent outing, Kwasiba pointed out one that sported two Negro men facing each other in stately pose. Lower parts of the facades are decorated with wondrous ornamental window frames, festoons and frontons. The skillful stonemasons who have created these carved sandstone front and shoulder pieces finish them off with a cream colour paint called "Bentheim yellow", as sandstone itself has the tendency to turn black.

Nearing two hundred thousand persons inhabit this busy seaport that was originally built on shifting lakes, soggy peat and swamplands. These marshlands around the place where the Amstel River flows into the sea were tamed with ditches and *dijks* and finally, one large, protective *zeedijk*, equipped with locks, to protect the inhabitants from the tumultuous tides of the Zuiderzee.

One would have the impression that everyone here is involved with the selling, storing, and shipping of products from all the major countries of the continent. Since the fourteenth century fish from the North and Baltic seas and grain from the European countries have been traded in Amsterdam markets, and much evidence remains of the wealth, culture, and forbearance that flourished here in the last century.

Today money changing and financial transactions are replacing trade and fishing as the city's grandest industry, and the commercial houses of Amsterdam are the bankers for European Kings who finance expensive wars with borrowed money. One such house is my own representative, Pieter Reydenius and Son.

This time I was prepared for the chilling Holland winter to come; Nanette and I purchased thick worsted stockings of a most enchanting blue with a gay pattern of red tulips. For the weather we have purchased for our personal servants to carry umbrellas of oiled muslin on narrow rattan poles—such articles will prove useful at home during the wet season. Nanette became enchanted with a wool mantle in wine red, and I acquired a similar one in purple. A simple gray mantle was purchased for Kwasiba and a wool jacket for Jakij, the twelve-year old black boy we had brought to assist Kwasiba. To protect our hands from the frigid air Nanette and I have luxurious beaver muffs and for our heads the very latest of fashion, large white beaver hats with very low crowns and silk cords that tie under the chin.

"Don't you think these hats look the best on us?" Inside our cozy lodgings on Prinsengracht, Nanette flounced in front of the mirror placing her new fur hat this way and that upon her head. She bound her nest of dark, spring-like curls up under the hat, then pulled them out again to try the hat with a few curls framing her face. I gave her a questioning look, to which she explained, "I mean, the white stands out more distinctly on black faces, don't you think?"

For certain my sister and I are not among the unnoticed, even in such a metropolitan city as Amsterdam. Persons of colour seen on the streets here are slaves or poor or both. To see two young black women in expensive dress and attended by their own black servants has caused more than one head to turn. Most likely casual observers assume we are the well-kept mistresses of some wealthy regent.

The lavishly decorated dresses we love in the Colony seem to have here faded from fashion. Dress is more simple, with a new emphasis on comfort and function. The gowns are all of one piece, tailored to enhance a lady's figure. The colours are more manly, it would seem: dark orange, shades of ochre, malachite, and blue in the hue of lapis lazuli.

Still, we have managed to make purchases in fine bright colours and stripes of hundreds of ells of garden silks, brocades, cloth of silver and gold, very nice Mantua silks for hoods and scarves, embossed Geneva velvet, and fine thread satins. For the working class we have acquired bolts of tickle berg linen for shirts, striped ticken for breeches, and one bolt of everlasting, a fabric made of worsted, for breeches and vests. This last, because of the weight of the fabric, will be favored at home only by the Society militiamen. My investment in these textiles, plus an assortment of needles, threads, buttons, and thin-boned stays, will see in the Colony a fine return.

For the Orangestraat house, I have selected long sheets of French distemper-coloured wall paper that have been stenciled and flocked in a delightful *paysage*, a country garden scene. These papers, as they are used in the décor of our lodging, are most charming. The seller of the wall papers demonstrated how to apply the paper to the wall with a coating of gelatinous substance called "sizing." This latter having a starch base, I will be curious to see if it can be reproduced using the starch of our native *kasaba* plant.

My sister and I returned to our lodging to have afternoon tea and await the delivery of some of our purchases. From a box I had personally carried, I unwrapped a wonderful gold laced, cocked hat.

"For Carl Otto?" Nanette asked.

"Aye, and won't he be handsome in it?" I whirled the hat in my hand and thought how fortunate I was to have Carl Otto in my life. How different all would have been had I never been able to return to the Colony, as the wicked prosecutor van Meel had planned.

Kwasiba came into our sitting room and handed to Nanette a packet wrapped in string. It had been delivered to us from the office of my business representative. "It looks like *meneer* Reydenius has sent over some letters just arrived from home," Nanette said.

I was excited to read a letter from Maria, dictated to and written by Anna. "Oh," I exclaimed. "There has been an accident at Vlaardingen, a small cane fire. Luckily it was averted by some of the men's quick thinking."

Nanette stopped fussing with some ribbons she had purchased and searched my face. "Dear God, was anyone hurt?"

"She doesn't say, so I suppose not." In the mind of every planter any blaze in the sugar cane fields is nigh equal to the threat of a slave uprising. "But there is good news. Quackoe's concubine has given birth to a boy, freeborn, and they have named him Dikje."

"A freeborn son." Nanette replaced the ribbons in their protective tissue and sighed. "Does Maria say the name of the concubine? What of Janetje? Is she the mother?"

"Curious. Maria doesn't say. He could have taken a new woman." On fingers in my mind I counted the months. "Aye, there must have been someone else, as Janetje was not returned to Vlaardingen err we departed the Colony."

I had a sudden image of our elder brother Charloo, the person responsible for the manumission of Quackoe himself. Even though at the time I was just thirteen, I remember Charloo painstakingly writing the letter to the Court of Police requesting to purchase the liberty of his brothers and sisters, Jakje, Quackoe, and Nanette, all slaveborn. He had been so proud to be able to read it out loud to all of us.

"Through hard work the dear God has bestowed on me temporary abundance through which I am the owner of the children of my mother, and humbly request your kind permission to purchase them out of their bondage."

And so it followed that Quackoe, through equal hard work, was able to buy out of slavery his own daughter, La Vallaire. With enough guilders to free only his daughter, his concubine Janetje, whom he had purchased from Salzhalen, had remained in bondage. Perhaps Janetje never forgave him for not freeing her first.

How poor sensitive Quackoe had cried when Charloo and his wife drowned in a tentboat accident. He was sad that Charloo had not lived to see him be able to manumit in return his own child, for one of the most prideful things a black man can do is free his children from slavery.

Yet well I know that freedom still doesn't always protect one from the vicissitudes of life.

Nanette handed me another letter, this one from my dear Carl Otto.

Upon opening the paper and reading his words I said, "I cannot believe this!"

"What is it?"

"The Oranjestraat house has suffered a thievery." My voice was heard in my ears to be rising in vexation, and I felt frustrated and helpless. Nanette's mouth was open in surprise, but she made no comment, waiting to hear more. "Three kilos of sugar have been taken, a gun, and a hundred and fifty guilders. Also 'trifling things,' but he doesn't say what those are."

Nanette found her voice. "Your own household slaves, do you think?"

"I don't know. He says a shutter was broken in, so perhaps

it was from outside, but who?"

"Maroons?"

"Not in *foto*, I should think. We've never had theft on this scale there before. One might rather expect it on a plantation, but..." My voice faltered for lack of sensible words. What explanation could there be for such brazen robbery? In the pit of my belly there was a growing knot of alarm. I felt an engulfing blackness about my family I could not name. I tried to think of spirits offended, ancestors ignored—perhaps some forgotten spell or curse that needed to be attended, but I could think of nothing that connected.

Yet I fear strongly that something may be going on that is more than mere household pilfering.

9

Amsterdam, May 1744

Now that spring approaches, we are amidst busy preparations to depart Amsterdam for home. Kwasiba performs her duties with a new energy, making no attempt to hide her pleasure at the prospect of returning to the tropical climate. I am not without reluctance, as I would like to see summer in this country again, this time to happily enjoy that most delightful and colourful of seasons in the Netherlands, but it is not to be. We must return with our investment of merchandise to the Colony.

It seems every nook and cranny of Amsterdam now sports pots of every shape and size filled with stately tulips on tall green stems. This afternoon was spent in visiting again the tulip merchant, whose shop is full to overflowing with the blooms, and arranging for Nanette's precious bulbs to be correctly packed for the sea voyage home to Suriname.

I have never known my sister to be so particular about such arrangements; she has truly been most attentive to every detail, even going so far as to examine the strength of the crate boards and the width of space between the nails that held them together. She gave strict orders that each bulb was to be individually wrapped in straw along with a piece of paper on which was written both the Latin name and type of bulb contained therein. This information was also to be handed to her in the form of a separate list, from which she can inventory her collection upon arrival in Suriname.

Returning to our lodgings after this exercise, there was received a letter from Maria, sent from the house on Waterkant that saying that she is anxious for our safe return. I foresee a happy reunion with my family, but a difficult time ahead for business transactions. My family will be the first to see the many goods Nanette and I have acquired, and will want to make from the hoard purchases for their own—at greatly reduced prices. How can I expect to make a decent profit on this excursion if I sell everything to my family? But conversely, how can I say no? I must admit I had not considered this dilemma, yet I should have anticipated it. It is fortunate that the ship will take such time to arrive that I will have adequate occasion to ponder my direction in this matter.

Maria also tells us that the white butcher Egbert Peltser is now the only game in town. The other butcher, *meneer* Temminck, has closed his shop and departed with his family to Holland "for the proper education of his young children." Granted, Temminck's cuts were not the best, but he provided us the opportunity to avoid buying from Peltser. It galls me to think that I must now give that odious man all my business if I want anything for my table other than the catch of my hunting and fishing slaves!

I held the letter in my hand long after I had finished reading it, thinking of home, my family, my plantations, and the tropical landscape I have so sorely missed. I longed for Carl Otto, my house, little Pansu, and the sheer pleasure of being surrounded by sights, furnishings, food, servants...all things familiar and comfortable.

I set the letter down on the inlaid *éscritoire* but continued to regard it, thinking how good it will be to once more taste *mope*. Yet I will never forget that there was a dark time when I could not have imagined I would ever again feel contented. It is easy to look out the window of this sumptuously-furnished hotel in Amsterdam, see a person of lesser circumstance clutch his garment against the chill of the late spring afternoon, and remember that unhappy time of my ordeal.

. . .

To his credit, Frederik never forgave himself for advising me to repeat to Governor Raye *vrouw* Peltser's treasonous words, which act resulted for me such a dire circumstance of public humiliation.

Two weeks after my visit to Governor Raye, matters had begun to develop that would prove of serious consequence to my person. One morning it was made known to me that I must show sufficient proof of my claims or be brought to the criminal Court of Justice for free persons. If unable to demonstrate proof of what I had heard the Peltsers say, I could be found guilty, flogged, branded and banished from the Colony.

"Outrageous!" exclaimed Maria, clasping her hands and pacing her drawing room in great vexation.

The mere thought of such punishment as could await me if I could not somehow prove that what Sophie Peltser had said in my presence was true caused an unbalance to my senses. A moment before I had thought I was hungry, and now I could not abide the idea of sitting at table before the midday meal.

Frederik's brows came together in a thoughtful frown. "You must have a lawyer in this," he advised me.

In complete overwhelm by this turn of events, I knew naught else to do but nod in agreement.

"Josephus de Cohue," Frederik said, snapping his fingers.

"The Jew," Maria added.

"All right." My voice sounded so strangely quiet to me as to not be my own. "If you think so, I'll go to see him."

"We'll go today." Frederik was determined to take immediate action. Maria retreated to her sofa with her needlework as her husband called for a carriage to be brought and ushered me by the elbow through the front door towards the street.

The office of Josephus de Cohue was in a stately house on the corner where Gravenstraat ends and the manicured grounds of the Governor's mansion begin. We walked up the red brick steps to the porch and were shown into a quiet foyer. Frederik had sent a slave ahead to announce our arrival, so we were not kept long waiting.

"This is indeed serious," the lawyer said, after Frederik explained what had happened. Josephus de Cohue, a squat man, had a short, manicured black beard that made his face appear harsh until he smiled. I admit I was admiring his even, white teeth, when he said, "*Mevrouw*, do you realize the consequences if the court convicts you of slander?"

This pronouncement jolted me back to reality. "They are lying," I declared. "How could I possibly be convicted of such a thing?"

The Jew de Cohue was kind and patient as he entered into a lengthy explanation of our judicial system, all of which I in my bewilderment did not readily comprehend. I kept thinking that if one tells the truth, as I had been taught in the Dutch Reformed Church, justice would prevail. I could picture the minister standing before our congregation expounding on the very subject. How wrong I was!

Three days later, when the Court of Police met and the Peltser situation was discussed, Josephus de Cohue was there to speak on my behalf.

"I let them know that this process was without justice," he told us afterwards. With a great foreboding I hung on every word he said. "I told them in no uncertain terms that my client has been accused of matters which cannot be proven."

"What did they say?"

De Cohue shrugged his round shoulders and made a disgusting noise. "The Court doesn't feel this matter is very important. That may be of good portent for you." He paused and smiled. "As a matter of fact, the Court was displeased with Governor Raye for summoning the Peltsers from their home and having them escorted by soldiers like criminals to Zeelandia."

"They *are* criminals!" I was fierce in this declaration.

"But wait till you hear what happened next!" De Cohue held up one hand. "His Excellency was indignant by the Court's lack of interest in such an important question as treasonous words denigrating the highest authority. He was so angry he stalked out of the meeting! He said it was unworthy of them to have him preside over the Court if they didn't think it necessary to discuss such insulting remarks from citizens."

"Oh!" I shook my head in amazement.

"The Court had to send out two of their members to persuade His Excellency to return, which they did."

"So the matter is ended?"

"Not quite." De Cohue frowned and combed his chin with his fingers as though arranging his beard. "The Court has both pacified the Governor and tabled the matter by calling for a full investigation."

I was tremendously downcast by this news. What was there to investigate? I had told a simple truth. How could any of this be proven other than by the words of both the guilty and the innocent? Even as I asked myself these questions, I had no concept of the answers, or of how long and anguished a time would pass before those answers were found.

His Excellency Governor General Johan Raye was not to be contented. Some months later, with dawdling progress on the investigation, he wrote a letter to the Directors of the governing Society of Suriname in the Dutch Republic, a copy of which found its way into the hands of my most excellent Jewish lawyer.

In his attempts to explain the insults done to him, His Excellency wrote, *I could have burned my hands if I doubt the evidence of such brave neighbors against the one witness of dubious reputation. Through lengthy experience we are learning that one cannot change black peoples. Freedom will not change their conditions; they will continue a hateful and conflicting behavior towards white people and Christian virtues.*

Such sentiments against Negroes were not in themselves surprising. That he had chosen to believe the innocence of the white Peltsers instead of me was no longer in doubt. What stunned me was the ferocity with which Governor Raye had turned against me. In closing his appeal to the Society of Suriname, he had written, *The gentlemen have to know that the free Black woman is known here as a public whore.*

10

Paramaribo, September 1744

On this day thanks to the grace of our almighty God returned safely to Paramaribo the ship *De Beekvliet*. It was a beautiful warm day without rain when we docked, as if *Mama Sranang* herself welcomed my return to her loving arms. The waterside was filled with carriages, cargo, workers, slaves and family to welcome us home as at the same time another ship at anchor was being loaded to depart. Such a grand confusion of slaves and ship owners screaming instructions, cargo animals braying, sellers of all sorts calling along the wharf—the largest anthill in the jungle could not have been more industrious. The mingled smells of smoke, fish, and that humid perfume that is peculiar to the tropical clime greeted our nostrils. All this served to welcome us heartily after so many long weeks at sea.

By the time we were ready to disembark, it was already the heat of the day, but neither Nanette nor I noticed the inconvenience of the cloaking humidity that embraced us, so thrilled were we to again see so many Coloured faces.

With carriages awaiting us were Maria, Nanoe and Liesbeth, La Vallaire with her two children, and of course, my beloved Carl Otto. I fairly flew into his arms, so glad was I to see his person. His grin made me feel ever so grateful that I had not been detained longer in Holland.

"Welcome home, my darling Betje," he whispered, bending his head to bury his face in the warmth of my neck.

"Nanette! Elisabeth! We are so happy you are back among us without harm." Maria hugged us close and then at once we were all laughing and crying. How right it felt to be returned to the bosom of my own dear family. Such familiar faces of warmth and affection!

"Did you buy clothes?" chorused Nanoe and Liesbeth. "When can we see?"

"What did you bring me?" This from La Vallaire's little three-year-old Pieter.

"Children, children, patience," scolded La Vallaire, her voice almost musical in the love it conveyed. "You will see everything and hear all in good time."

"Ah, Liesbeth, in sixteen months *joe kon so bigi*," I said, then laughed to remember the same Sranan words from the mouth of my own mother, Mariana. Where had I heard her say that? Aye, Maria's very wedding, where I had dreamed of someday having a wedding of my own just like hers.

Carl Otto caught my attention then, and I realized one of the servants had just handed him something, which he now held behind his back.

"Hold out your hand, Betje. Someone else wants to welcome you."

Into my upheld palm he placed the end of linked gold. I knew, before the movement of his arm, that what he secreted behind his back was my little squirrel monkey, Pansu. My pet's delight was equaled by my own, and Pansu twittered and scampered up my ruffled sleeve to sit upon my shoulder and examine the brilliant emerald earrings I wore. Nanette regarded the monkey with great distaste and moved a step away from me, in case Pansu decided he wanted to examine her attire as well. My little *monk-monki* rearranged his position on my shoulder and turned down and outward his leg and thigh in the erect penile display so common to his race.

As I stroked Pansu's long tail I looked around at my little family group and I could not ever remember feeling such general fine humor. But someone was missing.

"Quackoe? He is at Vlaardingen?" I asked, fearful to hear the answer.

Maria's smile faded under the shade of her hat. "Oh my

dear, Quackoe is not in good health at the moment. He remains at Vlaardingen and sends sad regards that he could not be here to welcome you home again. But we are assured that what ails him will soon pass."

La Vallaire picked up the encouraging note and grinned. "Just wait till you see the babe, Dietje. He's adorable. And so active! He has the entire household wrapped around his little finger. He will make a mark in this colony one day, to be sure." As she said this she put her hand on the wooly head of her little son, Jan Simon, nearly two years old now, who clung to her skirts.

"I can't wait to see him," said Nanette. Then she turned to Nanoe and Liesbeth. "I have brought you a wonderful surprise." I had to smile because I knew she was referring to her precious tulip bulbs, while I was sure the girls were dreaming of more wearable gifts of personal adornment.

All of our crates and boxes and trunks were delivered by slaves to the house on Oranjestraat. Refreshment was sent for so that an impromptu welcome home party could be enjoyed. Nanette and I were urged to rest, but we were both too enlivened by such loving presence to part from any one of them yet.

At length Maria and La Vallaire departed with the children, Carl Otto returned to the waterside to be sure the slaves had secured all our cargo, and Nanette and I took Nanoe and Liesbeth with us up to the bedrooms to see the things that had been unpacked from our personal trunks.

Liesbeth kicked off her shoes, flounced onto the mahogany bed and drew her bare feet up to arrange them cross-legged under her skirt. "We want to hear all about the French fashions," she announced.

"What French fashions can you possibly mean?"

"*Tante* Nanette, tell us!" exclaimed Nanoe, her face eager with anticipation. The girls had been waiting all day for this moment, I knew.

Nanette enjoyed teasing them. "Oh, there's nothing new that would interest you."

"*Please*—tell us!"

I pretended to raise with caution the lid of one trunk as if I expected an animal to bound out. "Perhaps, in here, there's a scarf..."

One by one Nanette and I pulled summer camlets, stomachers, fichues, and *saque*-backed gowns out of the trunks and spread them on various chests and chairs about the room. Nanoe and Liesbeth touched everything reverently, delighting in new colours and fabrics.

"What is this?" Nanoe picked up a round box made of pale blue shark-skin, embossed in gold, with tiny gold clasps and hinges.

"As a matter of fact, that's a gift for you," I said.

"Oh, *tante* Elisabeth..." Nanoe's voice softened as she opened the lid to discover the treasures inside.

"It's called a *nécessaire*. You can carry it in your pocket." Inside the box were miniscule items to make up a portable toilette. Liesbeth watched in fascination as one by one, Nanoe removed a tiny funnel, ear-cleaner, tongue scratch, and flask from silk-lined compartments.

"*C'est merveilleuse.*" Liesbeth reached for a tiny bottle. "And this?"

"An odor flask. That one contains a sweet water called *eau de Cologne*. It's from Germany. There is also a little ivory tablet there on which one can write notes at a ball."

I pointed within the *nécessaire* to a tiny jeweled box in the shape and design of an apple. "That is a pommander." I showed her how its sides fell down to open in quarters. "Inside is a scent ball of Bergamot rind. You wear it around your neck or in your pocket, like an amulet. The Europeans now want everything to give off a sweet scent."

Nanoe raised the *nécessaire* and sniffed the apple-shaped ball inside. "It smells very zesty." Her delicate fingers removed the apple-shaped, jeweled box. "Will this protect me like the *obia* that Gra'man Quassie makes?"

"Not in the same way, I think, but it is reputed to protect you from the plague. And it's much more aromatic than anything Gra'man Quassie has ever made!"

Liesbeth looked at me, the question she could hardly contain clearly visible in her eyes.

"Aye, there's something for you." I tousled her black hair

with smiling affection. From the nearest trunk, I withdrew an embroidered satin envelope wrapped with a gold cord. Nanoe lowered the *nécessaire* to her lap to watch her younger sister receive and unwrap her gift.

Liesbeth withdrew from the envelope a full face ladies' mask of embossed red velvet, decorated with black satin ribbons and aristocratic Alençon lace, jet stones, and lustrous pearls. On the satin-lined back of the mask at the mouth space was a silver platelet that fit between the teeth to hold the mask in place. "It's made without ties so as not to muss one's hair arrangement," I explained.

My niece put the mask to her face and between clenched teeth said, "I wouldn't think you could talk like this." We all laughed at the sound of her measured words.

"Masks like that are for very special occasions at court in England and France," Nanette said. "That kind of mask not only protects the hair arrangement, but also the pasted face because it doesn't rub so hard against it."

Liesbeth removed the mask and asked, "What pasted face?"

"Wealthy ladies paint their faces with a thick coat of white paste."

"Why?"

"To be fashionably beautiful, of course. They want their complexions to look white and smooth."

"But why would they do that?" Liesbeth persisted. "European ladies are already white."

"Many of them suffer horrible pits in their skin from the pox," I said. "The paste fills in the holes and smoothes their cheeks."

Nanette continued. "And then they take a bit of wet wool and daub red spots to their cheeks, and to their lips a stick of rouge mixed with plaster of Paris."

"Red painted on white." Liesbeth wrinkled her nose as she considered this fashion that was unknown in our Colony.

"The red colour provides a pleasing contrast to the pale powder of the face."

"I would like to try the red paste, but I wouldn't like the white," Nanoe said.

"You need neither. You are a young beauty as you are." In

truth, I thought Liesbeth more the beauty, but of course that was not the point. White faces on black bodies would look positively ludicrous.

"And their hair? How do they wear their hair?"

Nanette's eyes sparkled as she warmed to the attention of her young audience. "Oh, the hair," she said with mock mystery. "That is a big event!"

"She means the fashion just now is for hairstyles that entirely overwhelm the head," I said.

Nanette held up her hands to frame her head. "Elaborate arrangements that defy the imagination. In addition to their own curls, the ladies add separate pieces of hair, and even wigs to make their heads bigger."

"White women wear wigs as European men wear?" asked Liesbeth.

"Aye, but in colours close to that of their own hair."

"Doesn't that make it heavy on the head? And hot?"

"I would suppose. But that's not the most strange thing—they apply lard to their hair, then curl it with hot tongs and powder it and add feathers and small flowers. They do this once a month and in order to preserve such elaborate arrangements do not wash their hair between preparations."

"*Eeuuuh.*" Nanoe grimaced. The idea of such a behavior in our wet, humid climate was undesirable to us all. "Doesn't it smell?"

"Aye," said Nanette, "and I've heard tell that they attract more lice and fleas than young swains, and even attract—because of the lard—mice!"

"Mice in their hair?" Both Nanoe and Liesbeth were horrified.

Nanette and I laughed at the astonishment on their pretty, adolescent faces. "We shan't be adopting those fashions here."

"White ladies with white paste on their faces and mice in their hair," Liesbeth said. "That must be something to see!"

. . .

Carl Otto returned after dark from the waterside to report that everything appeared to be in order and well taken care of.

"Well, nearly everything," he added.

I looked up from where I sat at my toilette table, hair brush in hand. "What must I know?"

Carl Otto began to remove his breeches and shirt. "I fear Nanette's tulip bulbs are lost."

"Lost? The entire crate? How is it lost?" I was fairly certain that no one would steal a crate of tulip bulbs.

Carl Otto's handsome face was relaxed in a smile as if there were a great joke to be had. "The bulbs have rotted during the voyage."

I could see a humor in this. "Poor Nanette. She wrapped them so carefully."

"Well, perhaps she wrapped them too tightly. Also, seawater may have gotten to them. The captain was quite annoyed, calling the smell of decay in the hold 'disgusting.' You would think he would be more accustomed to such things."

"Oh, dear." I let out a little laugh. "Nanette will be quite dismayed."

"I'm not sure they would have grown well in our tropical climate anyway," Carl Otto said, sitting half-dressed on the edge of the bed.

I laid down my hair brush next to its matching silver comb, rose from my toilette table, and stood before him. "There's something about a military man wearing only his underdrawers..." I've always admired Carl Otto's bare arms and broad chest.

"Come here!" Carl Otto grabbed for my waist and, for a tease, I danced away beyond his reach.

"Catch me if you can."

"Ah, Betje, my sable vixen! You don't get away from me that easily." Quick as a *tigre* he had me pinned to the bed, my wrists gathered above my head. There were no more words as the fire ignited between us and we renewed the passionate warmth of our love after so many long months of lonesome separation.

It was after the midnight hour by the time we lay sweating at rest among the crumpled bed linens. It was then that my sweet state of post-love bliss was interrupted of a sudden by a disturbing thought. I remembered that earlier in the evening Carl Otto had made mention of some seeds of evil that have sprouted for my orphaned Negro niece and nephew, Cato and Jupiter. It distressed me that I could not recall exactly what he had said.

11

Paramaribo, December 1744

There is news that two of the richest personages of our Colony, namely Salomon du Plessis and Samuel Pichot, have been nominated to the Court of Police.

"This may not be good news for His Excellency," noted Carl Otto.

We were enjoying a late afternoon in the drawing room at home on Oranjestraat, drinking *sangaree* and smoking Virginia tobacco. It is the midst of the dry season and the heat is well upon us. My skin glows, and tiny beads of sweat gather at my temple, under my lower lip, in the hollow at the base of my throat, and must be often patted with a handkerchief. There was no breeze present this afternoon, and the tobacco smoke formed stilled layers in the air, where it would aid to keep mosquitoes and *mampira* at bay when the sun began to set.

"Du Plessis and Pichot are not friendly to Governor Mauricius?" I asked.

"I fear they won't help to end this simmering conflict between the plantocracy and His Excellency, who is after all the official representative of the Hollander Directors of the Society of Suriname. Du Plessis is competent and industrious, but also ambitious and violent. He's not popular, and His Excellency believes he bribed his way to nomination. The worst kind of Sephardim, who owes money to a friend of du Plessis, is believed to have influenced the nomination."

"Mauricius himself did not choose du Plessis, then?"

"He did not. But he favors Pichot because he's a moderate and modest man who has studied law."

I took a deep pull on the tobacco and with my silk fan waved the smoke from in front of my face. "We need the larger fans. I'll call Fortuijn." I rose from my chair and went to the bell-pull to make the house man's attention. In due time, the handsome young Mulatto, Fortuijn, arrived. His skin glistened from the moist heat and for a moment I envied his simple costume of blue cotton secured about his waist. I told him we needed to be fanned, and he left on quiet bare feet to find another slave to help him with the tall palm fans.

"Betje, I fear the French paper is not taking well to the wall," Carl Otto observed. "Perhaps we should have had the walls fanned for a lengthier period of time after the setting of the sizing."

Gesturing with his pipe, he directed my attention to a section of the wall just above the cedar China cabinet, where the wall paper appeared to be bulging away from the surface. Stepping closer to the wall I peered at the spot, then swept my vision along the entire wall, whereupon I frowned and said, "It appears to be coming away at the corners as well."

"I'll have the servants make repairs to that," Carl Otto said.

"Aye, would that we could repair as easily our governmental separations. Such turbulent politics." I sighed, returning to my brocade footstool, where I could sit at Carl Otto's feet with my back straight and my legs crossed in comfort under my skirts. Little Pansu arranged himself in my lap and began to doze. Carl Otto leaned back in his chair and rested his forearms on the carved wooden sides.

"They should all applaud His Excellency," I said. "Look at what he is doing on our behalf to increase our safety from attack by sea."

"Aye, the construction of Fort Nieuw Amsterdam is well underway."

"And shame on the planters for begrudging him the men to build it. While they grumble about not being paid for the use of their slaves, they leisure about in silken splendor enjoying all manner of merriment, wallowing in debauchery, and misusing their slaves most horrifically."

"These are our friends and neighbors," Carl Otto chided with good humor. "But His Excellency has little respect for them, I fear."

"I've heard he thinks of the colonial Dutchmen as former good-for-nothings in the Fatherland, and without a good upbringing."

"Hah," Carl Otto snorted smoke out of his nostrils. "That is not the half of it. He's written the most scurrilous words to the Society describing us. He says we have very mistaken ideas of religion and law, but especially that which is called order, decency, or modesty. He says we quarrel easily, and the slightest quarrel is bitter and irrevocable."

"It's true *vrouw* Mauricius makes her house girls cover their bosoms," I noted. But I was also remembering how bitter and nearly unalterable had become my quarrel with the Peltsers and the prosecutor Jon van Meel.

Carl Otto said, "His Excellency told me that as long as the planters remain in a lesser status they are peaceful and malleable and, even if strongly stirred up, have always shown an aversion to rebellion."

I waved back Fortuijn, who had approached too closely with the palm fan and with it nearly hit my head.

"Fetch us a fresh pitcher of *sangaree*," I said to the servant. "It's the planters in the Court of Police His Excellency has the most trouble with, then?"

"Aye. He complains that once gained of wealth or honor their heads are easily turned. There's talk of organizing a political group against Governor Mauricius."

Ah, the absurdity of Colonial society and politics. It seems to me our entertainments are too often slid over into vicious cruelty.

We changed our conversation then to a more agreeable topic, and began to speak of a plan to visit Vlaardingen, where Quackoe at this very moment lies ill with a cough and is suffering from a discharge of large quantities of fluid material. Maria and La Vallaire are very concerned for his health, as he has been lingering too long now with these maladies. I had seen among the populace these very symptoms during my first winter in Amsterdam, and as many did not fare good from them, we may well have reason to despair.

The six o'clock hour was upon us, and the sun reflected in gold upon the Governor's mansion, to the west of our house. Kwasiba and two other house girls came to close the shutters and expel the mosquitoes as best can be done, for they are rapacious this time of year. The girls removed their petticoats, becoming totally unclothed, and waved them about to make a wind with which to drive out the unwanted pests. In this way they lessened our discomfort, and by their rapid movements avoided attack by gnats and mosquitoes to their own naked bodies.

As Carl Otto and I retired to the dining parlour for the dinner repast, I was annoyed to discover the inside of my forearm had not escaped some tiny bite and now itched maddeningly.

"Kwasiba," I called, my voice high in irritation. "I've been bitten."

The bare girl walked into the dining parlour, carrying her chintz petticoat in her arms. "Aye, *misi*, I go bring patches."

Kwasiba stopped to step into her petticoat and secure it at her waist. Then from the cupboard she took out a gray paper and wetted it with spirits to secure it over the reddening swelling on my arm. Though I care not for the smell of the spirits, finding their odor to be cloying and sour, I felt immediate and welcome relief.

When the room was again occupied by only myself and Carl Otto, he said, "My dear, I fear I've received this afternoon some disturbing news. Jupiter has been arrested for theft."

Insect bites were forgotten. In great alarm I demanded, "What's happened?"

"It appears he's been stealing goods and selling them to the Maroons for money."

My heart went cold at these words, and I spoke with extreme reluctance. "From whom has he stolen these goods?"

"At least from our households, I presume. When he was captured he had in his possession an item from Maria's cupboard."

A swell of anger overcame me. Within our family the boy had had every opportunity to better himself, even learn to read and write Dutch, but his disposition had been of a lazy nature and now he would be unmercifully held to account for his indolent ways.

"Is he alone in this or working with the house slaves?" I asked.

"That isn't known just now. He's in a cell in Fort Zeelandia."

"And Cato?" I asked, holding my breath for the dreaded response. At nineteen, the girl is of an independent age with an insolent streak that I fear may bring down upon her a most terrible wickedness.

Carl Otto reached out and covered my hand with his own. "There is no news of Cato, Betje. Perhaps we'll know more on the morrow after Jupiter is interrogated."

I found it difficult to speak. "Who is doing the questioning?"

"Van Meel, just returned from Holland."

My anger merged with fear for my poor orphaned Negro nephew; how well I knew what it meant to be questioned at Zeelandia! And by the prosecutor van Meel, no less.

Jon van Meel, the white Dutchman, is of short stature and scarce four years older than I. His face is of hardened expression. Not born in our Colony, but having arrived from the Netherlands, one can only guess what misfortunes and indignities he suffered at a young age. A bachelor known to take a casual series of Negro and Mulatto mistresses, much *mofokoranti* surrounds him. He has been talked about as a man responsible for the disappearance of a young lady and such misuse of another that she could not without the greatest embarrassment return to her family. As prosecutor for the Court of Justice, he enjoys a powerful place in our legal and military society. Upon arrival at Fort Zeelandia he developed a reputation for a strict and intense method of interrogation of prisoners and criminals, and was seen as a man who would not hesitate to do what was necessary to extract the information he sought.

In my own case, he had begun with intimidation and threats. I had been tricked into appearing at a "special meeting related to my case" by having been advised that because of the informal nature of the meeting it would not be necessary for me to bring my lawyer. In my *naiveté*, I had gone willingly to the office of the military captain at Fort Zeelandia.

There van Meel and some of the military gentlemen guided me into a spare room in the lower level of the fort. I suspected this meeting was of an unusual nature when I saw the simple table and one chair, and this surmise was verified when one of the military gentlemen closed the door and locked it.

Van Meel shoved me into the chair and sat nearby on the table. A man of little gallantry, he went straight to his point.

"You think because you are associated with a *prominant*"—he fair spat the word—"family, you are above reproach, but such is not the case, my dear."

Distress welled within my person as I waited to see where this was leading.

"Do you understand that you have created a very unpleasant situation and thus leave us with no recourse but to charge you with bringing slander against His Excellency, Governor Raye?"

How could the man perpetrate such madness as to suggest I created the situation in which His Excellency now found himself? At this point my calm I managed to retain, though inwardly I seethed against the white prosecutor. "I have told you the simple truth."

"Truth? What can a black whore know of truth? You call His Excellency friend and suppose he will take your word against that of whites. He will not, I assure you."

At that moment I saw something about *meneer* van Meel that had not occurred to me. He was jealous of my family's friendship with Governor Raye. It came to me then that it was possible many white people in the Colony might not be happy with the presence of a Negro family of such financial advantage. I think I had always known this, but never before had reason to give it careful consideration.

"Have you interrogated Egbert Peltser?" This inquiry on my part was admittedly reckless.

"It is not necessary to now question a man of his stature. His Excellency himself questioned *meneer* Peltser and his wife when they were in Zeelandia."

It was clear that the prosecutor expected me to be of a

subservient demeanor, but this is not natural to me. Nonetheless I looked down at my pretty shoes, now soiled from the filth of the stone floors, in an attempt to gain time to think my way out of this predicament. My discomfort was exacerbated by the standing presence of the prosecutor so close to my body that I had the impression he stared at my bosom in such a way that he might hope to see well down the front of my bodice.

His voice was detached and formal. "Now you must confess that you have committed treason against the Governor, and in so doing, against the Society of Suriname and the Fatherland as well."

"I know nothing of the Fatherland," I muttered. I felt an unpleasant heat radiating from him and a flush to my face in response.

"You will if your whoring person is banished from this Colony," Van Meel threatened. His heightened tone of voice echoed off the thick stone walls and frightened me. What wickedness was this?

This was the first I had been directly threatened with any legal action. I raised my head and stared into the prosecutor's cold blue eyes. The great North Sea, of such cold repute, could not have appeared more frigid to me. What right did he have to call me whoring? I lived at home with my Mulatto sister and her white husband. Until this unpleasant business with the butcher and his wife, I had considered myself cultured and educated, and thus unaccustomed to such offensive references to my female person. Now I saw that this very cultured, educated nature about me was offensive to the white prosecutor—perhaps the sole reason for his present irritation.

Aye, I should never have come here without my brother-in-law and my lawyer!

"We have witnesses who have declared not to have heard *meneer* or *vrouw* Peltser utter during your conversation any of the words you accuse." Van Meel leaned over and grasped my bare arm, just below the elbow. In so doing he caught the lace of my sleeve and I heard a tearing sound.

"What witnesses?"

Van Meel hesitated, as if he had to make a decision about

sharing this information with me. Then he let my arm go. My skin felt a stinging from the release.

"She deserves to know," one of the military men said. He sounded most bored with the proceedings.

"Everhard Pleg and *vrouw* Vos," Van Meel said.

White witnesses, I thought. "Aye, they were there. They heard everything."

At this point the prosecutor lost all composure and raged at me. "They heard nothing! You have endangered the life of *meneer* Peltser because of your slander! The man could get the death penalty if he had truly said such things. You have committed perjury because these witnesses have declared not to have heard anything."

"I am innocent," I declared uselessly. Compared to their booming tones my voice seemed inadequate and small in the little fortress room.

This meeting-turned-interrogation went on for at least an hour. At length it came to my mind that they were not at the moment making formal charge against me, only accusing, fishing, and hoping I would slip on some detail in the telling of my story. I became emboldened by this realization and found the courage to stand up and challenge them.

"Gentlemen, I am a free-born Negress and I have answered your questions honestly and completely. If there is nothing further, I have family awaiting me at home and I shall take my leave." To my astonishment, though they frowned at me and exchanged glances, they made no move to stop me. "Now unlock this door and I shall be on my way."

And so on unsteady legs I walked out of the room, out of Fort Zeelandia, and home to Frederik and Maria's house on Waterkant.

It was only when I walked into the drawing room that I found myself shaking from my fright. I told Maria and Frederik of my detainment, and Frederik was livid against the prosecutor van Meel.

"He knows better! Such a sneaky devil to question you so brazenly, and without your lawyer!"

At once he sent a slave to the home of Josephus de Cohue to advise him of the event and secure his opinion.

When he arrived my lawyer explained, "The Governor has insisted that there should be a guilty party." I had calmed down somewhat with the help of a glass of Madeira and a well-tamped pipe bowl. We were all now gathered in the drawing room, where it was dusk and the shutters were being closed and the mosquitoes were being driven out by Maria's servant girls. No one paid the least attention to their nakedness and the flapping about of their petticoats.

In a quiet voice Maria concluded, "So. It appears to have been decided to make the guilty party the free black woman Elisabeth Samson."

Her husband paced, his heels clicking on the mahogany floor. "Nothing has been proven. This has all come to be outrageously out of hand."

"You're right, Frederik," said de Cohue. "I fear they plan to blame Elisabeth."

"Peltser would not have gotten the death penalty," Maria scoffed. "Granted an officer could insist on it because slander is treason, but the fact remains that *meneer* Peltser is white."

Frederik was so frustrated by my predicament that he began to obsess on the fading evening light. "The lamps, the lamps? Where are those slaves with the lamps?"

Was it possible that I could get the death penalty for this? The thought so startled and horrified me that I had not the breath to voice it. My lawyer would have the answer, but I could not force myself to ask such a dreadful question. The very idea that a white man could be so sentenced for slander meant that a Negro woman, no matter how free or rich, would be triply at risk. Everyone knew this, and no one had yet mentioned it; they did not want to alarm me, I felt sure.

The appearance of his house boys bearing the evening candles and oil lamps did not assuage my brother-in-law from his pacing. "This Governor..." He paused to choose his words with care. "The Court must be somehow persuaded to see Governor Raye returned to Holland. I fear his judgments are not without extreme prejudices."

A breath of air passing through the room caused the candle flames to flutter as if a *winti* spirit had come to call. I thought of the evening fire in the yard before Mariana's little house and felt a fierce desire to see my mother. I wanted to run to her and find solace in the warmth of her arms about me. But Mariana could not help me, and would most likely be embarrassed at such a childish display from a grown woman. She would advise me to consult Granman Quassie and have him make for me a special *obia*. Nay, there was no comfort to be had from either of those directions, though perhaps a talisman couldn't hurt.

12

<u>*Paramaribo, June 1745*</u>

Rain plummeted from warm, gray skies as Nanette, Carl Otto, and I stood on the porch and waited for the carriages to be brought from the carriage house. Even though we would not be walking to Maria's house, we would surely still be wet, but this is the season, and it too shall pass. Umbrellas were brought, I slipped my feet into my clogs, and was helped into the coach. As swiftly as it had begun, the rain subsided and, as it was still early in the morning, steam floated from the backs of the horses.

Nanoe and Liesbeth were already at the Waterkant house when we arrived. Maria complained of a morning chill and called for a heavier shawl to be brought.

"*Mi fersteri joe*," said Maria in Sranan Tongo, congratulating me on my thirtieth birthday.

Nanoe, just sixteen, said, "I can't wait till my next *bigi yari*." Her reference was to age twenty, for every tenth year of birthdays is called *bigi yari*, or big year. Her enthusiastic remark summoned forth a stern look from Maria.

At home on Oranjestraat Carl Otto and I had been in the midst of making a plan for a ball to celebrate both my birthday and his taking the oath to become a Captain Lieutenant when we had received despairing news. Maria had sent a slave to inform us of the passing of our brother Quackoe Samson. He was thirty-eight and had been malingering since his illness of the dry season past. His cough had worsened until he was vomiting blood, and it came to pass all knew he was dying of the consumption. Towards the end a concoction of laudanum was ordered to suppress his cough and, while it did not much for that malaise, his pain was nonetheless relieved.

Maria, appearing rather frail I fear for forty-five, is inconsolable. Quackoe was her favorite brother. In his testament he has made her sole heir to Vlaardingen and, as such, much to her relief, she will not have to go through the stress of an inventory. I would have thought Quackoe would have left his estate to his eldest child, La Vallaire. But then, it was Maria's husband in the first place who was so instrumental in Quackoe's acquisition of Vlaardingen. A few thousand guilders went to his son and a silver service to his darling La Vallaire. Since Vlaardingen is her home, she will continue to reside there and rule as mistress in Maria's absence. The plantation is doing well and any business can be conducted by La Vallaire and her plantation director. Everyone is at ease with these arrangements.

After greeting us and seeing to our refreshments, Maria took her leave and retired to her bed with a bit of laudanum to calm her nerves and help her sleep.

Some time was spent in reverent conversation about our dear, departed brother. As midday was upon us we became warmed by food, Madeira, and tobacco. But the rain resumed and, while varying at times in force, contributed to the somberness of the day.

It seemed we were doomed to gloom until Nanette cheered us by turning the subject to the latest *mofokoranti*. She herself has become the subject of conversation, as she has received a proposal to become "wife" to one of Carl Otto's fellow officers in a Suriname marriage, she being a free Negress and he being white.

"Emilius de Vries is a man with an upstanding reputation," said Carl Otto. "You could do worse."

"He's twenty years older than you," ventured Liesbeth. "But handsome."

While Liesbeth, as Nanette, was more the romantic, I pondered the legal side of this potential relationship. "You'll want to ask him to register at the notary your living in concubinage."

As a Negress, Nanette cannot marry him in any other way, and is debarred from the usual privileges of Christian ceremony. She will not be able to inherit property unless their concubinage is so registered at the notary. Yet this is a very desirable situation for Nanette, who will have her own house and a man to serve with the tenderness and fidelity as if he were a lawful husband. In these ways we pride ourselves to the shame of some great ladies and white planters' wives, who discard easily marital ties more sacred.

And of course, at age thirty-two, Nanette still hopes for children.

"Oh, the notary." Nanette shrugged off this piece of sound advice.

"Do you think he will agree?" Maria asked.

"Aye," said Carl Otto. "Emilius de Vries has no family. He'll agree."

We assume Nanette will accept de Vries' proposal. I'm happy for her. She's a sensitive creature, though sometimes more fun-loving than is practical, in that way much like our departed brother, Isaac. She deserves to have the opportunity for a family of her own. And as a free Negress, she can take pride in living with a European. Some might say that that is why I live with Carl Otto, but I loved Carl Otto before we came to live together. As a land- and slave-holder I already had wealth, so there was no financial advantage for me to take him as my consort. We love each other, and would marry in the church if the law allowed. Nanette will grow to love Emilius de Vries.

Liesbeth was mentioning that she had seen the butcher's daughter this morning, near the place of the father's business. I heard her say that Juliaana Peltser, now eighteen, flounced her skirts aside as if she did not want Liesbeth to touch them as she passed.

"She called me the niece of the free whore, Elisabeth," Liesbeth confided, her tone indicating that she did not know quite what to make of the words.

Will this never end? I wondered.

Nanette laughed. "If Juliaana weren't so blond with such blue eyes, I could have my maid spread the rumor the girl is Casties."

Carl Otto smiled, a teasing glint in his eyes. "She would have to be the child of Mesties and white, so you would have to add to the story, perhaps that Egbert wasn't her real father."

The preposterous idea caused much merriment among us. "This fantasy is indeed entertaining," cautioned Maria, "but see that it doesn't leave this room."

Seeing my family gathered in such warmth and camaraderie, even in the face of our recent tragic loss, made my eyes warm with tears. How these beloved people had rallied to my cause in my dark hour. Josephus de Cohue had indeed confirmed our suspicions that there were people in the Colony who resented me because I was young, educated, of means, unmarried, and black.

"Your fair beauty won't help your cause, either," de Cohue had said. Well, there was nothing to be done about any of that; I had been distraught enough about my then as yet undetermined fate.

. . .

In the afternoon Carl Otto and I set out to brave the weather and make a stop at Fort Zeelandia, particularly grim as it was grayed by the falling rain. Our task was somber, for my nephew Jupiter lay languishing in a dank cell.

Fort Zeelandia was built as a wooden fort in 1640 and named Fort Willoughby under the English. Captured by the Dutch in 1667, it has since been known as Fort Zeelandia, so named after Zeeland, one of the confederation of seven sovereign provinces of Holland. Of a pentagonal shape, the thick walls are shell-stone lined inside with red brick, and there are bastions on each of five corners. In addition to the protective cannons and powder house, the fort contains military offices and prison cells, some of these latter even smaller than the room in which I had undergone my own dismal interrogation.

When Jupiter was arrested he was imprisoned in a cell banking one side of the courtyard. He has not spoken of Cato, and it is sure that he will soon be tortured and punished for his crimes of aiding runaway slaves.

"Most likely Cato has fled to the forest and been welcomed

there by the Maroons," said Carl Otto. I dearly desire this proves to be true. The girl may well find an appropriate outlet for her lively personality in the company of such wild existence.

Though Jupiter greeted us with a stoic countenance, the condition of his body betrayed his situation. I had to look away from him so that he wouldn't see my tears on account of his scrapes and bruises. He fair devoured the food we brought; we stayed to watch him consume it, though it was painful to see how in haste he swallowed everything without seeming to chew. Had we not remained, the food might have been stolen from him or otherwise confiscated by the military guards who would feel barley soup, fresh baked buns, boiled plantain, oranges, and a dram of rum too fine a repast for prison scum.

It was with heavy hearts and no spoken words that Carl Otto and I departed, having to leave Jupiter to that place of miserable despair.

13

Plantation Welgemoed, September 1745

On a fine morning last week, over slices of papaya and mango and a strong morning tea with sugar in the breakfast room at Welgemoed, Maria, Nanette, and I enjoyed the wide view of the river and planned our coffee expansion.
"I want to grow chocolate in addition to sugar and coffee," announced Nanette, setting down her cup for the servant to refill. She touched the corner of her mouth with her lace-edged handkerchief.
Maria said, "What about planting *orleane* for red dye? And maybe some indigo."
"I like the idea," I said. "There's no reason all the land must go for one crop. Diversification is good—if one crop fails, we have others to fall back on."
His Excellency Governor Mauricius would like to see our free citizens establish more coffee plantations and to promote such endeavor has donated small parcels of land between existing large plantations along the Hoer-Helena Kreek. Already in possession of the coffee plantation Welgemoed, I deemed it prudent to make application and acquire additional parcels of land under this provision. Nanette and Maria also requested parcels, and we have been granted a total of three hundred hectares. Their parcels are adjacent to Welgemoed, and my parcel is a bit further up the Hoer-Helena Kreek.
"The first thing we need to do is get a good Dutch land surveyor out here to lay out the buildings and gardens. I want

the best man in the Colony for this." On a sheet of parchment I scratched notes with china ink. "This should have been begun in July when the rains lessened and the waters of the forest floor began to recede. We'll have to bring in extra slaves to make up for the time."

Maria gazed out over the grassy sward that lay between the plantation house and the edge of the river. "All the underbrush and trees need to be cleared. We'll have to order extra axes for the extra men."

My new coffee plantation will be called Toevlught. It will require most all of my attention for awhile, but I am eager for the task. Carl Otto and I want a large house. I dream of children's feet running through it. I thought of the plantation house at Vlaardingen and of La Vallaire, who has just given birth to Hendrik Petrus Planteau, her third son. While I am joyful, I wonder when Carl Otto and I will ever have children of our own.

La Vallaire is still content to live at Vlaardingen and be visited on week-ends by her married mulatto, Jean Planteau. She is free to marry anyone she wants, yet she is true to Jean, and not the least bothered by the existence of his *foto* family.

Changing the subject, I turned to Nanette, "Do you have news for us?"

My sister's face glowed with her broad smile as Maria and I anticipated her answer. "I have accepted Emilius de Vries. He has found us a house and we are moving there at the beginning of the month."

Maria, who has continued to wear black though her official time of mourning for Frederik is long past, rose from her chair and leaned down to hug Nanette. "I'm so happy for you, dear little sister." I thought that I would be happier for Nanette if she could enjoy a true Christian wedding, but held my tongue from saying so.

"I regret that we won't be able to live at the new plantation because of Emilius' military obligations. We'll be keeping house in *foto*."

And thus our conversation abandoned the plans for the new land for the more entertaining business of planning the furnishings and décor for Nanette's new house in Paramaribo.

. . .

It was well after dark that evening, with the plantation household settled and lulled by the sounds of the forest night creatures, when Carl Otto arrived in a small tent-boat from *foto*. The cook servant was summoned to prepare some food for him after his three-hour journey up the Hoer-Helena Kreek.

Having dined well earlier in the day, I was not hungry and so sipped merely a glass of Madeira at the table while he ate. As he placed the white linen napkin on his lap and regarded the plate of plantains, boiled *pingo*, *kasaba* bread, and sliced pineapple, he said, "Tomorrow, when we return to the city, we must take food again to Jupiter."

"How is he?" I asked. My voice was muted as if in fear to ask the question.

Carl Otto's jaw tightened, giving his face a pained expression. "I regret to report the news is not good. He's weakened. He received none of the foodstuff we sent over last week. It's evident we must deliver it in person each day."

In a vain hope that it would warm my dampened spirit, I took a long draught of my wine before I asked, "When will his punishment be pronounced?"

"It has been pronounced. He's to receive three hundred lashes." This was sore news, certainly, but hardly unexpected. Even so, an uncomfortable flush rose up my neck.

Carl Otto paused eating and laid down the silver fork. "Betje..." he began, raising a troubled face to look into my eyes.

I set down my wine goblet and put both hands flat on the table in front of me. "Do not spare me."

"A captured runaway has reported that Cato—the Maroons thought she was a paid spy for the Society troops—has been murdered and her body mutilated, her eyes burned out, and her hands cut off."

. . .

Our days have been well occupied with the arrangements for the establishment of the new plantations, and we do not speak of Cato's gruesome slaughter at the hands of the rebels living in the forests of the upper Saramacca River. It was reported that her poor burnt head, with the empty sockets from which her eyes had been torn out, was received at Zeelandia as a warning to the military government. Poor young Cato, hardly aware, I'm sure, of the danger in what she was doing. As for the idea of her being a spy, well, she was far too innocent and independent to engage in political intrigue. How easily everything could have gone the other way had she been willing to remain under the protection of our family. In truth I never had confidence in her success as an independent woman. But how unjust that she has paid such a heavy price for it.

Maria, Nanette, and I are often back and forth between *foto* and Welgemoed with tools, supplies, and furnishings. Though construction of the main plantation houses has not even begun, already we are buying draperies and decorations and storing them at my plantation house at Welgemoed, making for cramped quarters.

Trees and brush have been cut and burnt at Toevlught. The pile of charred remains from the bigger trees and trunks will be stored for firewood. A large, open-sided shelter has been built to quarter the slaves, with room for fifty hammocks.

My architect is a seasoned hydraulic engineer, and already the digging for the *dijk* around the cultivated area has begun. He reports that next will be built the sluice gates to channel the water during the wet season; all of this he seems to have under exact control and I am well pleased with the progress. After the land is prepared with top soil and peat moss, planting can begin at the end of the big dry season, just before Christmas.

When the architect had finished telling his report he was dismissed, and the family retired to the drawing room to enjoy a treat of roasted cashew nuts and a punch of rum and *mope*.

Emilius de Vries, who arrived from *foto* this afternoon, brought the most disturbing news that poor Jupiter has not only been sentenced to three hundred lashes, but he will receive them secured in the *Spaanse bok*.

"Like he's a common slave!" spat Nanette, outraged at this added humiliation.

The *Spaanse bok*, or Spanish Whip, is a treatment whereby the prisoner's wrists and ankles are tied together in front, then he sits with his knees drawn up to be surrounded by his bound arms. In this seated, hugging position, a rod is inserted through the opening between the knees and arms and then planted into the ground. The prisoner, lying on his side, is flogged on the buttocks with a guava or Tamarind rod.

"It's a common punishment," said Emilius, not prepared for the glares this comment elicited from the rest of the family. "I know it's a despicable torture," he added, "but there is every possibility he may live."

"Whether we like it or not, his point is well taken," said Carl Otto. "Jupiter fairs well not to be broken upon the rack or roasted alive chained to a stake."

To add proof to his new "brother-in law's" words, Emilius said, "This week five runaway Negro girls are recaptured, and they are already tied to the cross where they'll be broken alive. Their heads will be severed and exposed on stakes about the waterside."

"I don't care! It's still abominable!" raged Nanette. "Three hundred lashes alone are enough. The back is more able to tolerate the punishment than the buttocks." In her anxiety her hand fell by accident against the bowl of nuts so that it crashed to the floor. Nuts and shattered china exploded in every direction. Pansu shrieked at this sudden harsh noise. Nanette turned a glare upon the poor little monkey, who clutched my arm.

"Sshh," I murmured. I cupped the top of his little head with my hand. "It's all right now."

The vision of my own back in the mirror of my dressing room came to me. Forever burned into my memory is the day His Excellency Governor Raye himself ordered that I be flogged, branded, and removed from the colony.

Frederik had gone to talk with Governor Raye, and returned with the miserable news that His Excellency would not be dissuaded. Two days later the Court sanctioned his orders, calling me "an instigator" who should be from Suriname "removed until eternity" for the betterment of the Colony.

In the afternoon of that same day Frederik went with two witnesses to the Court of Criminal Justice to make a legal declaration that, "in the matter against the free black woman Elisabeth Samson," he would guarantee and pay bail so that I would not flee.

Indeed, to where would I flee? I had never traveled from my home and had never desired to do so. Suriname being bordered on two sides by British and French colonies, I would most likely not be welcomed in either place. I suppose I could flee into the forest, but how would I live? Certainly not among the Maroons, where as an educated woman I would be completely without skills and resources to survive. To be sure, the idea of living such a deprived existence was to me appalling.

Yet Governor Raye had declared that I should be banished from my home "until eternity." He meant that I should be sent to the Netherlands, a foreign place about which I knew very little.

I affected not to consider the flogging and branding, twin tortures I did not think I could bear. Yet while my Jewish lawyer made formal declarations to the Court that his client, the free Negress Elisabeth Samson, had been "severely disfavored by the sentencing," I could think of nothing else. When de Cohue told me he would request a revision from the States General in Den Hague, I was barely listening.

These gruesome memories were interrupted when I happened to glance across the room at Maria. As well as tired, she appeared much distressed.

"Our discussion of the vile *Spaanse bok* won't help our Jupiter," she said. "His sentence is irrevocable. We must now consider his future after that."

Should he survive, I thought.

Carl Otto tamped more tobacco into his long-stemmed pipe. "I believe I have a solution."

Maria's face relaxed into a grateful look. "I dearly hope so."

"He's just nineteen and has no trade to speak of. Except for occasional manual labor, I don't see how he can support himself living in *foto*. As a manumitted slave, he has the option to voluntarily return to slavery." Carl Otto took several short draws on his pipe while the rest of us contemplated this. "It's the only solution I see that will ultimately preserve his life."

But will Jupiter, youthful, strong-willed, and likely to be greatly embittered by his punishment, see the wisdom in this?

14

Paramaribo, October 1745

Two days before it arrives at Paramaribo one can smell the Guineaman with its human cargo and trail of sharks. On departing the Dutch possession of St. George d'Elmina on the African coast, a Dutch slave trader will hold three hundred miserable Negroes, and half the goods may die on the voyage. Yet every month a slave ship arrives with fresh cargo for the labor-hungry markets of the Dutch West Indies.

Liesbeth, who has been living with us at the house on Orangestraat, could not make up her mind what *araiement* to wear on the outing with me to Plattebrug, the place at the waterside where the recently-arrived Guineaman now sits at anchor, ready to auction off its human merchandise.

"Your oldest skirt," I advised. "This can be a dirty business when you get close to them."

This was the first time Liesbeth has accompanied us to Plattebrug. La Vallaire needs two replacements for Vlaardingen, where two women have been stolen by the Maroons, and I need more labor for the expansion at Toevlught. The director of Vlaardingen and my own Welgemoed director, N. Voorhees, accompanied us.

The Dutchman Voorhees arrived in Suriname fifteen years past aboard the *De Vrouw Magdalena* as a twenty-five-year-old assistant to Jan Malmberg, the well-known slave captain, *De Vrouw Magdalena* being a vessel of the slave trade. Said vessel belongs to the commercial company Coopstadt and

Rochussen, which has grown excessively wealthy from the triangle business. *De Vrouw Magdalena* carried goods from Holland to West Africa, there loaded with slaves in St. George d'Elmina, which then arrived in Suriname. Here the slaves are sold and the ship loaded with the coffee, cocoa, sugar, cotton and timber we send to the European markets.

Any slaves not purchased by Suriname's planters are dispatched in the last stop at Curaçao, further north in the Dutch West Indies, before the ship heads back to Amsterdam.

"I will never forget the stench of St. George d'Elmina," my director often says, not because he thinks the slave trade so awful but that he is thankful he was not obliged to remain in it.

In truth, I think my Welgemoed director finds plantation work a welcome haven from the temptations of *foto*. Voorhees says from the very beginning he found Paramaribo most agreeable. He did not find the swarm of merchant sailors, soldiers, Indians, Negroes, Jews, and planters who crowd the streets to be oppressive, but rather commented that "the place is very lively with music and coloured flags streaming in the wind." He noted the straight streets lined with odoriferous orange, shaddock, tamarind and lemon trees, and the bountiful yield thereof. He found the canals, where the way is often slow thanks to giant lily pads, with their profusion of waxy stalks topped with pointed blooms of ivory edged with pink, most pleasing. With great enthusiasm he remarked upon the well-kept white gravel and pink sea shell pavings, the elegant town hall covered with tiles, and the variety of churches for Protestants, Lutherans, and German and Portuguese Jews. He greatly admired the architecture of one of our most important buildings, the Lodge Concordia, where concerts and large parties are hosted in addition to the meetings of the freemasons.

"And the naked girls playing in the river at the waterside!" marveled *meneer* Voorhees, who had never before in his life seen the likes of the young Negro and Mulatto women who regularly bathed and washed clothes at the edge of the Suriname River.

This morning the wooden landing dock at Plattebrug was alive with white planters, free and slave blacks who would unload the cargo, eager merchants, and even an occasional street whore who managed to find her way to be close to the men. A cacophony of cries and clamorous conversation filled the air, which was foul with the odor of the Guineaman's waste and human cargo.

Meneer Voorhees' eyes lingered on the young wash girls at the riverside, their hips and thighs wrapped in the colourful cotton *pongees* according to their native African traditions. To the Dutchman this sight of bare bosoms constitutes complete nudity. Even though my director has free access to the beauties of Welgemoed, the landscape of Paramaribo, with its pretty vegetable gardens, well-kept church yards, and white wooden houses on red brick foundations with dark green shutters and ornate iron porch railings, holds a fascination for him.

A drove of Negroe men, women and a few children crowded the deck of the Guineaman that just this morning came to anchor. These were the ones already marked *WIC* upon the chest, showing their ownership by the Dutch West India Company, and making them easy to distinguish from the slaves of the English, French, and others, in whose company they sit. It also prevents an unfair exchange of good slaves for worse ones, a devious practice the attempt of which is all too common. Upon the deck of the ship they received good air, good slave-fare—well-boiled or roasted plantains—and were washed down.

"They look like walking skeletons," Liesbeth observed. She pulled the brim of her blue hat lower to shade her eyes from the fierce midday sun.

"During the middle passage for subsistence they only get horse beans and oil," said *meneer* Voorhees. To me he asked, "Have you heard about Salomon du Plessis and Samuel Pichot?" Virtually secluded on the plantation, when he comes to *foto* my director makes it his business to seek out the latest *mofokoranti*.

"In the Court of Police sessions they're behaving quite aggressively," I said. I was staring through the open gangway at what appeared to be a family among the slaves on the deck of the Guineaman. The woman was shaving the hair of the man in figures of stars and half moons, using a piece of broken bottle glass and no soap. A small, wild-eyed child clung to her bare leg.

"I'm told du Plessis has earned the reputation as His Excellency's most aggressive antagonist," said the Dutchman.

"I heard that when he was nominated," Liesbeth broke in, "an important Jewish family with twelve votes stayed home for fear of his friends."

"That's true," I said, impressed that the girl has such an understanding of the ways of our government.

The first small group of slaves was brought ashore for sale. A brief strip of cotton covered their parts, and they had been decorated by the captain with beads and cotton thread armbands. A few budding young girls he had graced with some gold coins for additional adornment; said coins, beads and armbands which would be returned to his chest upon the sale of the wearer.

"I heard du Plessis has become the leader of the opposition against His Excellency," Voorhees said. "One would think when the Governor chose him as Councilor of Police he would have responded by being less boorish."

"Hah! What a miscalculation on His Excellency's part," I said. "If anything, he's become worse. He shouts and screams and stamps his feet in the sessions, even threatens his neighbors. And Pichot, generally a modest man, is taken to following his lead."

"I wonder how long His Excellency will put up with such disturbance?" Liesbeth frowned, at her young age already concerned for our Colony's state of affairs.

As each group of Africans was being sold, the ones waiting on board the vessel were allowed to dance and sing and clap their hands at will. Such false merriment lent a festive air to the occasion which the captain intended to humor the planters and loosen their purse strings. It did little however, for the odor upon the air.

From my reticule I withdrew a bit of paper and chalk. "We need to be sure of our selections before we bargain with the captain."

"I like those two over there." Liesbeth pointed to two young men. One had just mounted a hogshead to be visited by the surgeon.

"You have a good eye, *misi*," said my director. "They appear to be among the most vigorous of the lot."

The surgeon began to examine the first boy, a handsome youth with a face reflecting the habit of his tribe to decorate the skin with ornamental incisions—such cicatrizations seen often among the Africans. The Surgeon determines the slave's soundness or unsoundness, after which said slave can be purchased or cast off, as the surgeon deems proper. Those cast-off, the *macrons* who had most deteriorated during the sea-voyage, are often traded to New England-bound vessels for rum.

Meneer Voorhees moved forward at my nod. In his hand he carried the silver stamp with my initials, ES, with which the mark is burned on furniture, cattle, and slaves to authenticate my ownership of the property. After some discussion between my director and the captain, a fair price of five hundred and seventy-five guilders for the two was paid. My new acquisitions were thus branded with the hot stamp on the thick of the shoulder, which marks will be healed in the space of two or three days of application with butter.

"What names do you want for them?" I asked Liesbeth. "You found them, so you may choose."

"I think October for the one, since that is the month. We don't have one already named October, do we?"

"Nay, my dear."

"And for the other, I like Adam." Liesbeth's pretty face beamed with satisfaction.

"So romantic, you are," I said. "Just so long as you don't see yourself as his Eve." The whims of young maids are not to be underestimated.

Liesbeth looked shocked. To her credit, her face warmed in a proper blush.

"They'll both go to Welgemoed," I said, "where they will be delivered up to two of the older men who will keep them clean and well fed, and instruct them for the space of six weeks."

With luck, today's purchases will be tamed and able to work by the time to plant. Every month *meneer* Voorhees reports well in advance if I need to make additional purchases, as deaths always outnumber slaves born; their work is demanding, and no matter how we feed them, regularly there are contagious illnesses among them.

"Will they learn Sranan?" asked Liesbeth.

"Aye, my dear. They know nothing of our speech now."

"And Dutch?"

"Of course not. It's against the law to teach slaves Dutch." I frowned at Liesbeth; surely she should have already known this.

I thought of Jupiter, who has been sent to Vlaardingen where he now legally belongs to that property. As a Dutch-speaking slave, will he attempt to teach it to the others? I wonder. At any rate, I doubt many of them would care to learn, but this is a concern of which I must make mention to La Vallaire so that she can be on the ready watch.

We made some other selections, purchasing in all nineteen men and five women, three with small children, at a total expenditure of 5,500 guilders. One of the women is barely fifteen, with a tiny babe still at her breast. Raw envy surged through my heart when first my sight fell upon her, and I knew at once I would have her. But would I, now twice her age, ever know that sweet maternal bliss of my own babe at my breast?

We could buy all the slave children we want, but what counts is the blood that is passed on through one's own offspring. Charloo had children by a slave concubine, and Quackoe and Isaac both fathered more than one child, while Maria, Nanette, and I remain childless. It is a great heartbreak to be barren. We pretend it's not so by being ever hopeful and engaging in the occasional secret charm, but none of us ever mentions it.

As we departed Plattebrug with its distinct stench and commotion, I gave one last look at the Dutch Guineaman riding high at anchor on the river. It was not much larger than *De Vrouw Dorothea*, the Dutch merchant ship I myself had sailed on when I was banished from the Colony. How the Peltser family had gloated when Governor Johan Raye himself apologized for his behavior, saying to them, "I have been too premature in my dealings with such a proper citizen; to have you and your wife be removed from your house was improper."

Governor Raye had written another letter to the Society, referring to me as *"the free black woman and slanderer."* He wrote that the situation had been investigated, and two white people had visited him. One was the assistant *meneer* Belards, who declared under oath that he had heard the slanderous words from Peltser. This statement struck a note of hope in my heart. The second witness declared to have heard from the apothecary that Peltser had yelled at the Governor, but he'd forgotten the exact words. Being secondhand, that was not of much value in my case.

The Governor wrote that I had asked for a revision of the court order, and that he understood clearly that the higher court would need to review the witness records, including the voluntary testimony from Belards. In his zeel to see me guilty-charged, the testimony of the assistant Belards had purposefully been ignored by van Meel.

Next the Governor went so far as to describe his difficulty in working together with van Meel and his colleagues. His Excellency wrote, *"A Governor who arrives in Paramaribo lies to himself if he thinks that all ongoing concerns can be directed by him without any fighting with the prosecutors; therefore a man who is afraid of their loud voices is to be pitied."* He ended his letter to the Society with a request that they find a more qualified individual to govern our Colony. He felt it would be *"a benefit (to him) because it is increasingly more clear that the demands of this job are lacking in me."*

In this way, His Excellency Governor General Johan Raye made attempt to cover himself politically with his employer, the Society of Suriname, should my lawyer's letter of appeal be delivered unto them from an earlier ship.

I tore my gaze from the guineaman and smiled at Liesbeth beside me in the carriage as it turned away from Plattebrug. In this way I made attempt to banish an unpleasant memory that had risen its ugly head in such an unexpected manner.

PART TWO

NO WAN PRIMISI FOE LIBI NA SRANANG (EXILE)

15

Paramaribo, December 1745

Bright morning sun streamed through the tall windows on the east wall of our bedroom, catching the bronze of the mahogany floor and the deep hues of the Turkish carpet so that they seemed to pulse with light. Kwasiba had brought fresh water, laid out my morning habit, and taken away the porcelain commode pot from under the bed. In a few minutes I would summon her to return to help me dress.

Standing naked before my long toilette mirror I was again wondering if I might be pregnant. I turned sideways to examine my belly. I placed my hands, fingers splayed, upon the slight mound and felt a great rush of warmth all over. I slid my hands in a small circle, glorying in the connection of skin to skin. My blood time is past due and now every day I awaken with both the dread that it will come and the hope for a new life within me. I want to remain calm for I fear anxiety may upset a babe, yet every hour I feel excitement well within me.

Until his arms encircled me I did not hear Carl Otto behind me; I had thought he still slumbered in the bed. He was barefoot and wore only his loose-fitting night shirt.

"Do you have something to tell me, Betje?" he whispered.

"Oh, you caught me! You know what I'm thinking." I smiled at his loving face reflected in the silvered glass. "Nay, that is, I'm not sure. Say nothing yet, if you will."

"I won't want to keep this secret long." His white fingers

played over my dark breasts and held there. He had not yet washed himself and I breathed deeply of his familiar man scent.

"Even more than marriage to you I desire a babe with you."

"Aye, my love."

We seldom spoke of our childlessness, and I sensed that he was more comfortable with it than I. Still, I was desperate to give him this living gift.

Carl Otto began to kiss my neck and my shoulders. I felt his urgency as he turned me to face the bed and moved my body towards that direction. I lay face down upon the bed and felt his hands familiarize all the curves of my back and buttocks. I should have been thinking sensual thoughts. Instead I thought of how ashamed I would have been to present that side of myself to a man I loved had my back born the terrible scars of van Meel's three hundred lashes.

In the end of my trial, Frederik had succeeded in bribing Governor Raye to forego the branding and the flogging in my sentence and settle for permanent exile. The guilders were paid in the form of an additional special bail, which everyone knew went into His Excellency's velvet pocket. I was not yet twenty-two and had never thought of being anywhere else in the world other than the Colony, and all I could think of was that I would never see my dear family nor my beloved Suriname again.

Carl Otto leaned down to kiss the side of my face and tasted the tears that patterned my cheek. "Betje, tell me what it is that makes you cry." He spoke these words in the most loving and gentle manner.

I rolled over and hugged him fiercely. "How nearly I lost you."

"What are you talking about?" He welcomed my embrace and rolled us onto our sides so that he could run his hand along my hip.

"If I had known you then as I know you now, I could never have born my exile to Holland," I said.

"Don't think about that now…" He made to silence my mouth with kisses, but I turned my face away.

"And if we had had little children that I had to leave behind…oh, the awfulness of the thought."

"Betje, stop," he said, his voice firm. His hand paused at my waist. "Please. Let the past rest. Think now only of this moment, and our future days together. How happy we are. I'm here and I'll always be here."

I sighed and let him kiss my lips to keep me from talking, and I felt pleased that he did.

. . .

Fragrant spermaceti candles warmed the light in the drawing room where we had gathered after dinner to play whist. From the drawer of the Georgian game table I withdrew the pack of cards and placed them upon the amboyna wood tabletop. Liesbeth brought forth three brocade stools for herself, Nanette and me, and Carl Otto arranged himself in a tall-backed, upholstered armchair. Emilius de Vries sat in a similar armchair next to him and crossed his legs. In contentment, Pansu twittered upon my shoulder, and Nanette moved her footstool to the other side of the table, away from the little creature.

Carl Otto began to tell us about the newest edict being discussed in the Court of Police regarding the punishment for any Negro caught poisoning man or animal.

"Death is useless. They're too firm in their belief that the happiness they can expect in the hereafter will more than make up for the tribulations of such a punishment. They must be dealt with more harshly."

"In the meantime, deal the cards," Nanette said.

Carl Otto gathered up the pack of cards and laid them out for play. "So the penalty won't be death, but rather the offender's ears and tongue will be cut off, he'll be branded upon the forehead, chained, and condemned to a life of solitary hard-labour at Fort New Amsterdam."

"Seems fitting," I murmured, regarding the hand of cards I held. "Did that discussion occupy the entire meeting?"

"Most nearly, and into the next day as well, and then finally we got to the business of His Excellency's candidates for the vacated posts." He went on to explain that yesterday candidates favored by Governor Mauricius were nominated to the Court of Police. For sometime now Salomon du Plessis has been pressuring the Jews to vote for the opposition's candidates, and this time he was not the least successful. After the nominations du Plessis went into a disgusting public rage.

"Such an obnoxious man," Carl Otto said. "Du Plessis greatly resents the Jews. Joined by Pichot, he screamed obscenities at several Jewish planters."

"What happened then?" inquired Nanette.

"Ironically they were joined by the Jew Isaac Carilho," Carl Otto said. From a gold snuffbox decorated in brilliants he selected a pinch of tobacco to add to his pipe-bowl.

I shook my head and made a little noise of repugnance. "Now not only is there conflict in the Courts but also in the Jewish community."

Nanette toyed with the lace ruching of her taffeta stomacher and made an indignant sniff. "And His Excellency has always so selflessly defended the Jews."

Carl Otto agreed. "He believes vehemently in the law and considers the Jewish privileges legally entrenched. He's always objected to any infringement of their rights, but he may change his mind regarding Isaac Carilho. The man's creating much the disturbance."

"Why would he do that?" asked Liesbeth.

Carl Otto explained to the girl that du Plessis and Pichot have organized the plantation aristocracy into an opposition group that now call themselves 'De Cabale'. Those who support His Excellency, among whom Carl Otto is a staunch member, are calling themselves the 'Mauritsridders'. Unfortunately, the latter, composed mostly of military men, many of them foreign mercenaries, often pose more problems than support. In his explanation Carl Otto neglected to tell of how regularly, after weekly exercises on the *Orangeplein*, they gather to enjoy some alcoholic beverages and while under said influence greatly harass those who oppose our Governor.

Liesbeth's pretty young face reflected her waning interest in politics and her gaze wandered about the room. "It's such a shame that your beautiful French paper wouldn't stick to the walls," she said. "Our clime is not very friendly to journals, either."

"Now the Cabale is calling the existence of the

Mauritsridders as proof of His Excellency's vanity," said Carl Otto.

I laid out my winning suit of cards upon the table. "Vanity? That's ludicrous."

"Ludicrous, aye." Carl Otto frowned when he saw my hand and threw down his own cards. "Now His Excellency is determined to see the Mauritsridders disbanded. I fear this poisonous conflict has not yet come to its worst."

16

Paramaribo, February 1746

    I fear my mind was in too melancholy a state to be the most gracious hostess to His Excellency and his lady, who today graced our table as honored guests. It was a fair and sunny Sunday for company at dinner, and Anna Buys-Julian had joined us as well. I would have reveled in the occasion had not my thoughts been distracted by a restless yearning for I knew not what, an uncomfortable feeling that everything and everyone around me was out of balance. Before they arrived I had had angry words with Kwasiba over an insignificant chore. Even the *gritjibi* birds in the trees and the *pikolets* in their hanging cages, normally a joy to hear, sounded strident and off harmony.
    "When the next merchant ship arrives, I want you to go with me, Elisabeth, to see what new things there are to purchase," *vrouw* Mauricius said to me.
    Carl Otto gave me an odd look and startled me out of my reverie. I answered with a rush of voice. "Of course. And I would like you to go with us to look at a country home, La Solitude, on the Landsweg. I've a mind to have it, but Carl Otto hasn't seen it yet, so perhaps we could all go together tomorrow?"
    His Excellency touched a linen napkin to one corner of his mouth and smiled at his wife. "It would be our pleasure."
    From behind her bamboo fan Nanette whispered in a loud tone to *vrouw* Mauricius. "You must be sure to make your

selections first, or Elisabeth will get the best for La Solitude."

This merriment caused everyone to laugh, but I could only manage the slightest of smiles. The bitter truth is that La Solitude may prove to be one more house full of beautiful fabrics and furniture, china, crystal, and brilliants, but hollow from the absence of children. I tried to console myself with the thought that dealing in these commodities has served me well, and how else would potential buyers know of their existence if I did not wear and show them? Indeed, at this moment the thought occurred to me of a twenty-four piece silver plate service of extraordinary engraving that I should like to sell to His Excellency's wife for her table.

These thoughts however were no comfort to that which I most longed to control—my own cold, barren womb.

Across the table I saw Emilius holding Nanette's hand in a most affectionate manner. My sister is thirty-three. Do they yet hope to have children together? I wondered.

It occurred to me then to question if the Christian God is punishing us for living in sin. Would all be different if Nanette and I were able to marry legally in the Dutch Reformed Church? Yet Maria, as a free Mulatto, had enjoyed such privileges and remained barren. Then I reminded myself of our brothers' virility with their concubines and shook my head, as if to throw off annoying flies or mosquitoes. Nothing seemed logical or just to me.

"Are you having any luck with persuading the planters to consider your policy of peace-making with the Maroons?" asked Emilius of the Governor. Now that he has captured Nanette in pleasurable concubinage, Emilius is reluctant to see any military confrontations with heathen runaways that will take him far from home.

His Excellency was untimely caught with a mouth full of food which prevented him from making immediate answer. With grace, Anna interjected, "I hope you can talk some *sensibilité* into them. I fear the Maroon problem is escalating. It seems every day I hear of a plantation that has been *mal affecté*."

Governor Mauricius set down the embossed silver fork and lifted his napkin to wipe his lips. To Anna he presented a brave smile. "I'm sorry to say, my dear, that they fight me tooth and nail on the issue."

At the end of the table there occurred an interrupting confrontation between Pansu and La Vallaire's oldest son. Six-year-old Pieter, holding loosely in his fingers a piece of pineapple, had lost it to the swiftness of the squirrel monkey's little hands, and bawled as Pansu scampered across the table, with his long gold chain upsetting china and crystal.

"Little sister, do something with that damned monkey," complained Nanette.

I chafed at her reference to me as "little sister" but chose to make no comment. *Vrouw* Mauricius was laughing at Pansu's antics, nonplussed by the fact that claret from one of the tipped goblets had spilled onto her ruffled sleeve, spreading a wide, dark stain. Liesbeth stood, grabbed Pansu, and lifted the offending chain from the table, gathering all deftly in her lap. There Pansu, who never let go of his pineapple prize, sucked the morsel as if nothing unusual had happened. La Vallaire frowned at Pieter, and his crying diminished to loud sniffles. Servants were called to bring towels and cold water and a generous amount of table salt to apply to the stain on the tablecloth and on *vrouw* Mauricius' sleeve.

With patience Carl Otto waited for this commotion to play itself out. Then he continued, "It would appear the Cabale and Your Excellency are steadfastly opposed regarding your philosophy about the Maroons."

Governor Mauricius sighed and helped himself to another slice of venison steeped in Madeira and flavored with mint leaves. "This sauce is excellent," he said. "On Jamaica, seven years past, a peace was made with the runaways and they were recognized as free black men and women."

"All of them?" asked Liesbeth.

"Aye."

Anna looked skeptical. "*Et c'etait le fin* of the attacks on the plantations?"

"The end, more or less. In any case I find it a progressive idea that can be here adapted, if we are diligent, to our unpleasant situation."

"My pardon, Your Excellency, but if the slaves were free,

who would work for us?" I inquired. "Though certainly I favor peace-making, I question the practicality of this idea of complete freedom for slaves." I also question the wisdom of this, but refrained from saying such.

"What I'm suggesting is a kind of amnesty, not complete freedom." Governor Mauricius smiled at me as a teacher might regard a bright, but unstudious child. "I recognize their contribution to the wealth and production of the Colony."

Emilius leaned so far forward with his keen interest that his ruffled linen stock graced the lace of the tablecloth. "How then would this peace work?" he asked.

"Naturally we would first have to identify and make contact with the Maroon leaders. Without a dialogue, there can be no peace. I think we have a pretty good idea of what they want—tools, food, to be left alone."

And women, I thought.

"So you would simply give them these things?" Emilius asked.

"Aye, a kind of treaty payment would be made annually. For certain it would be a small price to pay for the safety and productivity of our plantations."

"Small indeed," said Anna. "The price of two stolen slaves would buy a lot of tools and clothes and pots and pans, *n'est ce pas?*"

"May I have another serving of that delicious venison?" asked the Governor.

"Your waistline, my dear," scolded *vrouw* Mauricius in a kind tone.

I nodded, happy that His Excellency found my table so agreeable, and gestured to the food service boy who stood at attention by the door. He came to my side, and I gave instructions to bring more of the dish.

Emilius looked grim. "I can see why those rich planters oppose the idea. They won't pay a guilder to the Maroons voluntarily."

"They see the idea as caving in," said Carl Otto. "Surrendering in a war they think we can win by force and punishment." Like Emilius, he did not relish any idea of direct forceful conflict in the dark woods and tangled growth of the jungle.

His Excellency, a dutiful husband, and as much to avoid further comment on his appetite, changed the direction of the conversation to a discussion of his wife's reading society.

"I see European culture shifting to a broader toleration in many things. Isn't that so in your reading group?"

Vrouw Mauricius' blue eyes brightened. "Aye, the influence of enlightened ideas and toleration in such areas as freedom and religion is gaining ground. We've been fortunate in accumulating new books and periodicals with each shipment lately. I've even received some editions of the *Hollandsche Spectator*. And just this month I received volumes by Rousseau and Isaac de Pinto."

I was delighted to hear this and begged her to lend them to me before our humid climate makes its mark upon them, to which she agreed.

"Indeed our little literary society is growing," she said. "You ladies are all welcome to join us. And the gentlemen. We even have some Jews in our group."

In polite reply we smiled and nodded, because Maria can only write her name and read numbers and simple letters. Nanette is just beginning to learn letters. But Anna appeared to be very interested, and Liesbeth responded, "I should like to join you one day."

"Of course, my dear, you are more than welcome." The Governor's wife was sincere in her tone. Like her husband, she favors any further enlightenment among the inhabitants of our Colony.

Having dined well and fully, our group adjourned to the drawing room for games of whist, tric trac, and backgammon. Pieter and Pansu had come to terms and now amused each other on the Persian rug. Nanoe and Liesbeth settled cross-legged on two walnut stools with cabriole legs, little five-year-old Susanna on the floor between them. The girls proceeded to teach the child how to play *minchiate*, a popular Florentine trick-taking card game. The cedar tobacco case was unlocked and pipe-bowls were filled all around.

After a light dessert of fruits and sugar pastries, the ladies begged their leave to depart while Emilius and the Governor joined Carl Otto in the library where they would smoke more tobacco, enjoy a *digestif*, and no doubt continue their political conversations.

At the door Anna whispered to me, "*Ma chérie*, I'm so sorry you've been disappointed again."

I sighed and helped her with her silk mantelet. "I really thought this time we begat a babe. I was sure."

"There will be another time, my darling."

As I watched her descend the brick steps to her carriage, sudden envy enveloped me. I was startled by its ugliness. Dear Anna with her pretty Mulatto face and soft almond eyes, who has been nothing but a loyal friend to Maria and our family, did not deserve to be looked upon by the cold eyes of the coiling serpent that encircled my heart. I prayed to the Christian God and all the *winti* spirits that I could never deny her her white husband and sweet daughter if such were offered to me at her expense.

17

Paramaribo, May 1746

My sweet Liesbeth, already fifteen, attended this evening at the Governor's mansion her first formal ball. It took a special effort for us all to get there at the appointed hour, for her dress and toilette occupied a lengthy space of time.

Seated at my toilette table, Liesbeth frowned as Kwasiba worked her hair with awkward hands. Though I have made every effort to train the maid in the fine art of hairdressing, I must now admit that it appears not to be a talent natural born to her.

"Your hair will never do," I said to my neice. I sent Kwasiba away so that I might dress it myself. This took a bit longer, but when I was finished Liesbeth's hair was artfully arranged— rolled black curls supported by little hidden cushions. To this I added bows that matched the ones on her _saque_-dress.

A French piece of lovely rose brocade, the dress was embroidered with flowers and birds, with a line of red velvet bows descending from bosom to hem. There was a profusion of gold Alençon lace at her sleeves and all around the skirt hem. I knew she had selected this dress to accompany the red velvet Holland mask, and the pearls at her throat were matched in luster by the pearls adorning the mask.

My own gown of embossed Geneva velvet, in a dusky green hue, was more in keeping for a woman of my age, though I did freely adorn it with four strings of the most purely white pearls from the best water, clasped with a large emerald surrounded by twelve diamond drops. All this had been laid out on the mahogany four-poster in my bedroom. Kwasiba, aided by a house girl whose name escapes me, was present to help us make ready.

"It's time to depart," Carl Otto called from the stairs. Since our hallway was lined with a new Turkish carpet, we walked barefoot to the top of the stairs and there put on our shoes. Carl Otto was most handsome in his formal military dress of blue turned up with scarlet, the silver buttons on his short jacket newly polished. His jackboots gleamed from having been polished to within an inch of a slave's life.

As our carriage wheels crunched the shell gravel of the road leading to the Governor's mansion, Carl Otto said, "Liesbeth, you are radiant. You will be the star of the evening."

My niece broke into a bold grin. "Thank you, kind sir." I was amused to note a rather flirtatious manner to her reply.

From across the *Orangeplein* facing the mansion, it was clear the ball was already well in progress. Light poured from every window, and slaves in blue and gold livery could be seen walking everywhere among the crowd, fanning away the *mampira* and mosquitoes of the humid evening. Though we are now in the wet season, this night all was blessed with agreeable weather, as if the magic of the glowing mansion had spread out into the very universe itself.

Indeed, inside all was festivity and merriment. Crystal goblets edged in gilt sparkled with the most delicious wines. There was an abundance of all manner of delicacy and the meats were the choicest cuts of ham, salt pork, and venison, as well as a barbecued fish called *warapa*. Succulent cuts of pineapple and *pampelmoes* had been rolled in sugar and there were sliced papayas arrayed with sweet slices of orange, fried sugared plantains, and *markoesa* fruit marinated in rum. Set out on every table in cut crystal dishes were roasted cashew nuts and both salted and sugared peanuts.

Our neighbors were well set out in silks, brocades, and velvets of the richest manner, decorated with magnificent pearls, gems, golden chains, buttons, and medals—everything precious that could be bought in the world was in evidence. Everywhere people were engaged in the most fashionable conversation.

The musicians even were heard to be particularly energetic. Flute, clarinet, oboe, bassoon, and violin were joined by an extraordinary walnut clavicin, newly arrived to our Colony for the purpose of gracing the Governor's mansion. The musicians performed the popular music of the Frenchman Jean-Philippe Rameau—now living handsomely on an annual pension after performing a comedy-ballet at Versailles that was most successful with the King—and the lively *Four Seasons* concertos of the recently deceased Antonio Vivaldi. I find this latter to be most whimsical due to the composer's attempt to mimic birdsong and even a barking dog.

Nanette agrees with me in this and says, "The French are too serious. The Italians have always made better music."

Such are the luxurious entertainments we enjoy at Paramaribo, the capitol of the Colony.

Upon her masked entrance, Liesbeth, radiant with youth and beauty, attracted the attention of several Colonial officers. I watched her from a distance away that would not disturb the attention being paid to her. Now carrying the mask in one hand and fluttering her fan in a natural, feminine manner with the other, Liesbeth was a vision of lightness and fluidity as she swished the skirts of her dress this way and that. I was very greatly satisfied to see that while she found this discourse pleasing, she maintained the modesty befitting the education of such a young charmer.

"And who might be this beauteous maid?" Carl Otto whispered into my ear.

"Why, my darling niece, of course. She's the loveliest of creation."

Carl Otto laughed. "I meant you, my sable Betje."

"*Merci bien, monsieur*," I murmured, affecting a slight curtsy with my skirts. "But see how the officers show Liesbeth every courtesy."

"They'd better, or they'll answer to my sword."

I could have hugged Carl Otto then and there for the affection he extends to my family. For even as we gazed at each other I felt the eyes of some planters' wives condemning me as they do for living, to their mind, in sin.

We danced and partook of food and drink and when much

later I again saw my niece she was most giddy, with flushed cheeks.

"*Tante* Elisabeth, I'm having the best time," she said. As I caught a whiff of her breath I could tell that she had had the best of too much rum.

"Why don't we go upstairs and find a place for you to lie down for awhile," I suggested. "If you rest a bit now, you can dance again later."

A biddable creature in spite of her animated nature, Liesbeth nodded her cushioned curls and followed me as I headed towards the staircase.

Just then this stimulating evening was brutally interrupted by a heated exchange between Egbert Peltser and Emilius de Vries. I halted on the stairs and turned my head, the better to hear their angry words.

Meneer Peltser, a new member of du Plessis' Cabale, said in a voice heightened by drink, "...has signed a petition of complaints against the Governor."

"You think the Jew Isaac Carilho and his captains of the Civic Guard will have any impression with the Society?" Emilius demanded.

The butcher, a good head shorter than my sister's consort, stared upward at the taller man and from the stairs above I was thus able to see the fierceness in his face. "His Excellency thinks he can use the complaints from the Jewish *parnassim* against him to dismiss Carilho as captain of the Guard, but he won't get away with it! Carilho's petition will let the Society know what is really going on here."

Liesbeth had also paused to regard the two men below us. Their voices were rising and others standing nearby had stopped conversing to observe them.

"Your petition means nothing," scoffed Emilius, a Mauritsridder like Carl Otto. "Besides, the *parnassim* itself would like to see the Jew expelled from the Colony for his tactless behavior."

I noticed that several nearby listeners were indeed Jewish sugar planters. I nudged Liesbeth and we hurried upstairs, away from this most unpleasant confrontation. I wondered what could be the end result of this scrapping and squabbling between the government and the plantocracy, for even now, in the midst of a gracious evening, two white men of prominence, Edgar Peltser and Emilius de Vries, were without doubt ready to come to blows.

18

Plantation Toevlught, January 1747

At sixteen, now an accomplished seamstress and lacemaker, Liesbeth enjoys the passion of first love.

The object of said passion is the white Dutchman Samuel Loseke. He has just taken her, with all our approval, as concubine. Samuel only arrived at Paramaribo this past July, on the merchant ship *Adrichem*, undoubtedly destined for important government service due to the friendly family relationship between his mother's side, the Hanssens, and Governor Johan Jacob and *vrouw* Mauricius. I am told that the Hanssen and Mauricius families, with adjoining provincial estates in the Netherlands, share both political viewpoints and burgomaster positions.

Thus distinguished by the favor of His Excellency, and having bestowed upon Liesbeth every care and attention, we could have no objection to his proposed match with my dear niece. The girl, having implored Maria most heartily to allow his attentions, which on his side I must note were quite persevering, is besotted.

At lunch, Samuel Loseke was keenly interested in the operation of my coffee plantations Welgemoed and Toevlught here at Hoer-Helena Kreek.

"Why coffee rather than sugar," he inquired," already proven profitable and with an established European market?" As he asked this he held his fork, base resting on the table, pointed in an upward manner like a vertical exclamation mark.

I explained that coffee requires less soil than sugar. "And the European market is growing."

Samuel's reddish-brown eyebrows raised, and he shifted his body in his chair. "You expect coffee to replace tea as one's beverage of choice?"

"Oh, surely not," I said. "But the benefits of a regular drink of coffee in terms of aiding one's constitution are not to be discounted."

"I find it most agreeable," said Liesbeth. Her gaze at Samuel said coffee was not at all on her mind.

"Indeed," said her new consort, "the proof of your decision is evident in the success of these properties." He made a circle in the air with his fork to indicate his surroundings.

His flattering words were wonderfully charming to my ear. "Both are, I'm happy to say, doing very well."

"You don't have problems with runaways?" he inquired. Samuel Loseke's youthful countenance implied a sincere nature.

"Nay, we are fortunate here," I said. "The Maroons, though occasionally seen walking round the outskirts of the plantation, have so far excluded us from their pillaging forays."

"You are indeed fortunate, *vrouw* Samson, that you have for the most part been spared such misadventure."

"Please, Samuel, now that you are in our family you must call me Elisabeth."

It was easy to smile at the young man, as Liesbeth was doing, for Samuel Loseke is most pleasingly handsome. A tall, thin man with close-set bottle green eyes and well-formed features, he exudes energy and stamina. His skin is alabaster already turning to a golden cream from his exposure to our equatorial sun. Even the rather long port wine birthmark on the left side of his face in candlelight serves only to accent his manly features.

"You are most gracious." He gave me a courteous nod and the benefit of a quite disarming smile. "Yet I have heard tell that a fresh supply of troops have been requested of the Society, to protect the planters from the constant trouble with marauding Maroons."

"That's true," said Carl Otto, leaning back in his chair to allow the serving slave to pour more tea into his cup.

"The planters are feeling increasingly threatened, a state I believe they've brought on themselves by inhumanely damnable usage of their slaves. It's bound to result in a greater military presence in the Colony."

Liesbeth ventured, "They say Great Britain would free their colonial slaves."

Samuel laughed in his marvelous way and patted her hand. "And then where would their economy be? They will more likely lose their thirteen American colonies by making a free people into slaves."

"There'll be no abolition of the Guinea slave trade," said Carl Otto. "Fair-skinned Europeans and Indians as well are inadequate to the task of cultivating the land. Our Dutch countrymen must learn to value more carefully their black property so that our plantations can remain competitive against those of the English and French. The whole of the plantation condition could benefit from raising living conditions for the slaves and providing substantial food."

Liesbeth's consort nodded, considering the simple practicality of Carl Otto's words.

"It just makes good business," I said, "to take care of valuable property, so that it will serve you well. After all, it's why the silver is polished, so that the tarnish doesn't rot the metal."

"Besides," Carl Otto continued. "The Maroon concern won't matter if the Governor and the Courts of Police and Justice can't come to some understanding."

I considered this as I stroked the golden fur of Pansu, who lay slumbering in my lap after stuffing himself with sugared plantain and sips from my wineglass. Disputes in the Colony continue to become more volatile, with His Excellency less and less able to control them. Without some satisfaction on all sides, it would seem that all will soon be laid to ashes, as we wallow in a political dunghill of corruption and dire effects.

Recognizing that he can no longer treat the planters with too much indulgence, His Excellency has adopted a more authoritarian policy. In response, the Cabale has sent du Plessis to Holland with letters of complaint about the Governor for the States-General.

"The Jew Isaac Carilho continues to behave most indiscreetly," said Carl Otto. "The *parnassim* on more than one occasion has made formal request to His Excellency to remove him from the Colony."

"And His Excellency's reply?" asked Samuel.

"He declares the action legal on the strength of the Jewish privileges of 1669."

As Samuel nodded in agreement, Liesbeth made an inclination of her head to him and whispered something inaudible, causing him to grin most happily.

"More gingered pineapples?" I asked, passing a porcelain plate in their direction.

. . .

After the afternoon meal I placed Pansu, who has developed a decided taste for wine, to further his slumber in his cage near the back staircase. I closed the metal door and secured its tiny lock so that Pansu could not be stolen or otherwise carelessly allowed to escape, and retired to my bedroom where a soothing bath awaited me.

Long gauze curtains had been hung in the windows to lessen in the room the effects of the midday sunlight. The shoe-shaped copper bathing tub had been set up in one corner of the room, and filled with good Madeira heated on the cooking fires and hauled up the back stairs by the upstairs servants. I am the first person in the Colony to have imported from France such a bathing basin, and am wickedly satisfied to note *mofokoranti* about it is still in circulation.

I examined the redness of the water and instructed Kwasiba to heat more Madeira, for it did not seem that the bath contained enough of the spirit to properly refresh my skin. Kwasiba sent a girl to comply and then helped me out of my stomacher, skirts and embroidered camlet. I handed her my diamond earrings to put away in their silk envelope, which I would later lock in the armoire. Feeling fatigued and attributing it to the conversation at dinner, I welcomed the china cup of coffee the girl had placed on my toilette table. From a silver bowl I laced the drink amply with sugar. While I sipped the dark, hot liquid,

Kwasiba gathered up my hair and with an ornamental bodkin secured it atop my head in preparation for the bath.

I had just slid down well into my tub of warm, fragrant wine when Carl Otto entered the room. Kwasiba, having completed the necessary ministrations, retired. Carl Otto crossed the room and leaned down to kiss the top of my hair. "Are you feeling better, my beauty?" he murmured.

The heavy smell of the heated Madeira invaded my nostrils and emitted from me a langorous sigh. "Aye. Much better."

"It pleases me to hear it. I sensed you are attacked by some complaint."

I closed my eyes and he waited for a response. At length I whispered, "You are well intentioned, my love." I felt perforce obliged to confide a subject that well merited to be mentioned. "Nanette has met with a revelation of a most odious nature. It seems Governor Mauricius has written in his journal most disturbing words about white-black concubines."

"How can she know this?" he asked.

"A house servant with the knowledge of letters read it and passed it on."

"*Mofokoranti.*"

"Aye, indeed, yet a most disturbing *mofokoranti*. I don't think a slave would have the intelligence to invent what he says was written."

"And that is what, exactly?" Carl Otto lay down on the bed without removing his jackboots. When I sat up in the tub and pointed this out, he dismissed my comment with a wave of his hand. "Tell me what His Excellency wrote."

"His Excellency expressed concern about white men who keep carnal intercourse with black women. He says that even members of the Court of Police—who should know the law and know better—participate." When Carl Otto did not respond I added, "That's about two-thirds of the Court, if I count correctly."

Carl Otto sat up to remove his wig, which he discarded carelessly at his side on the bed, and made a lengthy sigh. I sensed he is as weary of this duplicity as I. Choosing his words with care, he said, "Of course His Excellency knows marriages between whites and blacks are forbidden by law…"

"And the Church regards living together without marriage to be living in sin."

"Aye." Carl Otto rose suddenly from the bed and got down on his knees beside my bathing tub. With gentleness he placed his hands on the sides of my face, forcing me to look into his devoted countenance. "Always remember, dear Betje, the love I have for you is not a sin."

I could not restrain the words that forced themselves to my throat. "Perhaps it is a sin and it's why we haven't been able to have a child."

His voice took on a harsher tone. "Nay! Betje, you yourself, as I, know many people who live as we do and have children. Don't let me hear such foolishness. I know you don't believe that."

He is right, of course; I don't hold such a Christian superstition. It would be more likely that some *winti* or ancestor spirit has a grievance against me that has not been recognized. It has been in the back of my mind to consult Granman Quassie about this, but I have procrastinated, for I fear that to speak out loud my concern in such a formal manner would give it the power of truth. Yet I cannot but wonder why God has chosen to pass me over by withholding the joy of motherhood. And why our Governor in his journal has found Suriname marriage to be worthy of such hate.

"Do you not fear that a scandal around this situation might taint the future of your military career?" I asked.

"Nay, my sable beauty." With great gentleness Carl Otto kissed me on the lips. "What I fear is that you will let the taunts of white planters' wives taint and thus weaken the strength of our love."

19

Paramaribo, August 1747

Samuel Loseke has become Inspection Master of the molasses hogsheads, one of the most important posts among the inspectors of the exportation of sugars. Samuel's appointment is, I'm sure, a recognition of his ability to make thorough analysis of things and easily remember every important detail. Everyone remarks upon his intellect and great retentive memory. Naysayers point out that he is particularly young for such grave responsibility, but of course we certainly have our share of those in the Colony.

Amazingly, I've heard no comment upon the fact that Samuel has a Negro concubine. His Excellency may believe that we are all living in sin, but in truth there is not much he can do about it when the practice of Suriname marriage is so widespread, even among, as he himself so cruelly noted, the Court of Police itself.

Samuel swore in front of Governor Mauricius. Normally inspection masters would not swear an oath in front of the Governor, but an exception was made for Samuel, a tribute to the affection and esteem with which His Excellency holds Samuel's mother's family.

Liesbeth beamed, her black skin set off pleasingly by her blue silk *saque*-dress. It's obvious she is quite proud of her handsome young consort, as well she should be. She has done well for making a selection at such a young age, and I am proud of her.

"I shall bear him a son," she confided to me. When she

noted my happy expression, she clarified, "Well, not yet, but soon I hope to be with child."

I marveled at her confidence, for I still wonder how it is that my brothers are so virile, while I and my sisters have so far proven barren? Kwasiba insists that someone has put a curse on all of my mother's daughters because we are beautiful and rich and therefore much envied. The reality tempts me to believe this. There is no shortage of Dutch women who might wish us ill luck. Yet common sense dictates that a white woman would not so readily rely on *wisi*—black magic—to achieve such an end. More likely it is a slave supposing to have in some way been wronged.

At the house on Oranjestraat we hosted this day a most lavish party for Samuel. Upon arriving at our house for the celebration, he gifted me with a bottle of continental gin, no doubt obtained through the conveniences of his new position. The dark green "horse hoof" bottle is quite special as it has a very deep heart with enough space to accommodate a music box, which begins to play when the bottle is lifted—a most amusing gift indeed.

I was happy to be able to debut my new gold service, with diamonds set into the hafts of the tableware, and to display a most abundant table. The multitude of candles from the overhead chandeliers and rococo wall sconces in the dining salon gave all a glow of warmth, agreeable security, and sumptuous comfort. Even my little Pansu, secured to my wrist with his golden chain, was on good behavior. Nanette says I'm allowing him to drink too much claret and Madeira, but it seems to calm him and he loves it so. More properly speaking, my dear sister is envious of the affection in which I hold the little fellow and the fond attentions I bestow upon him.

Only one thing served to poorly affect the disposition of the company: The conversation of the evening seemed unable to venture from the subject of the Cabale, which group of planters has taken every possible opportunity to ruin His Excellency. Of recent note was the systematic sabotage of a Court of Police meeting by the deliberate withhold from the Governor of vital information. All Paramaribo now talks of the open hostility between His Excellency and the plantocracy.

I slapped my fan upon the lace tablecloth in disgust. "Du Plessis has decried His Excellency's policy as despotic."

"In writing?" inquired Nanette, gesturing to the slave for another service of the *pingo* meat pie.

Carl Otto spoke. "In the very petition of 31 July he has made to the Society, I fear."

Emilius added, "Du Plessis has also requested that our Governor be summoned to Holland in order to answer for the quality of his Governorship. Du Plessis complains about the expulsion of Carilho and describes how the nominations for the Court of Police had been manipulated by the Governor. He claims he has abused the Jewish votes."

Samuel looked thoughtful and drummed his fingers atop the table. "I've heard tell that Carilho petitioned the States-General on the same day as du Plessis, claiming that the Governor dismissed him from his post at the request of the *parnassim* who are his personal enemies."

"I fear His Excellency will find it necessary to defend himself against these complaints." I thought of my own troubled history and felt a great sympathy for the man's distressful situation, for well I know the price of slander in guilders and tears.

"This affair with du Plessis and his Cabale has become exceedingly personal and distasteful," said Carl Otto, waving his hands about the air in an expressive manner. "His reproaches are absurd distortions! How is it possible to talk of making peace with the Maroons when there is no peace among ourselves?"

"However," Samuel offered in an intellectual tone, "Mauricius concedes that Carilho has been much more decent than the slanderer du Plessis."

"If du Plessis' words were spoken by any other who was not white, they would be called 'treason,'" I remarked. In spite of the sweet aftertaste from the delicious repast just consumed, bile rose in my throat at the bitter realization that there is no balance to life.

"True enough, I'm afraid." Carl Otto wiped his mouth with his linen napkin and took another swallow of his claret. Pansu made a move towards the goblet, but I distracted him by offering a sip from my own. "In any case," Carl Otto continued. "His Excellency considers Carilho's behavior to be strange, especially his contesting the validity of the Jewish privileges of 1669."

"Thanks to those very privileges," Emilius pointed out, "the Jews have two churches in *foto* as well as their own village at Joden Savanne, exclusively inhabited by Jews."

"Indeed, that is a phenomenon unique in the world," said Samuel.

It occurred to me that what was left unsaid in this conversation is that if the Society deigns to believe these accusations on the part of du Plessis and his Cabale and recall Governor Mauricius, I fear this might make dire consequences for Samuel's position as Inspector General.

In any case, with anxiety we await to see if in fact it will be requested that our Governor be summoned to Holland to answer for his governorship. For His Excellency I have the most sympathetic of feelings, having myself experienced the tribulation of being made to answer for false accusations. At least Governor Mauricius has friends and family abundant in the Netherlands to support his person and position. I am confident that he will find his way well, whatever the outcome.

His circumstance now made me think of dear Frederik Coenrad Bosse. I felt a warmth rise in me that spoke of how much I have missed my sister's husband, who after all was a virtual father to me. Indeed, he had saved me from the physical pain of branding and flogging, so that I was left to suffer only the emotional distress of separation from all that I held dear.

Frederik did eventually succeed in persuading the Court of Police to petition to have Governor Raye removed from the Colony. But before this event could take place, the Governor succumbed to a mortal attack of the dread malaria. As a result there was yet again, in the form of Gerard van de Schepper, a new white authority fresh from the Dutch Republic to govern the lives of the Colonists. However, this was after I had already been banished to Holland, and I was not yet to hear of it until the following year.

20

Paramaribo, July 1748

Two weeks past, Nanette appeared before the Court of Justice with her consort Emilius de Vries to make their will and testament. She requested that Carl Otto, as her "brother-in-law", act as her executor. And so my consort accompanied them in a sturdy carriage with oiled buckram drapes to protect them from the deluges of the wet season.

Nanette told me she was just signing her name to the papers in front of the notary when she saw Egbert Peltser and his daughter Juliaana, who at 21 years of age is still a beauty, though unmarried. The butcher barely nodded his acknowledgement of the black woman's presence, but his daughter seemed willing to converse. Nanette was relieved to see no sign of the presence of Sophie Peltser, for whom my half-sister has no admiration.

Egbert Peltser, Nanette reports, was not well. "His colour is that of *maripa* worms and his skin is rough as a *pampelmoes*. It's difficult for him to get his breath."

"Did he say what ails him?" I asked, though in truth I was indifferent to the answer.

"He did not, perhaps because Juliaana was all aflutter with her recent engagement to Pieter Visser."

I looked at my sister and I'm sure my eyebrows heightened in surprise. "Pieter Visser, of the Court of Police?"

"Aye, the very one."

"He is a strong opponent to Governor Mauricius," I said,

as if that had anything to do with a marriage. "Have the banns been posted? Has the date been yet set?"

"No date was mentioned, but I'm sure it will be soon. After all, the girl is not getting any younger." Nanette laughed heartily at her own words.

. . .

At the waterside this day we met a newly arrived Guineaman with a fresh cargo of slaves. Though it is still the wet season, the day promised fair. In his latest report from Welgemoed *meneer* Voorhees' mentioned being in dire need of additional help so I could no longer postpone the errand. Liesbeth and Samuel, Nanette and Emilius and two house slaves accompanied me. In truth, their fine company made the outing to Plattebrug promise to be agreeable business.

The ground about the waterside was awash with mud and pools of gray-brown water as a result of yesterday's heavy rain. Sailors, merchantmen, hawkers, Negroes, and planters were nearly indistinguishable one from the other, so covered over were they with the effects of the weather. Hurry and confusion surrounded us, as lengths of hardwood timber, hogsheads of molasses, European furniture, and boxes and crates and barrels of other goods were moved about, loaded, and unloaded. Every scent of horse, slave, river, and wood was sharp, a pungent reminder of the labor that supports our rich habits.

We passed a very large group of *kwatta* monkeys being unloaded from a rough, flat *periak* that had seen much better days. The monkeys had been captured in the wilds and housed in very close quarters during their lengthy trip downriver to *foto*. Their appearance was dull and listless—one or two were for certain near dead—and one screamed out in a noise of great agitation, most unpleasant to the ear. Most would be sold for meat and the occasional one might make it to Europe as a pampered pet. I did not see one among them that would make a suitable companion, and it is probably just as well, for little Pansu might not fair well in the company of the larger animal and they would have to be constantly kept apart.

When she saw my gaze upon the sad creatures, Nanette

wailed, "Please—no more monkeys, little sister."

I ignored her disagreeable tone and directed the driver to position our carriage as close to the auction block as possible so that we could observe the merchandise without the necessity of leaving the buckram canopy with its rolled-up side curtains that could be dropped in the event of a new rain torrent. Nanette held a fine silk handkerchief to her nose or sniffed repeatedly from a gold pommander containing a scent ball of orange rind. Liesbeth, with eyes only for Samuel, paid little attention to the wretched blacks displayed one by one.

Samuel and Emilius descended the carriage to better inspect the new slaves, and I was happy to let them take care of the business. At once they found their white silk stockings splattered from the muck. At their departure our carriage lurched off center in the uneven ground under the mud, causing Liesbeth to laugh and grab onto the frame while Nanette caught her breath in horror. When it seemed steady once more, we readjusted ourselves and sat without discourse to wait for their return.

After a short while, Samuel and Emilius returned, disappointed to have made just a few selections. "The merchandise was not as hearty as I would like," Emilius said. "But the captain says another ship was sighted and with fair weather should arrive next week."

Samuel Loseke had met up with some associates from the Office of Inspections and brought news that stunned us all. An acquaintance related to the gentlemen that four days ago the butcher Egbert Peltser died of a mysterious affliction for which no one knows the cause. Four days dead now—I wondered why it had taken so long for us to hear.

"Well, Nanette said he looked sickly two weeks ago when she saw him at the Court of Justice," I reminded them.

"What symptoms did he display?" asked Liesbeth.

Samuel frowned and wiped his forehead with his handkerchief. It came away in his hand smeared with the reddish brown dirt that seemed to be everywhere. "A putrid fever, spastic chills, and shivering, a sweat as of the ague for which bleeding and bathing in wine vinegar were of little success."

Upon hearing this I fell into a deep melancholy.

The symptoms, which came suddenly upon the butcher, do not relate to any of the common ailments with which we are familiar, thus there is always the fear in every heart that some new contagious disease has invaded the Colony. Who knows what ailments the Africans bring, for example? While malaria and consumption regularly take their toll, there are a myriad of infections and diseases for which even the best *dresiman*, Granman Quassie, has no cure. We have been blessed by God in the past few years not to have been visited upon by either plague or small pox, but who can foresee how long such good fortune will continue?

"Will *vrouw* Peltser continue her husband's butcher business, or do you think Juliaana's fiancé will take it over?" wondered Nanette.

"The man didn't have any knowledge of that," said Emilius, "but Juliaana's quite anguished as her mother has postponed her wedding date to next July in order to allow for a proper period of mourning."

"Just so," said Liesbeth. "But how distressing for Juliaana." As a free Negress, Liesbeth could never expect to enjoy a legal wedding of her own with Samuel, and sympathy for the white woman's disappointment was written upon her countenance.

My own heart, in truth, felt nothing for Juliaana's situation, not for the loss of her father or the delay in her marriage.

21

Plantation Welgemoed, September 1748

It was still dark all around when I arose from my bed at five a.m. I dressed in a simple garment and tied a large cotton apron about my waist. In its deep pockets I keep a pair of scissors, a cotton scarf, my fan, and the keys to house and cabinets. As I descended the stairs Pansu began fretting in his cage, as he had heard my step. His cries were piercing and insistent.

"I'm coming, little one," I muttered. "No need to awaken the dead."

As soon as I unlocked his cage and opened the door he leaped upon my arm and scampered up to his favorite position on my shoulder. Together we went out to the front porch and sat down at a large rattan table. The *keuken* girl brought me tea heavily laced with milk and sugar and some peanuts for Pansu.

While my breakfast was being prepared, I received my *bastiaans*, the four black supervisors who apportion and direct the day's work. Each *bastiaan*, wearing heavy boots, a sheathed machete and coiled whip at his waist, made his report on the work that was completed yesterday and which among the slaves was lazy or malingering, requiring some form of punishment.

"Extra hands have been assigned to the fields to guard against fire in the dry weeds among the coffee plants," said the tallest of the men, his hat held with respect in his hands.

The dry season is full upon us and fire is a constant dread.

Meneer Voorhees arrived, breathing hard and already wiping the sweat from his neck.

"You're late," I said, perplexed. My director is regularly quite punctual and organized. "Is something the matter?"

"*Mevrouw*," the man said in a hoarse voice. "I'm sorry to say there's been some fermentation of the pulp of the fruits that were collected five days ago. The beans inside will be useless. I did not discover this until just this morning."

"How was this allowed to happen?" In annoyance I tapped my pen against the open plantation ledger, making a large accidental ink mark.

"I will find the slave responsible," assured Voorhees.

"I certainly hope so."

The *bastiaans* stood to one side as a number of slaves were paraded before me, each one examined with care by the slave who serves in the capacity of doctor. In this way it was determined and thus recommended to me who was indeed sick and who was feigning illness.

Voorhees sat down across from me at the table and I directed to be brought for him a fresh pot of tea. "You do not look well yourself," I commented.

The man sighed, a great heaving motion that caused him to relax lower into the wicker chair. "I've not been sleeping well in this heat, *mevrouw*," he said.

I suggested he see the slave doctor for a concoction to drink before retiring or to otherwise engage himself in some personal activity with one of the female slaves so that he would be more relaxed at the end of the day and thus good sleep would more easily find him.

My director agreed to this and went on to make his report regarding the new seedlings that will be planted on twenty hectares at the south side of the plantation, close to the Hoer-Helena Kreek, when the wet season arrives. That will put all one hundred hectares into production, ninety-eight percent of it fine Arabica coffee plants. With seventy-six hectares already mature I may expect next year a yield of perhaps twenty thousand kilos of berries, a fine return for Welgemoed.

"When do you expect the new slaves to be ready to work

the fields?" I asked.

"In less than a fortnight, *mevrouw*."

"Good. But watch them to be sure they've learned to pluck the fruit correctly."

"Aye, *mevrouw*."

"And they recognize the right colour of the fruit, so that they only pick the ripe ones."

"Aye, *mevrouw*."

At this point I had finished my breakfast and the boy arrived who would accompany *meneer* Voorhees on his inspection of the fields. Following just behind the director, he would carry for him his tobacco, guns, and flask of rum.

They departed, and the breakfast China was cleared away. Pansu, who had been inspecting the food remains on a plate, screeched at the servant, who almost dropped the plates in his fright. I wiped my face with my napkin, beginning to feel the heat of the day. I had yet to meet with the houseman to discuss the day's interior work. But I put him off for an hour and chose this time to make entries into the journal kept for the business of the plantation, noting what had been reported that morning, the precise numbers involved, and bringing everything up to date.

I ordered for myself a tall pitcher of *sangaree* with extra nutmeg, a habit I had acquired after La Vallaire, and closed the plantation account book. When the pitcher was delivered I poured into a small cup a little of the *sangaree* for Pansu. The drink was particularly refreshing this morning and, as I gazed across the lawn at the solid wall of immense trees that mark the south boundary of Welgemoed, a feeling of contentment settled within me. All around me was order and luxury, and I felt the satisfaction that comes from seeing the results of work entered into with industry and perseverance.

But one thing troubled my mind: Governor Mauricius, after much diligence, may well persuade the Courts to mount an expedition to the territory of the Saramakas to make with them a peace treaty. His Excellency hopes this will be the first of several separate treaties with the various groups of runaways, and Carl Otto may well be named to lead the first expedition and begin the important negotiations.

Such an expedition, by its very nature, will be hazardous and fraught with peril. No matter the amount of billhooks, muskets, lead, and ball cartridges, men will certainly die. The climate will take its toll. The most learned surgeon can do little for the bloody flux, prickly heat, dry gripes, boils and corruptions that plague the men. Daily they will be visited upon by miserable scrapat-lice, cockroaches, wasps, chigoes, mosquitoes, and ants. Terrible swellings can result in amputation undertaken in the most wretched of circumstances. Nightly will be added to their misery the most annoying presence of vampire bats and screaming jaguars. For certain many of the European soldiers never comb, wash, shave, shift, or even put off their boots, till all about them reeks of raiments rotting from their bodies. I'm told the most evil *jorka*—spirit of a dead person—cannot rival their putrid persons. In addition, any Colonial military expedition is vulnerable to revolt at any time by the very Negroes recruited to carry the stores and provisions.

The thought of my beloved Carl Otto attempting to accomplish military glory under such conditions is dreadful. Despite the heat of the day, the very blood in my veins felt chill at the contemplation of these considerations. I found my fan had fallen to the floor and I was rubbing my forearms for extra warmth.

These dire musing were interrupted by shouting from the plantation's landing at the riverside. Welcoming the diversion, I gathered up Pansu in my arms, descended the brick steps and ran across the expanse of lawn to the water, where I could see that a tent boat had arrived.

I discovered my sister Nanette, frenzied and delirious with only one slave in attendance. In her ravings, having implored the curse of Heaven to rain down upon her, she cried out Emilius' name again and again. It was after some time that I was able to learn from the frightened Negro who accompanied her that Nanette's beloved consort has had his life given up to the malaria.

"Nothing could be done," she wailed. "*Gra'man* Quassie came—what a useless old man! How can everyone believe he has talents as a *dresiman*?" She went on to rail with bitterness against the Negro who attended so many families in times of need.

I pulled her into my arms and turned her body away from the tent-boat. "Come into the house," I urged.

I settled my distraught sister on one of the comfortable sofas in the drawing room and called for a drink of cider laced with rum. Nanette drank this obediently, and then asked for a draught of laudanum. Afterwards it was easy to coax her upstairs to a bedroom where she could rest until her frenzies lessened.

From a cane stool where I sat at her bedside, I watched Nanette fall into a fitful sleep. My own skin felt feverish and to breathe was difficult. Tears welled in my eyes when I thought of how happy Nanette had been with her consort. How distraught might I myself feel if it had been Carl Otto who succumbed to the malaria. This thought reminded me of his probable forthcoming expedition for His Excellency, who himself would never endanger his health by setting one foot into the wild jungle.

At length I retired to my own bedroom to lie restlessly upon the bed and ponder this misfortune that has happened to my sister.

A soup of *tayer* and salt pork had been ordered to be prepared by way of refreshment for Nanette's eventual awakening. But she would not touch it, and alternately spent her lungs and slept. Through her dreadful tears she begged me for another draught of laudanum, but I felt it wise to refuse. She became angry with me, screaming, "You cannot know my grief," and cursed me with all manner of unpleasantness. Her face has become ravaged by her sorrow. I was very glad to observe her at last fall back upon the bed in exhaustion, and closing the door behind me left her alone in the room.

From the Negro I elicited a most dreadful description of Emilius' declining energies, lack of appetite, and constant headache, and how his urine turned to a thick blood-red liquid. Neither Granman Quassie's amulets nor twice daily bathing—which Europeans rarely practice—nor strong leaf teas could stay the sad eventuality of Emilius' demise.

In my tenderness for my sister I myself am utterly exhausted by so much distress. Nanette had grown as passionately fond of Emilius as Liesbeth is of Samuel and had delighted in every minute spent with him. As with myself and Carl Otto, they had hoped for a child, but at thirty-five none had yet come to Nanette and it was the one dark shadow in their halcyon days.

In this manner of mad sorrow did she lay till today, being four days before she came to any sense, and then only with the help of medicinal spirits. Overwhelmed by her ravings, I relented and prepared for her a mixture of laudanum and honey, that her pangs may be alleviated for a time.

When I am more certain of her sound recovery, I will return to *foto* with the Negro servant to arrange for the disposition of Emilius' clothes and provisions. It will not be good for my sister to return to the house she shared with her consort, there to be faced with such sad duties.

Even as death is the specter with which we live on a regular basis, what with the bloody flux, lethargies, and all manner of fever which may result from insect, bat or viper, yet it is shocking to confront how faintly a life can be called by God to expire at any one moment.

22

La Solitude, December 1748

From the direction of the slave houses could be heard the soft, melodious song of a mother crooning to her child. I wondered which of the songs I knew might I sing to my own children?

Nanette, in mourning, now speaks often of the children she might have had with Emilius. Her babble annoys me greatly, for it serves to remind me of my own advancing age and barrenness. From the breakfast room I gazed out of the window in the direction of the sound of the singing and clutched little Pansu more closely to my bosom, until he squeaked and squirmed in distress.

"I tell you, when you have a child Carl Otto will make you get rid of that bothersome creature," Nanette snapped. I had not heard her enter the breakfast room and turned around to see her eyes, round and swollen, staring at my little *monk-monki* with open hostility.

My mouth opened to expel a stinging retort, but her black dress reminded me of her recent distress and, feeling somehow that I had failed to give her the proper sympathy, I said nothing. Instead I turned towards the drawing room and left my sister standing alone to contemplate the fruit and pastries set out on the breakfast table.

To expel the subject of children from my mind I contemplated plantation business. La Solitude, well situated on the Landsweg, has proven to be a fine investment and comfortable diversion from our Oranjestraat house. This year has seen added fifty-two cows, thirteen bulls, and thirty-two calves, and planted the last forty-seven hectares with fine Arabica coffee bushes.

The house is smaller than any of my other houses, just eleven by ten meters and two stories, but the porch is ample and the rooms finely furnished. In the master bedroom we now have two tin mirrors and a silk-embroidered coverlet for the bed. The *keuken* house even has an outdoor oven for baking. Next to the house is storage of about twenty meters long with room for a carriage. Part of this storage area may also serve as a stable. There is well-constructed slave housing with four windows, but I do not retain many slaves here, just five men, five women, and three children.

For this Christmas season has been added to the drawing rooms three mahogany tables, twenty-four new chairs, and to the dining salon twenty-four porcelain plates, twenty-four English plates, and crystal to replace what has been broken by careless servants.

Yesterday has seen completed the decorating of our little country home La Solitude for the Christmas dinner. The site of the drawing room in its holiday dress cheered my spirits. My most favorite decoration is the hand-carved scene of Christ in the Manger surrounded by sheep and wise men which occupies an entire table in the entry hall. Fresh garlands of orange boughs adorn windows, mirrors and paintings, and the air is sweet with their perfume. Every copper chandelier has been polished to make a fine reflection. Of significant aid to me in this endeavor of decoration have been my sister Maria accompanied by Liesbeth and Nanoe. They have also helped me bear the melancholy manner in which Nanette, wearing about her shoulders her mantle of grief, wanders about the house making attempts to be useful but resulting more often in depressing to the lowest ebb our spirits.

Maria took her morning tea in the drawing room, no doubt to avoid Nanette's heavy gloom. Upon completion of our Christmas decorating effort, left over materials, unused garlands, and boxes and tools had all been carried away and the floors again swept by the housemaids. Needlework in her lap, Maria had had a complete tea service brought from the *keuken* house.

"*Goedemorgen, tantes,*" called Liesbeth when she and her sister found us in the drawing room.

"Good morning to you, my dears." I kissed both girls and said, "Beware of your *tante* Nanette this morning. She's in a most foul mood."

"She won't spoil my morning," said Nanoe, heading for the breakfast room. Indeed, after eating, the girls managed to draw their aunt away from the fruit and pastries and lead her into the drawing room for some tea.

The drawing room faces a sunny, pleasant view of the coffee fields. Through the window I could see three dark-skinned field workers bowing their bare backs to the sun as they plucked the weeds that sprout so vigorously from tilled soil. Nanette seated herself in the room in such a direction that she might take comfort from the view of the flower gardens, where all manner of colorful tropical blossoms bloom.

"Her mother will not let her go," Maria said, continuing a conversation from the evening before.

"She must be devastated," murmured Nanette. The sad smile on her face spoke of her personal pain and belied any empathy she might have been perceived to have for the current situation of Juliaana Peltser.

"Still, *vrouw* Peltser is correct to make the judgment," I said, fanning myself in an attempt to stir the humid air that seemed even heavier than my sister's dejection. "The daughter cannot marry until the period of mourning for her father is over. The fact that the fiancé is now forced to leave the Colony is unfortunate timing."

The heat of the dry season is upon us and both the girl who appeared to refresh our tea and the girl who brought the silver salver of sweets had foregone all dress. Both are just at puberty and of form pleasing to the eye, and show great promise for a comfortable future as house servants. Already they know how to serve food and drink, keep their eyes lowered, and retire without inappropriate comment.

"I daresay we should all go about as bare as the day we are born," said Nanoe, waving her silk fan in front of her moist neck.

"Nanoe!" Maria gave a little gasp. "That would be most ungodly for ladies."

With mischief Nanoe's dark eyes sparkled and she winked at Liesbeth. "But oh, so much more comfortable than skirts and stomachers." As if to emphasize her point, she laid her fan in her lap, reached up and removed the white lace-edged cap from her head. Thick black hair tumbled to rest upon her shoulders.

"But not so much fun," I said. "Would you really want to give up your pretty clothes?" Maria gave me a sharp look, but I didn't care what she was thinking. The weather was simply too hot for serious discourse.

Nanoe laughed. "Of course not. But I must say I sometimes do envy the slaves their freedom of dress in this heat." Her eyes narrowed and the corners of her mouth stole upward. "I'll bet Juliaana wishes she were a slave right now so she would be able to accompany Pieter Visser to Holland without being married to him."

"Oh, I do doubt that." Maria managed an amused smile. "Sophie Peltser would die of Christian mortification if Juliaana went away with the man without being married. And after all, Juliaana is her mother's daughter."

"So you don't think it's possible Juliaana will run away with him?" Liesbeth was taken with the romantic notion of such an idea.

As she added more sugar to her tea, Maria's teaspoon clinked against the side of the china as if to emphasize her statement. "Nay. Believe me, Sophie Peltser will never let it happen."

From the silver salver I selected a small pastie. "Carl Otto tells me Visser and that other Council member, Brouer, were particularly vocal against the Governor's idea of making peace with the Maroons on the Saramacca River. He says the discussions in the Court of Police are hotter than the weather ten times over."

"Samuel says that's why His Excellency has used his authority as Governor to have them removed from the Colony," Liesbeth said.

"I told Carl Otto he should be on the Court of Police." It occurred to me that if he held such a position, he might not be seen as the most appropriate person to lead an expedition into the territory of the runaways. Thus I could keep him safe at home.

Maria nodded and made an accompanying gesture with her needlework in my direction. "What a splendid idea."

"He says he's of better use to help the Governor make peace with the Saramaka Maroons than to make peace with the members of the Court of Police!" I added, and my sisters and nieces laughed out loud.

. . .

Alone in my room this night, for Carl Otto will not arrive until three days hence, I sit at my little *escritoire*, smoke my pipe, and reflect upon the cursed inconveniences that thwart our most honorable endeavors. My poor Nanette, suffering from the loss of her consort, when all for her seemed a future of comfortable pleasures. The barrenness of our wombs. My own misfortunes at the hands of the cruel van Meel which so easily could have resulted in my very death.

I must call on Granman Quassie to make an *obia* for Carl Otto—something strong that will keep him brave and safe from the harms that plague the military. Aye, Mariana would have said that that is the best thing I can do to secure my own happiness. I will also pray to the Christian God, as I have been taught, so that any possible bad fortune may be called to account and thusly neutralized before the occurrence of the event itself.

At once I longed for my mother's presence, for the chance to sit at her knee and hear her tell of the time before I was born, when she lived at St. Christoffer, of the powerful magic of the *dresiman* and *wisiman* there. Though indeed she had seldom been present in my childhood, the few times she had shown me attention have not been easily forgotten. In truth I will never know why she abandoned me to Maria's household, and I will always bear ill against van Meel for depriving me of being at her bedside at the moment of her death.

It was a great surprise to me to discover that my face was wet with unchecked tears.

23

La Solitude, February 1749

The plantation director related how the dogs were first to raise the alarm. The sun was about to break over the treetops on the other side of the river when the attack came, and the dogs were the first targets, clubbed and stoned to death.

The plantation house at Lustrijk on the Cottica River was surrounded by Maroon rebels before the planter Daniel du Peijrou even knew of their presence. They set fire to the four outer corners of it, so that a young servant girl who ran from the house in panic rushed to certain death.

Du Peijrou was caught on the second landing, just emerging from his bedroom in a cotton nightshirt, nightcap still about his head. In front of his terrified wife the dark rebel leader slit the planter's throat, the while screaming, "That for the pains you suffered my wives and children! No more shall you abuse the black man and woman who wait upon you!" Then the ferocious man set fire to the nightdress of *vrouw* du Peijrou and laughed as she, in flames, fell screaming off the balcony to the courtyard below.

The plantation director, armed with a machete and in the hopes of hiding from the rebels while they pillaged the plantation, fled to the garret of the house and lay himself flat upon one of the beams there. To his utter horror, the rebels set the house afire and the heat became so insupportable that his options were to be thus burnt alive, or to leap from the high garret window to the midst of the enemy below. In sheer desperation this last he affected, and by good will landed to the ground unharmed from the fall, whereupon the Maroons slashed at him with sabers and billhooks as he fled to the riverside.

Though he could not swim, the director threw himself forthwith into the moving brown waters and, grasping some heaving vines, managed to secure himself among the mangrove roots in such a manner that he escaped immediate detection. There he remained submerged with madly beating heart and barely exposed mouth to breathe, until all human sounds of shouting and wailing had died away, and only the crackling of the flames remained to be heard.

Upon discovering the planter du Peijrou's entire family perished and the plantation house, outbuildings, and grounds laid to ashes, the director was after a time taken up by a boat and carried down the river to *foto*. He now rests in Paramaribo, being somewhat recovered from his very distressed situation.

"Thus, Sir, take care to be upon your guard," he told Carl Otto, who had stopped by a waterside tavern yesterday afternoon where the former director of plantation Lustrijk related his harrowing tale to every horrified listener. This affair has served to make a great alarm among the populace, for Lustrijk rests upon a very well traveled part of the Cottica River.

Thus here at La Solitude was it made known to me by my consort of the devastation at Lustrijk, situated next to Vlardingen and belonging to the same Dutch sugar cane planter who without affecting recompense murdered Quackoe's slave.

"What of La Vallaire and the children?" I asked, desperate for news of my family.

Carl Otto laid his hand to rest upon my arm. "Nay, Betje, all appears to be well at Vlaardingen. The rebel Maroons have disappeared into the jungle as stealthily as they came at Lustrijk. The slaves at Vlaardingen who have family among the rebels say there is no quarrel with Vlaardingen, or its *misi*."

I could not be quieted by his reassurances and paced about the room clutching Pansu, stroking him more to comfort myself than the chittering monkey.

Carl Otto's friend from his military company, Hendrik van Steenberch, arrived just then, distracting me from my worrisome thoughts.

"You must be thirsty after your ride," I said. Already a slave was seeing to the care of his horse.

Hendrik, a gangly man with arms and legs exceptionally long for his body, thanked me, and in just three strides entered the salon where Carl Otto was examining the position of several balls on the billiards table in preparation for a move. He set aside his cue to welcome his friend, and they settled in two armchairs to share some new tobacco Hendrik had brought. A repast of Bologna sausages, sliced bullocks' tongue, and some bottles of Rhenish was laid before our guest, and the mulled wine served well to calm our distress over the fate of Lustrijk and the du Peijrou family.

"Daniel du Peijrou was not a particularly respectable man," Carl Otto declared, "But he did not deserve such a foul end."

He raised his glass as if to toast the memory of the man when Hendrik countered, "Many would say he received his come-back, but certainly innocent were his wife and children. Ah, and to lose the entire plantation! It's said he had bottles of old Rhenish which had been in his cellar since 1726."

"Well, that is indeed a great loss." Carl Otto observed the mulled wine in the crystal goblet he held in his hand.

My thoughts otherwise occupied, I could not in truth determine the degree of sincerity on the part of these gentlemen.

"La Vallaire must bring the children here," I announced. "They can remain at La Solitude until the danger's passed. And what will the military do now to further protect us from such misfortune?"

Hendrik's response was solemn. "His Excellency has managed, as part of his attempts to forge a peace, to persuade the Court of Police to mount a massive expedition against the Maroons."

"Aye, that will help," I said, attempting a note of hope in my voice.

But Carl Otto was equally somber. "Chasing rebels through the jungle may well prove to be a long and frustrating campaign." In spite of my agonized look, he made further explanation.

"During the whole of the night the rebel Maroons in the neighborhood of a military force make noise with both horn and voice, so that no one can sleep and the resulting morning is one of utter exhaustion on both sides. And every expedition is frustrated with fevers and deliriums and badly contaminated food. If the enemy is indeed engaged, our Society soldiers, though brave to rally, are hardly in a good situation to win the day."

"These rebel groups with arms and supplies support one another." Hendrik's glass was empty and he held it up without even looking in the direction of the servant who came forward to pour more of the mulled wine. "We receive often conflicting reports from the field about the enemy. The Maroons have learned how to survive in the forest and to conduct a type of guerilla warfare against which hundreds of soldiers with the best of weapons will not in the end have a good effect."

"But runaways have been captured," I protested, unable to accept such a dismal picture of our Society troops' situation against the enemy. I was also much alarmed at the thought of Carl Otto engaged in such a discouraging campaign.

Hendrik took a sip of his Rhenish, crossed one lengthy leg over the other in his armchair, and shrugged. "So now and then we are able to capture a few runaways. Most likely the army will make expensive trips in the jungle to find only deserted villages and vegetable gardens, which they may then set about to fire."

Carl Otto nodded. "The rebels are known to even, at first sight of an approaching expeditionary force, set afire their own villages the better to escape unseen in the smoke and confusion."

"Still," said Hendrik. "Governor Mauricius wants this peace to be the first of separate treaties with each of the various groups of Maroons."

This conversation began to sound familiar and thus caused my thoughts to drift, to recall the inquiries about the Maroons I had received during my forced exile to the Netherlands. Many Amsterdam merchants had been quite concerned about the effects of *marronage* on the businesses of the plantations. It was not difficult to note that their interest stemmed from fear that the costs of sugar for their coffee, and even for the coffee itself, might rise significantly.

Though I had arrived in Amsterdam to begin my exile

without a friend in the world, I had carried with me some valuable letters of introduction from Frederik Coenraad Bosse. This was how I met the merchant who introduced me to Pieter Reydenius, of the august firm, Pieter Reydenius and Son in Amsterdam.

Pieter Reydenius is an older gentleman with a portly stance and a stout constitution, this in spite of his proclivity for indulgence in the Dutch habit of sitting down to a meal that may include as many as a hundred courses. Thus he suffers regularly from gout, but makes no complaint, and suffers also from a distressing habit of breaking wind with great frequency.

His greatest enjoyment was to escape from the rooms of his business and ride in his carriage through the narrow streets in Amsterdam. He begged me to accompany him on these jaunts, and he seemed not the least satisfied until he had heard tell of everything I had to say regarding Suriname.

"You must tell me, *vrouw* Samson," he said, "how fares the situation with the Maroons in the Colony."

In great detail I was made to describe the ways of the Africans, their most common methods of escape, their life in the wilds, and their punishments when recaptured.

From Pieter Reydenius' carriage I was shown many of the wonders of the city—the Weigh House at the Nieuwmarkt, one of the original city gates; the oldest building in Amsterdam, the Oude Kerk, which was formerly called, "Church of St. Nicholas" and which name was changed by zealous Protestant citizens after the Reformation to obliterate all references to Catholic saints; and the Royal Palace in the Dam square, with its decorations derived from classical antiquity, a most prestigious town hall.

Pieter Reydenius was a man true to his word, and became my most important benefactor, introducing me to several principal personages, and seeing to it that I was included in elaborate dinner and lecture gatherings. To his esteemed credit, he seemed to take not the least notice to the fact of my being a Negress. Thus was established what has proven to be a lengthy and fruitful arrangement. *Meneer* Reydenius serves me well as my representative in the Holland market.

"This is certainly a serious situation you are in, my dear," he said, upon reading the letter of banishment I carried from Josephus de Cohue. His eyes regarded me with care. "Your lawyer emphasizes that you are not guilty."

"Aye, sir. That is true. *Meneer* de Cohue wishes to have a request made to submit to the States General on my behalf for a revision of the judgment."

Reydenius cupped his round chin. "He says here he is sending all the documents from Paramaribo for further research of your situation."

"Aye. There was no time for everything to be ready before my departure."

By the end of September, my first month in exile, Pieter Reydenius had arranged, through his lawyer, one gentleman Hans Hoyer, for the request to be submitted, even though the documents from Paramaribo were not yet received. In the formal request *meneer* Hoyer laid emphasis on my innocence and asked for the revision of judgment.

By the end of January following, the parcel of copies was arrived and delivered forthwith to Den Hague. Along with the parcel came the news that Governor Johan Raye had died, and Governor General Gerard van de Schepper was in authority in our little Colony. I could only guess at how this change in leadership might affect my appeal with the States General.

By the by arrived from Den Hague the pronouncement that the parcel of documents was declared incomplete. At length I was long-suffering of the bitter cold winter season in the Netherlands, and my spirits were accordingly dreary. How much lower they would have been had I known how at home the prosecutor van Meel was barbarously proceeding to thwart de Cohue's efforts to collect the remaining documents necessary to my case. All I could think about was that no matter how many wool stockings and skirts I donned, nor how thick the mantle about my shoulder, nor how hearty the fire in the hearth, I could not be warm.

24

Paramaribo, September 1749

All Paramaribo still talks of the merchantman that arrived on 20 August last, for the captain bore news of the most tragic proportions.

At the Governor's mansion a grand party was in progress that dark, rainy evening. It was one of those social events based on some small accomplishment which made to serve as an excuse to gather planters and merchants together, exchange *mofokoranti*, eat, and drink at the government's expense, and hopefully further the cause of His Excellency's and his lady's pet projects and politics.

Carl Otto and I happened to be standing near to the front door when a small commotion was heard. The disheveled captain of the merchantman, with no regard for dignity or propriety, burst past the houseman and into the room, his demeanor quite determined and his soaked clothing dripping all over the luxurious carpeting and polished mahogany floor.

"The ship on which *meneer* Brouer set sail for Holland has been captured by the French," he announced in a booming voice that carried over the sounds of music and conversation.

All conviviality and mirth ceased and a quiet fell upon the gathering. For a time were heard only the rains of the wet season pounding house and grounds. He barely took a breath before he continued with even more distressing news that the ship upon which traveled Juliaana's fiancé, Pieter Visser, former member of the Court of Police and opponent to

Governor Mauricius, had been sunk down during the conflict and all on board taken unto Neptune's bosom.

Upon hearing this declaration, Juliaana uttered an anguished cry and fell to the floor in a faint. Her mother dropped to her side, her bosom heaving in a most lamentable state, and she screamed at no one slave in particular to bring posthaste a draught of laudanum.

The swooning Juliaana was helped to a nearby sofa, and her fan, dropped when she fell, was laid by her side. Her delicate brow was bathed with a handkerchief wet in wine vinegar and a hot tea boiled with licorice stick was brought. Her revival was so affected according to her youthful vigor, and she began to sob with such distressed suffering that *vrouw* Peltser demanded her daughter be carried to a room upstairs, where she might carry on her lament in a more private state.

The planters began to murmur among themselves and several of their wives were given over to open weeping. The military officers, unaccustomed to providing words of comfort and reassurance, especially to ladies, shifted about in obvious distress.

Myself, I labored under such an emotion as I hardly can describe. Certainly I was no friend to either Visser or Juliaana, so I was surprised to feel an overwhelming compassion for the girl. I asked myself how might I feel to have the love of my life torn from my heart in such a frightful manner.

I was alarmed to hear around me muttered the accusations, "This is all Mauricius' fault," and, "Better His Excellency himself had been aboard."

Resentment and fury swelled through the salon like the strong undercurrents of the high tide on the Suriname River. Some even went so far as to say that Johan Jacob Mauricius should be removed from the Colony. Without a doubt, there was much animosity among the company against His Excellency, which did not bode well for his future relations with the Court of Police.

Then I overheard a sugar cane grower's wife, resplendent of gown and sparkling with precious jewels, remark that one simply cannot buy good meat since the demise of the butcher Egbert Peltser.

. . .

"It's official, Betje," Carl Otto said. Seeing the alarm in my eyes he placed his hands on my arms and pulled me to him. "I've received the order to begin negotiating a peace treaty with the Saramaka Maroons."

This is an important command with significant possibilities for his future career, and it is with much self-force that I am able to maintain a calm façade in his presence. For in truth I am panic-stricken with thoughts of the hardships he will face on such an expedition.

This day began the gathering of the military and Negro slaves for the expedition to locate and meet with the runaways. From now till their departure, Carl Otto will be thus occupied with arrangements, and our house on Oranjestraat will be filled with people coming and going well into the evening.

Led by Carl Otto as Captain Lieutenant, the expedition will consist of two subalterns, two sergeants, four corporals, fifty privates, and a surgeon. They will seek from the plantations closest to *foto* a minimum of twenty Negro slaves, for whose employment their masters will be appropriately paid. The slaves will carry the spades, axes, kettles, medicines, and the officers' boxes, as well as beef, bread, and kill-devil—the new rum distilled from the dregs of sugar caldrons which is the only spirit allowed the Negro. Accompanying him to officially represent His Excellency as the Government negotiator will be the young ensign Louis Nepveu.

The intended destination of the expedition is a group of Saramaka villages located at the head waters of Agamadjá Creek. On the side of the Saramaka to duscuss the proposed ceasefire will be their principle leader, the runaway Negro Adoe. Not much is known of the man except by reputation, and that is that he is tall, a fierce defender of his groups, and skilled in the ways of survival in the wild jungles. The military has so far not been successful in locating another Negro who might be able to recognize the visage of the Saramaka leader, so that the expedition will be dependent on the whim of any such forest people they encounter to direct them to the right person.

Carl Otto began to set out onto our four-poster bed a case in which to pack clothes. "Surely you won't wear your beautiful uniform into the jungle," I said.

"Nay, we'll favor trousers and check shirts with short linen frocks, more adaptable to the humid climate." He tossed a wig aside. "And I'll gladly forego the campaign wig as well."

"I'd best set the sewing girls to making you more shirts," I said.

"There isn't time for that. What I already have will do." From the mahogany highboy he withdrew two pairs of heavy linen breeches. "I'll need to carry only musket, saber, and pistol. My man will carry the box and my hammock."

The instructions and conditions that Carl Otto has received from Governor Mauricius are that as part of a peace accord the Maroons are promised independence. They will even receive approval to conduct a commerce in a small way with white people, a bold condition on the part of His Excellency. I daresay His Excellency's future in the Colony may well dwell on the happy or unhappy outcome of this expedition.

. . .

So caught up have I been in the preparations for the governor's military campaign against the Saramaka Maroons that when Liesbeth began to talk of a distant cousin who has had another child I hardly paid the matter much attention.

A slave on the plantation Lankmoedigheid, where the Dutch director is reputed to be quite harsh, the new mother was just after the birth abducted by runaways who made a vicious attack against the estate. The men did not want to be slowed down in their retreat by a woman suckling a babe, and so the woman was forced at gunpoint to abandon her unfortunate little son, who has been named Quassie. Liesbeth is quite enraged by this kidnapping, and concerned for the poor abandoned babe.

However this news was overshadowed by Liesbeth's following announcement that she will soon bear a child, her first with Samuel Loseke.

"I cannot express how overjoyed I am," I said to Carl Otto,

"that my dear niece will not have to bear the sorrow of barrenness that I have so far experienced." We were walking side by side from the house on Oranjestraat to the grassy *Orangeplein* facing the Governor's mansion, where a goodly number of folk had gathered to see the Society expedition take leave.

Carl Otto was quiet this morning. I sensed his thoughts lay elsewhere and felt embarrassed that I had interjected so homily a subject as Liesbeth's pregnancy when the mind of my Captain was, I'm sure, occupied with the general safety of the Colony.

"Please take care to guard yourself well in the wild," I whispered, not expecting a response.

Carl Otto stopped and turned to face me. "You must not worry, Betje. See, I carry the *obia* Kwasiba gave me." He patted the place on his chest where a small bulge lay under his check shirt.

I pray that there might be some truth in Kwasiba's belief that this small pouch of hair and twig and leaf can protect a man from a lead musket ball or the vicious slice of a rusty saber. I know there are things beyond our knowledge and power in the world—it is not for me to say that one of the Christian God's mysterious ways may not be accomplished through a *dresiman's obia*.

At the *Orangeplein*, the Governor himself stood on a temporarily erected platform to bid our brave Society soldiers formal farewell and encouraging tidings, surrounded as they were by well-wishing but anxious family and friends. The Society expedition, led by Carl Otto, will march several kilometers by way of the Landsweg path to the banks of the Saramacca River, where a flotilla of dugout canoes and *periaks* commissioned from several plantations await to be loaded with the provisions and covered over with oiled cloth. On these the men will head on the high tide up the Saramacca as far as their mission will take them.

"I'm placing my trust in you, Captain," His Excellency said to Carl Otto as they shook hands. In spite of my own concerns, I feel a great pride at my consort's important responsibility in this matter.

The soldiers lined up and at Carl Otto's command rightly saluted His Excellency. As a proper military body they turned about face and, followed by the heavily-loaded blacks, marched off in the direction of the Landsweg. By the time all had disappeared from view the cheering of onlookers had faded to heavy sighs, the heat of the equatorial sun at midday being now well upon us. Thus I was glad that we had brought slaves to accompany us to carry the shading umbrellas, in particular for Liesbeth, now in a delicate condition, though exuberant for the outing.

It was also with great relief that Carl Otto had already departed when I found myself confronted by the grieving Juliaana Peltser, whom I suspect is not just now of right mind. Her gown appeared weary and the strands of blond hair that escaped from beneath her white house cap—she had not bothered with hat—were lifeless and dull. Sophie Peltser, accompanying her daughter, seemed tired and heavier of body than usual. I didn't notice how tightly she held to Juliaana's hand until her daughter started forward to me, nearly dragging her mother behind.

"Black whore," Juliaana hissed in my face, her voice low and hollow. One hand clutched to her bosom a gathered handful of her skirt, revealing a worn edge of frayed fabric.

In indignation I drew back a step and a great wave of soundless heat engulfed me. I could summon no voice with which to respond.

Juliaana's stare was glassy. "I send my black maid to *Gra'man* Quassie—he'll put a curse on your captain!" I was horrified to see her spit on the ground. "You too will lose the man you love!" she vowed.

Her words, loaded as they were with the pangs of loss and misery, lacked sense. I turned in alarm to see the shocked faces of Maria and Nanette. With a swift move, Samuel stepped between the wild young woman and myself, blocking her crazed face from my view.

"That'll be quite enough," he declared. "Take your daughter home, *vrouw* Peltser."

The strength in his deep voice seemed to break Juliaana's distraught spell and she leaned weeping into the arms of her mother. *Vrouw* Peltser with the utmost gentility led her whimpering daughter away from our presence.

But the damage was done. For me the day, beginning with Carl Otto's parting, was now reduced to despair. Only Kwasiba seemed not to be the least bit affected by Juliaana's outbreak of vituperation.

"That one, stupid girl," she said of Juliaana. "*Gra'man* Quassie canno make for her a spell. He *dresiman*, not *wisiman*." Kwasiba made a clear distinction between a doctor of white magic and a doctor of black magic.

"I can't imagine why she would even think to do such a thing," I murmured. "It's certainly not my fault Visser is lost at sea."

"Of course not, little sister," comforted Nanette. "She's jealous of you, that's all."

Despite my annoyance at Nanette's insistence upon calling me "little sister", I shook my head at the very idea that Juliaana Peltser could in any way envy my person. A beautiful young white girl who could marry any white man she so desired, jealous of an unfortunate Negress who is forbidden by law to marry the man she loves! Such absurdity by which we live.

"No worry, *misi*," assured Kwasiba. "White girl not have the power make a right spell." To Kwasiba's simple nature, no white person could put a spell on a Coloured person, while Coloured people could spell anyone anytime.

From that point on we walked without conversation back to the house on Oranjestraat which, without my Captain's manly presence, now seems quite empty.

25

Paramaribo, December 1749

    Not a day has gone by that I did not think of Carl Otto breaking his way through the strangling vines and clawing creepers facing God knows what handicap and hardship. One day came to La Solitude, to my happy satisfaction, a letter from my dear captain, laboring somewhere unknown in the steaming forest. He wrote in reassuring tones of his good humor and very little of the hardships of the expedition. Excepting for one brief account of an unfortunate German soldier who utterly from despair had hanged himself from the branches of a tree, as naked as the day he was born, all Carl Otto's words were of encouragement and confidence in the final outcome of the expedition.
    Yet I could well conjure up the vision of the body of the German soldier, hanging swollen by the heat of the climate and swarming in corruption, and imagine what unspoken miseries might have driven him to make such an end to his life.

. . .

    Some weeks passed most expediently due to the arrival of the merchant ship *Margaretha Johanna* bearing my latest shipment of goods from Europe. What with the registration, payment of duty fees, completion of papers, arrangement for delivery, and unpacking, my days were well occupied from dawn till long after dusk.

Among the most handsome of the goods are a knife, fork, and spoon box of veneered mahogany with satinwood ornament, a barometer with rectangular cistern and enamelled register plates in the rococo style, and a Tulip Wood double chest of drawers of the English cabinetmaker Thomas Chippendale. A wonderfully worked silver child's cup, plate, and spoon I plan to gift Liesbeth, now pregnant seven months. There is also a most beautiful writing box of inlaid oak and carved ivory set upon a matching stand. Its like has not before been seen in our little Colony, and the piece would fetch a handsome price.

Yet the more I gazed upon it, the more I felt a certain drawing to it that would make it difficult to part with. Indeed, already I could not envision it in anyone else's drawing room but my own. It is a remarkable work executed in the height of current fashion, yet there is something familiar about it. I was so drawn to it that I had it brought straight away to my bedroom at La Solitude, where I could reflect upon it at my leisure while deciding whether or not to make it available for sale.

Sitting alone in the bedroom, hearing the murmured voices of the housemaids at work downstairs and the afternoon activity of the birds in the orange trees outside my open window, I was quite aware of the absence of Carl Otto. I felt as alone as I had in my lodgings in Den Hague during my forced exile. I now recalled that there had been in that room an *escritoire* with carvings of ivory similar to this writing box.

. . .

To this day it's as clear to me as it was on that October morning, whence came to me via Pieter Reydenius the news that the States General had reversed the judgment against me.

After two and a half years in exile I had won my case.

It also came to light that, according to Pieter's lawyer, *meneer* Hoyer, one particular letter from Governor Raye, dated in May of the same year my mother died, had had removed from it a paragraph about the two other white witnesses. It did not surprise me then to realize that the foul van Meel had purposefully altered the paperwork before it was sent to the States General. In both happy tears and vengeful anger, I vowed never to forget his evil duplicity.

I set down on the *escritoire* the notice Hoyer had brought and stared out the window at a bleak fall day in Den Hague. I was free and instead of the gray rain and incessant chill on the other side of the glass I saw clearly before me the gentle palm, orange, and tamarind trees of Paramaribo, and felt the sweet, warm breezes blowing in from the river. My heart felt light for the first time since I had arrived in the Netherlands. I would throw a party for all the Dutch persons who here had befriended me and announce my intention to leave the country they hold so dear.

At long last I was free to return home to my beloved Suriname!

. . .

The *obia* with which Kwasiba gifted Carl Otto upon his departure has done its work in that it has brought my Captain home safely to me, but not without some misfortune.

At this late hour on the eve of Christmas, our house on Oranjestraat is quiet. All have retired, and Carl Otto sleeps fitfully upstairs in our four-poster bed. He suffers from a general weakness of constitution, and his poor body is severely affected with the ravages of chigoes and mosquitoes. The bites have been washed with lime acid and patched, he has consumed large quantities of an herbal tisane, and I pray to God that he does not carry the dreaded malarial infection.

The story of the expedition, related to me by my brave Captain, is one of disturbance and treachery, though not without a surprising outcome.

From the beginning, upon their arrival at the departure point on the Saramacca River, there was difficulty with the summons of boats belonging to private owners. This necessitated a stay at plantation Mayacabo and delayed by several days their departure from the river bank.

"Not one week upon the Saramacca River, several guns were found to be defective," Carl Otto said. "When a barrel of

Society meat was opened it was found to be a little more than half full, although it did not seem to have been opened. Four cases of dried codfish were found to be three-fourths full, and one keg of rum was found to contain water."

Carl Otto showed me where, in the journal he kept for his report to the Governor, he made note of the shorting of several supply lists:

"We note that the barrels and chests do not have the weight and size which is assigned to them in the lists that accompanied them. I had four chests opened, which were well nailed down and dry. Found no more than eight or nine jugs' measure inside, yet the list gives each as containing ten jugs' measure. A keg of Society barley, well-sealed and undamaged, is reported on the list as having in it 48 jugs; contains no more than 43 jugs. A barrel which appeared on the list as containing 50 had no more than 40. A barrel of rum which ought to contain 36 contains no more than 10 little kegs."

As I listened in unabashed horror, he related how in the rapids one of the *periaks* turned over and most provisions, including gun powder, washed away. "We happily recovered seven guns and a barrel of dried codfish—and no whites or Negroes drowned, thank God."

Carl Otto's voice had lowered to a veritable whisper, as if to relate these hardships was to relive their dreadfulness. I felt myself numbed to hear the harsh realities of this campaign against the Saramaka Maroons. Sinking to my knees at his bedside, I laid my cheek against the back of his hand.

"After a week of heavy rains," he said, "I found a case of tobacco and two of dried codfish mostly rotted by water, and that three kegs of rum had leaked out."

By October, the Commando had found and burned three villages, lost men to dysentery, snakebite, gunshot and drowning, and been attacked by hidden runaways who "fire more volleys at the whites than at the Negroes."

At about the same time the bread barrels, old and in bad condition, not heavy but too big, began falling apart. "A large quantity of bread was lost and the barrels could not be repaired because no cooper's nails, pitch, rye, or vinegar had been sent." Carl Otto had sprained his leg and was so unable to get about that for several days he had to allow himself to be carried by the Negroes.

Carl Otto paused in his narrative to sip more of the herbed tea which I desired desperately would prevent the malaria. When I made attempt to hold the China cup for him, he smiled and took it out of my hand. "I'm not so weak, dear Betje, that I cannot hold a teacup."

Then Carl Otto related how his Negro musketeers proved to be of little service. "They will not go out ahead and when attacked they go hide, and it takes hours of effort to get them together again. The bearers are even cleverer. They throw their burdens to the ground and run and hide, so that a considerable amount of provisions is lost and, when the danger has passed, they creep back to the Commando on their hands and knees."

"Such adversity in the Commando must cause uncommonly great dissatisfaction," I said, feeling a swell of dismay.

"Aye, my dear. I even had to punish one Kodjo with a *Spaanse bok* because he did not repair the boats according to orders and because he had run away."

"How many lashes did you give him?"

"Not enough. In truth I was torn between giving him the punishment he deserved and sparing him lightly because I desperately had need of every body that was even halfway healthy."

"But you did make progress?"

"Aye. The first week in November our guide Dosu brought news that the bush Negroes wanted to make peace with us. Indeed they brought as gifts a knife, a broadsword, and a white-painted bow and arrow. They wanted to meet alone with me, as they claimed to be afraid to meet all the whites together."

At these words my hand flew in fright to the lace at my bosom. "You met with them alone?"

Though he had decided to risk all, he explained, he took with him his two aids, a Corporal and the negotiator Ensign Nepveu, sending Dosu ahead.

When they encountered this group of Saramaka Maroons, they found their number to be about forty. Their chief, Adoe, himself called "Captain" by the runaways, was indeed a tall, emaciated Negro who nonetheless was well-muscled from a life in the wilds. He invited the whites to sit before his house whereupon Carl Otto, representing the highest authority in the land, in Sranan Tongo explained the terms of the proposed peace treaty. Afterwards this *kapten* Adoe summoned his wives to bring refreshment and all ate, drank and were merry together.

"Then the very next day," said Carl Otto, "Dosu came to me demanding the pair of gold shirt buttons I had promised him if he could show me the right villages. He also wanted me to buy him a Negro boy when we got to Paramaribo if all went well. I gave him the buttons and promised to buy the Negro boy also, in the hope that the Government will pay me back, since this has been done for its own well-being."

"Have you spoken to Commander Cromelin?" As of November 5, the Dutchman Wigbold Cromelin had been appointed as the new Commander of the Society troops in Suriname.

"I've sent a request and the response was favorable." Carl Otto lay back against the pillows, wearied from his tale of events.

"You must rest now, my dear," I said. "You have much strength to regain."

My hopes to avoid the malaria are buoyed by the fact that Carl Otto has been back to me now a full fortnight, and I have yet to see any of the sweats and fever that portent the disease. If he has indeed contracted the malaria, these symptoms may manifest themselves at any time now.

On behalf of the Governor of Suriname, Carl Otto had presented to *kapten* Adoe a fine large cane with a massive silver pommel on which is engraved the arms of Suriname, as a mark of their independence. This serves also as a preliminary to other presents that are to be sent out next year, as stipulated by the treaty, most particularly arms and ammunition.

Thus a treaty of peace consisting of twelve articles has been successfully concluded between the Saramaka Maroons and Governor Mauricius, as had been done before with the rebels on the island of Jamaica. The bow and case of arrows, which had been made by Adoe's own hands, was sent to the Governor as a token that, on his side, all enmity is ceased and at an end.

Would that I could make a treaty of peace that would end all enmity between myself and the white plantation wives. When Governor Mauricius held a holiday merriment to celebrate Carl Otto's successful negotiations, I felt the atmosphere to be as cold as winter in Den Hague. For Carl Otto is today a great military hero of the Colony, clearly in great favor with His Excellency, and the fact that he loves and lives in sin with a freeborn, wealthy Negress is a source of irritation to said wives, especially those with marriageable white daughters.

26

Paramaribo, March 1750

The candles in the brass sconces and chandeliers of the Governor's mansion burned again this evening with a grand party to honor the Society soldiers of the successful campaign against the Saramaka Maroons. Carl Otto, as Captain of the expedition, was the honored guest, and as such wore his cleanest wig and Society uniform.

Having readied ourselves for the evening, we stood on the porch awaiting the carriage to take us to the Governor's mansion.

"You still appear wane," I said to Carl Otto. "Let's not make of this a late night."

He did not look at me as he smoothed his short military jacket. "Agreed, my dear."

I regarded him with skepticism. The tone of his voice was noncommittal. I suspected he had responded with the words to appease my anxieties. Though he did not contract the malaria, his constitution has proved weakened by his ordeal.

Knowing I faced an evening of vicious looks from the white planters' wives, I wore the newest fashion I have been able to obtain from Paris, a most beauteous *saque*-dress of yellow embossed silk, the sleeves and hem finished in a wide edge of lavender satin and lace.

"No one can outdress you, little sister," remarked Nanette upon seeing my habit. I ignored her comment, not wanting to dwell upon its meaning and thus risk a pall upon the evening before it had even begun. I much preferred to regard the warmth in the eyes of Maria and Anna and Carl Otto.

To express his thanks and appreciation, Governor Mauricius, in great generousity, granted to the surviving men of the expedition both guilders and worldly goods. Carl Otto received a silver pitcher engraved in flowing calligraphy. Most importantly, he has received a land grant for a plantation at a most desirable location—the head of the Suriname River where its lighter brown water joins the darker headwaters of the Cottica River in a long, meandering line of light next to dark.

"Clevia," Carl Otto whispered in my ear. "I shall register the plantation named after my place of birth in Germany. And with the guilders we shall build a fine, two-story town house."

"At Wagenwegstraat and Heerenstraat?" This was land Carl Otto and I had accomplished the purchase of this year past. Part of Governor Mauricius' expansion of *foto*, the location is about ten streets behind our house on Oranjestraat.

"Aye, Betje. A fine large house, which you can fill with new furnishings." His eyes twinkled with love and merriment, knowing my predilection for fine textiles and décor.

I could already see the house in my mind's eye. I would have a high-ceilinged entrance hall for the ceremonial arrival and departure of my guests on formal occasions. I would have not one, but two drawing rooms for musical instruments, dances, and card games. I would have a library, gallery, billiard room, and conservatory. I might even consider a larger breakfast room in addition to the formal dining parlour. Of course, at the center of the entrance hall I will want a wide, tapering staircase leading to a minimum of eight upstairs bedrooms.

Yet no matter how elaborately filled with the things of fashion, a house like that can never be complete without children to make a grand noise as they play from room to room. An overwhelming longing seized me. At eighteen Liesbeth has given birth to her first child, a month premature, but strengthening daily, and I imagined the little Mulatto daughter spending many happy hours visiting me there.

Samuel Loseke is beside himself with delight and has told me he would marry Liesbeth were it not for the same law which forbids lawful union between myself and Carl Otto.

"Your *habit de soirée* is exceptional," commented Anna as we shared a moment at the buffet table.

To this dear friend I gave my warmest smile. "My thanks, and congratulations to you on your new marriage."

It had been Liesbeth who told me that Anna Buys-Julien is pregnant, though she has only just married her director of Buys-en-Vlijt, (the white) Willem Ouwater. The child is expected at the beginning of the dry season. Granted Anna is five years younger than I, yet at thirty-five I am still not ready to give up hope of bearing a child of my own.

Even Nanette, two years older than I, still hopes to bear a child. She has moved in to live with the director of the plantation Lankmoedigheid, Wijnand van Herpen, whom I freely admit I do not care for. The Dutchman van Herpen has a reputation as a particularly harsh slave master, one who would as soon ruin good merchandise by unmerciful misuse as exercise proper management. Indeed, the plantation from which Liesbeth's distant cousin was abducted during a vicious raid is one and the same. Poor Emilius has just been gone a year and a half, so Nanette is barely out of proper mourning. She never speaks of it, but if she is yet to bear a child she cannot waste any time waiting for a man to love as she did Emilius.

When I voiced to Carl Otto my disapproval of Nanette's liaison he replied, "Perhaps the white/black marriage law is fortunate in this case, since Nanette cannot marry him."

I scoffed at this. "What difference does it make when they are already together in a Suriname marriage?" But I already knew the answer, for in truth the laws that govern us and the reality in which we live are not necessarily one and the same.

Carl Otto and I moved among our neighboring planters and merchants, making idle conversation, sampling of this delicacy and that sweetmeat, enjoying the sounds of the melodic musical movements of the hired musicians and the taste of the best imported wines.

Vrouw Mauricius hailed us to join her in a group of white ladies with whom she was conversing. Carl Otto bowed to the group and received several warm comments of congratulation. Not one of the ladies addressed me, but I am accustomed to such behavior on their part and smiled at Carl Otto as if everything was completely normal. Inside I seethed that they should speak to him as if I were not even present.

"You must be quite proud of your Captain," *vrouw* Mauricius said, a gracious hostess attempting to draw me into the conversation.

"Indeed I am," I replied. "His brave actions serve the Colony well to keep us all safe and prosperous." I stared into the plump white face of the nearest planter's wife as I said this, and triumphed to see her turn her watery eyes away from me.

The Governor's wife was unsettled by the atmosphere surrounding this little discourse, as she is not as accustomed as I to such cool behavior. Carl Otto's expression told me he noticed nothing amiss, and I felt annoyed that he did not share my vexation towards these white women, *vrouw* Mauricius excepted. One by one the ladies excused themselves, including the Governor's wife.

"They would not treat me thus if we were lawfully married," I muttered to my consort.

Carl Otto said, "Let's have another drink, shall we?" He's heard this plaint too often, I fear.

"You know it's true," I persisted.

"Dear Betje, you're overreacting." His voice had that pleasant tone that told me he was comfortably sated by food and wine and would hear no words of distress.

Not wanting to spoil his good spirits, I refrained from speaking further on the subject. You're mine, I thought. They desire to possess everything in my life, including the man I love. It seems as if the Dutch Government and the entire plantocracy are working to undermine all that Carl Otto and I have worked for.

Even though everyone celebrated the success of Carl Otto's military campaign, with even the Governor himself rewarding him most handsomely, there are those who are displeased. As a result of the persevering endeavors of the Governor and Carl Otto for peace with the runaways, a new atmosphere of safe being has permeated our entire community; yet His Excellency's nemesis, the Cabale, was extremely upset about the peace accord affected by Carl Otto with the Saramaka Maroons. Last month, these opponents even wrote a lengthy letter of complaint to the Directors of the Society.

"They dared to criticize His Excellency's behavior," Carl Otto had declared, incensed at this. "They complain that the idea of a peace accord with Maroons is proof of cowardice!"

27

Plantation Toevlught, May 1750

"The Cabale is positively beside itself with smug triumph," said Hendrik van Steenberch.

Carl Otto did not look up from the tric trac game board when his friend spoke. Hendrik, Maria, and Liesbeth and Samuel have been two days visiting at Toevlught, having arrived by tent-boat on the 17th.

Heavy rains drowned the plantation for all of the afternoon hours. We ladies whiled away the time reading, smoking, and needleworking, while the men played games and made conversation. Liesbeth sat on a corner settee, giving her breast to little Suzanna Johanna, who made small gurgling noises as she nursed. Every time I look at them I take great comfort to have mother and child so near.

"The Society has made the decision," continued Carl Otto's friend, "to dispatch a committee of investigation to our Colony, as well as a military force of 400 men."

"We can certainly use the 400 men," said Carl Otto cynically. "Two hundred of them will die in the first six months."

Hendrik completed his next play in the game and said, "It would seem du Plessis has found willing ears at the Court of Orange."

Disturbed by this conversation, I held my needlework untouched in my lap, next to where Pansu lay sleeping after several sips of Madeira. "I have heard tell that Mauricius' desire to honor the promises made by you to the Saramakas has been overruled," I said to Carl Otto.

My captain considered his next move in the game. When he spoke his voice had a hard edge I seldom hear. "His Excellency's plan cannot succeed if it continues to be sabotaged by his political enemies."

"Not to mention being sabotaged by the Negroes themselves," Samuel added.

The detachment carrying the presents promised to the Saramakan Maroon *kapten* Adoe by Governor Mauricius and Carl Otto has met with a most foul end. When a desperate runaway called Zamzam encountered them he murdered every soul of them on the spot. This Negro, the head of another strong party of Maroons, had not been consulted at the peacemaking, and carried off the goods as his own private property. All of the tribute, consisting of arms, ammunition, lengths of checked linen and coloured cotton, gilt earrings, hats with gold edging, canvas cloth, hatchets, cooper's adzes, whipsaws and other carpenter's tools, besides salt beef, pork, spirits, etc. were thus lost.

Outside, the tropical rain increased its fury, as if to emphasize how by such an unfortunate accident the peace that had cost so much in hardship and human life has been broken.

"Is there no chance of finding this Zamzam and taking back what was stolen?" asked Maria.

Hendrik stood up from the game table and stretched his long frame. "It's not that easy, *mevrouw*," he said. "The jungle is a wild, tangled place with all manner of hiding places for both man and goods."

"And the Maroons cannot be counted on to tell the truth about the locations of men or villages," Carl Otto said.

"I'm afraid there'll be no affective peace with the runaways any time soon," Samuel said, his voice pervaded with gloom.

Pansu must have sensed my agitation from this conversation because in his drunken slumber he moved restlessly in my lap, as if he suffered from dreams of a violent and unsettling nature. "What does the Cabale think they can do now to resolve this situation?" I asked.

Hendrik shook his head and made a disgusted snort. "Du Plessis is a violent man by nature. He'd send no limit of military men to their deaths for the cause of murdering every runaway in the Colony."

Maria started at this, eyes widening in alarm. Even Liesbeth looked up from her nursing child with a worred look to Samuel.

"Surely there's no chance du Plessis can garner enough support to sway His Excellency and the Court of Police in that direction," I protested.

Carl Otto and Hendrik exchanged glances.

"We must do whatever it takes to see that he doesn't," Carl Otto said.

28

Plantation Toevlught, September 1750

The morning fog that had blanketed the Hoer-Helena Kreek dissipated as the sun rose in the sky, and so far the day promised no rain. One of the house slaves had raised the iron cage of the *pikolet* high to the porch's ceiling so that the little brown bird now gave forth a medley of melodious song, most pleasing to the ear.

My director at Toevlught, *Meneer* Huygens, stood before me this morning, hat in hand, as he made his daily morning report of what work was scheduled for the day, what slaves were too ill to work, and other activities of note in the business of operating the coffee plantation.

He reports that the largest section of coffee beans is ready for harvest and has requested me to acquire two additional slaves to handle the hand-pick work. When I inquired as to whether we could borrow the hands from Welgemoed, he answered that work there is already well assigned and no Negroes can be spared from that direction.

At the porch table I was making note of Huygens' request when out of the corner of my eye I became aware of someone running across the grassy lawn from the landing towards the house. I looked up from my account book and set down my pen on the lace tablecloth, next to the vase of yellow *palulu* and tiny white orchids on long green stems.

"Someone is coming," I said to Huygens. "See to it."

He descended the stairs and moved to meet the runner,

who was one of the gardeners. I watched the Negro intently as he made his report, head bowed, to my director.

When Huygens returned to the porch he said, "A tent-boat has been sighted. I sent the man to fetch another to aid him in carrying the baggage."

"Excellent. Let's walk down and give our visitors a proper greeting." Guests are always a welcome diversion on any plantation.

At the landing I seated myself on the yellow cushioned seats of the gazebo, from where I could already hear the sing-song chant of the rowers coming up the river tributary. Huygens paced the wooden boards of the dock, for he is not a man comfortable with social conversation and was plainly impatient to return to his work.

The tent-boat now approached the landing, coloured flags fluttering in a light morning breeze. I rose from my shaded seat and walked to the end of the little dock. I was elated to see coming into view the smiling faces of Maria, Liesbeth and Samuel. I laughed to hear little Suzanna Johanna crying lustily in competition with the Negroes' rowing song.

"Welcome! Welcome back to Toevlught!" I called, waving my straw hat in the air.

My two Negroes secured the tent-boat and Huygens helped the ladies alight.

"You must all be ready for some refreshment," I said. "Especially your little daughter!"

Liesbeth laughed and held up the baby, who upon observing my grinning face waved her dark, pudgy arms and from under her dress kicked her little bare feet, as if anxious to run towards her well-secured future. "We call her our sweet little 'Sutje,'" Liesbeth announced.

"Oh, let me carry her to the house," I begged. Liesbeth handed her to me and I buried my face in her ruffles and baby smell. All the way up to the house, to the amusement of everyone, I crooned little nonsense words to my darling Mulatto great-niece, Sutje. The babe grinned and wiggled and was thoroughly delightful to my arms. With great reluctance on the porch I handed her back to her mother.

Maria presented me with a welcomed packet of fresh

tobacco. "Newly imported straight from the English colony," she said.

"Virginia?"

"Aye, the very one."

A loose corner of the packet made for a convenient opening and I gave the contents a goodly sniff, inhaling the pleasant aroma of the rolled leaves, and thanked my sister for such a thoughtful gift.

"Pardon, *mevrouw*," said Huygens. "If you'll not be needing me more, I'll return to my duties."

"Of course," I answered, waving him off with my hand and nary a glance to his person. I would not see him again until the evening report at six o'clock.

I led my guests to seat themselves in the wicker chairs on the wide front porch and inside the door pulled the service bell for the *keuken* serving girl, who would bring us coffee, *sangaree*, fruit and fresh sugared buns. Little Sutje now nursed at Liesbeth's breast.

Since Carl Otto was away attending to the business of establishing Clevia, Samuel retired to one of the bedrooms to take an afternoon rest. It was natural therefore, since our little assemblage was feminine, to discuss topics not of interest to gentlemen.

Maria made the happy announcement that Anna, now Ouwater-Julien, has given birth to a beautiful daughter. "*Meneer* Ouwater of course, had hoped for a son, but once he saw the babe and how light she is, he's thrilled." Anna being Mulatto and her director white, the child is Mesties, only one-quarter black.

"Willem Ouwater is handsome," I said. "Without doubt, the girl will grow to be a beauty."

Maria and Liesbeth, who had exchanged their wide-brimmed traveling hats for house caps of white silk, nodded in agreement. Liesbeth, rocking as her daughter suckled, giggled. "There is even more interesting *mofokoranti*," she said.

Maria smiled and withdrew her clay pipe and some needlework from her brocade traveling bag. "Don't be slow in the telling, my dear. Elisabeth will find great entertainment in this."

After any period of time spent on the plantation, away from

the house slaves and merchants of *foto*, one is indeed always eager for the news that arrived with every tent-boat. "What else is there to tell?" I asked. As I spoke I arose and moved my chair a meter to avoid the direct sunlight creeping across the porch.

"Well," said Liesbeth with leisured tones. "Juliaana is with child."

"*P'sa?*" In my surprise I used the common Sranan expression of disbelief. "You must tell me—how did this happen?"

"The usual way," Liesbeth said, causing Maria to laugh out loud. Then my niece explained. "On August 21st past she was married to Jon van Meel."

This news left me aghast. At twenty-three of course the girl was lucky to find a husband, and the fact that she was already pregnant and the man is sixteen years older than she is of no real import. But Jon van Meel! The thought of being wedded to such a dreadful man was appalling to me. I felt as if God and all the *wintis* were rallying to plot some dire misfortune against me.

"Does she love him?" I whispered, not even conscious that the thought was in my mind. Nay, how could a woman come to love such a man?

Maria laughed again. "Who knows?"

My practical nature then asserted itself and I asked, "Will he take over her father's butcher business?"

"Nay," said Maria, "*Vrouw* Peltser has let the business out to someone else, a man new to the Colony. I cannot remember his name."

In spite of my astonishment at this news of Juliaana's marriage to the prosecutor van Meel, in shame I admit to envy of my white nemesis. By what *winti* spirit, Christian God and simple luck of birth can Juliaana Peltser have children and a lawful marriage while I, whose love and devotion to a good man has been proven, cannot?

All this good news of fortune for these women, both black and white, nevertheless left me on such a glorious day with a feeling of abject emptiness.

29

<u>*Paramaribo, December 1750*</u>

In an attempt to make the unpleasant investigation called for by the Society of Suriname will out in his favor, Governor Mauricius has hosted an elaborate reception to welcome the Dutch representatives of said body, in particular Major-General Hendrik Ernst Baron von Spörcke. During the course of the evening, His Excellency almost never left the gentleman's side, according to him all the courtesies of a guest of honor, plying him with food and drink which the little German consumed with gusto.

Major-General von Spörcke is of stout build, wide about the middle and a goodly head shorter than myself. His habit was all of one colour—a light fawn—from his jackboots to his jabot. His wig is immaculately dressed up off his wide forehead, the curls arranged in the pigeon-wing style of bunches at the sides of his face. He appears pale and not of good constitution, but as he is newly arrived to our climate it is too soon to assess the health of this European. While he seems agreeable enough, his voice is as his costume, the tone unvaried whilst he speaks endlessly of himself and his past accomplishments, not worthy of such attention, Carl Otto and I agree.

A single gentleman, von Spörcke exhibited an action that so disturbed me when I observed it that I was left suspicious of his character. At the sight of the beauteous Mulatto Anna Ouwater-Julien at the doorway, handing her mantelet to the

Negro butler, he stopped his conversation with Carl Otto and me and, cake still in hand, hurried over to make a greeting. This in itself would not have perplexed me except that he then focused his entire attention upon the lady, to the complete exclusion of Willem Ouwater, her lawful husband.

Anna, whose new daughter is now three months old, looked ever the picture of maternal health. Her long-sleeved satin gown, in the colour of pomegranate, was frilled with pale lace at neckline and cuff. Matching velvet ribbons flowed from her sleekly coiffed black hair. In her free hand she carried a tortoise-shell fan hand-painted with rococo leaves on the dark vellum.

If two other planters had not arrived on her footsteps, drawing his attention away from Anna, I daresay von Spörcke would have stayed by her side far longer than could be considered proper.

"How wonderful to see you looking so radiant, dear Anna." I greeted her with a kiss to both cheeks. "The babe is well?"

"You must come to see how she has grown," remarked Willem with great pride in his voice. "She is the most beautiful child in the Colony."

Carl Otto, shaking Willem's hand, grinned. "Your words are those of a true proud father. Your daughter is indeed assured of a pleasant future."

Because she's a light Mesties, I thought without resentment. Certainly, I'm most pleased that Anna's daughter will not have to struggle to attain a position in society and a fortunate marriage.

It came to me at this moment that as I had made my toilette for the evening I had again selected my habit according to how much I could impress the white ladies present. My blue silk dress was embroidered all over in silver thread with the leaves and flowers of the rococo design, a most costly application. Carl Otto commented on how much he enjoyed the view of roundness supplied by my décolletage. My hair, cut short in front, was dressed off my forehead with the ends set in curls supported by tiny black taffeta cushions stuffed with cotton and held in place by a dressing of pomatum and flour. Into this assemblage were liberally arranged, with the intent that their fragrance should accompany me throughout the evening, numerous yellow orchids. These were fixed into place by bodkins ended with large diamond studs. Diamonds and sapphires adorned the collarette at my throat as well as the toes and heels of my brocade slippers.

In truth, Nanette caused me some annoyance when she remarked as we left the house that I dressed thusly displaying my wealth to compensate for the fact that I am not married. She has no right to comment, living in sin as she is in Suriname marriage with that foul director of hers.

Vrouw Mauricius appeared pale and drawn and, ever loyal to her husband, confided to me her concerns about the investigators.

"Do you think they're pleased?" she asked. In a gesture of disquiet she toyed with the ends of the ribbons on her stomacher. "I'm worried at how this may come about."

"His Excellency has made significant accomplishments," I said, wanting to as politely as possible relieve her anxiety, for well I know what it is to be the unhappy subject of an undesirable investigation.

Indeed, Governor Mauricius, in addition to planning a successful expansion of our capital, has just last month reached a peace accord with the Ndjuka Maroons living along the Marowijne River. This settlement was also modeled, as Governor Mauricius intended, on the peace treaty used to pacify the runaways on Jamaica. As part of this agreement, the Maroons are required to hand over to the government any slave who escapes after the treaty became effective, and help to track down new bands of runaways. They must also promise never to combine forces with other pacified groups of Maroons.

Though this has all the air to be well and good, I wonder how we can tell how safe we really are? I hoped that His Excellency's wife did not sense my own doubts.

Under the guidance of Major-General von Spörcke, it is said that the commission intends to study the disagreements in Suriname, some staunch members of du Plessis' Cabale having submitted written documents containing more than fifty articles of complaint.

In an effort to distract *vrouw* Mauricius I touched her elbow and with my fan pointed in the direction of the musicians.

"Listen," I said to change the subject. "They are beginning a piece by Rameau. I'm told his first operas stirred up a storm of critical controversy. What do you think?"

Her face brightened and I felt a flush of social success, for I well knew her love of everything musical and literary. "It's true," she breathed. "Some decry the Frenchman's music as mechanical and unnatural. But I find I rather like it."

Thus we went on to discuss the relative merits of French versus Italian music, and for awhile her worries seemed forgotten.

By the by Carl Otto found me and we wandered to the dining table to sample the repast laid out on silver that glowed with warmth in the candlelight. "How is *vrouw* Mauricius bearing up?" he inquired.

My voice betrayed, I'm sure, my strong emotion for the woman's plight when I said, "Ah, Carl Otto, she tries indeed to be strong, but the strain is evident in the woman's bearing. I fear she's not well reassured by her husband's assertion that this political disturbance will come to naught."

"In truth, Governor Mauricius does not think the commission worthwhile," Carl Otto said in a low voice, as he did not want to be overheard by our neighbors discussing the Governor's affairs. "He is of the opinion that the commission members will be too often the guests of members of the Cabale to come to a fair outlook."

"That may well turn out to be the case, and make for a disagreeable result for His Excellency."

Carl Otto nodded at the same time as he feigned a great interest in selecting a few morsels from the table for his plate. "Let's see..."

It was no longer possible for me to put off speaking the question that has become uppermost in my mind: "Do you suppose they will discuss the living arrangements in Suriname between white men and black women?"

My consort did not even look up from his plate. "Perhaps in passing," he said, "but that is not their concern, as it is not the concern of the Cabale. However His Excellency feels about Suriname marriage, he has not been able to stop his best friends from such relationships. Most persons, I think, agree it's best to ignore such controversy. Certainly no rich plantation member is willing to change his private life to accommodate the wishes of the Governor."

"If he would change the black/white marriage law, there would be no controversy," I pressed.

Carl Otto smiled at me with familiar indulgence. "Betje, though he governs the land, you know he cannot change the law without the support of the Courts of Police and Justice, and they choose not to be concerned about an unlawful nature in the living together of white men and black women."

"Yet they purport to be Christian men," I persisted. "How can they not be concerned with relationships the church describes as sinful?"

Carl Otto shrugged. "The Dutch Reformed Church will never encourage white/black relationships. Both the church and the Courts agree that that's what they'd be doing if they relaxed the law."

30

Paramaribo, April 1751

Liesbeth is again with child, three and a half months now. Little Sutje, the delight of her father's eye, was one year old on 4 March, and proves to be an active child.

"I have asked my *djodjo* to speak to my *oemakra* on my behalf to favor a son for Samuel," Liesbeth told me, cooling herself with a pictured vellum fan on a delicate ivory frame. In the down-to-earth business of childbearing, Liesbeth has become more and more taken with the habits of the Negro slave women. She insists it cannot do any harm to acknowledge one's *djodjo*, or guardian spirit, and one's *oemakra*, or woman's soul.

She also related how she has gone to Granman Quassie for an *obia* against black magic that may happen to be directed at the child in her womb. He has given her a liquid in a tiny bottle to hang above the door of her bedroom, where the invisible spirit in the bottle will serve as guardian for Liesbeth against the entrance of a *bakru*, a carrier of evil that might be sent. Liesbeth, though baptized a Christian, is of the opinion that all ceremony must be observed in these matters, and I am in full agreement.

These machinations my niece related to me while visiting for tea at our new house on the corner of the Wagenwegstraat and the Heerenstraat, for this grand, new residence has just been completed last month.

Three stories and two attics in height, it is built upon a high, solid foundation of red brick and roofed with shingles.

A cooling basement was dug into the rock, as well as a well near the *keuken* house for the slaves and cattle. Our water needs are served by a large cistern that catches the rainwater. On the same land as the house are the *keuken* house and a storage building. On another lot next to the house have been built the slave quarters, and on the land across the way are the stables and guardhouse.

Our design is such that the entrance and iron front gate are positioned on the Wagenwegstraat. Our bedroom is positioned thus on the left in the rear, that room being most cool. All of the rooms are ample, with tall, wide windows to take advantage of all breezes. Unlike the Governor's mansion, this house has no long outside galleries as I wanted all the space possible for the interior, which I plan to fill as soon as able with paintings, silver, gilding, crystal chandeliers, cupboards, and cabinets. The rooms are already beautifully wainscoted with the most excellent joinery of Brazil wood and cedar.

Most conveniently, the new house contains an entire upper floor, after the fashion of Amsterdam merchants, available to contain my investments shipped from Holland. At present, awaiting distribution are 27 rolls of satin, taffeta, and fine India chintz to make skirts and 80 rolls of silk to line clothing that occupied a goodly space in our previous, smaller abode on Oranjestraat.

Already bearing scissors and watch, my chatelaine is now heavier with keys for all the new cupboards. In all, I have spent 22,500 guilders on the Heerenstraat house and have not yet taken complete delivery of the cabinets for the two drawing rooms.

"Where will you put all your cups and saucers?" inquired Liesbeth.

"I've no idea," I said. I am at a loss to find accommodation for nineteen dozen porcelain cups and saucers, all necessary for grand entertainments.

After tea Liesbeth departed, stepping with care around the Negro girls on their knees scouring the parlour floors with halves of oranges and lemons. I had set them to rub the boards, one half in each hand, till halves are void of juice. This is continuous work, accomplished whilst singing songs which I find, in addition to the sweet smell from the citrus, most pleasing.

Despite the occupation deemed necessary to set up our new household, Carl Otto and I are overjoyed with the progress. Now I found him upstairs, changing his habit in anticipation of receiving the evening's callers.

"What do you think about employing from Holland a decorator?" I asked. "I have collected quite a few trade cards from merchants. I'm overwhelmed by the kinds of furnishings available now."

Carl Otto, in front of the toilette mirror arranging his wig, said, "Whatever you like, my dear, but perhaps no more of the French paper for the walls."

"Nay," I admitted. "That decoration did not fare well in our tropical clime."

Carl Otto leaned closer to the toilette mirror to more closely inspect his reflection. "If you decide in haste that you want someone, there is still time to place a letter aboard the *Adrichem*."

"A capital idea. I'll write a letter to Pieter Redenius today to make the request."

"At the same time, order some things for Clevia."

"What do you need?"

"I'll give you a list of tools, plus whatever you want for the plantation house."

I laid down pen and paper and sighed. "I shall miss His Excellency and his lady."

"Aye. He could have done great things if he had had the full support of the plantocracy." Carl Otto's voice betrayed his annoyance with the men he viewed as spoiled Europeans who had never had to work to earn their place in society. "How did you find *vrouw* Mauricius today?"

I stared at the closed window and thought of the long sea journey that august lady must now endure. "My gift of silver scissors and lace handkerchiefs did not much to cheer her, I'm afraid. Her worries are now with whatever awaits them in Amsterdam, and she confided to me that His Excellency's spirit is at a decidedly low ebb."

Of a sudden, tears welled in my eyes and I could say no

more for the moment. For on 24 March, von Spörcke and his commissioners completed their report and were in agreement to send Governor Mauricius, to his bitter displeasure, back to Holland.

The bedroom felt stifling, the air of the evening still and heavy upon my brow. I picked up a cotton kerchief and patted my sweat-beaded forehead. Outside, the warm rain began to patter upon the shake roof.

"His Excellency was not surprised when the commission determined that the differences within the Court of Police were too great to be bridged and that it would be better that he leave the Colony," said Carl Otto rather matter-of-factly. "So tomorrow they sail on the *Adrichem* for Amsterdam. Now that he has passed leadership to von Spörcke, we shall support the German as we supported his predecessor."

Carl Otto's positive manner greatly annoyed me. "I'm concerned for Samuel's situation as Inspection Master," I murmured.

"I don't believe he's in danger of losing his position," Carl Otto said. "The Courts have no quarrel with the job he's doing, and the German doesn't seem to be one to make unnecessary changes. Though I daresay I believe the Court of Police will pressure him to reestablish the Jew, Isaac Carilho, in his post as Captain of the Civic Guard."

I dismissed the subject of the Jew with a wave of my hand. "Nevertheless, Samuel's mother's family is close to the Mauricius family, and von Spörcke has proven himself to be an enemy of Johan Jacob Mauricius."

"Aye." Carl Otto's voice lost some of its optimism. "Then there is the matter of the report of the widow van Hertsbergen. He must make some decision soon."

"I'll be very surprised if von Spörcke gives aid to her," I said.

Ester Francina van Hertsbergen, a grieving new widow, has petitioned a letter to our interim Governor General addressing the lamentable incident which befell her on the fifth of this month on her plantation, and making an appeal to be taken under government protection, *being the wife of a brave man who has been robbed of all her goods.*

Carl Otto said, "The Saramakas feel that they have been

betrayed by the whites. That's why there've been the raids on the plantations of the upper Suriname River."

"How the Maroons feel does not excuse what happened to poor *vrouw* van Hertsbergen. It's now the responsibility of von Spörcke to consume less bacon-ham and claret and deal with it."

During the early morning hours while her husband was away fishing on the Riverbank, *vrouw* van Hertsbergen and her fourteen-month-old son were stripped naked in the gallery of their own house in a most vicious attack upon their plantation, made by runaways who spoke Portuguese. There appeared among the hundred and fifty attackers some dissention and she and her child were thereafter imprisoned in the hencoop, while the Maroons plundered goods and violated the household. All the chairs and tables were broken to pieces, and the beds and cushions cut open, the feathers dumped out. The attackers then carried off by force all thirteen of her slaves. By the by leaving the hencoop, her person wrapped in nothing but a torn blanket, she managed to locate her husband in one of the Negro houses. He bore three mortal arrow wounds, his skull was crushed to a pulp, and he died in her arms after lingering on in torture for an hour and a half.

Now six days after, the German has made no response to the grieving widow.

Little Pansu, sensing my agitation, was restless upon my shoulder. "I don't like this interim Governor," I sniffed with indignation. "He's cold and contemptuous of us all, with perhaps the exception of Anna, and I don't care much at all for the way he looks at her."

Carl Otto raised an eyebrow. "Is this about his undisguised conviction that by being handed this governorship he has been banished in some way from the center of the civilized world, or is this about Anna?"

"It isn't enough for him to be named Provisional Governor-General of all the rivers and districts of the Colony of Suriname—he has to invade the family life of people we love." The very thought of von Spörcke as Governor caused a dreadful chill to overcome me.

"I hardly think the Ouwaters' marriage will be divided by

the Baron," Carl Otto said testily. "I'm more concerned about the treaty situation with the Maroons and how he will handle it. So far, he seems rather uninformed about events, as if he does not want to confront a situation he may not be able to handle. He never gets angry and is passionate about nothing."

In truth, I feel that it's Carl Otto who is uninformed as to the true nature of our provisional Governor. In addition to his unwelcome attentions to Anna, there are disturbing suggestions as to the German's personal proclivities. It seems he takes sensual pleasure in treating his body in such a way as to cause physical harm to his person. How this *mofokoranti* began I know not, yet the slaves talk and I sense there is some dark truth in it.

But I did not want to engage in further harsh words with Carl Otto, and so turned my attention to my letter of requisition for the goods and furnishings for the new houses, and a new wardrobe for this year's holidays.

31

Paramaribo, September 1751

The days pass for me now in a trance-like state, for I am overcome with grief. My family and my worthy captain can do naught to comfort me.

For two months, my beloved Liesbeth was taken to her bed with an unusual weakness, and the white doctor feared for the baby while I prayed for a fortunate birth. Granman Quassie made for Liesbeth a new *obia*, which she wore about her neck, following his instructions in good faith for the use of the talisman.

On the morning of Tuesday last, with the sun shining and the air sated with the noise of the *gritjibi* birds, Nanette, Maria and I were summoned posthaste to the home of Liesbeth and Samuel. In a room darkened by hanging cottons thought to repel *winti* spirits, my dear niece lay in a half-stupor, the effort of child-bearing having worn her to a greatly weakened state. She appeared to be sleeping when we arrived, and at first we were joyful to greet Samuel's long-hoped-for Mulatto son, Philip Samuel.

The house was unduly quiet, and I sensed that something was terribly wrong. An unnatural tightness engulfed my chest, as if a fist were clutched about my heart. The midwife's attitude was beyond the usual eyes of slave to the floor in front of the master—nay, she would not face any of us.

"Boy born feet first," she whispered, as if to say the words aloud would bring the curse upon all present in the room.

The blooded birth linens now being washed were copious, and yet more of them were being brought from the bedroom. The midwife had already sent one of the house girls to bury the afterbirth in the yard.

"A fowl not of the house's hencoop was seen in the yard," reported Nanette after speaking with one of the girls. This was discouraging news, as a chicken such discovered in a yard where a pregnant woman lives is understood to be a *bakru* bearing fatal mischief to the mistress of the house or her unborn child.

"Do not speak of this in front of Samuel," I advised my sister.

Samuel, tired and gaunt of appearance, paced the drawing room in an anxious state. Indeed, he drew on his pipe with such ferocity that the air following him was thick with smoke.

Maria placed a hand on the sleeve of his morning coat. "Samuel, you must come and sit down. When last have you eaten?"

"I've been awake all during the night," he said, shaking off her hand. "Call the girl to bring some food if you like. I'm not hungry."

Now thoroughly alarmed, I sought out the midwife in private. She tried to turn her wrapped head away from me, and her body quaked as if I had already applied to it the whip. Her fears were well grounded, for she might be reluctant to speak but I would have the truth.

"Tell me what is happening," I said, speaking in a cold voice. "Where is the babe?"

"In the *keuken* house."

"The *keuken* house? What is it doing there?" I demanded. "Where is the wet nurse?" Alarm was replaced by hot anger.

I placed my hand under the woman's chin and roughly turned her face so that she was forced to address me directly. In her eyes I saw a strange fright that had naught to do with the whip or the ordinary business of childbirth.

Her voice, when she spoke, was hoarse with trepidation. "No one will nurse the babe," she said.

A new feeling of panic enveloped me. If the newborn did

not soon nurse, it would die. "Find a wet nurse. Bring her to me now! And bring the babe from the *keuken* house."

The nervous midwife ran from the room and in minutes returned with the tiny bundle, which she placed into my waiting arms. Such a tiny thing, so quiet and innocent, Liesbeth and Samuel's long-awaited son! Oh, I felt such distress at the terrible thought that at any moment it might perish.

When a young woman with milk in her breasts was brought before me, I ordered her on pain of the lash or worse to nurse Liesbeth's son. Whether it was fear of the whip or compassion for the infant—who is truly fair—I know not, but the deed was accomplished. Seeing the babe's natural response to the breast, I began to relax a little.

"Elisabeth, come quickly." Maria's urgent voice interrupted the maternal scene I had created. She beckoned me to follow her to the upstairs bedroom where Liesbeth lay. A strange odor permeated the room and more cloths, soaked in blood, lay on the polished wooden floor at the foot of the bed. Liesbeth's young face was yellowed, but her eyes had opened and she did not seem to be in pain.

"May I have my mask?" she asked. Her voice sounded distant, as if she was already seeing the other world.

"Your mask?" I was surprised by this unexpected request. "The one you wore to the Governor's ball?"

"Aye. I would like to see it one more time." Her small voice carried a resigned tone.

Maria took in a sharp breath. "Liesbeth! Do not speak thusly. You will wear your mask again. You must rest now, so that you can regain your strength. Your son is beautiful and healthy. He's with the wet nurse now."

She did not seem to understand what Maria said. "My mask? Please?"

"Of course, my dear." If this simple pleasure would ease her mind so that she would rest more effortlessly, it was an easy enough thing to accomplish.

The embossed red velvet mask with the pearls and black satin ribbons was brought and placed in her delicate fingers. Moving her hand as if time had slowed, Liesbeth brought the mask to her face to smell the perfume lingering about it and smiled.

And as I watched in horror, Providence hath called her away, one hand clutching the mask and one hand at her breast having never left the *obia*, in which she had placed all her trust and confidence.

"Liesbeth!"

In abject distress I sank to my knees at the bedside. Behind me, Nanette gasped and burst forth with tears. Maria bent forward and touched the backs of her fingers to Liesbeth's parted lips, from where she could feel no breath emanating from the nostrils.

"Oh dear Lord," she whispered. "She's no more. We've lost her!"

None of the house girls moved, and for a long moment it was as if within the room time had indeed stopped. Outside, the calling of the *gritjibis* continued, as if nothing in the world had changed.

But my world had changed. My pain could not have been greater had I lost my own birth daughter. A great swelling of grief rose within me, yet for the moment I was too stunned to shed the tears that would come.

"Samuel." I murmured. "Someone must tell Samuel." My concern was not that a slave might do it first, as it was not the kind of news any slave would willingly impart. It was an unhappy message that properly required a family member to deliver.

"I'll go," said Maria, and departed the room.

Samuel, now no longer in danger of losing his post as Inspection Master, had been thrilled with the birth of a son, but had realized within minutes that all was not right with Liesbeth. He was therefore not surprised at the distressful news, and visited her alone in the bedroom to say his farewell with quiet dignity.

The entire slave household now whispers of nothing but the tragedy. Kwasiba, concerned for her own swollen belly, fears *wisi*-poison. In desperate need of action, I have consulted Granman Quassie on the matter.

After a rather brief ceremony, he said, "She not die of poison. Her death was the will of her own *wintis*."

I quitted his presence in disgust. I cannot accept that her

own *wintis* would have any reason to have caused her death. In truth, I can think of none who would wish Liesbeth or her family harm. Unless of course her family could be extended to include me. Certainly I have enemies, but would not any *wisi*-poison have been better directed at me? My blood runs cold with the thought that on my behalf death should befall my darling niece, who was never heard to utter an unkind word.

Frightening doubts fill my mind. Everywhere I suspect treachery. Though Granman Quassie is of wide repute as a man who can divine truth-saying from lies, how can I be sure of what he speaks?

In addition to this misfortune, Carl Otto and I are ourselves now ill of an unknown ailment leaving us weak from running fluids. We have therefore submitted with two witnesses closed testaments so that our affairs are in order. Denying any other possibility, I tell myself that certainly we suffer from a portion of sour fish rather than a spell of black magic directed towards us by outside forces.

The one light in all this depression and melancholy is that Liesbeth's child, may be cursedas the result of being born feet first, but the boy has a white father. I have confidence that Samuel will honor the memory of his concubine and continue to be a responsible father to his children.

32

La Solitude, June 1752

Nine months gone, yet a day does not pass that I see Liesbeth's sweet face or hear her melodious voice. I'm certain her *jorka*, her departed spirit, is near me.

Following Liesbeth's burial, a perfunctory Christian service was held at the Dutch Reformed Church with just the immediate family present. Samuel was stoic, black from head to toe in mourning attire, often turning his head a bit so that he could glance to the back of the room where the wetnurse, seated in a straight-backed cane chair, held his son. Nanoe wept openly with no attempt to hide her grief at the loss of her dear sister. Later at home prayers were offered for Liesbeth's *'kra*, her ancestors, and her personal *wintis*.

Thankfully, the child, Philip Samuel, grows well, and the wet nurse no longer fears him. *Meneer* Loseke goes about his business as Inspection Master, father, and master of his household with apparent ease, and wears only about his arm a mourning band.

A diversion from my sorrowful remembrances of Liesbeth has appeared in the form of an American artist, John Greenwood, recently come to our little Colony for the purpose, I believe, of escaping for a time a colder climate proving to be of ill health to him.

"I should like him to paint your portrait," announced Carl Otto one morning at breakfast. "You have spent too much time secluded at La Solitude. You must come back to *foto*."

"Portraits are for beautiful women," I objected, amazed and nearly moved to tears that Carl Otto should think me worthy of such an important expression. I thought that Liesbeth would have made a more worthy subject, but refrained from speaking of it. In the end I agreed to return with him to the big house on Heerenstraat, where we gave a reception for the artist.

John Greenwood proved to be a handsome young man with an engaging, if somewhat acidic, wit. Twenty-five years old and a bachelor, he already has caused to swoon several hearts in the Colony.

"I had no idea I would be so busy in Paramaribo with portrait commissions," he said over tea in our south drawing room. "It was not my intention to remain any amount of time in this port-of-call." His tone seemed falsely merry, making it clear he does not think much of our little Colony.

A native of Massachusetts and the son and grandson of Boston shipwrights, *meneer* Greenwood is not much comfortable with our slave economy.

"But is it not true that there is an abundance of slaves in your own southern-most colonies?" Carl Otto asked. "Surely the fine tobacco that comes from Virginia could not be produced, as our sugar cannot be produced, without the labor of the Africans."

Meneer Greenwood wore a grim expression. "Yes, but our plantation owners do not treat their slaves as the Dutch do."

Carl Otto raised an eyebrow at this comment. "How so?"

Maria was quite indignant. "All possible care is taken that they are not too deeply branded, especially the women, who are always somewhat delicate."

The artist ignored her comment and made his answer to Carl Otto. "It is said that in the tobacco colonies slaves are kept in line by the threat of being sold to a Dutchman, such is the reputation of your planters."

I laughed at this. "It would be quite irresponsible not to discipline the Africans."

John Greenwood frowned and said, "Yet you yourself are of the African descent, madame."

"That has nothing to do with it," said Carl Otto, striving to maintain a friendly tone. "She is a free Christian woman of property and accepts the responsibility that goes with it."

"By all accounts, the Africans are a conquered people," said Maria. "And the Holy Bible clearly states in Chapter 2, verse 19 of the Second Epistle of Peter: *'of someone who is conquered, a man-servant shall be made.'*"

"Do you not have Negroes who own plantations in Virginia?" I asked.

Meneer Greenwood was startled at the idea. "Why no, madame. It would be unheard of. The few freed blacks we have are quite poor, I assure you."

"So perhaps they would have been better off to remain slaves."

The artist, I'm sure sensing a wealthy commission at stake, smiled with condescension. "Perhaps just so, madame."

At this point in our conversation I realized that I had avoided any mention of my "Suriname marriage" status with Carl Otto. Now I sensed that the American would be quite shocked to learn of a legal marriage between an educated white man and an educated black woman.

He was explaining to Carl Otto an idea he was developing for a painting commissioned by a tavern at the waterside. "I admire the compositions of William Hogarth, the English engraver and painter, and would place twenty or so figures in a scene of the lighter moment of a merchant captain's life."

"That sounds much more complicated than a single portrait," I said.

"Yes, madame." His frank blue eyes fairly twinkled as he spoke of his contemplated work. "But I should like to portray some of the personages I know in the scene."

"You could call it 'Sea Captains Carousing in Suriname,'" I said, amused.

"Why, that is a capital idea, madame. I like it very much. A truly satirical piece. I have in mind one man cheating at cards by slipping one into his tricorn hat, another joining the festivities in his nightdress, and perhaps another, too tipsy to notice, oblivious to a candle burning his coat."

"That would certainly be a departure from a formal portrait," said Carl Otto, smiling at me.

His words caused me to have misgivings about my own portrait, for I should be deeply wounded should such ridicule be the least bit apparent in the American artist's portrayal of my person. While John Greenwood has set aside his prejudices and accepted the handsome commission offered by Carl Otto to paint my portrait, I daresay I'm sure I am the only woman of colour the man shall ever paint. And perhaps also the only one with a squirrel monkey perched upon her shoulder, for I insisted that little Pansu be part of the picture.

I should have been cheered by the prospect of Pansu and I being thus immortalized, but I am still disturbed by the *mofokoranti* surrounding the demise by *wisi*-poison of my dear niece. Kwasiba, now a mother in her own right, believes the curse of barrenness upon my sisters and me has been extended to other family women, and Liesbeth the proof of it.

Hearing this, I said severely, "You are not to say one word of this in the same sentence with little Suzanna Johanna's name!" She will grow up, together with her little brother, in Maria's house innocent and protected from black magic.

The custody of Liesbeth's children had been a difficult subject within our family. Samuel, while more than willing to meet the financial obligation of his children, at length did not want to stay in the house he had shared with Liesbeth, and had asked to place them with our family. I begged Carl Otto to take them into our home, to raise them as our own, but he refused, claiming a fear for my depression and reminding me of my responsibilities with the businesses of importing goods and managing the plantations. Maria also wanted them, and Carl Otto declared, "She is experienced from raising you, and a better choice as all she wants to do is to stay at home on Waterkant, so she will be there for the children."

I question my sister's ability to love them as I would, and I am hurt by his words. My heart, already heavy with the loss of Liesbeth, now feels an even larger well of emptiness. The meetings with my directors and managers, sorting of goods from Holland, and selling of textiles with which I busy myself cannot expell the poignant images of what might have been had little Sutje and Philip Samuel been invited to grow up in our big house on Heerenstraat.

I would never have thought Carl Otto would refuse me this simple request.

33

Paramaribo, September 1752

Carl Otto insisted our first party of the dry season be in celebration of the portrait of me painted by John Greenwood. Now completed, it hangs in the center of the salon in a very lovely rococo gilt frame. Each time I pass it I must admit to a secret smile, for he has indeed flattered me most admirably. The light upon the folds of my green gown are warm, reminding me of the leaves of orange trees as struck by the first golden rays of dawn. Little Pansu's leather collarette is studded with emeralds to match the ones I wear about my own throat and his expression is charmingly innocent.

The house fairly burst with the happy, mingled laughter of friends, family, and children. I was overjoyed to have a few minutes to entertain little Sutje while Philip Samuel slept in peace in his carved mahogany crib, well protected from the mosquitoes by a sheer white netting with a tiny edge of fine lace. I still envy Maria her new maternal role, and though I watch her with suspicion for any sign of neglect or carelessness, I can find no fault in her hand with Liesbeth's children.

Willem Hendrik van Steenberch has married a respectable young white girl, Maryk Hermelijn. When they arrived I kissed the lady three times upon the cheeks in a warm Suriname greeting. *Vrouw* van Steenberch is shorter by a head than her new husband, and just beginning to show evidence of expecting their first child. Carl Otto and I had been glad to attend their wedding in the Dutch Reformed Church. How I envied the girl! Her brides' dress had been most fashionable and all the attendant festivities were most merry.

"Your wedding was the highlight of the summer," I said. "Welcome to our house, my dear."

As the result of a near-accident with their carriage, Anna and Willem Ouwater arrived breathless and late. Anna was most anxious to see the portrait, but slowed her steps when she observed our interim Governor General, the little German Baron von Spörcke, standing in front of it, glass of rum punch in one hand and a sugar cake in the other.

"I'll wait to see it more closely," she murmured, fanning herself with rapid movements. Whether she did this from the unseasonable warmth of the evening or a personal discomfort to be in the near vicinity of von Spörcke was hard to tell.

Hendrik and his new wife were conversing with von Spörcke, so it did not appear he would move away from the spot very soon.

During dinner, when conversation ran high and merry, the artist John Greenwood could be observed to be sweating under his white wig. He was for the most part silent and rather reserved, but I suspect he has grown to like, or at least respect, our mixed family. He was particularly friendly to the children, for which admirable action I am more appreciative than the completion of my portrait.

To the amusement of all except my spoilsport sister, Nanette, Pansu scampered across the table, stealing samplings from the fruit platter. The children found this sudden entertainment particularly delightful, and when I made to protest the act, sounded choruses of, "Oh, let him be." I looked around the table and found many smiling faces, some persons already allowing the little monkey to sip heavily from their wine goblets.

Nanette seems happy with her consort, the rather brooding Lankmoedigheid director Wijnand van Herpen, though La Vallaire shares my dislike of the man. Indeed, she and I had seated ourselves as far down the table from van Herpen as possible. When he made reference to a particularly brutal slave punishment, Greenwood glared at him.

"I was obliged to cut through the large tendon above his

right heel with a knife, thus effectively hamstringing him," van Herpen said. "I considered having him quartered alive, but thought better to make what savings I could of the plantation's investment."

"No doubt Lankmoedigheid's owner will appreciate such a wise conclusion," I said.

Nevertheless, I thought van Herpen's tone arrogant, and did not encourage him to further conversation. He repeatedly pressed one side of his temple with his fingers as if he suffered from a terrible headache, which could have been from an overindulgence of claret. Yet when I studied him, I was struck with the malevolent thought that the man might have malaria. Indeed, his face appeared pale and he demonstrated little appetite. At once I felt remorseful, as Nanette appears to adore the man. But I could not suppress the idea that his slaves would undoubtedly prefer he not recover. I pondered the presence there of the little slave Quassie, now seven. Did he suffer much at the hand of the Lankmoedigheid director?

When van Herpen spoke at length to an enraptured acting Governor von Spörcke of several recent small raids by runaways against Lankmoedigheid, I gave the director my most ferocious stare. I did not want to hear such obscenities at my table this day.

Von Spörcke, now noticeably tipsy, lifted his wineglass and took a hearty drink while at the same time he rested his elbow awkwardly upon the table. "Verschuer has declared himself to be willing to take on the provisional government," he said.

It is well known that the German would welcome a speedy return to Holland. He's been shamelessly campaigning for someone else to take over the governing of the Colony. The Dutch Duke Verschuer, the highest military commander in the country, seems a likely candidate. He has shown himself to possess a firm hand, to see the balance of most things, and to demonstrate an eye that sees only what is politically appropriate to see.

"When will the Duke present himself to the Court of Police?" inquired Carl Otto.

Before von Spörcke could make to answer, a harsh cough escaped him, splattering some of the wine on the lace tablecloth.

All eyes at the table were now upon the man, who appeared to stiffen. His left hand clenched in a tight fist that gathered up the tablecloth and caused the plate and crystal around it to totter and fall with a clatter. His throat made a gurgling sound and he clutched at his left shoulder. This abrupt movement caused him to lose his balance in his chair, whereupon he fell against the arm of it in unexpected collapse.

Samuel, seated to the German's left, reached out to balance the man. Von Spörcke fell against Samuel, whose body served to cushion the German's heavy slide to the floor.

There was a great scraping of chairs and commotion as the men rushed to the aid of von Spörcke. The ladies remained in their seats, stiff with shocked silence. Even the children were wide-eyed and quiet, waiting to see what would happen next in order to make the least troublesome response. The American, John Greenwood, seemed thoughtful, as if he were considering a blank canvas. The servants also remained rooted where they stood, unwilling to involve themselves, but alert to any sudden order.

"Send for the doctor," Carl Otto commanded the nearest slave.

The man's eyes narrowed, but otherwise there was no change in expression on his black face. "Aye, *mas'ra*."

At this point eleven-month-old Philip Samuel began to wail and Maria called for the wet nurse to remove the child from the room.

Samuel unbuttoned Von Spörcke's waistcoat while Carl Otto tilted his head back so that the jaw and tongue were pulled forward. The breath that expelled itself from the German's throat was hoarse and noisy. Carl Otto moved close, running his finger into the man's mouth, but no morsel of food appeared to be lodged in the throat. The color of Von Spörcke's skin appeared reddened to me, yet admittedly it is often difficult to tell what is the healthful color of the white skin—indeed, white persons themselves are better able to recognize such condition in their own kind.

"His pulse is strong," observed Samuel, his fingers at Von Spörcke's wrist, "but slow. I fear he may be stricken with apoplexy."

With care he rolled Von Spörcke's head to the side. Nausea gripped my stomach as a bit of sallow spittle, a sickening combination of food and saliva, emerged from the mouth and oozed onto the mahogany floor.

Carl Otto looked at Samuel and said, "Let's carry him to the drawing room where he can be laid out more comfortably on the sofa."

Van Herpen helped and the three men lifted the inert body of our interim Governor and bore him out of the dining salon.

"Curb that vile creature," Nanette demanded. She made to swipe her napkin at Pansu as he reached for a sugared nut on the edge of her plate.

I gathered up the protesting squirrel monkey and made my excuse to take leave of the dining salon in order to cage him. No sooner had I put him inside than he nested his blanket, curled up, and collapsed into a deep slumber of little snores.

Indeed, I welcomed this diversion as an opportunity to collect my wits about me and consider the consequences of this unfortunate incident with the fat von Spörcke. Why couldn't the man have been stricken in his own home instead of mine? This will be yet another opportunity for the planters' wives to malign the free Negress Elisabeth Samson, and the *mofokoranti* will be relentless. No doubt, someone will mention *wisi* poison and even von Spörcke himself will suspect my household, when in fact this might not have happened if the German wasn't given to eating and drinking everything in sight.

Thoroughly disgusted, it occurred to me that now John Greenwood might be moved to paint a tableau of my dining salon with the rotund little German falling stricken from my table. My irritation at this ruination of my portrait debut was mounting when Carl Otto came up behind me.

"The doctor is here," he said. "You should come to the drawing room."

"Of course," I murmured. I took a deep breath to quell my rising anxiety and regain my nerves.

As soon as I entered the drawing room I knew that the situation was even worse than I had contemplated.

To my horror, Major-General Hendrik Ernst Baron von Spörcke had expired. As soon as the doctor had arrived he declared himself too late.

34

Paramaribo, January 1753

It is beyond my understanding why one would ignore the *winti* of his ancestors as well as his own *winti* and *'kra* when facing his final moment upon this earth. It is well and good to be a Christian, for the God of Christianity is powerful, yet it is never wise to turn one's back on the myriad of other spirits who can affect our lives in so many important ways.

Yet that is certainly what Wijnand van Herpen has done, and he and his soul have paid the price for it.

For over two months van Herpen drifted in and out of fever at Lankmoedigheid. The malaria which had stricken him at length manifested itself in the fevers alternating with the chills, each situation sometimes lasting for several days at a time. His face remained pale, his fingers lightened considerably, and the nails acquired a bluish tone.

When his water became thick and dark and he could barely rise from the bed where he was often drenched in sweat, Nanette said, "I want to call *Gra'man* Quassie. I should have done it when he showed the first symptom."

Maria and I agreed this was necessary. In my opinion Maria, who has developed a chronic cough, lost much weight and may be addicted to the use of emetics, could herself benefit from a visit to the *dresiman.*

Van Herpen, crazed by fever, raged against my sister with what little strength he had left. "I'll not have that black bastard touch me. I'll not have any mumbo-jumbo in my house."

The plantation house at Lankmoedigheid is not his house, but that is beside the point. "By God there'll be no pernicious alligator scum slinking around my bed to take advantage of me while I sleep!"

Nanette fretted with indecision. Van Herpen scratched himself until the puffy, inflamed areas of his skin bled, for lemon acid gave him no relief, and Nanette feared infection as well as delirium. Her consort had always refused to sleep under bed netting and had prided himself in tramping around in the swampy areas of the plantation with his back exposed.

I also suspect that some of the mosquito bites that were so numerous that his left leg was a swollen, reddened limb, were acquired by midnight visits to the house of a young Negress in the slave quarters. Nanette, in her loyalty to her lover, would not say how often he was gone from her bed, but the household talked. At the height of one of his fevers, van Herpen swore and raised the woman's name, driving my poor sister to flowing tears.

He accused Nanette of refusing him food, though in truth he took little of what was offered to him. Then it was discovered that when Nanette was not present, the house slaves had been indeed withholding nourishment from him. In distraught outrage, Nanette had them all flogged soundly and sent from household service to break their backs in field work done in the noonday sun. Her personal triumph was in discovering that one of the girls was the very one her consort had been visiting in the night, and this girl she mutilated further by having her lips cut away from her mouth.

In tears Nannette begged van Herpen to allow her to send for Granman Quassie, but the stubborn Dutchman would not have it. The white doctor bled him, and Nanette fed him a variety of herbal teas, but the jungle fever would have its toll. Just before Christmas, he died in her arms, mumbling and crying while soiling himself and her skirt.

When it was discovered that in his testament he had named as his principle heir his mother who lived in the Netherlands, I was incensed. Nanette Samson received only one hundred guilders, fifty-two Dutch silver guilders, a trunk with clothing, two gold buttons and some silver clasps. He had even named my sister as his executrix, thus further taking advantage of her love and loyalty.

An inventory has been made at Lankmoedigheid, requested by the plantation owner in Holland, who is writing a new testament and wants to be sure his recently deceased director, or his concubine (Nanette), has not stolen any property of value.

Nanette, in her sorrowful state, was doing the best she could to administer what is necessary, but it soon became clear that her thoughts were scattered and she was in desperate need of my assistance. There were items the owner deemed to be sold and I was of a mind to purchase two or three of Lankmoedigheid's slaves, so I arrived at the plantation on the day they were presented.

On the inventory list, I saw the name of Quassie, our little distant cousin.

"I will have him," I said to Nanette. "I'll send him to Vlaardingen, where La Vallaire will see to it that he will be able to grow up with family."

There appears in the eyes of these Lankmoedigheid slaves a strange, haunted light that leaves me unnerved. It is well known that Wijnand van Herpen did not care well for the slave property of the plantation; nay, even the smallest children appear starved and stunted. The adults, both men and women, are sullen and well scarred by the whip.

"I fear I cannot use any of them," I declared. "They are morose and badly trained, and of ill-abused condition."

Indeed, those who could manage it had already fled to the forest, and the remainder is not at all of fair health.

Nanette wiped her eyes, perpetually red now from weeping. "Lankmoedigheid is greatly in need of military protection."

"Our struggling Society troops are spread rather thinly about the Colony as it is," I said. "Besides, how can the government protect the colony when they can't even agree on who should govern?"

My sister, always bored with politics, turned away from me, mumbling, "Does it really matter who governs? The Courts do as they please, anyway."

Another thought arose in my already troubled mind.

"If ever there was a time ripe for uprising, this current climate of political instability may cause it."

"Little Quassie will be safer at Vlaardingen," Nanette said.

She was persuaded to return to *foto* with me when I left with the boy in the tent-boat. So at dinner at home on Heerenstraat this evening I had two sisters robed in somber black, as Maria, gaunt and coughing, has never stopped mourning since Frederik left us eight years ago.

My bright spot was the presence of the two children in her care. Two-year-old Philip Samuel squirmed in my arms when I lifted and hugged him. Darling Sutje is a spritely three-year-old whom I would love even if she didn't look heartbreakingly like my dear Liesbeth.

Maria ate little and never stopped smoking, as she had brought her pipe to the table. Her demeanor is of great concern to me for she cannot forego a pipestem in her mouth even in order to partake of food. She coughed again, and wiped her mouth with an already-soiled silk handkerchief. It is clear she suffers from a chronic ailment.

Unable to hold my tongue I leaned towards her and whispered, "Have you seen *Gra'man* Quassie or the white doctor for whatever ails you?"

"It's nothing," said Maria. She turned away from me to fuss with the napkin of one of the children. She had not answered my question, but this was not the place or time to press.

Carl Otto was just saying, "The Princess-Regent as well as the Directors of the Society have made it known they do not approve the manner in which the Court of Police handled the succession to von Spörcke."

"Indeed," I said. "I understand that Duke Verschuer has been ordered to turn over governorship to the military commander Wigbold Cromelin."

In truth, such discussion at the moment held no interest for me. I looked at Maria and worried for the future of Liesbeth's children should her condition prove mortal. In the case of such an unhappy event, once again there would need to be a conversation about who would care for them. I looked at Carl Otto, now offering Maria his clean handkerchief, and remembered his hurtful words. I felt wounded and vulnerable. Surely he could not again refuse our home to these two beautiful children.

Then and there at the dining table I was moved to tears. I looked down to where little Pansu lay sleeping in my lap. A cloak of chill enveloped me, causing me to shudder. The body of my little squirrel monkey was cold to the touch, and when I made to prod his tiny hand, it was limp with death.

I must have screamed, for when I looked up conversation had ceased and the whole assembly was staring at me. My mouth opened, but no words came out.

"Betje—what is it?" Carl Otto set down his wine goblet and put his hand to my arm.

In mute response I reached for his hand and put it on the body of Pansu. At once he devined the situation and took the little monkey from my lap.

"Your pardon," he said to the group and left the table carrying Pansu away from me.

The tears that had brimmed in my eyes now broke forth in full volume. The shudder in my body had developed into an unstoppable shivering. I rushed from the table, not caring that the chair in which I'd been sitting fell backwards to the hardwood floor in a strident racket. My ear was further assaulted by Nanette's cruel mockery.

"It was only a stupid, drunken monkey. You should lose the man you love."

35

Plantation Clevia, August 1753

The sun was low in the sky over the outlying jungle, edging billowing white clouds with the bright orange and scarlet colours of twilight. At six p.m. Carl Otto and I settled ourselves in the wicker chairs on the porch of the plantation house to receive our director and the *bastiaans* and review together the work of the day. The evening report was satisfactory, and an air of contentment seemed to float about us on the gathering breeze. Afterwards, in the darkened house, candles were lit and we played whist before retiring for the night.

Barking dogs awakened us. The bedroom lay in semi-darkness, moonlight casting sliced light through half-closed shutters. When Carl Otto sat up I shivered as his warmth beside me was disturbed.

"What is it?" I asked, not really alarmed, but annoyed at having my slumber bothered. Outside the dogs continued to bark, a harsh, insistent sound.

In seconds Carl Otto was at the door, pistol in hand. He put his finger to his lips to caution my silence, opened the door and disappeared into the hallway. It seemed like hours passed, agonizing time spent imagining all manner of disaster except for the one I least expected.

When Carl Otto returned, the words he spoke were laced with urgency. "Come down to the drawing room. Nanette is just arrived."

I threw a dressing gown over my nightdress and followed

him in bare feet down the carpeted stairs. Candles had been lit in the drawing room, and Carl Otto ordered a carafe of brandy to be brought.

Nanette's black habit spoke of the news she bore. Even in candlelight I could see that her eyes were red-rimmed and tired. "When you didn't appear in *foto*," she said, "I could only assume you hadn't received the slave I sent."

We had been a month at Clevia, and were hungry for news from *foto*, but not bad news. A long dreadful moment passed before Carl Otto said, "Have a draught of brandy, Nanette, but please continue."

My sister swallowed hard, and then coughed from the sting of the liquor on her parched throat. "It hasn't been a good trip on the river. In our haste, drinking water was forgotten." She raised sad eyes to me and said, "I'm afraid Maria is with us no more."

"Maria?" I repeated.

In a stronger voice she said, "Maria began coughing blood two weeks past. Her constitution appeared to be broken beyond repair. She refused to be bled, and the overall appearance of her skin became scrofulous."

Carl Otto saw me sway upon my feet, and helped me to the sofa next to Nanette. My sister leaned into me in an uncharacteristically dependent movement and sighed. Not knowing how to respond, I put my arm about her shoulders. That small gesture caused her to break down in quiet little sobs that caused her nose to run. Carl Otto handed me his handkerchief, and with it I wiped her face as I would wipe that of a child who has scraped her knee in a tripping fall.

Indeed, when last I had seen Maria I had been impressed that she had lost such an amount of weight that her bones could be seen through her papery skin.

"I went every day to the house on Waterkant," Nanette whimpered, as if this was reason enough for Maria to recover. Her ample body quivered with emotion.

Nanette related how as Maria lay dying, she was most distressed that she would never see her much-loved Salzhalen again. Even though in recent years Maria hardly ever has visited the plantation, it evoked for her memories of her life there with first Pierre Mivela and later Frederik Coenraad Bosse. These two gentlemen had been kind and good to our sister.

"A room has been readied for you," I said to Nanette. "Come upstairs. A good night's sleep will do you a world of good."

Nanette leaned heavily against me as if she could not rise on her own, and Carl Otto helped me pull her to her feet. As the three of us ascended the stairs, she whispered in a tired voice, "Do you have any laudanum?"

. . .

Nanette and I have inherited together half of Salzhalen. The other half belongs to the white Dutchman, J.W. van der Linden. This news was given to me by Nanette over a late breakfast the following morning. Carl Otto had risen early for the morning plantation meeting, allowing me to sleep a little longer. When he'd finished, he joined us in the breakfast room.

"The overseeing and administration of Salzhalen has been difficult since Frederik passed," Nanette explained. Her entire face was much fuller than usual, the skin around her mouth and eyes puffy and bloated. "I'm afraid Maria felt forced to seek help."

"But why outside the family?" I wondered out loud. This morning I joined Nanette in lacing my coffee with a generous portion of rum.

Carl Otto dismissed my question, saying, "We'll never know. It's not important now, anyway."

When Carl Otto and I had at length returned to bed the night before I had wept with shame for Maria.

"She was a mother to me when my own mother was unable to care for me," I said to Carl Otto. Indeed, I am more sorely moved by the death of Maria than I ever was at the departure of Mariana. Of all my brothers and sisters, I now have only Nanette left. To lose them one by one as we all get older must be the curse of being the youngest child in the family.

"What of the burial?" I asked Nanette.

"A headstone has been purchased for the yard of the Dutch

Reformed Church. She was laid in the ground yesterday and it should be ready by next week. Anna organized a very nice service." My sister raised anguished eyes to mine. "I should have sent a more responsible slave to tell you."

"Who did you send?" I asked.

"A man from Maria's household. Coujo."

"I know him not," I said, trying to remember if our director had mentioned anyone recently arriving from *foto*. "I've had no word, so I suspect he never arrived at Clevia."

"I'm sure that's the case," said Carl Otto. "We would have been informed."

Nanette shrugged, and helped herself to another generous draught from the rum bottle. It was certainly not the first time a slave had been lost upon the river, and would not be the last.

"Hendrik Van Steenberch has written you a letter," she said to Carl Otto. She made a little apologetic smile. "I almost forget. I'll get it for you."

With some effort Nanette lifted her ample body from her chair and was gone only a few minutes. When she returned she handed a folded sheet to Carl Otto. He broke the wax seal and read the message while he drank his coffee.

I would have been eager to hear whatever news it contained, but I felt so depleted from the news of Maria's death that I had no energy in that direction.

At length Carl Otto said, "The first of the month came to Suriname the news that our good friend, Johan Jacob Mauricius, has won his case in Holland. He succeeded in defending himself in Den Hague and was cleared of all blame on 15 May. He additionally obtained the right to prosecute—most likely for slander—du Plessis, who was actually imprisoned at Den Hague, but then pardoned."

"That is some good news," I said.

"Even so, neither of them will be allowed to return to the Colony," he said.

"How fortunate I count myself that I was able to return from my ordeal." Without thinking I had spoken my thoughts out loud.

Oblivious to my sentiments regarding the similarity of the

unfortunate circumstances undergone by myself and our former Governor, Carl Otto said, "A new Court of Police has been chosen directly by the Princess-Regent."

Nanette, her spirits no doubt warmed by rum and coffee, took unusual interest in this discourse, adding, "I'm told the return of Carilho to his post has rekindled dissension amongst the Jews."

And so the politicians continue to circle around each other like dancing orange cocks-of-the-rock.

. . .

The day proved bleak with overcast clouds and dark threats of rain at any moment. I spent a good deal of time wandering from room to room, upstairs and downstairs, in an attempt to find some measure of comfort in idle occupation. In the drawing room I sat by an open window with a beautiful view of the plantation grounds, picked up my needlework, watched an iridescent rose and green lizard make its way across a log under a tree, put down my needlework without making one stitch, and got up again.

Images of Maria crowded my mind: resplendent in her wedding dress when she married Frederik in the church, bringing me sugar tea to comfort me as a child, scolding me when I pestered Frederik with questions, envying me my quickness with numbers as Frederik and I together reviewed the plantation journal for Salzhalen. Feeling a measure of guilt at the motherly feelings I felt for Maria, I tried to envision Mariana in a similar way, but her image was unclear, faded with the distance of time passed and little spent in the company of one another.

Carl Otto, uncomfortable with my restlessness and agitation, retreated to the outside grounds on the excuse of plantation business. I knew he had gone hunting, but it seemed of no importance to make issue with him over the business. When he returned in the afternoon bearing a gift of a freshly-killed *powisi* bird, I made every effort to appear refreshed and sociable.

The *powisi* made an excellent stew, and Nanette, Carl Otto

and I dined heartily, if silently. All of us consumed too much claret, which would normally have brought up some harsh words between my sister and me. Now every word and motion seemed dulled by an unknown attendance. I wondered if Maria's *jorka* had followed Nanette down the river from *foto*, but dismissed the idea since there had been no overt sign of its presence. Nonetheless, what meager conversation occurred during the meal passed between all in the most polite tones.

With no further interest in conversation or games and drowsy from food and wine, we passed on entertainments and retired early to bed. Yet I was still restless and spent a goodly length of time on the silly business of selecting a nightdress to wear.

"Come to bed, Betje," Carl Otto coaxed. "I'm weary of this day."

I crawled into the four-poster and found it difficult to settle myself in comfort. At length I spoke what had been invading my mind with every sip of wine at dinner.

"Maria died without issue," I wailed to Carl Otto. "Am I destined to die old and alone as well?" I thought of my little squirrel monkey, Pansu, lying cold within the ground behind the house, and felt sorry for myself that I did not even have him to cuddle in my arms.

In spite of his own inebriation Carl Otto's logical nature caused him to evaluate my words literally. "You are the youngest of six children, Elisabeth. You have nieces and nephews, and even grand nieces and nephews. You have friends. You are a beautiful woman. I hardly think you will die old and alone."

"But I'm thirty-eight years old. I have no children of my own." This was the first time I had said such a thing out loud, and the actual sound of the words sent me rolling into his arms where I buried my face from his sight and sobbed wretchedly.

Carl Otto was rather taken aback by this hysterical display. Is it pity he feels for me? I felt such misery and gloom. Yet his arms encircled me so that for the moment I succumbed to the lure of feeling protected and safe.

"Betje," he murmured. "I so hate to see you upset like this. How can you imagine such a thing?" His voice was calming and I could hear a reassuring smile in it. "Will it help if we take Liesbeth's children to live with us?"

"Oh, Carl Otto! Do you mean it?"

If there was hesitation in his voice, he hid it well. "If it will make you happy, I'll see to it."

Indeed, I'm sure I make no sense to him. As much as I want to have little Sutje and the babe Philip Samuel, how can he understand the thing that eats away at my very soul, the shame of not birthing him the children we both desire. All my life I have wanted only two things: children and marriage. It appears the former may never be mine. But there is still time for marriage. All I have to do is figure out how to change the law.

And if Carl Otto truly loves me, he'll help me in this.

36

Paramaribo, November 1753

On 29 October Hendrik van Steenberch came to call in the afternoon, a definite air of excitement about him. We gathered in the drawing room and lit our long-stemmed pipes, the better to enjoy the visit.

"Matters are changing dramatically," he announced, placing himself in a chair across from Carl Otto. Hendrik's lengthy arms and legs seemed to drape about the chair. "Governor Cromelin has received a letter from Holland in which all members of the Court of Police are fired!"

Carl Otto sat bolt upright. "They are *all* out?"

"To a man." Hendrik slapped his knee and his face was broad with a grin that revealed yellowed teeth. "When informed, they actually told His Excellency it was a pleasure to be fired because the job had given them nothing but difficulty and bother."

Upon hearing this we all shook our heads in disbelief.

"And you and I are going to be named by His Excellency to the new Court!"

I gasped at his declaration, thrilled for this opportunity for Carl Otto. This was indeed an exciting announcement. Governor Wigbold Cromelin obviously appreciated what Carl Otto had accomplished with the Saramaka Maroons before the broken treaty. After all, my Captain was the first man to make, on behalf of the Society of Suriname, a formal peace with runaways.

Finally I can be assured that living with a black woman has not held such a worthy white gentleman back from high government appointment.

Now—oh happy event—the most wonderful opportunity presents itself for Carl Otto, working within the Court of Police itself, to affect the very change in the law that I both dream and desire!

Indeed four days later the announcement was official. The birthday of the Princess-Regent on 2 November was an occasion of much merriment at the Governor's mansion. Wigbold Cromelin has been Governor General for nigh eight months and has responded well to his duties. He is also taken to extravagant celebration, for which habit the planters adore him.

"Your gown is resplendent, *ma chérie*," whispered Anna at the festivity. "You do know how to show up the white ladies." Though she said this with the greatest affection, her words spoiled somewhat my elation for the evening. They continued to stay with me as I received condolences on the passing of Maria, as well as congratulations on Carl Otto's appointment. I found myself hiding my mouth behind my silver lace fan; I thought of Liesbeth's red embossed velvet mask and wished the fashion were such that we could always hide our sentiments behind a formal mask.

All around me conversation glittered on the subjects of interest to Colonial planters, the least of which was the Dutch Princess-Regent's birthday.

Unfortunately, a rather serious illness had bestruck my handsome Captain, preventing him from celebrating his own good fortune. I fear to admit his constitution has never fully recovered to the strength he enjoyed before his suffering during the expedition against the Saramaka, now four years past.

. . .

This day, 17 November, in the year of our Lord 1753, Carl Otto Creutz and Hendrik van Steenberch, dressed out in complete military attire, swore their oaths of office before the Governor. There followed a grand reception in the drawing room of the mansion that spilled out onto the wide galleries, as the weather was most gracious.

"Now, with a complete change of members," Carl Otto said

in triumph, "there will be a brave, new atmosphere at the meetings of the Court of Police!"

Then he fell into a spell of coughing which greatly alarmed me. Maria, whose counsel I sorely miss, coughed blood before she left us, and when Carl Otto's attention was elsewhere, I carefully inspected his linen handkerchief. Thankfully, there was no red evidence of greater disease.

"I must beg my leave," he said in a hollow voice. "Call the carriage."

"I'll go with you."

"No, Betje. I'll be fine," he insisted. "Go back and enjoy the festivities His Excellency has planned."

The carriage came and Carl Otto, now rather pale, climbed inside, where he reclined with a heavy sigh. I stood alone at the top of the brick stairs and followed the departing carriage with my eyes, thinking I should have accompanied him home after all.

When I turned around to return to the drawing room, I came face-to-face with the woman now destined to remind me that I am still barren while she has born two, Juliaana van Meel Peltser. She casually held the arm of her husband, the prosecutor, who himself had not taken notice of me. Juliaana tightened her grip on his arm and steered him pointedly away from me, towards a far end of the gallery.

Already during the ceremony I had been snubbed by two of the white planters' wives, and seeing my nemesis now behaving so contemptuously towards my person caused the bile of anger to rise in my throat. Inside the mansion I wandered from person to person, making meaningless conversation with my neighbors, in truth drinking too much claret. I could not shake off the feeling that Juliaana's look was ill luck, indeed. I remembered her ravings of madness on the greens of the *Orangeplein* in front of the mansion when she had threatened to have her girl put a curse on Carl Otto. The image of him coughing uncontrollably nagged me. Food and conversation and even drink would not bring my mind to be put to ease.

After this several pages appear to have been eaten by insects and rats, or otherwise rotted away, and there is no other entry until seven years later. Ed.

PART THREE

TROWMISI SA NO ABI PRIMISI
(FORBIDDEN BRIDE)

37

<u>Paramaribo, November 1760</u>

Carl Otto's cousin, Helena Antoinette Creutz, doesn't speak to him because he lives in sin with a black woman. We last saw her on 20 October in front of the Court of Justice, an encounter I shall not soon forget—or forgive. The German woman was there to file a prenuptual agreement with a Dutch fiancé, J. G. Grebber.

"Greetings, cousin," Carl Otto began, in a natural attempt to make friendly overture.

The woman stared him in the face, sneered at me, murmured "whore", and turned down the steps.

"We must be inside by five o'clock to make our testaments," I said to Carl Otto, urging him towards the massive entry door. It had been a long time since I'd been called *whore* within my hearing, and I was justly annoyed. It seems that just when I've forgotten such insensitivities, something happens to remind me.

Inside the staid brick building, the sworn civil servant, *meneer* Goede, together with two witnesses, recorded our matter and afterwards closed and sealed the documents. I was wary of their looks, after our unpleasant encounter outside with Helena Antoinette Creutz, but the gentlemen were cordial enough. No doubt they appreciate the fact that Carl Otto is a respected member of the Court of Police. And they should also appreciate the fact that my annual income is several times over those of lowly civil servants.

"Good day, *mevrouw*," Goede said politely as he escorted us to the door when our business was complete.

In the carriage I turned to Carl Otto, for the legal business had left me feeling agitated.

"We must be able to do more than make a notarized testament of our properties. Why is it so important to record our properties and legatee intentions in a notarized manner before the law, yet our loving faithfulness cannot be legalized in front of God?"

Carl Otto did not look at me, but stared out the open sides of the carriage.

"Betje, my dear sable beauty," he said. "The Governor and the Court of Police are concerned with far more important matters regarding our very safety and wealth. Marriage laws are set, and not about to be changed any time soon."

"Don't you see that the very marriage laws we observe, made by the government, are in direct conflict with respectable marriage in the eyes of God as taught by our own Dutch Reformed Church?"

Carl Otto turned his gaze in the direction of the waterside, where a newly arrived Guineaman was just now being unloaded of its fresh cargo from the African coast.

"When Willem died," I began, "Anna was able to have a proper ceremony in the Dutch Reformed Church. Granted she has inherited, but she also has all the respect a widow deserves."

Anna Ouwater-Julien is now seven weeks in mourning for her husband, Willem Ouwater. People still arrive often at the house on Waterkant to pay their respects, and Susanna Buys, now nineteen, and the ten-year-old Elisabeth Ouwater share in grace with their widowed mother the receiving duties.

Carl Otto tamped tobacco in his pipe bowl, bade the carriage driver to stop so he could light it, and took several long puffs before he answered.

"This obsession of yours with the marriage laws cannot lead to any good. It will only serve to alienate you from the rest of the colonists," he said, a severe tone to his voice.

. . .

The following day Nanette came to show me an elaborately carved pipe she had purchased from the latest shipment from Holland. We sat smoking in my drawing room when for no apparent reason she announced, "I never loved Wijnand as I did Emilius."

I watched her work at lighting her new pipe-bowl, surprised at her comment. "Why do you tell me this?"

She smiled. "Emilius is concerned with your pressure on Carl Otto regarding this marriage business."

Though she does not affect the visible display of mourning, Nanette has taken to setting aside the Christian way and turning to the traditional Negro spirit beliefs. At one end of her drawing room she has established a formal ancestor shrine to the *jorkas*, or departed soul spirits, of her consorts as well as others of our family who have gone before us.

I sighed and closed my eyes, feeling a slight tightness at my temples. "You should have been able to marry Emilius. I'm sure he would have had you."

Without unclenching her teeth from the long stem of her pipe, Nanette rolled her eyes and made a noncommittal noise. "Mmmmm...."

I pointed my pipe-stem at her. "I know you think it's absurd, but how can the Church expect us to create a respectable household when the law forbids marriage between black and white? They were happy enough to take your money for Emilius' burial."

"Elisabeth, you must let this marriage thing go. The Church and the Courts choose to look the other way, and so does Carl Otto."

"When living in sin is the only choice, does that make those persons sinners?" I asked.

Nanette sighed, annoyed at this direction in our conversation. "That's a question for the white clergy. You should be satisfied with being free and rich and able to marry any free Coloured or Negro man you want."

"I don't want any free Coloured or Negro man! I *want* Carl Otto." The air in the room of a sudden burned with my impatience. I felt smothered and found it difficult to breathe.

My sister sat forward in her chair and glared at me.

"You have his complete love and devotion. Is that not enough?"

"No! It's not enough."

"It's more than I have today." Tears welled in Nanette's limpid eyes.

How could I answer her? I still chafe at Carl Otto's refusal to be concerned with our marital status. As he had predicted, things went well in the Court of Police—there have been no more fights and business is being handled in a proper and timely manner. The time is perfect, in my opinion, to raise the subject of changes in the marriage law.

"The law is wrong to forbid us lawful Christian marriage," I persisted.

"Tell that to the Governor, or better still—" Nanette said, "tell Carl Otto to tell it to the Court of Police. There's nothing you can do."

"Perhaps. Perhaps not."

"What are you thinking?" She gave me a queer look of suspicion.

"Nothing in particular," I said. "Yet if we are indeed to become an enlightened society, must not some things change?" Indeed, why couldn't I myself tell it to the Court of Police?

"Be kind to Carl Otto, little sister," Nanette said. "You cannot know what the future holds. One day the most important part of your life is gone, and no matter what you do, you cannot call his *jorka* back."

"You seem to have no problem talking to *jorkas*," I retorted.

"I talk to the *jorkas* of them both," Nanette said.

"Emilius and Wijnand?"

Nanette nodded with complete sincerity. At that moment I feared for her sanity.

She regarded me with a great sadness in her eyes. "Be kind to Carl Otto," she repeated.

. . .

On Sunday last Carl Otto and I hosted a splendid party for Governor Cromelin and his wife, the occasion to celebrate the completion of a project as dear to Carl Otto, as a Captain-Lieutenant of the Society troops, as to His Excellency himself.

The dogs did not come out to bark their usual welcome for the carriages as they arrived, preferring to loll against the bricks of the porch as the air was excessively humid, November being well into the dry season. Slaves fanned the air above the tables to keep the flies from the fruits, stews, and sweetmeats that were set out for our guests. Governor Cromelin's wife, a lady of ample proportions, hovered about the table like a very large hummingbird, repeatedly nibbling.

"I'm afraid I had my fill earlier," protested His Excellency as he scanned the table. His face was flushed and he sweated under his wig. Compared to his wife, he is far more in a state of discomfort from our wet climate.

"A rum punch then," I said. "Or perhaps a glass of claret?"

When I gestured towards the mahogany wine cistern he nodded graciously. So that I could pour for him I directed one of the servants to open a bottle.

"Congratulations, Your Excellency, on the completion of the hospital."

"Aye, it is gratefully appreciated by the soldiers," said Carl Otto.

"And the civilians as well," I added. With the increased number of military personnel sent by the Society, my Captain agreed it was necessary to build a military hospital that would not only accommodate the soldiers but also, for the sake of Colonial politics, civilians. Begun two years ago the impressive structure, built entirely of the Brown Heart timber, is this month ready for operation.

"Now if we only had adequate staff to take care of the sick," said Governor Cromelin, wiping his brow with his lace sleeve.

"Perhaps I can help, Your Excellency." Anna, who had been standing just behind him, fanned herself with vigor as she spoke. "I have more slaves than I need for *la saison*. May I send, say, twenty-five to work in your *hôpital?*"

"My dear *vrouw* Ouwater, that would indeed be a splendid contribution, well appreciated by the surgeon, I'm sure."

Now that Willem is gone and the beautiful Mesties, Susanna Buys, is engaged to be married, Anna has lost interest in the plantation Buys-en-Vlijt and let several of her fields overgrow this past season. She made sure however to plant enough to sustain her and see to the expenses of Susanna's marriage.

"In the past few months we've lost over fifty men to the ills of the climate," said Carl Otto. "The hospital is a godsend, I can tell you."

"*Vrouw* van Meel was to give birth there," said Governor Cromelin. "but at the last minute she remained at home." It was left unsaid that the white doctors still advised the wealthy to avoid the hospital.

Hendrik van Steenberch made a merry gesture of counting on his fingers. "Two daughters, a firstborn son named Wigbold, after Governor Cromelin, a three-year-old named after Pieter Albert van der Meer, and now another beautiful daughter." Van der Meer was an older member of the Court of Justice, of which van Meel himself is now a member. "The van Meels certainly know how to climb a social ladder."

"Juliaana knows how to get what she wants," said Nanette.

"Why her?" I raged. "How can I have so much wealth, have accomplished so much in business, and yet she has what I most long for in the world?" Everyone peered at me as if I were of a sudden stricken ill. Even I was shocked at my outburst, but I couldn't stop myself. "Five children!" In a most unladylike manner, I flung my fan across the room.

"And don't forget the white husband," Nanette murmured, most cruelly.

"Forget? I could never forget!"

Carl Otto rose from his chair to retrieve my fan. "Can we not just be happy for the girl?" he asked.

"At least she named the new *enfant* Agnes," mused Anna. "Not after another high-ranking person." As soon as she had said it, the look on her face said she regretted it.

His Excellency was most gracious in covering her faux pas. "Her children should be named after those in her own family," he said.

The dainty on the plate in front of me could have been covered over with ants, so unappealing had it become. My stomach still clenched at the mention of Juliaana's name. Aye, I searched my heart for even a small a measure of happiness for Juliaana van Meel-Peltser, the white woman I despise most in all the world. When I looked into Carl Otto's face as he handed me the fan I had so impetuously discarded, I saw only devotion and concern for the well-being of my mind.

My sister, on the other hand, regarded me with a look near to contempt. This served to flare my anger. How can Nanette ever know the depth of misery and desolation I experienced at the hands of the Peltser family and the hated prosecutor, van Meel? She may dismiss the years I suffered in Holland in unhappy exile, but I shall never forget! Those were youthful years I could have been with Carl Otto, who might then have fathered my child. For how can I be certain that perhaps there is not something about the European climate that is unfriendly to the constitution of maidens born in a tropical clime— something that might render such a woman incapable of childbearing?

For this Granman Quassie has no clear answer, and all the potions, *obias*, and fertility charms in this world have proven impotent for my sisters and me. Nanette may choose to behave as if she has no care to raise children but I have heard her weep in the night and I no longer care to put forth such a pretense. If tomorrow all Paramaribo—and planters' wives—make comment upon my emotional display today, what matter is it to me?

In the end, I fell into a despair, silently acknowledging that in this matter of Juliaana van Meel-Peltser and her family there is no Christian charity in my heart.

"Please excuse me," I whispered, and left the group to find a chair, preferably by an open window. There I sat for several minutes collecting my wits about me. Feeling great unease, I helped myself to another glass of fortifying claret. When I returned to Carl Otto's side I was somewhat flushed, but feeling better in control of my senses.

Carl Otto and several officers of the military were in earnest discourse with Governor Cromelin regarding the state of the peace treaty with the runaway Maroon rebels of the forest. Owing to naught but their being so cruelly treated by their masters, a new revolt has broken out in the past few years among the Negroes inhabiting the plantations along the Tempaty Creek. A recent count on the part of the military puts the joined runaways at over 1,600, and they have established eight different villages along the banks of the Ndjuka Creek beween the Tempaty and the Marowijne River. Another parlay this year having been proposed by the colonists, all are encouraged by the apparent desire on the part of the runaways to conclude a peace treaty, no doubt more for the purpose of acquiring a handsome quantity of firearms and ammunition than anything else.

We give careful attention to the happenings in the easternmost part of Suriname, for any traffic from that area must pass by Clevia to reach the capital. In spite of his setbacks of health, Carl Otto has turned Clevia into a beautiful, successful sugar plantation with an elegant dwelling house, sturdy sleuces, and canals well-constructed by 200 slaves. He has directed the countryside to be burned and planted with sugar, bananas, rice, citrus, cotton, and indigo. This past year he has seen constructed a fine stone mill operated by cattle, so that it is always ready for use and the sugar can be ground at any time, rather than waiting for the opportunity of the spring tides, as was necessary with the previous water mill.

"A peace treaty is not an easy thing to accomplish," said the military Lieutenant Collerus, a man not much younger than Carl Otto. It could be seen on Carl Otto's face as he listened to the man's words that he wished fervently to have been included in the latest expedition.

Carl Otto prefers more and more to relax at Clevia, where the sea breezes at the mouth of the river are particularly fresh and pleasant. He often complains of a general weakness of body, and though his appetite is good and he passes clear water without difficulty, still I have a growing concern; he was so seriously unwell for two years that I fear a relapse.

Nevertheless he listened eagerly as Lieutenant Collerus related his experience.

"On 24 September, to the Maroon camps at the Ndjuka Creek, numbering about eight to ten villages in total, Governor Cromelin sent two commissioners, Sober and Abercrombie, under my command. We were accompanied by a peace patrol of 206 soldiers, two physicians, and some Negro bearers. We carried with us a letter to the primary chief, a handsome Negro called Granman Araby, and a small bundle of advance presents, to be distributed if the runaways were indeed still interested in a peace parlay. In turn we were assured that we need not fear any harm as we were arrived on such good a cause."

Lieutenant Collerus told of how a Maroon captain, one Boston van Tampatij, read the letter to Granman Araby.

"All went well until it was discovered that the preliminary presents were only a few knives, scissors, combs, and small looking-glasses rather than gunpowder and firearms."

"Do you think we can live on a comb and a looking-glass?" Boston van Tampatij had challenged the commissioners thunderously, causing them to feel much alarm, when another captain called Quacoo hastened to point out that the gentlemen were only the Governor's messengers and therefore should be sent back to *foto* unharmed.

"Van Tampatij had the arrogance to criticize the Europeans," said Lieutenant Collerus, "saying we only pretend to be a civilized nation, when by our inhuman cruelties towards our slaves we make the occasion of our own ruin."

The gentlemen laughed at this, but I felt a certain tension about this response that made their laughter seem as if to cover a grave anxiety.

There had been much discussion among the Ndjuka Maroons, after which the white men were given leave peaceably on 8 October to return with the allowance that the Governor and Court would have a year to deliberate on what they would have—peace or war. A lengthy list of requirements on the part of the rebels was sent back with the commissioners, along with a severe admonition.

According to Lieutenant Collerus, Boston van Tampatij had said, "We desire you to tell your Governor and your Court that if they want to raise no new groups of rebels, they ought to take care that the planters keep a more watchful eye over their own property and not so often trust them to the hands of drunken managers and overseers. These latter, who wrongfully whip the Negroes, debauch their wives and children, and neglect the sick, are the ruin of the Colony and willfully drive to the woods such quantities of stout, handsome people who by their sweat got your subsistence and without whose hands your Colony must drop to nothing—and to whom at last in this pitiful manner you are glad to come and ply for friendship."

This warning was currently the talk of all Paramaribo, along with the reference to slavery in Suriname by the French writer Voltaire.

In his latest novel, *Candide*, a satire on philosophical optimism, he has gone so far as to use our Colony as an example for his views of New World slavery. For indeed, he has written: *Candide spoke in Dutch to a Negro with no left leg and no right hand wearing only a pair of blue cotton drawers lying on the ground by the road. When he inquired what the man was doing in that horrible state, the Negro replied, 'It is the custom. We are given a pair of cotton drawers twice a year as clothing. When we work in the sugar mills and the grindstone catches a finger, they cut off the hand; when we try to run away, they cut off a leg. Both these things happened to me. This is the price paid for the sugar you eat in Europe.'*

Such audacity paints ill a picture of our hard work and endeavor to keep up with the demands for our products in Europe. Where before I admired Voltaire, now I despise him as a philosopher sold out to politics.

To the young Lieutenant I said, "I understand the article of the treaty about pursuing runaway slaves for the Dutch is still a point of contention."

"Aye," he answered, "but this could be modified for situations where the slaves were ill-treated and for those who lived already for a long time in the jungle."

"In any case," said Governor Cromelin, "a peace settlement with the Ndjuka Maroons implies by its very nature that they are now allies of the Dutch government."

Though sorry he missed the expedition, Carl Otto is now an important member of the Court of Police, and acknowledges his health has been such that he could probably not have survived a hazardous jungle trek. Still, he maintains great interest in anything that has to do with the accomplishment of Governor Mauricius' idea of peace.

"This is not ended just yet," he cautions, "The rebels may well change their minds, and a year is a lengthy amount of time during which any number of things might happen."

38

La Solitude, January 1762

In a back upstairs game room that I had made over for them, I sat on a low stool next to Sutje and Philip Samuel. They are learning to play whist and the three of us had been thus occupied for the better part of an hour. Outside, the tropical afternoon rain drummed the roof of the house, a comfortable tapping drone.

"*Tante* Elisabeth, you are cheating!" declared Liesbeth's son. A precocious child who has just celebrated his eleventh birthday, he regarded me with serious intent.

"*Moi?*" In mock surprise I put my hand to my bosom. Sutje leaned forward to examine the cards, which stood out in stark contrast against the dark *broen ati* hardwood of the low table, carved in the formal designs of the Maroon style.

"I don't see it," she said, looking up at me.

"That's because it isn't true. I won fair and square, but that was a nice try, my boy."

Philip Samuel yawned, as if to let me know he didn't take the game seriously. "I'm hungry. Can we have some more of those sweet buns Dorotea made this morning?"

"I don't think there are any left, but let's go see if there's some fruit." I stretched out my legs, then got up from the stool. "Sutje, put the cards away."

"Why me?" she asked. "It's his turn."

"Sutje, do as you're told."

I tried to make my voice firm, but I fear I've spoiled these two to the extent that they rarely mind me. They well know they are a joy in my life. On the one hand I want to raise obedient children, yet on the other I marvel at their different personalities and desires for independence. Still, they show themselves to be somewhat unreserved in conversation.

At twelve years, Sutje shows a great delicacy of heart and is already a real Mulatto beauty. Her studies are excellent, and in addition to reading and writing in Dutch, she is becoming versed in French as well. There will be plenty of time later for her to learn to mind a husband. I'm so grateful that Carl Otto agreed to have Liesbeth's children come to live with us, but all too soon I fear this happy domesticity will end. I dare not think of how I shall get along without them in the house.

Downstairs in the drawing room, Carl Otto was seated in a comfortable velvet armchair reading a well-worn book I had not seen before. I sent the children to find the nearest servant to bring us all some fruit, and arranged myself at the end of the sofa nearest to him.

"What are you reading?" I asked.

Carl Otto sighed and closed the book. "A novel by an Englishwoman named Aphra Behn. It's called *Oroonoko*."

"Not good?"

"It begins in Africa and comes to Suriname, but she wrote it eighty years ago so it's dated, but an amusing history." Carl Otto smiled, but his face wore an expression of boredom. "It romances the slaves a great deal."

I took the book from his hands and opened the cover. "How did you come by it?"

"Maryk had it. She enjoyed it very much and I couldn't say 'nay' when she offered to lend it to me."

We both looked up as Sutje and Philip Samuel burst into the room, followed by a servant boy bearing a carved wooden tray loaded with sliced oranges, pineapples and mangoes. We had just begun to sample the fare when the houseman came to make an announcement. He addressed Carl Otto, as the man of the house.

"A carriage arrives, *masera*."

Posthaste the fruit was abandoned in the interest of determining who our visitors might be. As one we rose from our seats and hurried to the front door. The rain had stopped and the sun was bright and hot. Everywhere water dripped from palm and foliage and flower to the spongy ground, and the air gave off a heavy fragrance of pungent earth and jungle decay.

How delighted we were to see Hendrik van Steenberch with his little family. He is now the proud father of two sons, quite handsome and lively, and a new baby daughter. The boys bounded up the brick stairs to the porch, laughing and happy to greet Sutje and Philip Samuel. Maryk is an easy mother and Willem calls her "a most agreeable wife." They were welcomed into the drawing room and tea was called for.

In his exhilaration to see his old friend, after calling "Hello" Carl Otto fell into a fit of coughing. This habit has become more frequent in the past year, and each time it occurs my concern increases.

A most agreeable visit followed, with the four children begging permission to take their leave to pursue more adventurous activities outdoors. Upon their departure, our discourse took a serious direction, with Hendrik bringing with him news of yet another military expedition to Ndjuka territory.

"What an opportunity to explore the area and put the eight known villages on the map!" Carl Otto exclaimed. He sucked heavily on his pipe stem as he listened to his friend describe the details of the government's latest attempt to establish the peace with the Maroons.

"And to bring the promised tribute to the chiefs?" I asked.

Hendrik scoffed. "In the past fourteen months, almost all the meetings where gifts have been distributed have ended in filthy brawls and complaints."

"I can understand why no one is anxious to serve as *posthouder* in any of the villages," Carl Otto said. One of the articles of the peace treaty required the posting of military inspectors in Ndjuka villages. These *posthouders* would report any treaty violations.

"I think it's a good thing that in exchange the sons of the chiefs will come to Paramaribo to study how to read and write," I said. "And won't the Reformed Dutch Church want to educate them about the laws against multiple wives?"

According to Maroon custom, though kinship and the law of inheritance are determined by the bloodline of the mother, a man may take as many wives as he can afford to keep.

Carl Otto puffed on his tobacco and said nothing. Hendrik made a little laugh. "Ah—multiple wives." The idea seemed to amuse him. "Perhaps if the *posthouder* himself could have more than one woman under his roof to serve him hand and foot, our young officers would flock to the post."

Hendrik's little joke offended me. When I looked at Maryk her expression was as if she hadn't heard. I reached for the cedar tobacco box and yanked the lid open. A glance in the direction of Carl Otto told me he well knew my feelings on the subject. Even so, he smiled at his friend's jest.

. . .

Later in the evening, alone in our bedroom, I sat at my toilette table and fingered the embossed edges of the red velvet of Liesbeth's mask. "You are sorely missed, my dear," I murmured. "And soon so shall be your dear children."

The mosquito net over the big four poster fluttered with a night breeze, for I had opened the shutters of two windows to gain some relief from the oppressive weather. La Solitude was surrounded by the night songs of the insects and frogs of the forest.

"You are here?" I sensed her *jorka* in the room. "So you know," I whispered. "He has married a Dutchwoman, Geertruida Bleij, a divorcée. She owns the plantations Bleijenhoop and Bleijenrust and has a sickly little daughter."

The mask in my hands felt heavy. But you already know this, I thought.

I stood up and, clutching the mask, began to pace the hardwood floor. How could Samuel Loseke not marry Liesbeth whom he loved? But of course I knew the answer well enough. Samuel has given Hanssen, the family name of his mother, to his daughter and son by Liesbeth. Soon he will take them from my bosom into the house he'll now share with Geertruida. He will see that Sutje and Philip Samuel continue to be educated, and make a good marriage for the girl when she is grown.

While as a divorced woman Geertruida does not have the best reputation, she is happy to accept Samuel's two Mulatto children for the privileges and money she will now enjoy.

My morose thoughts were interrupted when Carl Otto entered the bedroom. He stopped in the doorway, as if he too felt the presence in the room of Liesbeth's *jorka*. He shook his head as if to shake off a waking fog, and asked, "With whom were you speaking?"

I stared at the mask, then set it on my toilette table and shrugged.

"What do you think of Geertruida Bleij?"

Carl Otto's eyes narrowed. "She will make Samuel happy, I think. He needs a mother for his children."

"They've been well in our house." I whirled around to face him. "And Liesbeth made him happy!"

"Betje, Liesbeth is dead." The look on Carl Otto's face was hard. "I'm happy Samuel has found someone agreeable."

"If only he could have married Liesbeth..."

Carl Otto sighed, made two hoarse coughs, and sat down in one of the brocaded armchairs. "Ring for a servant to remove my boots."

"Do you think he didn't want to marry her?"

"Of course he wanted to marry her."

"Do you want to marry me?"

Carl Otto placed his hands on his knees and stared at me. Why didn't he answer? Was he weighing his words, concerned for their effect?

"Are you going to ring for the servant or are you going to remove my boots?"

Even as I turned towards the bell-pull to do his bidding, I said, "I suppose it's better that you're not legally married to a Negress whore, no matter how free or rich."

Carl Otto regarded me with a look of disdain. "We've been over this subject too many times," he said in a slow, careful voice.

I jerked the bell pull. "When will you speak to the Court of Police? Surely, as a respected member, you can speak up now."

"It's not that..." his words trailed off.

"Then *what?*" I demanded, my voice louder and more

high-pitched than I'd intended.

"Now is not the time. His Excellency's cares are otherwise occupied."

"And when *will* be the time? It's certainly too late for Liesbeth and Samuel and Nanette and Emilius, but what about you and me?"

The pained look on Carl Otto's face caused me to freeze where I stood.

"You never wanted to be married to a black woman!" I accused, my voice harsh with emotion. Before my eyes the room took on a red tint.

The Negro slave had just entered the room. Carl Otto rose from the armchair, brushed the man aside and strode for the door, his boots resounding on the mahogany floor.

"You will *not* give up! I'm tired. I'll not hear more."

He slammed the door behind him, and I screamed, *"If you won't do it, I will!"*

39

Paramaribo, April 1762

When the heavens open to deliver their watery gift of the wet season, the far side of the Suriname River is obscured. The resulting feeling of being closed in leaves me irritable and restless.

The hostages and chief officers of the Ndjuka and Saramaka Maroons arrived this day in Paramaribo and were invited to be entertained at the Governor's own table. A treaty of fourteen articles has been signed by two white commissioners and sixteen of Granman Araby's Ndjuka captains. A peace has also been concluded for the third time between the Colony and the Saramaka Maroons, who are now governed by a Negro called Wii instead of their former *kapten*, Adoe, who has died this past year.

They were paraded in state through the town in His Excellency's private carriage and, though wetly bedraggled, thin, and giving off a musky odor, I thought they carried about their shoulders an air of insolent pride. On the porch of the governor's mansion the Maroons had to be dried off by His Excellency's own slaves so that water would not be carried onto the polished hardwood floors of the entry way.

The rebels ate of the hearty fare laid out before them ravenously and without shame. Carl Otto made a discreet cough into his lace handkerchief and watched them from across the table. Though he is still weak he had insisted upon accepting the opportunity of attendance to this banquet.

I found the rebels to be of curious interest. "Why would people prefer to endure such a perilous and uncertain existence in the dangerous jungle," I whispered to Carl Otto, "when they could sleep in comfort surrounded by wives and children and family and friends in a sturdy plantation cabin?"

He shook his head. It is obvious from the way their black skin stretched over their bones that hunger has been their constant companion. What misery must they feel to watch their babes and those they love whimper and cry for lack of regular sustenance? I wondered as I was served a dish of roast venison stew. To be hungry must surely be of the most unpleasant discomfort.

There was another atmosphere about the gathering that had nothing to do with the peace with the Saramaka rebels. It was apparent that people are talking about us, as both Carl Otto and I garnered querying looks and unusual stares from our neighbors. After enjoying the meal and adjourning to the drawing room, I commented on this to Carl Otto.

"Isn't it obvious?" he asked.

Carl Otto had at length agreed to speak to the Court of Police about the marriage laws, I suspect to prevent me from doing it myself. How vexed I was with him when he reported that the Court of Police had laughed at him when he mentioned the subject of unjust marriage laws.

"I'll have you know I was greatly chastised for wasting valuable Council time on such an issue of domesticity," he said. "Betje, no one but you is interested in changing these laws."

A flush came over me and I searched around the stuffed cushions of the sofa for the fan I had just had in my hand. How could I have thought these (white) people would ever allow a white person to marry a full-blooded Negro? These laws, nearly one hundred years established, are too ingrained in our little Colonial society to warrant serious inspection by such men. Nevertheless I am determined to pursue my course, for I am entitled to have Carl Otto as my husband.

The Governor's hired musicians began to play an oratorio by Georg Friedrich Handel, and the attendant members of our society paid scant attention. Indeed, they continued to gossip and chatter among themselves. The Ndjukas and Saramakas, however, appeared to be stunned by the sounds emanating from the violins, flutes, clavicin, and especially the oboe. They stared in a kind of untamed rapture, like animals stilling themselves in the forest to await the next move of the predator. Even after the musical movements came to an end and there was slight applause, they made no visible response.

"Ah, here you are."

I looked up to see Nanette's round face smiling at me, her pink silk fan in one hand and a full glass of claret in the other. She flounced her skirts about in a great show of arrangement as she sat down next to me. Carl Otto bowed and excused himself, no doubt to pursue more political conversation among his collegues.

Nanette lowered her voice. "I was speaking to Anna about poor Geertruida," she said. The death of Geertruida Loseke's little daughter is the talk of the moment. It came upon the child after just a few days of fever and delirium. There was hardly time to consult a white doctor, let alone send for Granman Quassie.

"Geertruida and Samuel are heartbroken," Nanette said. Her look was accusing, as if she thought I felt nothing.

"I am saddened by the death of any child, even that of a white woman such as *vrouw* Geertruida," I said, feeling defensive.

"*Gra'man* Quassie says the girl had a very sad *'kra*, and many *wintis* in conflict with each other."

"That would make anyone ill."

"You scoff, little sister, while all around you the spirit forces make their bidding, whether or not you care." She shook her pink fan at me.

Her words were as vinegar to my tongue. "Don't call me 'little sister.' I'm forty-seven years old! I detest such childish talk."

Nanette shrugged, laid down her fan and opened her reticule to search for her clay pipe. I rose, leaving her alone on the sofa, and moved towards the other side of the room in hopes that movement would dispel my vexation.

Carl Otto appeared at my side. His pallor was pale, and he touched his hand to the lace cuff at my elbow. "Let us depart, my dear. I've seen enough of the rebels and I'm weary of such diversion."

I shook off his hand, and smoothed my skirts. "Call for the carriage, then."

"You'll not come with me?"

"Nay. I have business here that is incomplete."

He opened his mouth, then closed it, as if he'd thought better of speaking. He nodded, and coughed. "As you wish, *mevrouw*." His tone was polite and indifferent.

His posture was very erect as he walked away. I wanted to call him back, but in truth I had nothing further to say to him. I could think of little else than my chosen road, the one that would lead me to success or ruin. Yet how could my reputation be any further sullied than it already is? What value is the title of free Negress when it is so often bastardized by my neighbors as *free whore?*

Across the room, Governor Cromelin stood speaking with Hendrik and two other members of the Court of Police, de Beauveser and Marlin.

They nodded in acknowledgment of my approach.

"A word with you, gentlemen," I announced, vowing to speak boldly my intentions.

"*Vrouw* Samson," said His Excellency. His expression was polite, his eyes unreadable. With great effort I focused my thoughts on the one direction over which I've spent so many moments in serious contemplation.

"I have a matter of concern I would like to petition before the Court of Police," I said.

The four men whose attention I now had waited for me to continue. My mouth was dry, and I wished I'd had another glass of claret before speaking.

"It is a matter of the marriage laws that I believe needs be addressed."

The two gentlemen on Hendrik's left smiled, while the Governor's expression remained impassive. Hendrik, I suspect, privy as I'm sure he is to Carl Otto's business, knew well what was coming.

Governor Cromelin asked, "What is it, *mevrouw*?"

"The marriage laws are unfair to women such as myself

and I would see them changed."

The heat rose in my bosom as one of the Council men rolled his eyes to the ceiling.

His Excellency, ever the smooth politician, recognized sincerity in the urgency of my tone. Rather than encourage me further, however, he said, "Would you be so kind, *vrouw* Samson, as to make a formal petition in writing for our consideration?"

He underestimates me if he thinks I cannot write and in this manner hopes to put me off. I also recognized when I was being dismissed from the conversation.

"An excellent suggestion, Your Excellency." I bowed my withdrawal. "You may be assured that I shall take it to heart."

<u>40</u>

<u>Plantation Clevia, November 1762</u>

I'll not soon forget how Carl Otto reacted when I told him of my conversation with Governor Cromelin and my intention to write a petition to the Court of Police to affect a change in the colonial marriage laws.

"Are you mad?" he cried, then fell into a fit of coughing that left him weak and frightened me greatly. When he could continue, his voice was hoarse. "Cannot you leave well enough alone? Our affairs are in order! We live well together and I desire no other woman. Why is that not enough for you?"

I do not know whether I backed down because my desire made him so unhappy or, as happens during the demanding dry season, other matters pressed upon my time. In any case, months went by and I did nothing about a petition.

How remote the matter of living in sin seems to me now. Nine days past, I have lost the very one most dear in all the world! Granted that Carl Otto's constitution had not been strong in recent years, but I had given no thought to the day I might experience his loss.

Just two Tuesday mornings past in our grand house on Heerenstraat we breakfasted together on chocolate and sliced mangos. I babbled away about the current state of our various businesses, when from across the breakfast table I heard a whisper of passing breath. It was so soft I might have thought it was Liesbeth's *jorka*, had I not looked up. I saw Carl Otto relax, and his head fall to one shoulder. A great shock passed through me, as if black storm clouds had opened and a jagged scar of lightening had sought me out. I cried out and servants came running. Someone sent for the white doctor. By the time he arrived they had Carl Otto laid out upon the sofa in the drawing room, a linen cloth shrouding his form.

For a long time after the doctor left I sat in the armchair across the room, running my fingers back and forth over the various indentations of the emboss upon the velvet, and stared at the still form on the sofa.

My great regret—my one regret—is that I do not have a child by which to remember my love, a son or daughter to comfort me in my hour of grief and to be a comfort to me for the remainder of my life upon this earth. Oh, Carl Otto, what forces of mystery conspired to torture us by withholding the thing our wealth could not buy? What God did we offend—what ancestor ignore? I cannot just now even think about how I will live in the future, alone without the man who stood by me for so many years, no matter my mood or fancy.

My dear consort's body now rests in the burial ground at the *Nieuwe Oranjetuin* cemetery. I have ordered a most elaborate marble headstone to be made, and the stonecarver assures me he will begin the work immediately upon the arrival of marble block from the next merchantman. The service was held at the Dutch Reformed Church, with all my family in attendance. La Vallaire even came in from Vlaardingen with her four Samboe children, now tall young men and girls of marriageable age. In a mourning shroud of black veils I was grateful to be able to hide my face from public view. I thus passed through the service with a feeling of not really being in attendance, but rather observing everything from a faraway place.

Oh, what I would give just now to lie up in my bed, numb my feelings with laudanum, and wait while the world slips by, but whether I will it or not, there are responsibilities which must be acknowledged. All our properties needed to be inventoried. As executor, Carl Otto's friend Hendrik van Steenberch gave the sworn civil servant, *meneer* Dozen, the order to inventory the estate with *meneer* Kock, the planter Vieira, and Hendrik himself as witnesses. Of course as owner of half of the estate, I had input, and Hendrik has been thorough, if remote. His voice was courteous when he announced, "Your assets total over 200,000 guilders, *mevrouw*."

Before Carl Otto's demise Hendrik and Maryk had called me Elisabeth, and I wondered what had happened to so affect our friendship, but I made no comment upon it.

"The brothers of Carl Otto Creutz inherit half of Clevia and half of La Solitude," said Hendrik. "I will see to the letters that must be sent to them in Germany."

"Aye, so be it," I murmured, picking up a porcelain figurine of English hunting dogs that Carl Otto had treasured. Again I felt flood my body the heat that foretold tears to come. How can I bear to look at each of our possessions and know his fingers will never caress them again? How can I look upon my own flesh in the long toilette glass in our bedroom and know I will never see him standing behind me, sliding his hands over the curves of my bare body?

The business of the inventory at Clevia occupied three miserable, sultry days. Nanette, who had been so inconsolable as to be incapacitated at the deaths of her own consorts, now came to Clevia to lend me sisterly support, bearing the mourning clothes she no longer wore.

"You know you must rest during the heat of the day," she said, upon seeing me. "Your dress is damp and needs be changed."

In truth, I had not considered my habit, which I had not changed since early morning. I had no interest in the clothes she brought, as they are way too voluminous for my figure. Instead of answering, I waved my hand in weak acknowledgement. I wandered the room in circles, unsure of what needed to be done next.

"I can see the weather is affecting you," she scolded. "Upstairs now, little sister."

Heedless of the hated expression she used, I let her lead me to the bedroom, where she shooed away the house slaves and made me remove my stomacher and skirts. The fabric felt limp and sticky in my hands.

"I must write to Amsterdam for bolts of black satin and lace," I murmured. Nanette made motherly shussing sounds and gently pushed me back upon the pillows. She prepared a draught of laudanum and honey, after which she left and I fell asleep, vowing that I shall forever mourn for Carl Otto in spite of the fact that he never became my legal husband.

. . .

When Hendrik van Steenberch first came to our house on Heerenstraat to discuss Carl Otto's estate, he recounted an incident he had witnessed which would have dearly upset my Society Captain. In horror I thought, I'm glad Carl Otto did not live to see this.

"The Maroons have become positively insolent," Hendrik said. This did not seem to be an appropriate time for such a discourse, but perhaps he began this recital to distract my mind from my sorrow. I forced myself to consider his words.

"No doubt this is their reaction to the treaty, which many planters believe still to be a grave mistake. By way of derision and independence, the behavior of the excused runaways has become overbearing."

The back of the chair felt unforgiving against the small of my back and to be polite I nodded, knowing he would continue nonplussed.

"Just yesterday I saw one of them brandish his new, silver-headed cane under the nose of the planter C.N. Detweiler and his wife. They were accompanied by *vrouw* Peltser and her daughter."

He paused to wait for me to acknowledge that I knew them. I just stared at him, and he continued. "From *meneer* Zobre he demanded liquor and money. Do you know the black was even so bold as to remind them that as a slave he had murdered their parents and friends and husbands?"

I started at this, thinking that for such offense Carl Otto would have struck such an upstart, no matter his colour, smartly about the shoulders. Hendrik went on to talk of how Governor Cromelin's own coffee plantation has been plundered by Saramaka runaways, which he called "the Nassij Negroes" in reference to their owner.

What did I care that two of His Excellency's slaves, Kofi

and Jupiter, were taken by runaways who may have been from the Jew Nassij's plantation? Or that *vrouw* Peltser and Juliaana had been held up on the street for tribute? These happenings are nothing to me.

In truth I do not feel anything for anyone else, my own *'kra* consumed with the loss of my beloved Carl Otto.

41

Paramaribo, February 1763

"Nanette wants to buy a summer house at Pad van Wanica," I said aloud, fingering the bolt of black silk that had just arrived from France via the Holland merchant ship. Hazy afternoon sunlight filtered through the orange trees outside to splatter the mahogany floor of the bedroom with speckles of light. I had been alone at my knee-hole desk all the day, making coorespondence, consulting my accounts, and considering the summer house purchase.

"What do you think of the idea?"

Did the pleasant breeze from the river shift in response?

"Can you show me a sign?"

I unfolded several ells of the fine fabric and, posing in front of the long toilette glass, draped them about my hips. Carl Otto had loved the ormulu carvings adorning the top of this mirror frame. A reflection dim in the silvered backing of the plate glass appeared—it was Carl Otto, so handsomely dressed in his short jacket, military wig and leather cap, all the blue and scarlet of the Society uniform, Carl Otto standing at attention. I fancied a look upon his face that said he approved of my selection for yet another mourning dress.

I have this day written a letter to Pieter Reydenius in Amsterdam to buy the halves of Clevia and La Solitude inherited by the brothers Creutz. I'm happy that Carl Otto approves of this, for I have instructed my solicitor to be as free as necessary with the price.

"Now I must know what you think of the summer house purchase."

Nanette presses me daily to make a decision about the property at Pad van Wanica, upon which she now has her heart set. In truth I haven't made time to see it, as it doesn't matter much what it is like. I doubt I myself will spend much time there.

Though three months now in his grave at the Dutch Reformed Church cemetery of *Nieuwe Oranjetuin*, Carl Otto is still with me. His *jorka* is strong in my presence. At first I was somewhat surprised by this, but not unnerved. It's natural that he who was so bonded with me in life should continue to be bonded with me now.

"He's still disturbed by your persistance in that marriage business," claims Nanette. She speaks with such clarity I wonder how she can be so sure.

"Oh, nay," I objected. "More likely he is reluctant to leave everything he has loved so much." Then I recalled that she enjoys regular conversations with the *jorkas* of Emilius and Wijnand so perhaps she has spoken to Carl Otto as well. This does not seem strange to me now.

But there is a gnawing thing in my belly that belies this declaration. In truth I wish I had not pressed him so much, yet then I wish I had been more persistent. I ask myself how a legal marriage would have changed my situation now? I would still be without the man on whom I have spent all my life's affections.

I wiped the moisture from my eyes. The matter is that Carl Otto was a good man and did not deserve to hear his neighbors call *whore* the woman with whom he lived.

So of my own mind have I been these past months that I fear I was no comfort to Nanette or the rest of my family when La Vallaire departed this earth in January. I attended the church service, but only in body, I fear. Again layered in black from head to shoe, I paid scant attention to her children, Pieter, Jan Simon Petrus, Hendrik Petrus and Nanette Suzanna, all now of marriage age. Looking upon them serves to remind me of my own advancing age, and all that might have been.

"You should rent Toevlught to Pieter Planteau," advised

Hendrik in a meeting shortly after La Vallaire's passing. The man has become one of my close advisors, though he still does not call me Elisabeth. "Pieter is distraught at his mother's death and wants to leave *foto*, but not to live at Vlaardingen, and you need to free yourself of so many responsibilities."

Hendrik is thinking that I'm no longer a young woman, I know. But the white doctor says my constitution is strong and my water clear, and indeed I have few physical complaints. In any case, I will probably act upon this advice, for in truth I have little inclination to business.

"The season has been fortunate, your crops healthy and abundant," he added.

At Welgemoed, just as the coffee harvest commenced, a babe of my nephew Dikje was born to the fifteen-year-old Adjoeba, his childhood friend and now concubine. The child is also my property since Adjoeba has belonged to me since the day she was born at Welgemoed. If she were free, Dikje might marry her, even though he has a free wife in Paramaribo, with whom he has yet to have children. Uneducated Africans who are slaves or Maroons and free Negroes often take more than one wife according to what they can afford, but the Dutch Reformed Church objects, and Colonial law says he cannot marry a slave.

"What of the carriage house?" I asked. The rooms above the carriage house, where the stableman usually lives, have been vacant for several months now.

"The church organist desires to let the place," Hendrik said.

"The unmarried Braband?"

"Aye, the one."

"He lives alone?"

"Aye."

"I don't want to rent to an unmarried man without a concubine," I said. "They make all manner of mischief, and do not keep good house."

"He's in his forties, a pious man," Hendrik assured me. "He has a good position as director for a lumber company, and he owns Nuda, the country home on the Pad van Wanica that is situated adjacent to the summer house Nanette wants."

"The three hundred hectares to the south? Why, I believe

there are more than twenty slaves working there."

Hendrik nodded, adding, "Braband has a good reputation."

"Christoph Policarpus Braband has no reputation that I know of," I said. "That is, 'tis true I've not heard anyone speak ill of him. All right. See to the matter."

"And what of—"

I pressed my thumb and forefinger to my temples. "Oh, I've had enough of business for today. Cannot more matters wait until tomorrow?"

Hendrik looked up from the open ledgers. "Aye, *mevrouw*, as you wish."

Before he departed my house he made mention of bans posted at the Dutch Reformed Church. "Anna Buys Ouwater-Julien has just married for the third time, to the Dutch planter Johan Godfried Clemen."

As the door closed behind him I was thankful for the quiet in the house.

"A third white husband!" I moaned out loud.

I am sure the words I heard in response came from Carl Otto's *jorka*.

At forty-three, she's still a most handsome Mulatto woman.

42

Pad van Wanica, June 1763

The new summer home at Pad van Wanica, though smaller, reminds me of the dwelling house at the plantation La Diligence, which I visited on 23 June, in the bend of the Suriname River at Joden Savanne. I mention the excursion itself, the occasion being to visit some of my great-nieces and nephews and friends in the vicinity, to note a meeting with a most charming young Captain of the Society troops, one J.C. Dörig.

At dinner he was found to be quite agreeable, insisting I call him by his given name, Jacobus. Being thus seated next to one another, we enjoyed a merry discourse that continued late into the evening with our host and hostess serving brandy and tobacco on the very fine mahogany dumb-waiter in the drawing room.

Our host is recently the recipient of a fine English terrestrial globe on a tripod stand of oak which he insisted on presenting forth for our edification.

"Here is Suriname, and here flows the upper Suriname River," said Captain Dörig. He took my hand in his own and led my fingers to indicate the spot.

"Where is your destination?" I asked.

"This far." He indicated a point on the varnished composition surface. "From which point we shall cross overland to the upper Saramacca River."

"Could not you have gone all the way up the Saramacca as

previous expeditions have?" I was thinking of Carl Otto's expedition of 1749.

The young Captain Jacobus Dörig smiled at me. "There have proven to be a greater abundance of *sulas* on the Saramacca, making this route now a more practical one."

"Aye," I murmured. "I've heard tell of the treacherous rapids of the upper Saramacca."

Captain Dörig's mission is to fulfill the most respected resolution of the Honorable Court of Police dated 2 October 1762, whereby was inserted the instructions for how to behave with the Bush Negroes of the Upper Saramacca. His instructions are to stay with them and to negotiate peace with the two remaining villages and try to persuade them to agree, and having done this, to get them to swear to it.

Upon my return I related this to Nanette and Christoph, who were eager to hear any news of such a peace-making expedition.

Christoph Policarpus Braband has become quite friendly to Nanette and I. He has proven to be a most interesting man, pretty and fastidious. We delight in the company of our neighbor as he is seldom without an amusing story to tell. I have even confided to him that I am again thinking of confronting the Court of Police to have the marriage laws changed. Since he sees humor in most every situation, I had suspected he might laugh at this, but he did not.

This evening was passed most enjoyably, as the three of us smoked our pipes, enjoyed several bottles of claret, and played games in the drawing-room of the summer house.

"You must join us for Nanette's *bigi yari*," I said to Christoph.

His limpid blue eyes twinkled. "It would be my pleasure to join you anytime, *Vrouw* Elisabeth."

"I want my *bigi yari* birthday party here," declared Nanette, now fifty, yet sporting just a few springy grey curls upon her temples.

"One as bright as your orange dress?" I teased. Nanette still prefers in her habit bright, happy colours.

She tucked an errant curl of hair, appearing like spun silver, under her lace cap and smiled.

"Aye, and why not?"

"Aye, why not indeed?" inquired Christoph. "And how

about a full orchestra for musical entertainment?" He waved his hands about as he hummed a quick little air and tapped his foot in time under the walnut games table.

"You could be our guest organist," I suggested.

"I want an abundance of orange blossoms and orchids tied up in silver ribbons," Nanette announced. "And no new slaves! I want experienced house servants."

Christoph said, "Certainly not anyone who looks like those wretches you bought last week with the tribal markings all over their faces."

Christoph accompanied me on a recent outing to Plattebrug when no one else was available at the moment. I was able to enjoy his conversation as I conducted my business of purchasing Africans newly arrived in the Colony. Our discourse had been merry, and I had found it easy to indulge in pleasurable laughter.

At midnight, our charming neighbor took his leave and returned to Nuda. I was waiting for the house slaves to finish putting away the silver so I could lock the cabinet when Nanette commented, "*Meneer* Braband admires you greatly."

"What do you think of Captain Dörig?" I asked, remembering the man I had met the night I had spent at La Diligence.

"What about him?"

"I should like to find a suitable white man to marry," I said.

Nanette frowned and twisted her rotund body, weary of the tightness of the stomacher she had worn all day. "If you'll pardon my saying so, I thought that business was ended when Carl Otto left us."

"Well, why should it be ended?" I asked, annoyed by her remark. "Why should I not make them change the law anyway? I deserve to have a white husband as much as any Dutch planter's wife."

"And you are thinking that Captain J.C. Dörig is a good candidate for a legal marriage?"

"Why not?"

"Little sister, you only met him once. He may not be willing."

"Don't call me little sister!" I exclaimed, my face heating in anger. "He'll be willing enough when he learns how financially comfortable I am."

"But you don't love him." Disapproval was evident on Nanette's round face.

"I'll never love again," I said. "But I will have a white husband."

43

Plantation Clevia, September 1763

Under the guise of the very necessary act of overseeing the cutting of a section of cane sugar, I have this afternoon arrived by tent-boat at Clevia. The travel has exhausted me, as even though it is the dry season we were deluged upon by a thunderous rainstorm that lasted the better part of midday. The tilt-windows were secured, but a leak was discovered in the roof of the tent-boat that resulted in muddy water that sloshed about my feet and a damp chill that permeated my being. On the walk from the landing to the plantation house I lost my footing on a muddy step where the gravel had washed away, and was unable to recover my balance. One clogged foot flew out from under me. I fell aground, soiling my habit and causing a severe strain to my ankle.

"You're hiding," Nanette had scoffed, when I had informed her yesterday of my intended journey.

"Perhaps." In truth I couldn't wait to quit the activity and bustle of the town. "In any case you're welcome to accompany me."

"Not now," she said, yawning and fanning herself in warm and humid air. "I'll remain here in *foto* and fend off the *mofokoranti*."

"There's no need to be sarcastic," I said, fuming at her attitude.

My sister had laughed. " 'Successfully arrived this day at Paramaribo is Captain J.C. Dörig and his family,' " she said, imitating the announcement of Hendrik, who had brought the news.

Captain Dörig, having arrived at the military post at plantation Victoria on 17 September, met up there with his wife and child. He had with him two hostages of the Saramaka allies and eight of their representatives. Their party continued on with overnight stops at plantations Blauwe Berg, Rama and La Diligence, arriving Paramaribo at 10:30 the evening of Wednesday, 21 September.

All *foto* now talks of my *faux pas,* along with the curiousity called "Twofinger" which the Captain brought back from his expedition to show the Honorable Court. According to the Saramakas met by Captain Dörig, a group of people has been discovered to the south of the Maroon villages at the heads of the Saramacca and Suriname Rivers. They called these black people "Twofingers" because they have just two fingers each on their hands and feet. The Saramakas describe them as very big people who deal with the Devil both by day and by night, can run faster than they through the forest, and answer to a female chief. I have not personally seen the speciman the good Captain brought back with him, but am told he has braided hair bound about his head.

"So I didn't know Jacobus Dörig was already married," I snapped. "At dinner at La Diligence he made no mention of wife or children."

"A natural error," Nanette said. Her ebony eyes were merry with this humour.

"Aye, a natural error." In my urgency to identify a white man worthy to consider as husband, my error had been in speaking aloud of my interest before learning fully of the man.

This unfortunate mistake on my part would not be so hurtful if Christoph had not related to me how hilarious Juliaana van Meel-Peltser had found the situation when she heard. My neighbor himself was now delighted to repeat the story to me, little knowing of my unpleasant history with the woman and her prosecutor husband.

To his credit, Christoph was kind and consoling when he saw that I did not respond in good humor.

"It will pass, Elisabeth," he said with great gentility.

"Tomorrow, as more people view the Twofinger, they will forget your error."

To distract me, he then told a wondrous tale of a carpenter he knew who had caused, by a miscalculation, a porch to collapse right out from under the person of a corpulent sugar cane planter.

The greenery of Clevia, with its sea breeze and orderly fields provides just the succor I need to plan another course of action. Thankfully, the dark storm had passed by the time I arrived, and when the sun returned late this afternoon, every leaf, stem and vine glinted with jewels of dew as if diamonds had been scattered about. I had planned a walk at dusk along the shell-graveled path atop the *dijk*, but my ankle had swollen so that I was forced to remain seated in a wicker chair on the porch instead. The sun disappeared in a blaze of orange and purple and I watched a fat moon rise while it was still dusk. A sweet breeze came up, so fragrant and comfortable that I felt sure I was accompanied by Carl Otto's *jorka*.

Aloud I mused, "I must now give this serious consideration. I cannot approach the Court of Police without a white husband to claim. Though given their reaction to your request, perhaps indeed this might not be the way to approach the situation."

Perhaps I should consider an appeal above their heads to a higher authority.

As I pondered that action, the breeze turned cool, and I sent for a shawl to wrap about my shoulders.

44

Paramaribo, February 1764

    I held my straw hat tilted at a low angle to shade my eyes from the sun, now high in the sky of late morning. As our carriage turned the corner onto the shell-gravel road leading to the office of the Commission of Marital Affairs I gripped the hand-railing to steady myself. When the carriage halted my driver alighted to help me down. The hand he extended was as dark as my own, but whereas mine was damp with sweat, his was cool and steady.
    Though my mind was clear of purpose, the world around me seemed to flutter with uncertainty. The leaves of the palms and tamarinds and mahogany trees danced in the breeze, nervous birds flitted from branch to branch, and even the carriage horse shook its mane in a shivering alertness. About me everything in the warm morning was moving, as I myself moved up the brick steps to enter the place where I would begin my journey to the final realization of my fondest desire.
    My arm was held steady by Christoph as we entered the somber interior of the staid building. Its imposing two-story ediface of red brick with its tall windows trimmed in black shutters seemed to me to reflect all that is organized and systematic about the Dutch Europeans. While I must have passed this building without thought countless times in my travels about the town, I did not realize until this moment how significant it could present itself.
    "The papers, boy."

My Negro servant who carried the oilcloth umbrella handed me the leather pouch containing the formal request, prepared by my solicitor, of the intention of Christoph and I to marry.

At the desk of the civil servant handling marriage requests, I took a handkerchief from the pocket of my burgundy satin skirt and held it to my nose. I handed the pouch to Christoph who in turn handed it to the civil servant. How long has it been, I wondered, since this representative of our Colonial government has bathed?

"*Vrouw* Elisabeth Samson." The man read my name at the top of the first document removed from the pouch and looked up, a question poised on his face.

"Aye."

"Christoph Policarpus Braband?" As he stared at Christoph his bushy grey brows collided with each other across his frown.

"Aye."

"This document appears to be a request of your intention to marry."

I nodded and Christoph said, "That's correct."

"Each other?" the man asked.

"Can you read?" I snapped. I had known this might be an occasion of unease, but had given no thought to the uncomprehending mentality of a civil servant.

The little white man, for he is easily a head shorter than myself, searched his desk for some spectacles with which to more closely examine the documents. As he perused the words again, his discomfort became apparent.

"*Vrouw* Samson," he began, then took a deep breath. "Are you not the free Negress Elisabeth Samson?"

"Aye, indeed I am."

"If you will excuse my saying so, *mevrouw*, it would appear that you and this white gentleman are wanting to marry, and I do believe such a marriage in the Colony is not permitted." His expression as he made this announcement took on a pompous air.

Christoph, who absently twirled a curl of his wig with his fingers, laughed at this.

"My dear man, we care not for your opinion in this matter. I do believe your duty is to file papers."

"Indeed, *meneer*," the flustered little man murmured, in haste recovering his composure. "It's no business of mine whom you want to marry."

In indignation, I had turned my back to them both, for in truth I could not bear the degrading tone of this discourse. Why must the lowliest civil clerk always brandish his small power in such a grandiose manner?

The questions that followed were appropriately relevent to the occasion, and when the paperwork was completed, we left the office of the Commission of Marital Affairs, I in great relief.

As he hailed our carriage, Christoph said with a dismissing laugh, "Such arrogance!"

. . .

Now you have succeeded in raising the issue to the height of public controversy and debate.

Carl Otto's *jorka* would not be still. On this bright sunny morning, two weeks after Christoph and I had visited the office of the Commission of Marital Affairs to file our intention to marry, I entered the building where the Court of Police met. I wanted to scream at the voice I understood so clearly, but instead I tightened my hold to the arm of my lawyer.

The Court of Police can be a most intimidating body, but the building itself is not unlike the Dutch Colonial architecture we see everywhere in *foto*—the well-built white clapboard with dark green trim on doors and windows, with perhaps a wider red brick stoop than most and ornate iron railings at each side. The interior courtroom itself is quite expansive, lined on two sides with tall windows through which the daylight poured, hazy from the heat. I did not know if the sweat atop my bosom was from the heat and humidity or the natural nervous anxiety within me.

Josephus de Cohue's neat, trimmed beard was no longer black, but cotton white. He looked up at me and patted my hand. "We have been down this road before, *mevrouw*, and we shall again prevail."

Confident words, I thought, coming from a man who

himself, as a Jew, is forbidden a seat in Colonial government. Twenty-five years ago I had believed every word he uttered. Now well I know the duplicity of government, and my belief in the impartiality of the gentlemen I was about to face was as dead as my dear brother-in-law, Frederik Coenraad Bosse.

With much perseverance de Cohue had gained an appearance for us before the Court to argue my case for legal marriage. This was more likely granted to cause the gentlemen of the Court to appear balanced and unbiased, their reputations intact, if later questioned on the issue by the Society.

Whatever the outcome, I hope you find satisfaction.

De Cohue escorted me to a seat where I would be next to him at the heavy wooden table facing the dais of the Leader of the Court. I held my head high with purpose as I smiled and nodded greetings to the gentlemen already in attendance and those now entering the large room. Every one of the planters who sits on the Court of Police is known to me, as well as many of the members of the Commission of Marital Affairs, also represented here today. Hendrik Van Steenberch and Johan Vieira are old friends of Carl Otto's who were most helpful in the settling of the inventory of his estate. I felt sure I could count on them for support.

His Excellency Governor Wigbold Cromelin, his wig already limp from the humid air, arrived and took his place to the right of the Leader of the Court. I fiddled with my closed fan while we waited for two members, Gallerman and Roux, who were late in arriving. His Excellency, who condones a relaxed gathering, did not make any note of disapproval.

De Cohue handed a sheaf of papers to the Leader of the Court, Aart Nepveu. The leader made a great ceremony of polishing and setting his spectacles upon his nose, but it seemed to me he paid little attention to the papers before him.

He began by saying, "We are gathered here today to discuss the request of the free Negress Elisabeth Samson and Christoph Polycarpus Braband to enter into legal marriage. This decision will affect the entire Colony, what with some members approving and some not approving such a marriage."

De Cohue stood and said, "His Excellency the Governor and the esteemed gentlemen of this Court are of the opinion that a law from the period of Governor Cornelis van Aerssen, Lord of Sommelsdijk, forbids marriages between a black person and a white person." His voice was clear as he still has all his teeth, though he is now a gentleman of advanced age.

"Aye," said Nepveu. "The text of the original laws of the Colony established by van Sommelsdijk state clearly, that 'All inhabitants are strictly forbidden to have relationships with black women or Indians.' We understand this very clearly to mean that sexual relations of any kind between free persons and slaves are naturally forbidden."

As these words were spoken I looked at Klaas Vieira, who had witnessed the inventory of my estates, who everyone knows keeps not one, but two black slaves as concubines, and not hidden away on his plantation, but right here in *foto*. Vieira's face wore no readable expression. In any case, I thought with disgust, I am not, nor ever have been, a slave.

My lawyer continued, "Your Honor, the text also forbids sexual relations between white and free Indians, but it doesn't mention relations between whites and free black women."

The planters looked at one another, until at length old de Beauveser tilted back his head the better to see through his spectacles, cleared his throat and said, "In the time of van Sommelsdijk's governorship, such a category no doubt did not exist!"

"Is it true, gentlemen, that nowhere is the document of this particular law to be found?" Governor Cromelin, beginning to look somewhat uncomfortable, searched the faces of the Council members and then turned to the commissioners of Marital Affairs. When no one spoke, he boomed, "Well?"

"Ahem. Your Excellency." The spokesman for the commissioners stood up, reluctance clear upon his face. "We, ah, have been forced to assume that said documents, which we are, in truth, unable to locate exactly, may well have been eaten by house lice."

Hendrik, seated to my left, rolled his eyes to the roof and leaned back in his chair, stretching his long legs out under the front of the table.

Roux, not the least flustered for having held up proceedings by arriving late, now spoke. "The reason for such a marriage today is that those black people, as they live with one another, otherwise live in sin. Mulattos and all sorts of combinations of people live in unapproved relationships, avoiding the church's wisdom and judgment."

Mulattos and combinations created by white men, I thought. *Indeed, as we would happily have done.*

"We assume that these two persons who are requesting to be married will do the same if we do not approve this marriage."

Voices rose as the members spoke out loud their reactions to Roux's declaration.

The sugar cane planter and Court member J. Marlin shouted, "Through this marriage she will mingle with white people, which is not the problem. Free black people who have too much power may create future problems! It will give our slaves the idea that they can become as we are!"

The commissioner who sat next to him, whom I had expected to sleep during the entire proceeding, murmured, "This Elisabeth Samson should stay amongst black people."

I felt my face flush, and de Cohue, aware of my discomforture, placed his hand upon my forearm.

Marlin continued, "We have a better and more noble character than they. While living in the midst of such strange people it is imperative that we maintain our might! It is ludicrous to think that she who is free, by attaching herself through a solemn marriage ceremony, can be like us and their children be our equals. Where is our responsibility as a higher race of whites?"

Nepveu began, "The Samson situation—"

This is what I'm now called? The *Samson situation*?

Governor Cromelin raised his hands and implored, "Gentlemen, gentlemen. Let us speak one at a time. Everyone will be heard."

This calmed the room, but only for a moment.

"The marriage from a judicial standpoint is a doubtful case." declared Nepveu, "Of course black people are like we, except they have different hairstyles, attitudes, and skin colour. Theologically, they are our brothers and sisters. We are all Adam's children."

Through a tall open window I observed three capuchin monkeys cavorting across the limbs of the tallest mahogany tree. See no evil, I thought.

De Cohue stated with a smile, "Your Honor. Let us not forget to consider that in any event this marriage is a financial advantage for the young man because the free black woman Elisabeth Samson is already very rich. Among her family are no expectations to inherit and it may even be assumed she will become increasingly wealthy in the coming years."

There's a great argument, I thought. As much as I admired my lawyer, I knew it was just a matter of time before my wealth entered into "the Samson situation."

Now Gallerman was acknowledged by the Leader of the Court. With exaggerated dignity, the white planter rose and said in a hardy voice that echoed off the high ceilings, "The reason against such a marriage is that it is disgusting! It's scandalous for a white person that he might because of lust or because of financial advantage consider such a marriage."

Oh, such cruel words!

Again the room erupted with raised voices.

"We are seeing in our time scandalous mingling unlike previously when our governor Johan de Goyer punished white women, if they were unmarried, with flogging, and married women who forgot themselves would be similarly brandished, with the death sentence ordered for the slaves."

In a loud voice, Hendrik addressed His Excellency. "It seems to me the issue here is the existing law that states 'no one of the Colony can marry with black people, and it is also against the law to have a concubine.' It is true that we cannot find this law in our archives as documents containing many of the laws have been lost."

"However," interjected de Cohue, "we can determine that the strange mixture of proper Europeans and mingling with local population has taken place. It is also a concern, Your Honor, that there are marriages without proper ceremonies."

"Would a white woman not want to go after black slaves," yelled a commissioner from the back of the room, "free them, and subsequently marry them? Or want to marry free black men?"

De Cohue waved his hand in a vain attempt to make himself heard, but no one listened now. The planters, whom I had heretofore thought of as somewhat civilized neighbors, shouted back and forth at one another their debatable opinions.

"The fact remains that marriages between white and black are prohibited and it's based on good argument!" the Leader of the Court said when the shouting wore down. "We see no solution for this dilemma. We therefore recommend...to pass on the final decision to the Directors of the Society."

I smiled to myself and nodded to my lawyer, for indeed that is just what I have already done.

Ah, Betje, my sable beauty, I fear you go too far.

"That would also allow us more time to review our archives"—Nepveu glared particularly at the Commissioners of Marital Affairs—"to see if there indeed exists a copy of the initial declaration of van Sommelsdijk."

The rest of this exhausting, humiliating day was spent in arguing over the appropriate verbage of a letter of appeal to refer the decision to the Directors of the Society of Suriname.

In the end, the draft to the Society read, *Honorable Gentlemen: We commission members have received from the marriage bureau a request for marriage from Christoph Polycarbus Braband, organ player in our Reformed Church, with the free black woman Elisabeth Samson, the one being a young man in his prime and the selected bride fifty years old. Our members of both the Court of Police and Commission of Marital Affairs found this request to be extraordinary and without precedent, and as such have determined that you must determine the outcome. We write Your Honors because we have discussed at great length to resolve this request, and we trust that you will be able to determine what the best solution would be: to permit such a marriage, or to prohibit such a marriage. We simply propose that you make a decision with the best interest of the country and church in mind.*

The letter went on in great detail to describe the marriage situation as seen by the white members of the Court and Commission.

Political ordinance indicates that Suriname marriages, according to God's law, are sinful and incestuous and all such marriages considered a disadvantage for society, including marriages which could be considered incestuous according to our principles. So that there is no doubt, Your Honors, we could create a law or renew a law forbidding such marriages as outlined in this request, but in such a loving and serious situation as a marriage we prefer that you, Your Honors, determine after lengthy pondering and consideration how to proceed.

In the meantime, in consideration for the future, we cannot allow persons conducting marriages outside the colony with black people to return. We also request that if this marriage is permitted all whites who commit such a marriage will be punished with incapacity, and will not be permitted to serve in our Colony. This is necessary in order to conserve the purity of Europeans. At the very least those working in government need to be white; these positions may not be filled by people of colour.

Respectfully submitted and requesting a favorable response.

We use this opportunity to compliment Your Honors and to complete our archives request to receive copies of minutes and resolutions.

Paramaribo 23 February, 1764

. . .

It was quite late in the afternoon by the time this missive was completed, and the gentlemen of the Court and Commission were weary of the proceedings. Voices were less forceful and several wigs appeared limp and askew. Many a coat had been removed, and ruffled silk and linen shirts were streaked with the white men's sweat.

Across the room I regarded Johan Vieira and Hendrik van Steenberch, who at this moment were in close conversation with each other. Hendrik, as former executor of Carl Otto's testament, trusted Johan Vieira, a witness during the inventory. Both gentlemen had been very good friends to Carl Otto and had been frequent guests in our home. Yet as members of the Court of Police they hedge and refuse to honor my desire for a legal marriage.

When I first realized this I thought their opinions might have been influenced by loyalty to my beloved Carl Otto, but now I see that they hold convictions of white supremacy. They all fear chaos, madness, and ruin.

Josephus de Cohue reached out to grab my arm to prevent me from rising. But he was too late and I now stood alone before His Excellency and the Leader of the Court. I stiffened and dug my nails into my palms, oblivious to the pain this caused. All eyes were upon me, and conversation halted.

With the bitter taste of bile in my mouth and no forethought, I shouted, "You force us to live in sin against the teachings of Jesus Christ and the Church! You should honor my desire for this legal marriage because I have no heirs, and when I die the property you so covet would thus return into white hands!"

To my utter horror, when I collapsed back into my chair, I was made to listen in disbelief as the honorable white gentlemen, in discourse amongst themselves, began to consider this as reasonable.

Well, so be it.

<u>45</u>

<u>La Solitude, July 1764</u>

 The familiar rains of the wet season that pounded the earth outside the house could not drown out the thoughts swirling in my mind of an act so abhorrent as to be indescribable. My morning tea sat cold in the china cup as I listened to the solicitor inform me in a most mechanical manner that my sister Nanette and I have inherited everything. The slaves Premier, Akoeba, Blanka, Willem, and Sander have been told they are to be bought free according to the testament, but two of them cannot be found. The remainder are no doubt at this very minute planning the new names they will take for themselves.
 Seventeen days past, the Maroons in the vicinity of the Kabbeskreek committed the most terrible carnage upon four plantations there, among them, Catharinas'burg, a plantation belonging to a distant cousin of Charloo's. The attacks, completely unexpected, had come at dawn. In the quiet of the same afternoon, when slaves and dogs and children had scattered and the fires began to abate, the bodies of the ravaged and dead lay already swollen and covered with flies. Two white plantation owners, three directors and the cousin, Catharina Opperman, were among them.
 Our family was never close to this woman, and I had never met her or visited her plantation, and now we benefit from this cousin without issue because she has fallen victim to ferocious adversity. I am again reminded that there is no balance in the world, and I wonder if this insane war between

the plantocracy and the runaways will ever end.

"You must write the request for manumission for the slaves," said the estate's solicitor. "They will be bought free out of the available monies."

Of a sudden, a vision of Lankmoedigheid came to mind. That plantation, next to Vlaardingen, had years ago finally been destroyed, burned to the ground by Maroons, and I am thankful that we were able to save little Quassie, now fifteen years old and learning a carpenter's trade at Vlaardingen. It seemed that everywhere along the snaking brown rivers our family is connected in some way by plantation land, planters, slaves, and runaways.

I rose from the breakfast table. "Are we quite finished?"

The solicitor for Catharinas'burg shuffled some papers and answered, "If you wish, *mevrouw*. The rest of this can wait a day or so."

I rang for a house servant to show the man to the door. I heard the slave's voice shouting to someone, and then the solicitor's footsteps as he braved the rain in a sprint from porch to carriage through clinging mud.

Was it raining the morning of the attack on Catharinas'burg? Did our cousin suffer greatly before her demise? The thought of the horrors perpetrated upon plantation women, both white and Coloured, in such events left me feeling as cold as the dark liquid left in the china cup. I must not allow myself to think of such things. As I watched the rain outside, I felt the need for human company, for even the familiarity of Carl Otto's *jorka*, which has replaced that of Liesbeth, is of little comfort.

"Bring my umbrella and fetch my carriage," I said to Kwasiba when she answered my summons. "I shall go calling this afternoon."

Even in the rain, I found myself turned away by one excuse or another from four of my neighbors. Hours later, discouraged, I returned to La Solitude and allowed Kwasiba to help me out of my dampened habit. Thus attired only in a fresh, dry teagown, I dismissed the girl and lay down upon the bed. The rococo moldings of the high white ceiling blurred as my eyes welled with tears of rage and frustration.

I well know why I was told my neighbors were not at home.

It's been nigh five months since Christoph and I flouted convention by submitting to the Commission of Marital Affairs our formal request of intention to marry, and everyone waits to see what the outcome will be.

The Dutch Reformed Church is in a quarrel over the situation. His Excellency would rather lose money on more music lessons for his daughters than risk his friendships and support among the planters by deciding in my favor, and so they all wait and hope the Society will make any unpleasant decision for them.

Needless to say, with such controversy surrounding my name, I have avoided even attending church services to hear divine worship. The first time I had appeared on the arm of Christoph had been a disaster, as Sophie Peltser had made outrageous comments to me regarding "the engagement." Even as Christoph played the organ for the service, I felt hot from the looks I garnered from the white planters' wives. Angered by an unwarranted sense of shame, I left the service before it was completed and walked alone all the way home to Heerenstraat.

And so, I have remained at home on Heerenstraat or here at La Solitude. My days are full enough with the business of the plantations. Christoph has occupied his time with duties to the lumber company and the remodeling of Nuda, and seems unbothered by disapproving glances and *mofokoranti*.

I find myself often wandering from room to room as if in an unfamiliar house. My mind is bothered with a thousand imaginations, and in truth there is none I can share them with who would understand the depth of my concerns.

Carl Otto's *jorka*, whose presence I often feel about me, has been quiet, as if he too waits to see what outcome will prevail. I think of Liesbeth, in such love with Samuel that she cared not about the marriage laws, and taken from this life so early. I think of the childlessness of Maria, Nanette, and myself, and wonder again if indeed Mariana's daughters have in some way been cursed.

In the big mahogany four-poster bed so very aware of my loneliness that sleep eluded me, I was thus wide awake when Kwasiba tiptoed into the room to tell me Christoph had arrived.

"Greetings, Elisabeth," he said when I appeared downstairs in the entrance hall. "How fare's your day?"

"Well enough," I answered, dismissing his inquiry with a vague wave of my hand.

We entered the dining parlour, where two slaves brought us cashew nuts, a fine fish stew, and a variety of tropical fruits for refreshment. Christoph helped me to my seat at the head of the long mahogany table, in the place which had usually been reserved for Carl Otto. I dared not disturb his *jorka* by placing another man there. I directed Christoph to seat himself at my right hand.

"I commend you," Christoph said as he fastidiously placed his linen napkin in his lap, "for seeing quickly to your duty to manumit the slaves named at Catharinas'burg."

"I'll not free the two who have not come forward," I said in a severe tone.

"As well you should not. It very much appears they ran away during the melee and joined the Maroons."

"If I find out they had anything to do with our cousin's murder," I exclaimed, "I'll personally see them broken upon the rack and fed to the vultures by the fort!"

"Of course," he said. "That's only just."

The fish stew was delicious and my appetite took the better of me, so that I helped myself with a second ladle. "Indeed, I would rejoice to see it, but it would not bring Catharina Opperman's death into balance."

In a solicitous manner, Christoph changed the subject, telling an amusing story of two planters' wives. It seems that one, visiting the other with her husband, had lost her way in an upstairs hallway in the dead of night, and wandered in her nightdress into the plantation master's bedroom. Whereupon her host took full advantage of her, while his wife snored peacefully under the influence of a sleeping dose of laudanum. The woman of subject, hardly a lady in any case, had appeared the following morning at table as if all was well with the world.

"Such are the manners of the Dutch aristocracy," said Christoph.

He had just finished this discourse when a slave came to announce that a carriage bearing Nanette had just arrived in the drive at the front of the house. Before we could arise she was shown into the dining parlour, where she joined us at table. As she detests fish stew, she she ate several handfuls of cashews and a mango.

After having eaten our fill, we adjourned to the drawing room for dessert, brandy, and tobacco. Nanette, her arms growing rounder by the day it seems to me, helped herself heartily to the sweets laid out on the three-tiered, Chippendale dumb-waiter.

"I think it's a good idea if we purchase more slaves," Christoph was saying, "and hire some military soldiers, so that what has befallen Catharinas'burg and the three other plantations at Kabbeskreek does not befall our own properties."

While I admire Christoph's Christian reserve and practical, forthright nature, he does have a marked affinity for knowing how to spend the guilders.

Nanette smirked when she caught my eye on her fingers reaching for another sweet.

"Your plans to wed, little sister, are still the *mofokoranti* of most interest to everyone!"

It was difficult to curb my temper, as I wanted to slap my sister for her insolence. With a forced calm I did not feel, I withdrew some threads of tobacco from the cedar box on the side table.

"I know everyone is talking. I don't care."

Christoph, as usual, found Nanette's comment most amusing, but his smile was for me. "Your decision to submit a request to the States General through your business adviser in Amsterdam has indeed upset the gentlemen of the Court of Police," he said.

With great concentration I put the flame to the tobacco in my pipe-bowl and drew in a deep breath. In spite of my vexation with my sister, I was very careful when I let out the smoke to send it in a direction away from her face so as not to insult her.

"I followed the required procedures by submitting the request in the same way as the letter to the Court of Police. That those cowardly planters who make up the Court chose to ignore it by deferring it to His Excellency, and now the Society, is not my concern."

Indeed my letter of 4 June had been submitted through Pieter Reydenius, as special envoy on our behalf. He was clear to mention that I am a free-born black woman, confirmed at the Christian Dutch Reformed Church, and because of God's grace blessed with earthly goods and proud to be one of the most wealthy citizens of the aforementioned Colony. He stated in detail that Christoph and I plan to marry each other in a lawful and Christian marriage, and to this end had already submitted said request to the Commission of Marital Affairs at Paramaribo.

Christoph's blue eyes were merry. "He nearly went so far as to also call His Excellency a coward."

"Those could be treasonous words," giggled Nanette. "But I know you don't mean them."

"Of course not."

The planters of the Court of Police are all cowards. They do not want to be responsible for a decision that may have consequences they will regret. It is also well in their nature to ponder, worry, debate, and make paperwork so that action is interminably delayed. At first I was incensed at this endless postponement, but I learned well enough during Governor Raye's reign how to plan an action against the Court of Police, and my patience is strong.

"So let them talk," I said with outward confidence. "It's out of their hands now, and up to a higher authority where I'm sure the right thing will be done."

In truth, I am not sure at all. Carl Otto's *jorka* regularly reminds me that I may well have fired a situation that I shall live to regret.

46

Paramaribo, December 1764

"A token for you, Elisabeth."

Christoph held out a small box wrapped in the tissue of Christmas. Inside lay an object which completely captivated me.

"Your sentiment is appreciated." Such delight I felt as to bestow upon him my most grateful smile.

What I held in my hand was a silver brides' box, its six sides surprisingly cool to my fingertips. The box was a most elegant work of rococo swirls and leaves, each shining side engraved with allegorical figures.

"They depict tenderness and love," Christoph said, "along with trust, hope, prudence, and fidelity." When his limpid blue eyes met mine I was charmed to see complete devotion.

"I ordered it from a most renowned silversmith in Friesland," he continued. "See inside." A great state of excitement had taken hold of him, a childlike mixture of love of surprise and simple pleasure.

My breath caught as I raised the silver lid. The weight of the box in my hands revealed itself to be a full contents of golden ducats.

"Christoph," I murmured. "This is an impressive marriage sovereign." For the first time I noticed that when he grins his narrow cheeks dimple in the sweetest manner.

"Your acceptance, of course," he teased, "means that you intend to marry me, and that your intention is legally binding."

By way of agreement I bestowed a kiss upon one dimpled cheek of my "suitor."

Thus it was that when we departed my house on Heerenstraat for the bright lights of the Governor's mansion, attired in our elaborate Christmas finery, my heart was in high spirits indeed.

I do so love the appearance of the Governor's mansion alight with the candelabra, swags, and decorations of Christmas. Seen from across the *Orangeplein* it reminded me of a most wondrous cake framed among the stately *mawrisee* trees of the palm gardens.

Inside the formal dining parlour the magnificence of His Excellency's table answered very well to that of the splendid dress of the company. The drawing rooms and galleries were crowded with the elite of the colony, all grateful for the balmy evening God hath granted us for the occasion of the Governor's Christmas *fête*.

We had just been inside for a few minutes and Christoph was handing me a crystal glass of claret when he was bumped from behind. To my horror the glass flew from his hand. Thus startled, I stepped back and in turn fell against a gentleman standing too near behind me. Wine splashed to the floor, and some of it soaked the ample rows of Alençon lace at the hem of my *panier* skirt. The gentleman with whom I had in turn collided recovered himself and now held me firmly about the waist, so as to aid me in steadying myself.

"Oh! I do beg your pardon!" said a melodious voice behind Christoph.

Christoph turned to respond to the lady speaking and I was shocked to see the yellow hair and white face of my nemesis. Juliaana's blue eyes widened with mock innocence as I stared, then her eyelashes fluttered as she smiled her apology.

"Such a clumsy accident." She looked down at my hem. "And such a dreadful mark upon your dress. My most humble regrets."

Such sweet words of remorse spilled from her mouth as to cause the most doubting of hearts to believe. But I'll not be so easily fooled—I'm confident she committed this "accident" with knowing deliberation.

My savior from behind asked, "Are you all right, *mevrouw*?"

"Aye, thanks to you."

My fiancé bowed to Juliaana in happy acceptance of her apology, so as to appear unconcerned by her impertinent style.

"I do believe we have not been formally introduced," Juliaana said sweetly.

"C. P. Braband," I said, indicating Christoph beside me. With cold speculation I regarded the white woman, for certainly she had more malcreance in mind. Indeed, she already knows Christoph is our church organist, and I found it impossible to believe she has never before been introduced.

The gentleman who had rescued me from falling bowed and said, "Hermanus Daniel Zobre, at your service."

Juliaana's blue eyes crinkled and her smile now spread to a smirk directed at Christoph. "Ah, the fiancé!"

It was necessary for us to step back to make room for two serving Negroes who wiped up the floor and cleared away the broken crystal fragments about our feet.

Christoph again bowed, and said, "*Vrouw* van Meel," for he knows well enough who the woman is.

Turning her pretty white face to my rescuer, she said in a loud whisper, "These two are engaged to be married."

"Indeed," the young man answered. "My congratulations."

"Zobre. Might you be in some way related to Jacques Rudolph Zobre?" Christoph asked. "The Society Captain of the sugar plantation Guilgal involved with the peace accord of the Aucaner bush Negroes?"

"Aye, Sir. I was his eldest nephew."

"Then your father would be Jean Henny Zobre?" I asked, for of a sudden I recognized him.

His answer in the form of a formal bow told me I surmised correctly.

Thus it was with warm recollection that I recognized this twenty-seven-year old white man as the same babe I had held upon my knee before a great fire on a cold winter's eve in Den Hague during my first year in exile. The Dutchman Jean Henny Zobre and his wife were newly parents when I was introduced to them by Pieter Reydenius. The Zobres, ignorant of my scandalous past, had welcomed me into their home. There I subsequently spent many a happy hour admiring their little son and dreaming about the babes I would someday have of my own.

"Elisabeth Samson," I said by way of personal introduction. "Though I doubt you would remember a lady who visited your home when you were a mere toddler."

Zobre smiled, causing his dark moustache to spread across his face. "But of course, *mevrouw*. I do remember you."

"Your parents are well? In Holland?"

"Aye. After leaving the Colony in '33, my father never returned. My mother has no desire to live here."

"They were good friends to me in Amsterdam. I was sorry to learn four years past of the passing of your uncle."

"When he left this world I inherited Guilgal, which I call home today."

I was grateful Zobre was too young to remember how I had fled their home in Den Hague in embarrassment when my situation had been brought to light.

Juliaana's mere presence more than reminded me of that unhappy time.

"Have you had word from the Society regarding your marriage?" she asked, her bold blue eyes narrowing with mischief.

Of course, word spreading as quickly as it does in our little Colony, she would well know if a decision had been reached. Alas, since our request to the Commission of Marital Affairs in February and my letter of June to the Society, there has been no word.

With the utmost civility I formed my answer. "Any day I expect a formal letter to arrive."

"The Society will never approve of such a marriage," she sniffed. Then I felt her cold blue eyes fall upon my bosom. "Such a surprisingly rich dress calls for immediate repair. Send it round to my house and I'll see to it that my best cleaning Negro puts it in goodly order." Her emphasis of the word *Negro* was not lost upon me.

In my turn, I dismissed her attentions with a muttered curse which no one but she could hear. Her hand flew to her mouth in surprise, and I stalked away towards the staircase leading to the upstairs rooms where I hoped to recover myself. Inside an unoccupied room, I slammed the door behind me and flung myself in tears upon the settee in front of the open window. My head throbbed and my back stiffened when I thought of all the ladies in our little Colony of malicious caprice such as Juliaana van Meel-Peltser. They would not dare to treat me with such insolent disregard if I had a white husband!

Soon after this Christoph sent a wait-servant to inquire after my state of mind. In due course I was obliged to retrieve my good humor and return to the *fête*, Juliaana's words still stinging my ears.

At some time during the evening, not only wine but candle wax had spilt on the lacy hem of my satin skirt. I was regarding it with dismay when I heard the whisper of Carl Otto's *jorka*.

Their approval of the marriage doesn't matter, my sable beauty. It's too late for us.

47

Paramaribo, April 1765

How is it that something so well planned could end up in such disaster?

The occasion was my 50th birthday, a *bigi yari* indeed! Nanette and Christoph and I worked for weeks on the party we would have for our family and guests at the house on Heerenstraat. For days the cleaning Negroes have been on their hands and knees, bare breasts brushing their worn chintz skirts, polishing the mahogany floors with citrus halves and soft cotton cloths. Fresh orange boughs were cut, and the smell that permeated every room, both upstairs and downstairs, is heavenly to note.

I experienced disappointment—but not surprise—when the gowns I had ordered from Amsterdam did not arrive in time. Hendrik van Steenberch, as my solicitor, had made his report to me this morning in a most reluctant manner.

"There is no word, *mevrouw*. I've not been able to confirm if the ship has come upon some misfortune in the middle passage, or even if your shipment was loaded."

"I understand," I sighed.

I didn't need to ask if there was in addition perhaps word of my marriage request, submitted over a year ago. No one speaks of it, but I know it's still on everyone's mind. To his credit Christoph, who is attentive to my every need, has not approached the subject of a more intimate relationship between us. Such a Christian man is he that he appears to be agreeable to waiting for the wedding before indulging in such bedroom activities, and in truth I do not feel much the need.

"I regret to say there is more bad news." Hendrik lit his long-stemmed pipe before continuing. "Your letters appear to have been lost."

I had spent the better part of the past week composing letters to various suppliers in Holland requesting accessories and new bolts of silks and velvets for wedding clothes for myself and Christoph, as well as for this year's Christmas holidays.

"Do you mean to tell me they have been lost before they could be delivered to the ship captain?"

"Aye, *mevrouw*. Such appears to be the case."

"How is this possible?" I demanded. I set down my coffee cup with such force that it rattled on its porcelain saucer.

Hendrik regarded a smudge at the corner of his coat, and scratched under the back of his wig. "I'm not sure, *mevrouw*. I have not been able to determine which slave was responsible."

"Oh! The letters will all need to be rewritten." I held a discomforting hand to my forehead where I felt sweat brought on by the dampness of the morning air. A flash of heat flooded my body. I also felt the beginning of a small throbbing that foretold a headache.

Resigned to the additional work and to not having a beautiful new habit for my *bigi yari*, I instructed Kwasiba to begin filling the oaken bathing tub with heated Madeira. Having sent my shoe-shaped copper bathing tub to La Solitude, I had had a new oaken one made for the Heerenstraat house.

Imagine my horror when later I entered my bedroom and discovered one of the boards of the tub had split, causing a disastrous leakage! My Turkish carpet was soaked with the dark red liquid, which crept in spreading pools as I stared in disbelief.

"*Kwasiba!*" I screamed. There was no immediate answer and I whirled down the hallway to the back stairs to find the girl. Why hadn't she been watching? She was supposed to attend to the tub and not leave the room. I have spoiled her by giving her slaves of her own. Now that she had others to heat and carry the Madeira for her, she had become lax in her responsibility, and she would pay dearly for it.

Kwasiba was to be found in the *keuken* house gossiping and laughing with Dorotea. I strode up to Kwasiba and slapped her smartly across the face.

"Now that I have your attention—both of you—come and see what you've done!" In my anger, my own voice sounded hoarse to me.

In fearful silence, the girls followed me across the yard and back into the house, where the pungent stench of hot wine had begun to hang upon the humid air. Dorotea let out an anguished cry when she saw the mess on the bedroom floor. Kwasiba steeled herself and said nothing, for she knew well now what to expect.

"Rags! Quickly, girl!" I grabbed her arm. "Get this mess cleaned up! Dorotea, get some men to help you remove the carpet."

At length the tub was removed, the floor mopped, and the Turkish carpet hanging on a sturdy line in the rear yard where the servants attempted to wash the wine out of the weaving before the stains became permanent.

So knotted was my stomach over the incident that I gave no thought before I summoned my Samboe butler to punish Kwasiba and Dorotea.

"Two hundred lashes each, and since they like it there so, banishment from the house to the *keukenhuis*. Let them work there. I don't want to see their faces again."

"Aye, *misi*," the man murmured, and left the room.

I paced the dark mahogany floor, unable to determine what to do next with myself.

"Forty house slaves," I hissed, "and *still* I lose a bathtub full of Madeira!"

There is plenty of Madeira, my sable beauty.

"Not the point! Those girls are lazy."

You've indeed spoiled them.

"No longer."

I rang for someone else to help me dress. At least I had the evening's entertainments to look forward to.

Yet awaiting me downstairs was a situation with the

musicians. Two of them appeared to be ill, so pale of complexion were they, and three remained absent by the time my guests began to arrive. The families of La Vallaire and Samuel Loseke fairly burst upon the drawing room, and the house was soon filled with conversation and the joyous laughter of children and young people at play. I was happy to be able to provide a bilbo catcher, tin soldiers, clay marbles, and a game of draughts for their amusement. La Vallaire's youngest, Nanette Suzanna Peterse, has become a charming young lady of eighteen with a most appealing nature, and will cause the breaking of a few more young gallants' hearts before she makes her final selection.

"The weather is monstrous," Nanette Suzanna told me. "Even the shell roads are soggy, and the rest are rivers of red mud." She turned up her nose in distaste, kicked off her mud-covered clogs, and raised her *panier* skirt to inspect the condition of her shoes.

"I expect your shoes survived," I said with revived good humor. "Have some refreshment and make yourself at home."

The musicians now began to play. They were out of tune, their concertos strident and disconcerting.

"Our musicians might benefit from a glass or two of claret before playing," mused Christoph.

"Or they suffer from it," I muttered.

As I walked from drawing rooms to dining parlour to billiard room, I discovered that half our invited guests appeared to be absent. Did they remain home deterred by bad roads and a little rain? Or was it something else? Have my marriage plans so upset the entire Colony that my neighbors would avoid my *bigi yari*? Everyone in this colony loves an extravagant entertainment, and I had spared no expense to see that they would have it.

A strident squeal from the drawing room where the musicians attempted to make music served to interrupt my depressing thoughts. Two crying children ran past me as I hurried to see what accident had occurred. The music had come to a halt when the strings of one of the violins had snapped, stinging the face of a child standing too near to the seated musician. The child was not seriously injured, but the suddenness of the accident had startled everyone and greatly frightened the children.

To the neglect of my other guests, I summoned all the children to a corner of the dining parlour where I had set up a dumb-waiter of sweetmeats just for them. I poured them all a bit of *sangaree* and encouraged them to indulge themselves. This served to calm their spirits so that snapping violin strings were forgotten. The children, all turned out in miniature habits mimicking the current French fashions, were in truth a pretty delight to behold.

None of the children mine.

A fearful pain stabbed my heart.

You will have the marriage, but you will never have the children.

Oh, Carl Otto, how cruel of you to remind me of this just now.

I fled the presence of the children for the distraction of a bottle of old Rhenish in the wine cistern at one end of the dining table. I helped myself to a goodly swallow in order to still the voice that plagues me.

"Will you share that bottle with me?" Nanette, her ample bosom bursting above her stomacher, spoke with her mouth still full of roasted *pingo*.

"Why not?" I poured a second glass for her. "Proost! To my *bigi yari!*"

The crystal glasses chimed a pleasant sound as they touched in a traditional toast, and I longed for Carl Otto—not his troublesome *jorka*, but the dear man himself in warm flesh. If he were only here to stand beside me so that I would not feel such loneliness—to be beside me as I stand up to the Governor and the Commission of Marital Affairs and the Court of Police. How I miss the simple comfort provided by his presence.

Nanette downed her glass of mulled wine and turned back to the dining table, where she nibbled and minced her way through two new salvers of meats just presented to table.

To my dismay, I realized that His Excellency, Governor Cromelin, and his two lovely daughters had yet to make an appearance. My beautiful Chantilly Le Noir clock chimed the midnight hour, and as I regarded its porcelain face it was clear they had, for some unknown reason, stayed away. No regrets had been received and considering this wearied me.

I have reason to wish this day to end, I thought.

Not yet, my sable beauty.

In the drawing room, I was happy to see Christoph charming the ladies with his stories and carrying on polite discourse with the few gentlemen who remained. I had joined them for just a short while when they began to beg their leave.

In the entrance hall I waited with them for their carriages to be brought round, and received more agreeable *bigi yari* felicitations. Then Nanette appeared, unsteady upon her feet. With great dread, I watched her step forward to say a word, then lean over and clutch her belly. In front of God and my guests, my sister proceeded to cast her stomach upon the luxurious pile of the carpet. It was obvious she was in a very weakly condition resulting from the consumption of too goodly an amount of drink and rich food laced with spices.

Her act was so unpardonable as to render me ill myself. In a trance-like state I forced myself to call for two Negroes to clean up the foul, stinking mess. Just as they appeared, a besotted Nanette swayed and passed out, collapsing in a heap at the foot of the staircase.

"Upstairs," I directed two serving Negroes, who bore her glutted body posthaste to an upstairs bedroom.

Without knowing whereof I spoke, I bid good-night to my silently disapproving guests and fled to my own bedroom.

What have you wrought upon yourself, my sable beauty?

Oh, that I should suffer such misuse by God and the spirits! Where is the balance, that I should be so smote for the simple desire to be lawfully married as directed by the Christian God according to the Dutch Reformed Church? For surely, I am being dreadfully sabotaged!

You have made your enemies.

Van Meel? Do you think he has something to do with this interminable delay? Oh, how can I tolerate yet again his damnable influence upon my person?

Indeed, you should have had news by now.

I'll write again to Pieter Reydenius. He'll find out what is happening with the States-General. He'll tell me the truth.

I paced the polished wooden floor, tearing at the Belgian lace at the sleeve of my *saque*-dress.

For love, what is the truth, my sable beauty?
I give you all my love.
Yet you would wed another.
It means nothing! I must have a white husband! I'm weary of being called 'the free whore' behind my back! I'll no longer tolerate their impudent looks!
It's out of your hands. The States-General will decide.
They must see reason in my request. In Holland, there's no law against white marrying black or Coloured!
You are not in Holland, my dear Betje. You are subject to the laws of the Colony, as long-established by the Society of Suriname and the States General.
Oh! How dare they tell me how to live!

In exasperation I picked up a glass-pot of powder from the toilet-case and threw it across the room. A dusty white cloud exploded with the glass. Everything in my view was now vulnerable to my rage. I grabbed hats, shoes, fans and lacquered tabletop boxes and threw them every which way.

At last, having spent the storm of my fury, I fell exhausted upon the four-poster and sobbed until I remembered no more.

48

Paramaribo, November 1765

For two days all Paramaribo has suffered from the increasing odor upon the breeze. Bets were taken in the taverns along Waterkant as to which hour the guineaman *de Goede Hoop* would arrive. On the last day the ante was upped as the bets were now for the exact minute the first mooring rope of *de Goede Hoop* would touch the dock at Plattebrug.

Having successfully navigated the middle passage, *de Goede Hoop* carried a cargo of muskets and powder, ivory tusks, gold and silver plate, Holland trousers, silk stockings, precious jewels, and 178 survived African men and women in iron shackles.

Since I was not purchasing slaves this day, there was no need to brave the stench and be the first to arrive at the dock to inspect the shipment. I waited until both decks and Africans were doused and rinsed, and the air surrounding them thus slightly more tolerable. Then I set out to Plattebrug accompanied by four of the livery Negroes and my houseman, the Mulatto Nero.

It was already noon and the tropical sun was high and bright. Clouds fluffy as balls of new cotton dotted the blue sky from horizon to horizon. In spite of the heat of the dry season, there was a slow drift of breeze upon the river.

At the waterside I took the shading umbrella from my servant and sent the black to fetch *de Goede Hoop's* captain. When the captain came to me, he took a long time to consult his thick manifest.

"Aye, *mevrouw*. I have merchandise listed as destined for 'The Free Negress, Elisabeth Samson.' You be she?"

This captain, a burly man whom I had never seen before, regarded me with frank disbelief. He had large pop-eyes that blinked often, I suspected more from his surprise than from the piercing sunlight. He made no attempt to hide the insolence of his look as he moved those eyes down the length of my person all the way to my clogs and up again in a most indelicate and unnerving manner. Certainly he was not accustomed to the sight of a black-skinned woman dressed in such finery and speaking a language forbidden to slaves.

"A moment, *mevrouw*," he said. As I watched in irritation, the captain sought out the nearest white planter. They hovered so near together that I could not hear their words, but it was obvious this captain sought to confirm that I am indeed the woman deserving to receive the goods. Oh, such affrontery! This would never happen if I were in the company of a white husband! The presence of Christoph would have well served the purpose, but he had been several days absent, visiting friends up river at Joden Savanne.

At last I was able to take possession of my shipment. I bade my Negroes open every crate and box to confirm that they did indeed contain, complete and undamaged, the goods and fabric I had ordered for my wedding clothes: Geneva velvets, Norwich crepes, one bolt of Italian needle lace, fifty ells on bolts of India chintz, a set of Sevres porcelain dishes, silk embroidered tablecloth and napkins, and a pair of Red Morroco slippers for Christoph. With an exaggerated show of supremacy, I handed the sun umbrella back to my servant so that I could sign off on the Captain's manifest without unnecessary discourse. At last, as he made no further offer of additional packages for me, I was forced to ask, "Do you have in your packet of letters any correspondence addressed to me?"

"Nay, *mevrouw*."

His curt tone and cold eyes made me suspicious enough to repeat my query. In desperation I await word from the Society and States General regarding the situation of my marriage request.

"You have not one letter addressed to Elisabeth Samson? I expect a communication from Pieter Reydenius and Son in Amsterdam."

It had been at least seven months since I had received any communication from Pieter Reydenius and I was awash with unease. Accustomed as we are to the length of communications with Holland, I felt growing within me a grave annoyance towards the Honored gentlemen of the Society and States General. When no law prohibiting marriage between black and white exists in the Netherlands, how could it take them so long to make this decision that is so significant to me? What matter can it be what law governs relations between man and woman in a Colony so many thousands of kilometers across the sea? Oh, how my mind reeled with the injustice I felt.

The mention of such an important Netherlands business house as Pieter Reydenius and Son caused not a flicker of recognition upon the weathered face of the captain of *de Goede Hoop*. A wave of frustration engulfed me and I turned away from the man, so as not to reveal to him the moisture that gathered in my eyes. I found Nero and my other slaves finishing the loading of crates upon our wagon. Nero helped me climb into the seat where I hid my face behind my umbrella as we turned up Heerenstraat and away from Waterkant.

As if the day had not already held a disappointment, unhappy news awaited me at home. Nanette, her bulk amplified by the width of her swaying *panier* skirt, clasped her hands in mine as soon as I reached the front entry.

"Christoph has arrived, little sister," she whispered, "but he is badly incapacitated."

My heart leaped with such concern that I dismissed her hated nickname for me. "Where is he?"

"Upstairs, the first bedroom on the right."

I brushed past her and, lifting my skirts, took the wide stairs by twos. The door to the room she had indicated was open. At once I saw the white doctor standing beside the bed. From a glass jar he withdrew two fat, black leeches. The putrid smell of bodily injury permeated the room.

"What has happened?" I demanded.

Doctor Wekker turned round, gave me a querulous look, and nodded, but said nothing. He is the most respected—and expensive—white doctor in the Colony. He attends almost exclusively white patients, especially the planters' wives who constantly complain of bad humours and miseries most usually brought upon themselves by bad personal usage, boredom, and decadent behaviours. In silence he went about his business of placing with care the leeches upon the black and swollen arm of the man on the bed.

In absolute fright, I hardly recognized the face and limbs of Christoph. Every visible part of his skin was abused in some way. He lay on his back upon the edge of the bed, one still-booted leg straight out on the spread and the other bent at the knee over the edge so that the toe of his boot touched the floor. His body appeared so damaged as to remind me of a lizard I had once observed caught in the beak of a *gritjibi*. The bird had dashed the reptile repeatedly against a log, the better to break its bones and make it swallowable.

At length Doctor Wekker turned to me and in low voice said, "I will speak to you downstairs," thus dismissing me from the room.

In the drawing room Nanette poured us both a hefty dram of dark rum. I gulped it, mindless of the flaming sensation such action caused in my throat.

"The boats were attacked by ferocious Maroons," she said. "He is the only white survivor. He escaped them thanks to the swiftness of the current and their running out of powder."

My mind swirled with the vision of Christoph half-submerged in the brown water of the Suriname River, one battered arm clutching a length of drifting branch. He was fortunate indeed that before he was rescued by Indian fisherman his injuries did not attract the vicious piranha which inhabit these waters. For three days the Indians had nursed his wounds with their bush medicine, then delivered him into the hands of some Dutch hunters who were on their way back to *foto*.

The Dutch doctor Wekker now fears the possibility that Christoph has suffered from some unseen internal wounds. The doctor has not been able to affect the fever that keeps Christoph's body hot and weak. I sent a slave to determine the whereabouts of Granman Quassie, but have heard naught from that direction.

As the sun was just beginning to set, turning to vivid orange the palm garden and the facade of the Governor's mansion, a man came to my house to deliver to me a letter from Pieter Reydenius.

"From whence came this letter?" I asked in puzzlement.

"Why, from *de Goede Hoop, mevrouw*. Just landed this day."

This letter could only have been among the contents of the captain's letter packet after all. Oh, and I had trusted that the captain had spoken to me in truth!

I bid the man *goedenavond* and took the letter with me to the drawing room, where this time I poured myself a healthy glass of old Rhenish. I sat down in the upholstered chair and regarded the letter in my lap, ignoring the little nagging ache that was beginning to plague my forehead. At long last, a letter from my representative! For a moment I sat, staring at the letter as if it were from the Princess-Regent Herself. At length, with my favorite silver, ivory-handled letter knife I slit the edge above the seal.

After inquiring as to the state of my well-being, my representative went on to describe the political delays in communications between the Society Directors and the States General. In closure he had written, *We understand your situation and beg you to remain patient. All is being appropriately considered. Yours sincerely, P. Reydenius.*

I threw the letter to the carpet. As dusk descended into darkness, I sat staring out the window, drinking the rest of the mulled wine that of a sudden tasted bitter to my mouth.

Now I sit alone in my bedroom surrounded by shadows, with the yellowed light of the candles to comfort me, and have time to think upon this latest mishap on the river. If Christoph had not been awake enough to tell me in his own feeble voice that indeed his party was attacked by Maroons, I might have suspected foul play on the part of the Dutch hunters.

You have come to suspect enemies everywhere.

Nay, who would be able to say whether or not they told the truth about Christoph's condition when they found him? I know I have enemies everywhere. This could be some new sabotage on their part.

Sabotage.

But might not the Maroons who perpetrated this foul deed

been in the pay of the Dutch hunters? It has not been established who the runaways were. In the wild jungle anything is possible.

That white men might hate you, my sable beauty, enough to harm one of their own is inconceivable.

I hear you, yet in my heart I cannot be sure.

49

Pad van Wanica, January 1766

In my family's pew inside the white wooden Dutch Reformed Church I sat and stared at the white man who had taken Christoph's place as organist. His fingers were lost among the black and white keys, and when he played all the chords of the Christian hymns ran one into the other.

In the church I felt a measure of peace, for so far it has proven to be the one place I am not followed by Carl Otto's *jorka*.

I prayed to God to bring peace to Christoph's *jorka*. I simply could not bear to be haunted by so many ghosts. So many times have I prayed to the Christian God—for peace in the Colony, the well-being of my family, a child of my own, a white husband, and that Christoph's constitution might rally. It appears that the *jorkas* of our ancestors, the *wintis* within our bodies, and even the smallest *winti* spirits around us are more powerful than the Christian God. He has never answered any of my most fervent prayers. Yet seated on the hard, mahogany pew built by my eldest brother, Charloo, I prayed one more time to Him for peace for Christoph.

For many weeks Christoph had lain in fever after his terrible ordeal on the Suriname River. When the white Dutch doctor Wekker was not around, Granman Quassie had come and made *obias* for the restoration of Christoph's health. Doctor Wekker continued to bleed Christoph, yet his constitution ebbed and a pale mortality began to take place. At a most lamentable rate his injured arm began to rot, until the diseased tissue gave forth with great frequency a brown, foul-smelling secretion. No matter the leeches, the *obias*, and the prayers, Christoph's condition continued to slip.

A saving grace was that, as a result of sipping the tea of Granman Quassie's root compounds, Christoph suffered little. His limpid blue eyes, when they gazed upon me, were free of pain, and a great sadness shown there.

Now ten days past, after lingering with fever since the end of November, Christoph Polycarpus Braband, my white fiancé, has succumbed to earthly damage. His body rests in the Church yard, and my soul is numb with loss.

I hide myself at Pad van Wanica, where Nanette, who insisted upon accompanying me, has become the scourge of my every waking moment. Her incessant appetite for food and drink, along with her chattering tongue, repeatedly mar my peace.

"How long will you wear mourning for Christoph? One month should be sufficient, since you were only 'engaged' and never lived together." Nanette eyed the fare of the breakfast table.

"Indeed." My response was without thought.

Between bites of meat and fruit she said, "You know that last *obia* that Gra'man Quassie made disappeared from the sick room."

"What are you talking about?"

"I tell you, someone stole the *obia*, so that Christoph did not benefit from its presence. My *winti* told me."

I felt confusion and then a greater suspicion. "The white doctor?"

"Perhaps. Who can say? Perhaps a slave removed it."

"Bah," I scoffed. "The slaves would fear it too much to tamper with it."

"Unless the slave acted under the direction of someone he feared more."

The breakfast chocolate tasted flat upon my tongue. "What are you suggesting? That someone who hates and envies me bade a slave remove the healing talisman that might save Christoph's life?" Such a fear was already fomenting in my belly.

Nanette shrugged. Her already round cheeks bulged as she chewed.

So unnerved was I by this speculative prattle on the part of my sister that I set aside the dish of chocolate and reached for my pipe and tin. The good Virginia tobacco would soothe me. As the threads caught fire, I sucked hard at the mouth of the stem.

"*Gra'man* Quassie should have known the *obia* was stolen and come immediately to replace it," Nanette said.

This talk wearied me. "If God Himself doesn't know what's going on in the Colony, how can one old black man? In any case, I doubt the talisman would have saved his life." In truth I did not feel the conviction of my words.

"But perhaps," she insisted.

I picked up my pipe and tobacco and left the table, leaving to my sister what uneaten food remained.

Not ten minutes had I been smoking alone, seated in a rattan chair at the far end of the porch, when Nanette appeared to disturb my small comfort. She carried a tall glass of *sangaree* and plumped herself down in the opposite chair.

"We must decide what we will wear to the wedding," she announced.

"Whose wedding?"

"Why, Elisabeth Buys and Jan Nepveu, of course." Nanette's voice was thick with exasperation. "You will attend. You cannot resist a lavish wedding, little sister."

I flared at her. "What do I have to do to get you to stop calling me 'little sister?' Die?"

The sound of Nanette's laughter rivaled the noise of the *gritjibis* in the bushes surrounding the house. "You won't die," she said. "You'll wear a lavish habit that will surely upstage the bride."

I thought of the bride, the Mesties daughter of Anna Ouwater-Julien and Willem Ouwater. At sixteen, she will marry the handsome young Society Lieutenant Jan Nepveu. Already established with a reputable career and good connections, the man is most likely destined someday for governorship of the Colony. It will remain to be seen how his career may be affected by the presence of a Mesties wife.

"Since Willem is dead, who will give away the bride?" I wondered.

"*Meneer* Clemen, Anna's present husband, I should imagine."

In my mind's eye, Christoph's face replaced that of the bridegroom, and I had a momentary vision of him as he would have appeared on our wedding day, waiting for me at the front of the Church. His good cheer and amusing stories are sorely missed.

He was a good friend to you.

I froze in the midst of relighting my pipe, then took a deep breath in an attempt to relax. After four years I'm more aware than ever of Carl Otto's *jorka*. Next month it will be two years since my marriage request was submitted to the Society in Amsterdam.

It's finished, then.

"Nay, it is *not* finished," I said aloud.

Nanette started. "What?"

I waved my hand as much to blow smoke from my face as to dismiss the comment. But Nanette would not be put off.

"What did you say?" she repeated.

I would not tell her I had spoken to Carl Otto's *jorka*. "I was thinking aloud about my marriage request."

"Oh, that." Nanette shrugged with disinterest.

"As unhappy as I am about Christoph's demise," I said, "I must not let it keep me from my objective."

"Aye, you are determined to have a white husband." Nanette's tone was laced with sarcasm.

"Eventually I must receive an answer from the Society. I must forge ahead with a new plan."

Nanette shook her head and made no response.

It's not to be, my sable beauty.

50

Plantation Clevia, July 1766

    Disturbed by a new noise, a flock of *sabaku*, the white herons that are everywhere about the coastline, rose up en masse from the mangroves and mudbanks at the foot of the jungle and passed overhead. There was such an abundance of the birds that for a moment it seemed they filled the sky, their whiteness competing with that of the clouds that floated above.
    From the landing I shaded my eyes with my hand in an effort to better see the tent-boat coming up the river. Across the water I could hear the chanting call-and-response song of the rowing slaves.
    The sun was already high in the sky and the moist heat upon us when the tent-boat landed at Clevia containing the provisions I had ordered from *foto*. Also aboard were Hendrik van Steenberch with Maryk and their three children, my sister Nanette, and the young man with whom I had become reacquainted two years ago at Christmas, Hermanus Daniel Zobre.
    Since I saw him last, Zobre has achieved a pleasing maturity, and still sports his handsome, broad mustache. He is taller than I remembered, or perhaps I shrink with old age! Nanette seems taken with him, and it was she who invited him to join their little party.
    "He's most gentile," she whispered to me as we walked across the lawn from the landing to the main house. It occured to me to suspect that she might fancy the young man.

The visit by the van Steenberch family caused me some surprise, for though Hendrik has been an attentive solicitor, he has been distant with me since the death of his friend and colleague, my beloved Carl Otto. Well, perhaps Carl Otto's *jorka* has visited Hendrik and made inquiries to mend whatever distance has come between us, for surely I have not been able to do so.

All were welcomed, even my sister Nanette with her ability to annoy me. For indeed I was wearied of the daily duties associated with the sugar cane harvest and in need of some merry diversion. I wished for something to take my mind off the accident just after dawn this morning in the mill, where the slave who entered the canes into the rollers caught his fingers between them. The hatchet kept ready to chop off the limb in such an occurance had disappeared—thus the working of the mill was forced to a halt. The shattered arm was removed by the means of a billhook, the injured worker carried away to the slave quarters and replaced by another so that the mill could resume production. Though not an uncommon occurance, I was still disturbed by such a permanent disfigurement that easily might have been avoided had the mill Negro exercised more care.

With happy delight, I watched the van Steenberch girl, five-year-old Doelsie, race for the end of the long porch where I keep Clevia's menagerie of forest creatures. She clapped her hands at the parrots and toucans and was charmed by the small, infant *keskesi*, the capuchin monkey that is a recent addition. I showed her where the fruits and nuts were kept below the cage-stands and how to present small tidbits safely to the birds. She jumped back in a start when one of the toucans emitted its *ku ya ke* call, then she laughed with glee.

From a distance, Zobre watched Doelsie with smiling eyes. His attention was diverted by the arrival of the serving slave with silver trays of drinks and refreshment.

Leaving Doelsie with the menagerie, I joined my guests as each found a place of comfort among the brightly-cushioned wicker armchairs.

"Please make yourselves at home at Clevia," I said.

The serving Negro moved among them in silence as natural

as the sun beating down upon the shingle roof protecting the porch with pleasing shade. I seated myself with my back to the wall, so that I could converse with my guests while enjoying the view of the greenery that grew untamed on the far side of the canal surrounding the plantation.

Hendrik looked in the direction of my gaze and commented, "Hard to believe anyone could survive there in such primitive fashion." He was referring of course, to our Colony's chronic situation with runaway plantation Negroes.

"There are no Maroon villages near here." As I said this I smiled at Maryk, who seemed ill at ease.

"That you know of," Zobre said. Seated near to Maryk, he offered her some sugared cashews from a serving bowl.

I gave them both my most reassuring smile. "It would be very difficult for them to establish themselves without my hunting and fishing slaves becoming aware of their presence."

My solicitor looked thoughtful as he helped himself to a second glass of *sangaree*. "True enough, I suppose."

For the past seven years, since the peace treaty with the Ndjuka Maroons, most of the planters have felt relatively safe. Yet Christoph's unfortunate demise came to mind. I resolved to avoid mention of this so as not to further unnerve Maryk.

"We have patrols along the perimeter at night," I said. "You may be assured your family is safe here. Every precaution has been taken."

In truth, though we tell ourselves the attack on Christoph's party was an isolated incident, our biggest concern will always be a massive uprising so long as slaves outnumber whites by ten to one.

"Is your patrol made up of Society militiamen?" inquired my solicitor.

"Nay, I pay just for two such arms-bearing men. The rest are trusted Clevia Negroes."

"Surely," Maryk interrupted with alarm, "you don't give them muskets?"

"Of course, not, my dear," I said. "Here is the service tray. Would you care for more *sangaree*?" It has been my experience that a guest well-fed and fortified with drink is more easily calmed, no matter the direction of any conversation.

"The planters complain of the financial burden they must carry to provide military protection for their sugar production," Hendrik noted. "Could not Clevia benefit from a greater expense in that area?"

"We've had no trouble in the neighborhood, but your suggestion is well-taken. I shall take up the matter with my director in the morning."

Hendrik seemed insistent to pursue the subject. "In accordance to the treaty agreements, the Maroons continue to hand over new runaways, but just enough to pacify the military. How many slaves have you lost to the Maroons in the past year?"

Before I could answer Nanette said, "My little sister"—I glared at her for her blatant use of the hated phrase—"is too consumed with the answer to her marriage request to concern herself with marauding runaways."

Maryk raised her eyes from the needlework at her lap, but said nothing. At the end of the porch little Doelsie could be heard making clucking sounds to the toucans. To his credit, *meneer* Zobre seemed much more interested in the state of his fingernails than Nanette's comment.

"My representative in Amsterdam assures me everything is proceeding as it should," I said, straining to keep my voice even and without emotion. "Let me see to the serving of our midday meal."

As I rose to summon a house Negro, Hendrik said, "*Mevrouw*, another woman of your financial success and social standing would be content to spend her declining years enjoying the fruits of her labor rather than concerning herself with Colonial politics."

First Nanette persists in calling me "little sister" and now Carl Otto's friend and my solicitor refers to my "declining years!" Will these insults, even under my own roof, never cease?

Your interest lies in a dangerous area.

"I ask you," I challenged Hendrik, "why cannot a woman of my financial success and social standing have whatever she desires?"

"Indeed," said Zobre, glancing inside the window at the

lavish furnishings of the drawing room, "you would seem to have every luxury money can buy."

Nanette, who was beginning to show the effects of too many glasses of *sangaree* to which she had made a generous addition of dark rum, said, "Money, so far, has not been able to buy those luxuries of an intimate nature that other plantation wives enjoy."

Hendrik shifted in his wicker chair, while *meneer* Zobre chuckled. "But those luxuries 'of an intimate nature' as you call them, can easily be bought," he said.

"For a man, perhaps," Nanette said. "A lady needs be more discreet. Although we have all known several European wives to indulge in mischief and debauchery."

At that moment my houseman arrived to inform us that the meal was ready to be served in the dining parlour.

Thus we adjourned to the inside of the house which, warmer than the porch, required servants to fan us while we dined. Set out on fine linen and porcelain, a sumptuous feast awaited us, with the best my larder could provide. The wine cistern had been filled so that we were able to enjoy a cooled claret with our meal.

Nanette, to no small surprise, heaped her plate with meat, fried plantains, cheeses, and fruit as if this were her final meal on earth.

When the young girl who brought fresh water appeared with her earthen jug, Nanette paused, loaded fork in front of her mouth. The girl's chintz skirt was striped in red, yellow, blue and purple, and her head was swathed up in a length of tamarind-coloured cotton. Just emerging from the roundness of childhood, she already had high, firm breasts. Nanette watched *meneer* Zobre's eyes as they wandered after the little beauty circling the table.

Grinning, she said, "Those dark mounds can be yours for the taking, if she pleases you."

I had expected Zobre to blush at this blunt offer, but he did not. Instead he asked, "How old would the girl be?"

"I believe she has just turned thirteen," I said.

"Ah, the blush of sweet youth." As soon as she had made this statement, my sister hiccupped.

With gentlemanly reserve, *meneer* Zobre said, "The girl promises to be a beauty."

"So." Nanette leaned forward towards him and waved her wine glass in a loose gesture. "Do you desire her?"

He raised his wine glass in a manner of salute, and downed the rest of its contents in one long swallow.

Hendrik, who had busied himself with cutting meat for his little daughter, said to me, "Your house slaves are most handsome, *mevrouw*. Are any of them for sale?"

"They are always for sale—for the right price."

My solicitor laughed out loud at this, for he knows that if presented the opportunity I will make a hard bargain.

His wife, whose voice is firm for one so diminutive, said, "Hendrik, I hardly think we can afford any new slaves just now."

"I was thinking of a gift for van Meel," he said.

I froze at the mention of this hated name. Was my solicitor in some way wanting to curry favor with the prosecutor? If so, why?

"Ah," said his wife, shaking her head, "an admirable idea, but still, I think, beyond our present means."

"What needs van Meel of such a gift?" asked Nanette.

To hide undue interest in this question on my part, I set about refolding the napkin in my lap, arranging it with all the lace points evenly displayed.

Maryk's reply was soft and tinged with a somber sadness. "The perils of childbirth have claimed his wife," she said.

"Juliaana has died?" Nanette's face, flushed from the claret, showed the mildest of interest.

"Aye. Tuesday past. Her husband is frantic with only the old mother-in-law to look after his children."

So. The white woman has proven not to be of sturdy enough constitution for continuous child-bearing.

Your nemesis is no more.

I might have felt compassion for the passing of a woman who would never hold the babe that survived. But in truth, I felt nothing for the loss. Age may often soften old hurts, but I admit to the same loathing this day as I had twenty-five years ago for Juliaana van Meel-Peltser.

Remembering her last words to me at the Governor's

Christmas fête, I sighed, an ache filling my chest.
The Society will never approve of such a marriage.
Aye, that is what she had said. How dare she make such a declaration public.
There are others, dear Betje, who are of the same opinion.
I don't need you to remind me!
Without speaking I rose from the table in such haste as to knock over a water goblet. Whatever the direction of the conversation, I no longer heard. Water spread across the damask cloth and servants came to repair the damage. I fled outside to the far end of the porch, where a slight breeze and the chattering of the parrots and *pikolets* might serve to distract me. I looked at the little brown capuchin monkey, with which I had thought to replace my Pansu, but I felt nothing for this creature.
Christoph is gone, and I must find another to take his place. Maria is gone, without issue, and I must face the probability that such a fate may come to me any year now. Nanette, if I precede her in death, will anticipate an inheritance, but the children of my half-brothers have not such expectation. It would be well worth half my fortune to have a white husband to bring me equality with other planters' wives.
Now, to whom can I turn?
If you are thus determined, what matter is it which white man you choose?
I must consider with care before I choose. After the affair of J.C. Dörig, I do not wish to add again to the general mirth of the whole Colony.

51

Paramaribo, April 1767

Having enjoyed several days in a row of fair weather, Governor Cromelin's daughters persuaded him to hold a lawn party on the *Orangeplein*. A military exercise had already been planned for this day and the daughters were of a mind to use the opportunity to further their father's favor with the plantocracy. Yellow and white striped tents were erected to protect the delicate white women from the equatorial sun, and the Society soldiers wore their least frayed formal uniforms. The officers were finished out in their handsome short jackets, jackboots, and campaign wigs.

I was eager to attend this outing, so joyous have I been these past five weeks. By the time breakfast was finished and the sun rising in the sky the habit I'd selected with care had been laid out by my maid. I hummed a little tune as she secured in place my most expensive stomacher. With great satisfaction, I imagined how the sun would cause the yellow diamonds studded on its little decorative bows to blind the eyes of the planters' wives.

By now, all Paramaribo would have heard the news. My triumph is at hand, though Josephus de Cohue has cautioned me that until the Court of Police meets again, the permission which arrived in February is not yet final.

Poor Christoph had been gone just over a year when the letter from Pieter Reydenius and Son arrived. From the odor emanating from the paper Pieter had taken to the use of strong perfumes, no doubt to counteract the effects of his regularly flatulent condition. With this letter Pieter had enclosed a copy of the letter from the States General via the Directors of the Society to Governor Cromelin. After three years they had come to the conclusion that since in the Dutch Republic there was no law forbidding a marriage between white and persons of any other colour, the decision should be passed back to the Governor *"to handle the matter as (he) thinks appropriate."* However the Directors did give the advice to approve my marriage request!

When I showed the letter to Nanette, she said, "Now all you have to do is find a white man to marry."

Indeed, I have not come to any conclusion regarding a candidate, but I have not given up. I will be equal to the planters' wives—I will have a white husband! Never again will I be called the "whore" Elisabeth Samson!

You're not called "whore" for living alone with only your sister.

Oh, God keep me from living my last years all alone with Nanette's unbridled tongue!

Just this morning, as I came down from my bedroom dressed out in all my finery, with hat and fan and matching sun umbrella, feeling mistress to all the world, I encountered Nanette waiting at the foot of the stairs.

"Perhaps today will be the day you find the man you seek," she said, smiling at her idea of a jest. "Why don't you bring the Society letter with you to wave under the noses of the white women?"

Determined not to be taken in today by my sister's provocations, I said, "The letter is locked away for better use."

Following behind me out through the tall double entry doors, she said, "Hendrik is right. We are beyond child-bearing, we are rich, we have everything money can buy. What's the point of marriage?"

"You don't understand," I said in a stiff voice.

Nanette, who of late had seemed less troublesome, said, "Why don't you marry the handsome young Hermanus Zobre? He can be the son you never had!"

My heart cringed to hear such cruel words from my own sister!

At that moment the pretty young black boy I had selected

to carry my sun umbrella appeared at the foot of the porch. Tall for his age of twelve, he wore a white shirt, short jacket and clean breeches above bare calves and feet. I handed him my sun umbrella as we climbed into the waiting carriage.

The *Orangeplein* was already frequented with the elite of the Colony and their attendants: White Dutch planters in smart vests and cutaway waistcoats, so dressed out in elegance and soft speech as to be taken by the uninformed for Italians, the white wives no less eminently dressed. Several other persons also had a slave, one or two as ornately dressed as his owner's family, to hold high their sun umbrellas. Everywhere children, no matter how finely dressed, ran in and out of and around chairs and tables and tent-poles, laughing and teasing one another with unleashed gaiety.

Bare-foot male and female slaves of pretty countenance circulated among the gathering, presenting a wondrous variety of food and drink. The sun rivaled all the glittering jewels in evidence as it glinted off the salvers of massy gold upon which all was served. Its reflection shimmered atop the water served in golden bowls which were offered for the purpose of rinsing one's hands between dainty samplings. All was opulence and abundance and thoroughly enjoyable.

As I passed among the gathering, greeting neighbors, merchants and distant relatives, I regarded with scrutiny the men in their close-fitted breeches and finely turned calves in white silk hose. Particular attention I paid to those whom I suspected to be unmarried, and my face never tired at smiling.

At length my gaze fell upon the person of Hermanus Daniel Zobre.

"Good-day," I said, extending to him a formal curtsy. "Do you find the heat of the climate not to your liking?"

Meneer Zobre had flaunted conventional dress by removing his vest and waistcoat. His white shirt was decorated with hand ruffles and had finely plaited sleeves. Indeed, I wished to be able to remove my own collarette of bow-knots and diamonds, for the newness of the fabric had become an irritation to my moist neck.

In greeting *meneer* Zobre touched his hand to the gold braid edging his velvet tricorn hat with its jaunty ostrich feather and smiled. His person smelled pleasantly of tobacco and lavender.

"*Vrouw* Samson, what a pleasure to see you again." He swept his other hand in a wide gesture. "Such stodgy neighbors we have, do you not agree?"

Looking around, I had to laugh in agreement with him. Having now the leisure to enter into a gentle discourse with the man, I held out my arm to be taken in his. He responded in a most polite manner and we strolled across the grass to the nearest tent. There we helped ourselves to a few refreshments.

At length the new corps of Marines, having been sent by His Serene Highness the Prince of Orange to assist the planters, was ready to engage in their parade in front of the Governor's mansion. To no one's surprise some of the white soldiers fell to a faint from the heat during their maneuvers, it being now in the heart of the short dry season.

"They have no idea what they're in for," said *meneer* Zobre, shaking his head.

Hermanus Daniel Zobre is thirty and unmarried.

The words of the *jorka* startled me, and I turned my head to regard the man beside me in a different light. I remembered Nanette's cruel words following her suggestion that I propose marriage to him. Yet at the heart of the comment, her idea might be sound, after all. A wild impulse overcame me, and without further thought I spoke.

"*Meneer* Zobre..." I began. "I have a proposition that may well interest you."

Consider with care before you choose.

It was a reckless urgency that seized me—thus it was easy to ignore the cautionary words of a *jorka*. To calm my beating heart, I rubbed the pearl tassels of my fan between my fingers.

Seeing that I now had the young man's attention, I said, "It would be a great benefit to me to marry. Being blessed with every comfort, I have now a special wish that I have not been able to, as yet, fulfill. I wish to marry a white man—a gentleman—such as yourself."

"I beg your pardon, *mevrouw*, but is not such a marriage forbidden in the Colony?"

"A practical concern, I agree," I said. "However, I am in possession of a copy of a letter from the States General, via the Society Directors, addressed to the Governor himself, wherein it is recommended that His Excellency approve such a marriage on my part."

When I searched his face for some hint of his response, I found his countenance impassive.

"That you should think so well of me as to consider me a worthy candidate for your proposal is an honor," he said. There appeared to be no affectation in his words.

Beware, my sable beauty, there'll be no love lost in this direction.

"I don't expect an immediate answer." I smiled and kept my voice light. "Please give it your utmost consideration. There is some wealth at stake, as I'm sure you know. Why don't you arrange to visit me at Clevia, where we might discuss it at length?"

To my unutterable surprise, he bent forward in a bow and kissed my hand. "This day has been most entertaining. I shall indeed ponder at length upon your situation."

Whereupon Hermanus Daniel Zobre begged leave to return to his lodgings and withdrew from the *Orangeplein* in his own carriage.

A feeling of high exuberance stayed with me for the rest of the day, which was spent in grand entertainment without the least disturbance, to the great satisfaction of the Colonial plantocracy.

In spite of this, my one perturbation was the annoying awareness of Carl Otto's *jorka*. When I heard his voice, it was as if the world around me receded behind a silent, filmy mosquito curtain. The movement of the sweet salt-scented breeze from the river stilled. Colours softened and singing, laughter, and conversation were a very great distance from me.

You would marry a man who doesn't love you.

Aye, indeed I will. This is no longer about love.

It is now all about pride.

It's about position! Fiercely I clasped my fan at the persistent thought of how close I am to my ultimate achievement.

In the end it will be about your fortune.

So be it. What worth is my fortune if I don't have what I most desire?

At that moment I saw that His Excellency Governor Cromelin was standing just a few steps in front of me.

The wine, the sun's heat, the rush of confidence after my proposal to *meneer* Zobre, and the needling *jorka* all served to propel me forward at that moment.

With no polite preamble, I tapped my fan on His Excellency's shoulder and spoke out loud in a most unladylike voice: "The Court of Police is avoiding a discussion of my marriage permission. You have your instructions to recommend they approve it and I suggest you do so with the utmost haste...*Your Excellency*."

52

Paramaribo, December 1767

    For seven months Hermanus Daniel Zobre was preoccupied with his own plantation Guilgal, so that it was November and well into the dry season before he was able to visit me at Clevia.
    As I awaited his answer to my proposition, an anxiety grew in me to think that he might have forgotten all about it. Pondering the situation, I concluded that I could not very well approach another without first receiving a defining answer from *meneer* Zobre. Almost daily I think of my advanced age, and wonder how much time I have left in which to accomplish this deed. God has blessed me with a strong constitution, but one never knows what ill fates await elsewhere in this life.
    When at length a letter came from *meneer* Zobre to announce his intention of the visit, my spirits were renewed. In frantic anticipation I set about to put everything at Clevia in the most presentable order. No expense was spared for food and wine and I sent to the house on Heerenstraat for my most expensive, silk-embroidered table linens.
    The day came when the man arrived, accompanied by two Negro servants. They brought provisions for my table, and *meneer* Zobre presented me with a most interesting gift of smooth cowrie shells worked with silver in the form of an elaborate neckpiece.
    "It symbolizes beauty and power," he explained. "It's a bridal necklace from the coast of West Africa."
    Christoph's silver bride box came to mind, and I pushed

away the memory it evoked. Such a warm smile graced *meneer* Zobre's handsome young face that he made it easy to focus upon only him.

"A fine piece of workmanship. My sincere thanks for your thoughtfulness."

I showed him to the large corner bedroom with the little anteroom entrance I had set aside for his use and bade him rest or otherwise occupy his leisure until dinner.

The meal that evening at Clevia was unparalleled in comfort. It seemed to me the *pingo* stew never tasted so delicious, the silver never shown more brightly, and the candlelight cast new warmth in its yellowed glow. Our conversation was light and without effort. We talked of family, of Holland, of music and books, and even of Colonial politics, but nothing unduly unpleasant. All was undemanding, and though the business that at length would need to be discussed was never far from my mind, I was distracted so as to overlook for a time the reason for his presence at Clevia. Indeed, the evening passed in the most pleasant of circumstances.

The following morning dawned with a feathery mist kissing the surface of the brown river. I was happy to see *meneer* Zobre was an early riser. Indeed, he showed eager anticipation to view the grounds of Clevia, asking questions of the mill Negroes, *keuken* slaves, and even the small Coloured children who trailed behind us as we walked.

"Your operation is much larger than what I have at Guilgal," he said. "I look forward to learning more about how you manage the grounds and process the cane."

Arm in arm we strolled down a graveled path between two fields. On each side of us, the thick rows of matured sugar cane reached above our heads, so that it was as if we walked between two green walls. Even so, the sun was high overhead so that the path was without shade, and I was glad I had worn my largest straw hat. The topsoil and peat moss added for better cultivation gave the earth a fresh, rich smell.

"How many hectares does Clevia occupy?" *meneer* Zobre asked.

"Almost three hundred. There are over five hundred field slaves alone."

"And in the house?"

"Oh, around seventy or eighty, I believe. Come this way. You must see the mill."

I led him towards the area where the cane was processed into the rich, dark molasses that we so prize, and which contributes greatly to my annual income. In the cool darkness of the mill-house, I pointed out how the mill was powered by water to crush the cane.

"It's the most expedient way with the least expense, and my engineers have designed a holding canal in such a way that the usual whims of the tides do not adversely affect production."

To my great satisfaction, Hermanus Daniel Zobre appeared quite impressed.

"We are still using horses and mules at Guilgal," he said.

"We have horses and mules, but they're now kept for other work."

"Are the Maroons active in the neighborhood?"

"There has been no problem at Clevia with *marronage*," I was happy to be able to say with confidence, "but I know the slaves practice a certain amount of traffic with the runaways in the neighborhood. Many of them have relatives in the bush who have escaped from other plantations. The trick is to monitor their daytime and nighttime activities so that it doesn't get out of hand."

After a leisurely midday meal, we sat together on the porch, smoked our pipes, and arrived to the business at hand.

"As you are aware, I'm sure, I have no children to inherit my holdings." I refrained from mentioning my age in actual numbers of years. "May I assume your presence here and your interest in the operation of Clevia reflect a positive consideration of my proposal of a marriage between us?"

There it was then, the question I had been forming in my mind since his arrival. The beating of my heart seemed to stop as I waited for his answer. It occured to me that this might be my last chance to have a white husband. The ghost of Carl Otto was present with us there on the porch, watching me, but its voice was silent and so for the moment I was able to put it to the back of my mind.

At length Hermanus Daniel Zobre's mustache spread in a

quite enigmatic smile.

"Elisabeth, if I may so address you"—I nodded instant agreement—"it will be my very great honor to enter with you into a legal marriage."

. . .

It happened that as we departed this afternoon the office of the Commission of Marital Affairs after submitting the legal request for approval of an impending marriage between us, we encountered His Excellency Governor Cromelin, accompanied by his two daughters. The girls fidgeted with their hat ribbons as we entered into conversation with their father. For a brief moment, I saw in their disquieted blue eyes the reflection of a third man, in military dress, standing beside me.

Governor Cromelin did not seem surprised when *meneer* Zobre informed him of our declaration. Nay, when I began to again insist His Excellency further pressure the Court of Police, he made the most astonishing announcement.

"*Vrouw* Samson, the Court of Police in truth wishes to avoid further problems. The gentlemen this very day have officially approved your marriage."

EPILOGUE

Paramaribo, 17 December 1767

The day following the wedding in the Dutch Reformed Church of the free Negress Elisabeth Samson to Hermanus Daniel Zobre, a white man twenty-two years younger, a letter was written describing the nuptuals. Liesbeth's mulatto daughter, the seventeen-year-old Suzanna Johanna (Sutje) Hanssen, wrote to her elder brother Philip Samuel Hanssen, being educated in Holland.

Dearest brother:

This letter is written in the hopes that you are enjoying your studies and planning soon your return to our Colony where you are sorely missed by all who hold you dear.

You will be interested to learn that since last I have written, our great-aunt, Elisabeth, has yesterday married in the Dutch Reformed Church the white planter, Hermanus Daniel Zobre.

Two days following the signing of the contract in the presence of a notary and the publishing of the wedding banns, at her house was held a betrothal dinner. Both family and intimate friends were in attendance at Heerenstraat, which house exhibited exceptionally festive decorations.

At the bann dinner brandied raisins in a silver bowl were passed all around while we sang many wedding songs to the accompaniment of the harpsichord and violin.

Yesterday morning, before the couple left for the church, we scattered flowers all about the pathway and porch before the entry. Meneer Zobre's friends decorated the bridegroom's pipe with ribbons and garlands, which after the wedding he will most likely display in the large corner curio cabinet in the dining parlour of the house. You remember the one—tante Elisabeth was beside herself when at the age of four you marred it with your wheeled toy.

The bride's present to the young bridegroom consisted of a delicate collar and cuffs of the Italian hand-lace, which were presented in one of the baskets made by Indians.

Our great-aunt was most resplendent in her bride's dress of blue the shade of the traditional designs you see on the best Delftware. The profusion of gold lace at her elbows was the same as that of her long veil. Of course, she carried the traditional perfumed gloves and fan, and was followed by a pretty young Samboe girl as bride's servant.

The bridal party entered the church quite unattended by family—that is, due to their advanced age, no parents were present to give them away. The pastor began the marriage ceremony by reading in his gravelly voice the formulas of marriage followed by parts of the Epistles of Saint Paul, and we sang Psalms between the lessons. My favorite part of such ceremonies, the bonding kiss to exchange a winti to live in the new spouse's soul, I'm sorry to say, lacked the warmth of youth. After the ceremony a collection was taken up for the poor.

From the church to the house was strewn by the bridal servants from Indian baskets young palm branches and spidery yellow orchids. There was a grand open house at Heerenstraat, where the refreshments were sumptuous and plentiful indeed; all manner of game was abundant, as well as fruit and pasties. The centerpiece of the table was a molasses cake of three tiers adorned with garlands of orchids lavender in colour. In addition to the sugar cake, there were sugared almonds and cashews, sugared beans, marchpan, and many sorts of sweet cordials. There was the traditional bridal sugar sweetmeat, of course.

With so many people about and therefore none to notice, I admit to consuming two portions of the "bride's tears" drink. To a very pale rum had been added cinnamon and tiny flecks of real gold which floated about in the liquid as delicately as the scent of perfume about the air.

In truth, there was such an abundance of food, merrymaking, and liquor as I have never before seen. Late in the afternoon, when such a goodly amount of liquor had been consumed so as to render the celebrants particularly gay, the Governor General took advantage by collecting money for a new powder house at Fort New Amsterdam.

In this he was aided by the old Councilman Jon van Meel, whose aged mother-in-law, I might mention, was rather entertaining. Well into her cups, she was quite besotted to be sure.

Now I would have expected this from our great-aunt Nanette, but to her credit she showed herself to be singularly courteous. Great-aunt Elisabeth, of regal bearing befitting her advanced age, was seen to eat and drink little; nay, she seemed thus brightly affected solely by the events of the day. Her triumph was paraded for all the Colony to see, if her voice somewhat shrill and her manner breathless.

Indeed it was as if her thoughts as she gazed at her new white husband were as bitter as Granman Quassie's leaves.

I would be remiss not to note the presence of a shadow about the bride. In truth, it should have been Captain-Lieutenant Creutz who stood beside her this day, but the fates have been such that it was not to be. The family whispers that she sees his jorka everywhere, and is heard regularly to converse with it.

With much anticipation of your safe return, I remain
your loving sister Sutje

. . .

Elisabeth Samson's triumph was short-lived. Between the evening of April 21 and the morning of April 22, 1771 Elisabeth Samson died at the age of fifty-five. Official records of the Dutch Reformed Church state, *On April 22, 1771 H.D. Zobre paid 50 guilders in funeral costs and 21 guilders and 14 cents in other fees for the burial for his wife, Elisabeth Samson, in the (cemetery) Nieuwe Oranjetuin.*

Since her husband was her universal heir and there was no division of inheritance, no inventory was made of the vast holdings. A small bequest of 23,000 guilders was distributed to family heirs.

Even though Governor Cromelin found the couple's engagement so notable that he wrote about it in his journal, Governor Jan Nepveu made no mention of her passing in his journals for April 1771.

One month after Elisabeth's death, Pieter Reydenius and Son granted to her husband a mortgage for 200,000 guilders on Belwaarde, a plantation the couple had purchased with

Nanette. Beginning the previous year devastating harvest failures had plagued the wealthy planters of Suriname.

At the same time, prices for cocoa and coffee in Europe fell disastrously. Many planters heavily mortgaged their estates waiting for a market to improve that took much longer than they anticipated.

Like many of his neighbors, Hermanus Daniel Zobre continued to heavily mortgage the houses and plantations he had inherited from his free Negro wife in order to continue to live in the style to which he had become accustomed. In 1773, the plantations and homes which constituted his holdings were valued at 1,872,486 guilders.

Zobre accomplished the mortgage on Belwaarde without Nanette Samson's knowledge. The mortgage was to have been paid off in four years' time. By October 1774, when not one payment on principle or interest had been made in almost three and a half years, a letter was sent to the secretary in Suriname to begin legal proceedings against Zobre and Samson as owners of Belwaarde. A demand was made for the mortgage and all interest payments to be paid in full by May 30, 1775, and the mortgage would not be extended.

Zobre did not respond at all to this, but a surprised Nanette Samson assigned Hendrik Schouten—married to Liesbeth's daughter Sutje—to protest. Pieter Reydenius responded in writing to Nanette that both halves of plantation Belwaarde were affected by the mortgage and that the debt applied to her as well as her brother-in-law.

Meantime Zobre had changed his Amsterdam representative from Pieter Reydenius and Son to the commercial house of Marselis. Nanette, who had stayed with Reydenius, had mortgaged her other holdings in 1774 to buy the plantations Toevlught and Welgemoed from Zobre. On March 24, 1775, she also purchased Zobre's half of Belwaarde, along with the mortgage debt of 200,000 guilders, plus the interest. She asked that the existing mortgage be replaced with a new mortgage; Reydenius had the plantation inventoried and appraised for tax purposes.

Though plantations were not profitable at this time, Nanette, like other planters, was sure they were still a good investment. In this way, she created increasing debt.

Zobre, however, with a better understanding of business, sold at the right time those plantations that were not profitable as well as those, such as Belwaarde, carrying heavy debt. Thanks to these sales, he managed to survive the crisis. Zobre used the money to provide personal guarantees for the production of other plantations. Several years later, the economic situation did improve and Suriname plantations once again became profitable. But by that time, several planters had lost their holdings to Zobre.

By 1776 Nanette could not meet her payments and continued to request mortgage after mortgage in a vain attempt to survive financially. Two years later, unable to pay back her mortgages, she was declared bankrupt. Though she lost her plantations, she still owned some homes in Paramaribo and continued to live, along with some nieces and nephews, in her sister's house on Heerenstraat until she died in 1793.

Hermanus Daniel Zobre continued to live in the house on Heerenstraat as well until his death on October 6, 1784. Though deep in debt, he had managed to avoid bankruptcy. At his death he owned the Suriname River plantations Clevia, De Goede Vreede, Klein Perou, the country home La Solitude, 50 percent of the Para River wood plantation Onverwacht, 50 percent of Vlaardingen, 50 percent of Catharinas'burg, 25 percent of Salzhalen, homes in Paramaribo, and 50 percent of six other homes in the capitol. Zobre was also the administrator of plantation Reijnzand for the commercial house Marselis and plantation Zoelen for the commercial house Coopstadt and Rochussen. Of note, the house on the corner of Heerenstraat and Wagenwegstraat was not listed among his properties.

The heir to the fortune and executor of Zobre's will was his brother, Johan Anthonie Zobre, but Johan refused to accept the inheritance because of the excessive mortgage debt.

Thus commercial businessmen Jan and Theodoor Marselis in Amsterdam became the owners of all the plantations and homes that constituted the wealth of the free-born Negress Elisabeth Samson. What the members of the Court of Police had hoped for had become a reality: this fabulous wealth had returned to white people.

Even though Hermanus Daniel Zobre, after a marriage of just four years, inherited an estate worth nearly two million guilders, he did not purchase a tombstone for his wife.

The exact location of Elisabeth Samson's grave has never been found.

THE END

Author's notes:

Liesbeth's son, Philip Samuel Hanssen, became a lawyer.

The raids and wars between the plantocracy and the Maroons in Suriname continued to escalate and did not end until emancipation in 1863.

The colony referred to by its inhabitants as Suriname and formally named Dutch Guiana gained independence from the Netherlands in 1975. Today the country is officially the Republic of Suriname.

Surinam is the English spelling and Suriname is the Dutch spelling.

ELISABETH SAMSON, FORBIDDEN BRIDE
BIBLIOGRAPHY

Boinsky, Sue, *De Apen Van Suriname*, Stichting Natuurbehoed Suriname, Paramaribo, 2002

Clancy-Smith, Julia and Gouda, Frances, *Domesticating the Empire—Race, Gender, and Family Life in French and Dutch Colonialism*, University Press of Virginia, Charlottesville and London, 1998

Cohen, R. ed., *The Jewish Nation in Surinam*, S. Emmering, Amsterdam, 1982

Herskovits, M.J. and F.S., *Surinam Folk-lore*, AMS Press, New York, 1969

Hippocrene Books, Inc., New York, *Dutch-English/English-Dutch Dictionary*, 1990

Hoogbergen, *The Boni Maroon Wars in Suriname*, Brill, Leiden; New York, 1990

Howarth, David Armine, *The Men-of-war*, Time-Life Books, Alexandria, VA, 1978

Hughes, Bernard and Therle, *Small Antique Furniture*, Frederick A. Praeger, New York, 1968

Jacob, Margaret C., and Mijnhardt, Wijnand W., ed., *The Dutch Republic in the Eighteenth Century: Decline, Enlightenment, and Revolution*, Cornell University Press, Ithaca, N.Y., 1992

McLeod, Cynthia, *Elisabeth Samson, Een Vrije Zwarte Vrouw in Het Achttiende-eeluwse Suriname*, Vaco Press, Paramaribo, 1994

Price, Richard and Price, Sally, Ed. *Stedman's Surinam; Life in an Eighteenth-Century Slave Society*, The Johns Hopkins University Press, Baltimore, 1992

Price, Richard, *To Slay the Hydra: Dutch Colonial Perspectives on the Saramaka Wars*, Karoma , Ann Arbor, Michigan, 1983

Price, Sally and Price, Richard, *Maroon Arts: Cultural Vitality in the African Diaspora*, Beacon Press, Boston, 1999

Schama, Simon, *The Embarrassment of Riches*, Vintage Books, New York, 1997

Stichting Natuurbehoed Suriname, *De Wilde Vogels van Paramaribo*, Paramaribo, 2000

Stichting Surinaamse Musea, Mededelingen No. 38, December 1982, *About the Original Religion of the Creoles in Suriname*, pp 6-48

Stichting Surinaamse Musea, Mededelingen No. 17 & 18, Oktober 1976, *The Boni Maroon War 1765-1793, Suriname and French Guyana*, pp 6-27

Stichting Surinaamse Musea, Mededelingen No. 44, Mei 1989, *Skeletons of Slaves*, pp 29-30

Stichting Surinaamse Musea, Mededelingen No. 12, December 1973, *Manumissie in Suriname* (1733-1863) pp. 8-33

Stichting Surinaamse Musea, Mededelingen No 13, *Antique Bottles in Surinam*, pp 1-16

Stichting Surinaamse Musea, Mededelingen No 34, Augustus 1981, *The Branding of Negro Slaves in Suriname*, pp 5-13

Stichting Volkslectuur Suriname, *Woordenlijst/Wordlist*, Vaco Press, Paramaribo, 1961

Suralco Magazine, 2001 Jaargang/Volume 23 nr. 1, *Paramaribo, the Capital of Suriname*, pp 2-27

Suralco Magazine, 1986 Jaargang/Volume 18 nr. 1, *The Protection of Suriname's Side-entrance*, pp 1-6, *Suriname's Wild Plants*, pp 10-15

Suralco Magazine, 1985, Jaargang/Volume 17 nr. 2, *The Saramacca Canal*, pp 16-25

Tannahill, Reay, *Sex In History*, Scarborough House, New York, 1992

Tjin, Roy and Schellekens, Els, *The Guide To Suriname*, Brasas Publishers, Amsterdam, 1999

Turner Wilcox, R., *The Mode in Costume*, Charles Scribner's Sons, New York, 1958

Werner, David, with Thuman, Carol and Maxwell, Jane, *Where There Is No Doctor*, The Hesperian Foundation, Berkeley, California 1992

Printed in the United States
21993LVS00003B/1-24